MW01436773

THE SOUND OF A SHOT

WHEN A WAR GOES WRONG, SOMEONE MUST PAY THE PRICE

EDWARD AEGIDIUS

ISBN: 979-8-35095-879-9 (paperback)
ISBN: 979-8-35095-880-5 (ebook)

For Anna, who waited for me

"If they knew they were dying uselessly here, it would be like shooting them in the belly and kicking them in the behind at the same time."

—A French colonel in the First Indochina War

CONTENTS

1
THE VISITOR

The city's morning newspaper was bleeding to death, and no one knew what to do about it. Dwindling subscriptions and shrinking ad revenue had provoked budget cuts, staff layoffs, and severance packages. Morale in the newsroom was terrible, and as assistant managing editor, Jack Hoffman was both the chaplain and the executioner. He loved the paper but hated his job.

When Susan, his wife of thirty-five years, died after a long battle with cancer, he'd had enough. He needed a change, some time to recover and sort things out, maybe even quit his job and open a yogurt shop. The publisher was sympathetic and urged him to take a break, return to reporting for a while. When the police beat opened up, he took it. In "the cop shop," at least, he would find the solitude he craved and be responsible for no one but himself.

The press bureau at Central Precinct was a stuffy, windowless room with just enough space for a desk and a couple of chairs. Ceiling-high shelves on one wall sagged under the weight of paperbacks left by predecessors on the beat: mysteries, westerns, science fiction, pot boilers, antidotes to the mind-numbing babble of the scanner. Hoffman arrived for work at 5:00 p.m., replacing the day reporter, and worked until midnight.

As the hours passed, the coded exchanges between the units on the street and the dispatcher reflected the mundane misdeeds of a city at night: narcotics violations, auto theft, burglary, domestic disturbances, and random gunfire. When the chatter suggested some more newsworthy indictment of the human condition, off he'd go, notebook in hand, to pursue a story.

Hoffman was on a first-name basis with most of the detectives. It took months to demonstrate that he would respect confidentiality and avoid screwing them in print, a confidence he needed them to have. Seldom did a night pass that someone didn't wander down the hall to chat about their kids, fishing, the struggles of the Mariners and Sonics. Occasionally after work, he hung out with off-duty staff in a lounge a few blocks away.

It was late March, and a few days of emerald and blue portended the passing of the monochrome months of winter on Puget Sound. A rash of gang-related shootings and drug busts had kept Hoffman busy in recent weeks. Did seeds of malice germinate in the spring? The setting sun gilded the Space Needle as he drove to his post in the cop shop after a staff meeting at the newspaper.

The first hour passed uneventfully. He was finishing Graham Greene's *A Burnt-Out Case* when he sensed someone's presence. A young woman, tall, slender, and attractive, stood in the open doorway. Though he didn't recognize her, he speculated she might be one of the women recruited to the police bureau in recent years. "Excuse me, are you Jack Hoffman?" she asked. "They told me I might find him here."

"They told you right," Hoffman said, pulling his feet from the desktop and standing up to greet her. Her handshake was firm, her eyes fixed on his.

"I'm Tess Danton," she said. "Does the name Danton mean anything to you?"

"Good God," Hoffman said, stunned. "If you mean Alan Danton . . ."

"My father," she said.

"Well, I'll be damned," Hoffman stammered, trying to collect himself. He last saw Alan Danton three decades earlier, in a Cambodian jungle.

"I apologize for barging in on you like this," she said. "I'm in Seattle for a law seminar, and I don't have much time. Had to fib a bit to get into the building, told them I was your niece."

"I doubt they believed you, but you don't look dangerous," he grinned, removing a stack of newspapers from a chair. "Please sit down."

Had Alan Danton mentioned a daughter? He studied her for clues, much as one might examine suspects in a lineup. Alan Danton's face floated in his mind like a hologram, as clear as yesterday. She was about the same age he was then. Yes, he saw the likeness now, the intensely blue eyes, the appearance of someone supremely sure of herself.

"You must have been just a kid when he . . ."

"I was five. I have very little memory of him. You were with him when he died."

Hoffman flashed back, two bodies together, the evidence of a desperate struggle. "Yes."

"Your name was in after-action reports in the national archives. Amazing what they store in cardboard boxes. And Jim Northrup remembered you."

"Oh, he did, did he?" Hoffman said somewhat dismissively. Captain Northrup was his first company commander in the Nam, a guy on his second tour who couldn't get out of the bush to a rear job fast enough. It broke no one's heart when he moved on.

"Jim wasn't there when my father was killed," Tess Danton said. "Of course, you would know that. I was hoping you might tell me what you recall . . . about my dad, about what happened that day."

"It's in the reports, I assume," Hoffman said uncomfortably. "I mean I'm not sure I can add anything. It was a long time ago."

"Whatever you remember would be helpful," she persisted.

Hoffman took a deep breath and exhaled through pursed lips. "Well, I must say Alan's daughter is the last person I expected to walk in the door." He needed time to think. "How did you find me?"

"I searched online and came across some of your bylines—oh, and a collection of your poems."

A small publishing company had printed five thousand copies of Hoffman's verse, most of it inspired by growing up on the shores of Puget Sound. It ended up on the bargain tables of Seattle's bookstores and didn't earn him enough to keep him in coffee for a week.

She said, "It's late, and you're busy, but I wonder if we could get together in the next few days to talk. There's so much I'd like to know, I mean from someone who knew him, someone who was actually with him. I have some questions about what happened. The records are . . . Well . . . let's just say they're less than satisfying."

What could Hoffman possibly tell her that the Army didn't see fit to do? The man was posthumously awarded a Distinguished Service Cross, the second-highest medal for valor. It must have come with the usual epic testimonial. Leave it be.

She said, "I could skip out on the seminar for an hour or two tomorrow if that would work for you."

Hoffman's nearly overwhelming impulse was to tell her he couldn't help her and send her on her way. But if the war left him anything worth honoring, it was the sacrifice of those who gave their lives. Alan Danton lost his life, but Jack Hoffman didn't. If it was his own daughter standing in front of Alan Danton, Danton surely would have done what he could to help her.

"We could meet for lunch tomorrow," Hoffman said. "Where are you staying?"

"The Harbor View."

"I'll meet you in the lobby at eleven thirty."

"Perfect."

With that, she thanked him and left.

He served with many men in Vietnam, some for months, some for only a few days. Everyone arrived as a replacement, and you never spent a full one-year tour of duty with anyone. Time had reduced the soldiers he served with in Delta Company to nameless young faces in Instamatic photos. But Alan Danton was different. Alan Danton was a man you didn't forget.

2
TON SON NHUT, OCTOBER 1969

A Boeing 707 bounced hard on the runway and floated, obstinately refusing to land. In the threadbare seats of the Braniff charter, 180 men sat silently, with no cheers, no expressions of relief that a long flight was ending. The plane taxied past F-4 Phantoms nested in revetments like brooding hens. A Huey "slick" taxied on an adjacent runway, gathered speed, dropped its nose, and climbed away. The big aircraft came to a stop near a makeshift terminal in what might have been an old storage building.

The flight had left the airbase in Sacramento twenty-four hours earlier, arriving in Vietnam after a stop in Japan for refueling and repair of a jammed cargo door. The passengers, most of them junior officers, stood and stretched. They were hungry, jet-lagged, and anxious. Only a year and a half separated most of them the day they checked into a basic training company at some dreary fort in the States. They had voluntarily traded safe and secure lives for one that just might get them killed. Crazy, but best not to dwell on that. A flight attendant threw open the cabin door to a blast of hot air.

The whistles, jeers, and epithets that greeted the new arrivals gave them no comfort. Nearly two hundred soldiers sat on benches outside the terminal, waiting for the "Freedom Bird" that would take them back to the States, and it was late.

"Glad you could make it, cherry boys," one of them yelled as the new men descended the stairs to the tarmac.

"Yeah, Charlie expecting y'all," chimed in another.

"Three-sixty-five and a wake-up," jibed someone to uproarious laughter.

The lean, bronze-faced veterans appeared perfectly cool under a blistering sun. They had turned in their green jungle fatigues for khakis. Combat Infantry Badges and rows of ribbons told each one's story of survival in "the Green Monster," the grunt's honorific for the jungle. Hoffman averted his eyes; the year that separated him from a plane ride home seemed an eternity.

Inside the terminal, each man searched through a mountain of duffel bags for the one with his name stenciled on the side. An NCO in charge of transport to the army post at Long Binh urged them to "make it snappy; we ain't got all fuckin' day." Hoffman decided the prudent course was to wait for the pile to melt. He spotted his bag, threw it over his shoulder, and climbed aboard the last bus in a line of six idling outside. The heavy wire mesh that covered the windows didn't escape his notice.

The little convoy jounced and, where possible, sped on a road choked with bicycles, pedicabs, and motorcycles. Lambrettas loaded with cargo and clinging passengers sputtered along, spewing clouds of purple smoke. The bus drivers leaned on their horns, parting the noisy throng like a flock of sheep. Shanties constructed of salvaged war materials lined the route. Anything salvageable from the detritus of the American occupier was put to use: sides of ammo boxes used for walls, discarded sheet metal for roofs, flattened beer and soda cans for shingles.

Everywhere, pedestrians carried goods on their heads or on shoulder poles. Naked children with swollen bellies played in the dust at the roadside, while grandparents watched lethargically from open doorways. Men and women in conical straw hats and ao ba ba, the loose-fitting shirt and pants common in the south of the country, crowded the shops, while women of means sped by on motor scooters, their faces covered against the sun and colorful ao dais sailing behind.

The bus was a sauna. Hoffman's shirt adhered to him like a second clammy skin. Then, the saturated air outside could hold no more and turned liquid with a thunder clap. A cloudburst drove the roadside folk to shelter, all except the children who gleefully splashed in muddy pools. Mothers seized the opportunity to soap and rinse their toddlers in the torrent. To Hoffman, it was a scene in a movie, one in which he never dreamed he would be an actor.

The buses arrived at the heavily guarded gates of Long Binh post where they stopped at the headquarters of the 90th Replacement Battalion. The hopscotch passage to Vietnam took Hoffman from Fort Benning, Georgia, to Seattle on leave, to San Francisco for a flight to Panama for two weeks of Jungle Operations School, and back to Mather Air Force Base near Sacramento for the flight to Southeast Asia. At Long Binh, he would be issued the tropical combat uniform of jungle fatigues and canvass-topped boots. He would receive orders to report to an infantry unit somewhere in Vietnam.

At last, he could begin counting down the days until he returned home, though it was like emptying a swimming pool with a teacup.

By the time he checked in at the replacement center, it was 1800 hours, and he was hungry. The transients ate in a large mess hall, silently bolting down chow and running to see if their assignments were posted at the headquarters building. A gaggle of men milled around a bulletin board, killing time until a clerk appeared with a new set of orders. No predicting when an individual's orders might appear on a list, thus the Army's usual "hurry up and wait."

In the last forty-eight hours, Hoffman managed only a snooze on the plane, but he was too wired now to sleep. He hung around the headquarters building. Hours passed, several postings occurred, night fell, and still no Hoffman on the list of assignees. At 0200, with the next posting three hours away, he went to the transient barracks to get off his feet. The building was as dark and humid as a cave. He groped between rows of iron bunks, looking for a vacancy. Mosquito nets made it difficult. Feeling his way, he found one, but no: "Hey, asshole, occupied."

Finally, an empty upper bunk. He climbed in, lay on his back, and closed his eyes. Sour breath and body odor fouled the air. Who in his right mind would choose this? And yet, he had. He had walked away from decisions about a career, graduate school, marriage, and family, all the issues that seemed so important just a short time ago. Now his future was uncertain, his very survival at stake. Oddly, the powerlessness of his position brought him a certain peace.

Men shuffled in and out of the barrack in the darkness. Indignant shouts and curses greeted some fool who made the mistake of turning on the lights. His nerves taut as guitar strings, and despairing of getting any rest, he rejoined the troops wandering in the transient area. He lit a cigarette and headed for the combination latrine and bath house to relieve himself.

In the steamy shower room, a dozen naked men bathed, while nearby, soldiers stood at urinals. Several Vietnamese women mopped floors and replenished the supply of soap and towels. Two more sat on their haunches in a corner, polishing the leather portion of jungle boots. The presence of women struck Hoffman as strange, but they seemed cool with what was going on around them.

As dawn broke, the smell of bacon and eggs drifted from the mess hall. Hoffman's stomach was queasy and he wasn't hungry, but he poured himself a cup of coffee. Word came that another set of assignments just went up, and he rushed out to the bulletin board. From the midst of the gaggle, someone yowled, "MACV Headquarters in Saigon. Lady Luck smilin' on me." Others ambled off grimly to collect their gear. Finally, Hoffman saw his name: "01 Jack Hoffman, 24th Infantry Division, Camp Farrell, Pleiku. Report for transport 0630 hours."

The Twenty-fourth? Responsible for patrolling the mountainous wilderness of II Corps, which was the largest of the four tactical zones of Vietnam. Now his training at the jungle school in Panama made sense. For two weeks, he had slogged through the rainforests, rafted the Chagres River, rappelled waterfalls, practiced escape and evasion, and ate monkey meat. Gigantic rusting steam shovels abandoned by Ferdinand de Lesseps demonstrated the jungle's capacity to reject foreign objects.

With ten other replacements, he boarded a C-123 for the half-hour flight to Pleiku. The plane climbed steeply and headed up the coast: on the right, the cerulean South China Sea, and on the left, a sparkling green quilt of flooded paddies. Here and there, the neat thatched roofs of hamlets, water buffaloes grazing along dikes, and peasants planting rice belied the fact that, somewhere down there, a war was going on.

The plane wasn't airborne long when it banked west, leaving the sea behind and climbing over mountains rising abruptly from the coastal plain. Jungle lay like a thick blanket of green wool over undulating mountains and ridges. Rivers fell through steep canyons to falls. He saw small patches of cleared forest, but otherwise, nothing to suggest human presence, no roads, no villages, no plantations, just a vast trackless wilderness stretching to the hazy horizons.

The drone of the engines and the vibration of the plane had a narcotic effect on the passengers sitting in slings along the walls of the cabin. Their heads drooped and swayed with the rocking of the plane. Hoffman closed his eyes and thought about Clara. They had met in high school, gone steady, and never seriously dated anyone else. He missed her terribly.

A change in the engine tempo and the sensation of descent woke Hoffman from a light sleep. He turned and peered through a window behind him. The plane banked over a large military installation. Row upon row of long squat buildings filled a perimeter devoid of vegetation. Deuce-and-a-half trucks crawled like toys on dirt roads. Here and there, black smoke from small fires rose and spread like smog. A chain of bunkers and concertina wire encircled the entire camp. Antennae crowned a hill just outside the defensive fortifications.

The plane's intercom crackled: "Gentlemen, welcome to the tropical resort known as Camp Farrell. We sincerely hope you enjoy your accommodations here. If not, don't blame us. We're just following orders."

No one laughed. This was the last stop in their long journey forward. They would remain at the division base camp only long enough to receive their assignments to companies. Hoffman reported to his battalion headquarters, the Third Battalion, Twenty-seventh Infantry "Desert Devils," a regiment with roots in Arizona. He sent a perfunctory telegram to Clara. She would want to know he was okay. He asked her to inform his parents that he had arrived safely. Then he visited the post exchange and purchased stationery and envelopes.

Most of his orientation consisted of briefings on such topics as the necessity of taking atabrine tablets against malaria and avoiding trench foot and venereal disease. He checked out a rucksack and web gear from the supply building and signed for an M-16 in the armory.

A Jeep driver took him and two others to the firing range to sight-in their weapons. They passed through various brigade and battalion areas. The base camp seemed larger than it looked from the air, a virtual clapboard and plywood city, large enough to house and support a population of more than twenty thousand. Limited electricity and no plumbing meant minimal creature comforts. In each unit's designated area, soldiers used engineer stakes to stir a flambe of kerosene and human excrement in halved fifty-five-gallon drums. So that was the source of that black acrid smoke that hung over the post.

On day two, Hoffman joined a group of replacements for an "orientation patrol." A few hundred meters outside the wire, they came upon a small Montagnard village. Several women hawked strings of love beads and brass bracelets melted from shell casings. Smiling mischievously, their teeth shockingly red from chewing betel, the women offered a snack of dried grasshoppers, which hung on strings from their waists. They got no takers and obviously expected none.

With the preliminaries out of the way, Hoffman and nine other officers gathered in a briefing room to receive their company assignments. A major entered. They jumped to attention. He looked too young to hold that rank, but a Combat Infantry Badge, Jump Wings, and Special Forces and Ranger patches demanded respect. "As you were, gentlemen," he said, opening a folder and removing a typewritten sheet. "I won't keep you long. I know you're champing at the bit to join your units in the bush." He read off their assignments. Hoffman was to join Delta Company, guarding an airstrip near the village of Buon Binh.

The major said, "Before I dismiss you, take a good look at one another. Go ahead; look around." The men did as they were instructed, wondering the point of it. All of them were in their early twenties, with clean-shaven "white-sidewall" haircuts. One was African-American, one Hispanic, and the rest Caucasian. All were physically fit. "Statistically," the major said, "half of you aren't going to make it out of here on your two feet. I'm doing you a favor by telling you this. Keep your heads down and your shit tight, and you'll be just fine. Now get out of here, and Godspeed."

At noon the following day, Hoffman went to the chopper pad at the airstrip for the last leg of his journey forward. Mirages gave the illusion of small lakes at the far end of the runway. A slick landed and idled, while shirtless men, their backs gleaming with sweat, loaded cartons of C-rations and ammo boxes headed for Bravo Company, not Delta, Hoffman's destination. Twenty minutes later, another chopper arrived, this one delivering supplies to Delta. Hoffman threw his ruck on board and sat on a stack of C-rations. The bird lifted off and turned south.

3
FUCKING NEW GUY

The highland forests and plains of South Vietnam provide a habitat for numerous species of tropical fauna. In the French colonial days, the puppet emperor Bao Dai built a hunting lodge in Buon Binh. Theodore Roosevelt had once visited to hunt the Indochinese tiger from the back of an elephant. The grand bungalow now housed a detachment of Green Berets more interested in hunting men than big game.

The Montagnards, whom the ethnic Vietnamese contemptuously referred to as "moi," or "savages," foraged the wilderness of the Central Highlands. Until the 1950s, the hill tribes enjoyed peace and relative isolation in the dark, virgin jungle of the Annamite Mountain Range. The French and American wars ended that. In order to exert control over the area, the Vietnamese government under Ngo Dinh Diem resettled thousands of ethnic Vietnamese, lowland people, in the Highlands. The Montagnards found themselves entangled in Vietnamese wars that brought them nothing but misery. They embraced the Americans as allies and protectors in the 1960s, but it was to be an alliance as expedient as the one they struck with the French, with a similar result.

Interlocking sheets of matting called PSP, pierced steel planking, clad the runway at Buon Binh. The Americans used the airstrip as a refueling station. A small detachment of observation helicopters and gunships flew missions from there, as did a few Cessna O-2 Skymasters, or "Oscar Deuces," fixed-wing surveillance aircraft. Hoffman's "slick," an arcane term grunts used to refer to a Huey supply helicopter, landed near a small circle of bunkers adjacent to the runway. A soldier with a radio was waiting for him.

"Lieutenant Hoffman?" the soldier shouted over the noise of the chopper.

"Roger that," Hoffman said. "Looking for Delta's C-O, Captain Northrup."

"Follow me."

The soldier identified himself as Gonzalez, Captain James Northrup's RTO, or radio telephone operator. Hoffman knew from a briefing at Camp Farrell that Delta was licking its wounds after a firefight in the Bu Prang Massif, a spine of rugged, heavily forested mountains extending into Cambodia and a perennial sanctuary of North Vietnamese troops. He asked Gonzalez about it. "It was some bad shit," the soldier said. "Every time we go there, we get our butts kicked. They keep sending us anyway."

Around the perimeter, the grunts appeared to be on light duty. Some sat shirtless on ammo boxes, playing cards. Others chatted as they cleaned weapons or sat on their bunkers writing letters. A transistor radio blared, "Break another little bit of my heart, now, darling. Yeah, yeah, yeah, yeah . . . You know you got it, child, if it makes you feel good." Hoffman sensed eyes furtively sizing him up as he walked along the bunker line. He felt every bit an FNG—fucking new guy—and a butter-bar second lieutenant to boot. How long would it take him to demonstrate his bona fides to these battle-tested men?

Gonzalez proceeded with the new lieutenant toward Northrup's large bunker, located in the center of the perimeter. Hoffman saw something that stopped him in his tracks. A soldier sat on a wall of sand bags with his leg propped up, while another stood over him with a helmet in his hands. The latter raised the steel pot high and brought it down sharply on the boot of the former. The steel pot struck with a hallow thud, and the recipient of the blow howled a stream of expletives.

"More?" the wielder of the helmet asked.

"Yeah, but Jesus, dude, hit me in the damn ankle like I told you."

The steel pot fell once more on the fabric portion of the shrieking soldier's jungle boot. Grunts nearby seemed unconcerned, but not Hoffman. "What the hell are they doing?" he demanded of Gonzalez.

"Oh, that's just Finkelman getting his ticket to the rear punched," Gonzalez shrugged. "They reserve a bunk for him at the hospital. The Fink could write a book on self-inflicted wounds."

"Well, I'm going to put a stop to this," Hoffman asserted, dismayed by Gonzalez's indifference.

"Won't do no good, LT. Anyway, in the boonies, he's as useless as a limp dick in a whore house."

Hoffman wouldn't let it go. "Hey, you two, knock it off," he shouted.

The striker looked up, shrugged, returned his steel pot to his head, and sauntered toward the bunker line. Finkelman hobbled off toward the medic's bunker.

Gonzalez rolled his eyes and raised his radio's handset to his ear. "Pinky, tell LT Unnerfeld the Fink is at it again. Yeah. Sorry muthafucka's getting his leg hammered with a steel pot. Yup . . . Yup . . . I know, I know, but tell him anyhow. Out."

"So now what?" Hoffman demanded.

"So now, not much," Gonzalez said. "It don't mean nothin.'"

Hoffman would take it up with Captain Northrup, about whom he knew only what the battalion executive officer at Camp Farrell had told him, that the captain was on his second tour and had been with the company three months. An experienced CO on his second tour--—that was encouraging.

"Here's the command post, LT," Gonzalez said, turning away. "You'll find Captain Northrup playing cards."

Four men sat at a folding table in the shade of a tarp. Hoffman dropped his gear. No one looked up from their hands, so he waited. The betting started. Two players folded, and the remaining two stared at one another defiantly. One was heavyset. A blue paisley bandana adorned his neck. The other was lanky and perhaps a bit older than the other men. His cheek bulged with chew. He turned his head and spat a brown gob.

"Damn it, Al, I wish you wouldn't do that here," said the stocky one. "It's nasty. Besides, how is it possible to hold that stuff in your mouth and drink beer at the same time?"

"Years of practice, my man," said Al. Hoffman noticed a Bowie knife strapped to Al's leg.

"Well, it's unsanitary, not to mention annoying," the larger man further objected.

"One takes small pleasures as one can," said Al.

"Wonderful, just fucking wonderful," said the larger man, shaking his head. "Raise you ten."

"See your ten, and call," Al said, ceremoniously laying down three jacks and two aces.

"Damn it, you're unconscious today," said the other, throwing down his cards.

"When you hot, you hot, chief," Al crowed, sweeping up a mess of military pay currency.

The "chief" must be Captain Northrup, Hoffman assumed, but asked to be sure. "Which of you gentlemen is Captain Northrup?"

Al cracked a sarcastic grin and launched another stream into the dirt. "Ain't seen no gentlemen 'round here lately," he said. "Any of you know if we got any gentlemen in this goddamn outfit?"

"Only by an act of congress," said one of the others, "which leaves me out."

Real comedians, Hoffman thought. "I'm Lieutenant Hoffman, Jack Hoffman."

Ignoring him, Al said to the man to his right, "Horner, be a good chap and grab me another can of that warm piss, will you?"

The soldier got up and retrieved a Coors from an open case. The big fellow with the bandana stood up. "Well, that's enough abuse for one day. Have to go to work. We've been expecting you, Lieutenant Hoffman. Bet you're just tickled to death to be here."

"Oh, good one, chief," Al said.

Hoffman saluted. "Thank you, sir."

“Hey, never salute an officer in the field,” Al snapped. “You want to get captain here greased by a sniper?”

“Absolutely not,” Hoffman said, fed up with the kidding. “Wouldn’t want to get off to a bad start.”

Al fixed his cold blue eyes on Hoffman. “Think it’s funny, lieutenant? I’m serious.”

“Cut the new man some slack, Al,” Northrup interjected. “I’m Jim Northrup, and this congenial fellow is Lieutenant Alan Danton, company executive officer. He snarls a lot, but he’s toothless. Isn’t that right, Al?”

“If you say so, sir,” Danton said, smirking.

“Take a seat and crack a brew,” Northrup said, kicking a chair toward Hoffman. “They’re warm, but they’re wet. We get a ration here, a reward of sorts for good behavior.”

Hoffman took a can from the case and pulled the tab. Its contents foamed over his hand. Northrup offered him a Camel, not Hoffman’s brand, but he took it to be sociable. It went with the beer, hot and stale.

Northrup said, “I am assigning you to the second platoon. You’ll find them yonder.” He pointed to the north side of the perimeter. “Sergeant Galvin is your platoon sergeant. You’ll do well to listen to him. He’ll provide you with a roster. We’re a little short-handed after the contact last week. I’ve sent two replacements to your platoon, and we’ve got more coming.”

Northrup didn’t offer an explanation. He said only that the company was providing a few weeks of security on the air strip, after which it would rejoin the battalion on an operation. The duty was light but not without its moments. The strip had been mortared the previous day, just a couple of rounds, nothing serious. A few months earlier, sappers slipped in and lit up two choppers with satchel charges.

"Just make sure the bunkers are manned at all times. Keep 'em busy with details. Other than that, none of your men goes into town without authorization. They'll try to sneak out, so be vigilant. Anything to add, Al?"

"Keep the whores outside the wire," Alan Danton said. "One set up for business in a bunker last night. The boys think I don't notice, but there isn't a trick I haven't seen, pardon the pun. You are the duty officer tonight. That means you walk the bunker line every hour on the hour. The password is 'Marilyn,' and the response is 'Monroe.' Anyone caught sleeping on guard gets an Article 15," he said referring to a nonjudicial punishment. "No exceptions."

Northrup sucked on his can of beer and belched. "And oh, one more thing. The locals gather at the gate to do business. Everything from knockoff wrist watches to porn. No military pay currency should be going into their grubby little civilian paws. I just got a directive from division concerning the black market, so watch for it." Northrup had a habit of constantly flicking his cigarette. He paused, looking at the burning tip. "What have I forgotten, Al?"

Danton said, "Formation, 0700 tomorrow for an equipment inspection. Every swinging dick's weapon and ammo should be clean. I want to go blind looking down a shiny barrel. We just got in fresh radio batteries, frags, and a few light anti-tank weapons to distribute. And make sure they aren't using up their C-4 to brew coffee."

The plastic explosive burned white hot when lit with a match. The grunts had a habit of pinching off bits of it to heat their C-rations. Removing the stuff from their Claymore mines could reduce the device's lethal explosion to an anemic pop.

It was noon, and the heat of the day had arrived when Hoffman approached his first command on the bunker line. A detail was adding a ring of razor wire to the perimeter. They stretched the coils and anchored them to the ground with steel engineer stakes. They pounded in the stakes with a sledge hammer, striking a 105-mm artillery casing placed over the top to make a larger hitting surface. The brass rang like a bell.

"Looking for Sergeant Galvin," Hoffman said to a black soldier cleaning an M-60 machine gun. The parts covered his poncho liner like pieces of a mechanical puzzle. "Over there," he said perfunctorily, pointing in the direction of two soldiers near a water trailer. One of them stood naked on an ammo crate, soaping himself while the other poured water on him from a bucket.

"Sergeant Galvin?" Hoffman inquired of the two.

"That's me," said the bather.

"I'm Lieutenant Hoffman."

"Yes, sir. Saw your bird come in." He stepped off the crate and dried himself with a green towel. "I'm Ray Galvin, but everyone calls me Razor, usually preceded by Fuckin', as in, 'Fuckin' Razor said so.'" He pulled on his pants.

"I'll omit the Fuckin'," Hoffman said. "Hope I didn't interrupt your shower."

"Not much of a shower but field expedient. Been over a month since we've seen a bar of soap and enough clean water to drown a cat."

Hoffman was staring at the scabrous, weeping sores on Galvin's forearms and shins. "You seen the medic about that?"

"US Army jungle rot." Jungle rot was a fungal infection of cuts and abrasions of the skin, caused by pushing through thick jungle, Galvin explained. "You'll get your standard issue of pussy sores soon enough. Exposure to the sun is the best remedy. Step inside my bunker, and I'll show you where you'll be sleeping or trying to."

Galvin pulled back a tarp covering the entrance to an igloo-like structure of stacked sandbags. The air inside was damp and sour but at least cool. Weak light crept through gun ports.

"You can drop your gear there, in the corner," the sergeant said. "I'll go over the roster with you; then I suggest we assemble a little formation to introduce you if that's okay."

Galvin appeared to be in his early twenties, not much older than the troops he supervised. He seemed pleasantly unpretentious and easygoing. He recited the names of the four squad leaders. "They're all good men, seasoned grunts. They'll give you no trouble, and they know what to do when the shit flies."

"Understand you had a rough go of it on your last operation," Hoffman said.

"We walked into a trap."

"How did it happen?"

"Long story," Galvin said, frowning. "Ask Lieutenant Danton."

Galvin obviously didn't want to talk about it, and Hoffman decided not to press him. Some grieving was going on, and Hoffman was not yet a member of the family.

Galvin said, "Replacements for our KIAs arrived yesterday. They are worthless until they get their shit together. Usually takes a few months. Oh, no offense, sir."

Hoffman laughed. "No offense taken, sergeant. I expect you to be honest with me." The buck sergeant was at least as capable of leading the platoon as he was.

Galvin said, "You'll get honesty from me. I'm way too short to bullshit you."

"How short?"

"Ninety-one and a wakeup."

This was a comfort Hoffman. He would be with the platoon for three months. The lieutenant said, "I have some dumb questions. If some of them sound stupid, humor me."

"Fire away."

"These troops look like a bunch of hippies: love beads, peace symbols, brass bracelets. Not exactly regulation."

"Don't try to enforce a dress code, LT. That stuff is for luck, and these grunts need all they can get."

"All those helmets on backward. What's that all about?"

"Two reasons. The front rim of the steel pot blocks the M-16's elevated sight. Why they replaced the good ol' M-14 with a piece of plastic shit made by Mattel, I can't explain. The other reason is equally important. It pisses off the lifers."

"I'd better turn mine around then."

"And one more thing, LT. In those new fatigues, you look like a recruiting poster. I'll get you a used set out of the laundry bag. And if you're wearing boxers, toss 'em unless you want to start a fungus farm in your crotch. I hope I'm not offending you, just trying to get you squared away."

"No, sergeant, I asked, and your advice is appreciated. Anything else?"

"Those dog tags hangin' from your neck. They rattle and catch on undergrowth in the bush. Lace the tags into your boots. That way, if all they find are pieces, they'll know it's you."

"Not a prediction, I hope."

"Just a possibility. Here's the roster."

Galvin read down the list. Two were in the hospital at Qui Nhon with shrapnel wounds and a third with malaria. Two were on R&R, leaving eighteen to hump out on the next operation. "That's pretty much full strength for us: twenty men, give or take a few."

"Half a platoon," Hoffman said, stating the obvious.

"Way it is. The geniuses upstairs want us lean and mean, snoopin' and poopin'. We rarely see large units of NVA anymore. If we do, it's because they see us first, and that ain't good. It wasn't like that on my first tour back in '67. We usually humped in battalion strength, but doing that in these mountains is impossible. Let's go see if we can scare up some other platoon leaders."

The two men emerged from the bunker into the blinding sunlight. Galvin slipped on his Ray-Bans and lit a cigarette. A light observation chopper buzzed low overhead, made a ninety-degree turn, and circled like an angry wasp over a Cobra gunship warming up on the runway.

"We've got a pretty squared-away crew right now," Galvin said. "Always a few duds to babysit, of course. A couple of months ago, we had a fucking Audie Murphy. Stood right up in the middle of a firefight, and a B-40 rocket knocked his helmet clean off. It was a dud. Pure dumb luck. It didn't decapitate him, but he had a hell of a headache. God protects fools, drunks, and the United States Infantry, I guess."

"Good to know God's on our side."

"When He's in the mood."

"Speaking of moods, what's this guy Danton's story, anyway?"

"You meet him at the company CP?"

"Yeah. Charming fellow."

"Wouldn't win no popularity contest around here, that's for sure. The dude is looking for more fruitcake on his Class A uniform and is not too worried about what it costs. On our last operation, he put us on a suicide trail."

"Suicide trail?"

"Reeked of rotten fish and charcoal, the Dink smell. Fresh footprints everywhere. I told him it was crazy, but the man didn't listen to anybody. We walked right into an L-shaped ambush."

Galvin was distracted by a soldier sitting on top of a sandbagged bunker, leafing through a *Playboy* magazine. "That the November issue, Jules?"

"Roger that. Kraut just brought it from the rear. Miss November, she got some fine tits I must say."

"Drop it by my bunker when you're done."

"End of the line, Razor."

"Shit burning detail for anyone rips out the centerfold."

"Yeah, yeah, yeah."

The two passed the mortar pits. The crew was busy swabbing barrels and stacking ammo. A lean, bear-chested grunt shouted, "Hey Razor, the LT says we might get some hot chow tonight. Heard anything?"

"Not today, Indian. Maybe tomorrow."

"Tomorrow, reservation time," the man called Indian laughed. "That mean maybe never."

"Indian?" Hoffman said.

"Yeah. Blackfoot from Montana. Good man. The mortar crew was busy for a while last night. Someone said they saw movement outside the wire and called for a fire mission."

"Confirm anything?"

"Danton had us run a sweep this morning. We didn't find diddly squat."

"Northrup and Danton seem tight," Hoffman said.

"Northrup thinks Danton shits silver dollars. It's all about the body count. The gooks drag their dead away, so the higher highers have us digging up fresh graves. That's hard up, man. And for what? There are rumors that some units are deploying back to the States pretty soon. Of course, you can't believe half of what you hear."

"I heard the talk before I got over here," Hoffman said.

"Declare victory and get the hell out I say," Galvin said.

"What about the ARVN?" Hoffman wondered.

"Worthless. There's a company of 'em on the other side of the airstrip. They rarely leave their fortified position, and why should they? We go out in that stinking jungle and do the fighting for 'em. No, don't buy that Vietnamization crap, LT. Only Vietnamization gonna be done 'round here's by Uncle Ho, soon as we leave. Just a matter of time before he's slurping his pho in Saigon."

If this soldier, on his second tour, was that negative about what he was doing here, morale must be terrible, Hoffman surmised. A Chinook hovered above them with a water trailer spinning from its undercarriage on a tether. A soldier tossed a smoke grenade to mark the spot for the trailer, then ran into the blade wash to release the cable. Galvin identified the soldier as First Lieutenant Todd Unnerfeld.

Unnerfeld was tall and muscular, in college days a tight end at the Citadel. A bandana tied on his forehead, a Fu Manchu mustache, squinty eyes, and a trace of a goatee gave him a Genghis Khan look. "Who you got there, Razor, the new lieutenant?" Unnerfeld asked when the chopper was gone and quiet returned to the bunker line.

"Yes, sir. Just got in," Galvin said.

"Welcome to our humble little war," Unnerfeld said, shaking hands in the elaborate pattern Hoffman had observed but performed awkwardly. "Ain't much of a war, but as they say, it ain't much of a war." He invited his visitors through a curtain into his bunker. Marijuana and incense sweetened the stale air. Four cots and a table fashioned from ammo crates furnished the hole.

"Plant your bottoms, boys, and help yourselves to my Southern hospitality," Unnerfeld said. "Traded with the Air Force for these cots. Only cost me two Montagnard machetes. Those boys live like kings, and they do like their souvenirs for lying purposes back home."

He opened a pack of Swisher Sweets blunts and poured Old Grand Dad into a canteen, then opened a bag of pretzels. Hoffman took an immediate liking to Unnerfeld. "How long have you been in the country?"

"Six months, twenty-two days, and," he looked at his watch and added, "a little over twelve hours. A fucking lifetime and still not short. Time goes faster in King Tut's tomb. Ain't that right, Razor? But you, my man, are short enough to dance with Minnie Mouse."

"I don't like to talk about it," Galvin said bluntly.

"Oh, sorry. You see, Hoffman, we have our little superstitions. Dig it."

"Uhh huh," Hoffman said, lighting up a cigar.

"You get a standard issue of luck, and the rest of it is up to you," Unnerfeld said. "Just keep your shit wired tight, and don't go looking for trouble. It will find you soon enough. Right, Razor?"

"That would be a roger," Galvin said.

"It's really not complicated," Unnerfeld said. "Uncle Ho knows high school physics. He'll exert only enough force to keep an object moving in the direction it's already going. In our case, that's right on out of Vietnam. So, go with the flow, man."

Hoffman had never heard an officer talk that way. Back at Fort Benning, it was still all about winning.

"And don't let that asshole Danton bother you. Thinks he can tell the rest of us how to fight this goddamn war. Fucking know-it-all. Well, he can go fuck himself far as I'm concerned, and I've told him so. When you're in the boonies, ain't no one but God can tell you what to do."

"What about Northrup?"

"Lifer. Came up through the ranks and didn't want to spoil his career by getting killed. Put in for a transfer to Signal Corps. Much safer there."

After sharing a little "back in The World" rap, Hoffman and Galvin headed to the platoon's command post. They came upon four men setting trip flares outside the wire. One of them was Tom Sullivan, whom Galvin identified as Hoffman's RTO, though the lieutenant could choose someone else if he wanted.

"Sully's got brains, college degree and all," Galvin said. "Only one in the platoon finished college. He'll do a good job for you."

A Huey slick arrived with mail and supplies. The door gunner handed a packet of mail to Galvin, and the grunts pressed in around him, hoping to hear their names called. The fortunate rushed off to find some privacy; the rest drooped away to resume their tasks. There was no letter for Hoffman, but he didn't expect any. It would take the mail a while to find him.

Nature was calling. He spotted four men perched like birds on a platform, their pants down around their boots. Nearby, another soldier poured kerosene into several halved fifty-five-gallon drums he had removed from beneath the platform, while another lit the contents and stirred them with an engineer's stake. Black putrid smoke darkened the air.

But near the company command post, what appeared to be a small outhouse caught Hoffman's eye. The door slammed behind him. He dropped his pants and made himself comfortable with a copy of *Field & Stream* he found on the bench. He was just getting started when he heard a knock on the door.

"LT, you in there?"

"Yeah. Won't be long."

"No, LT, you have to leave. Now."

"I'm not done."

"This is the captain's private shitter. LT Danton told me to tell you to snap it off and use the latrine."

"Is this some kind of joke?"

"Afraid not, sir."

"Tell Danton his shit stinks too, and I'll see him when I'm finished."

"Yes, sir."

Hoffman's blood was boiling as he approached the command post where Danton was waiting, grinning, his hands on his hips.

"Okay, Danton, what's your problem?" Hoffman demanded.

"Oh, is our Ivy League too good for the common shitter?"

"Look, I don't know what your beef is, but let's get it settled right now."

"At ease, lieutenant. No sense of humor?"

"Find some other way to entertain yourself."

"My, my, your jaw is tight. You'll learn how we do things around here. Until then, use the common latrine. The captain doesn't like to wait when he's gotta go."

Hoffman stomped off, cursing under his breath. He had let Danton get under his skin, and he regretted it.

The second platoon was gathering for its daily briefing. Hoffman joined Razor Galvin atop a bunker and surveyed his new charges. They were just kids, most too young to vote, but their eyes were old and tired. Gaunt and haggard, in baggy, filthy jungle fatigues, they had the appearance of an army in retreat. Galvin told them there would be a red alert that night, prompted by intelligence from the CIA, that the local VC—the Vietcong—were planning a sapper attack on the airfield. The men groaned. The alert would mean doubling the guard and little, if any, sleep.

Galvin said, "I know, I know. I don't like it either. Just make sure you aren't looking at the back of your eyelids. Lieutenant Danton will be checking, and if he catches you napping, there'll be hell to pay. But on to more important things. This is our new platoon leader, Lieutenant Jack Hoffman. LT, you got something to say?"

Hoffman wanted to make a good first impression, but what does a green second lieutenant say to men who've been blooded in battle?

"Thank you, sergeant. Like Razor said, I'm Lieutenant John Hoffman, from Seattle."

"Hoorahh," someone shouted.

"Okay, a homey. Any others?"

No one answered.

"Well, we're all eating the same shit sandwich here." He paused and wondered if he was trying too hard. "Sergeant Galvin tells me you lost some men in the mountains last week. I'm very sorry to hear that, and I want you to know the most important part of my job is keeping us alive, to the extent that's possible." He wondered if that sounded patronizing. "I'm going to rely heavily on the sergeant here. All I ask of you is that we work together. If you've got a bitch, bring it. If there's anything I can do to resolve it, I will." He wanted to keep it short. "Any thoughts, questions?"

"Yeah," said a baby-faced kid in the back.

"Yes, *sir*," Galvin corrected.

"Yes, sir. Do I get to keep the monkey?"

There were giggles from the others.

"Okay, knock it off," Galvin said. "Beezley, I've told you a hundred times you can't hump with a fucking monkey on your shoulder. Just leave the little lush here with a can of beer, and he'll be happy."

This elicited laughter, as the monkey was known to drink the beer the men gave it.

"Awe, Razor, he doesn't bother no one. He needs a tribe. The first one we see, I'll turn him loose. Promise."

"Take him back to the main gate, and the locals will look after him."

"They'll eat him."

There was more laughter.

"You heard me, Beezley."

Galvin informed the platoon to prepared for a full equipment inspection at 0800 the next morning. Lieutenant Hoffman was the duty officer and would be checking the bunker line all night, every hour on the hour. Danton too would be sneaking around. They should use the password for the night. With that, he dismissed them.

Darkness fell on Hoffman's first day with his platoon. Did he leave a good impression? There had been no instruction on platoon management at the officer candidate school. He made his first check of the bunker line and found everyone at their posts, doing what soldiers do most of the time: wait. This was not the garrison army he knew in the States but an army in the field, one that dispensed with customary military courtesies. It was also a demoralized army, fighting with no objective but staying alive long enough to get home.

As night surrendered to dewy dawn, poncho-draped figures moved about like monks in the gauzy light, chatting in muffled voices, brewing powdered coffee over heat tabs. Hoffman sat atop his bunker, fighting off sleep. His wristwatch told him it was almost 0500. No need for another check of the bunker line because everyone seemed to be up. He lit a cigarette.

"Time to get ready for inspection, LT," Galvin said, passing by the bunker. "We should have a dry run before Danton gets here."

Hoffman yawned and stretched. "Can we be ready by zero eight hundred?"

"Yes, sir. I've already instructed the squad leaders."

Hoffman thanked fate for delivering Sergeant Ray Galvin. He knew exactly what to do. When he said, "Move," the men moved. In less than an hour, everyone was standing tall in formation, their rucks, ammo, and weapons laid out at their feet. With Galvin, Hoffman took a quick inventory: a five-day supply of C-rations, a canteen and a five-quart blivit, Claymore mines, C-4 plastic explosives, fragmentation grenades, parachute and trip flares, mosquito repellent and cleaning equipment for weapons, belts of machine gun ammo, several light anti-tank weapons, a coil of climbing rope, and a Starlight Scope, a night vision device about the size and weight of a Presto log.

These items were borne by riflemen and grenadiers; machine gunners, two of them, had special burdens. "The pig," as the M-60 was referred to, weighted twenty-three pounds and usually ended up in the hands of the strongest men in the platoon. They also had to carry the feed for their bullet-hungry pigs, thousand-round belts of linked cartridges slung Pancho Villa style across their chests and more girdled around their waists.

In jungle operations, an infantryman carried everything he needed to fight and survive between resupplies by helicopter, which happened once a week, weather and circumstances permitting. Hoffman had a lot to learn about how all of this was done. Much of the standard operating procedure developed organically, over time, in the field. U.S. Army Infantry School classes covered none of it. He noted every detail in anticipation of assembling his own kit.

4
THE NEED TO KNOW

It was nearly 2:00 a.m. when Hoffman turned out the light in the little press room at Central Precinct and drove through a sleeping city to his home in Ballard. "Alan Danton's daughter," he mumbled to himself incredulously. First Lieutenant Alan Danton was dead, and First Lieutenant Jack Hoffman ceased to exist when he hung up his uniform for the last time. Few knew he had ever been other than an average guy with a family, a mortgage, and a job at the newspaper. He felt like a fugitive betrayed after years of living under an assumed identity.

The house was dark and cold. He seldom turned up the thermostat since Susan was gone. In the kitchen, he poured himself half a glass of Scotch, took it to his bedroom, and put it on the bed stand. He stripped, dropped his clothes on the floor, and crawled in naked. The sheets were cold. He sat up, drained the glass, and felt the booze warm his body.

His phone rang at 7:00 a.m., and it could mean only one thing at that hour. He fumbled for the receiver.

"Jack, get your butt out of bed," said the city editor. "We've got a report of a body found on some unused port property, a young woman. A fellow walking his dog stumbled on to it. Cops are investigating now. How fast can you get going?"

Hoffman said, "Probably some derelict. What am I going to find out that I can't get before the deadline from my sources at the department?"

"Not this time, Jack. She apparently was just a kid and pregnant."

He threw on some clothes, jumped in his car, and headed to Central Precinct where he met two homicide detectives in the hall. They were on their way to a crumbling industrial area near the bay. He drove through a patch of morning fog to the port and parked behind several squad cars on the side of the road. Tired and vaguely depressed by a dream he couldn't remember, he proceeded to the crime-scene tape and a uniformed officer. The officer recognized him and allowed him to pass.

About fifty feet up the path, he found a detective, the coroner, and a police photographer standing over the body of the woman. She was Asian, small, delicate, and very young. She had a bullet wound in her left temple, and there was a lot of blood. She was fully dressed and pregnant. Hoffman blanched and turned away, trying not to vomit. An officer noticed his uneasiness.

"Pretty little thing, and with child too," the officer said. "Not easy to look at, is it?"

"No," Hoffman said, "not easy."

"Never really get used to it."

"I suppose not. Any idea who she is?"

The cop shrugged. "No ID."

Hoffman forced himself to look again. The body lay in the mud and weeds like a discarded rag doll. Had she fallen into the Stygian world of drugs and prostitution? She was dressed conservatively and well, not in the cheap, tawdry way of a prostitute. For now, there was little to report in the first edition. He returned to the newsroom, made some phone calls, and checked the missing person's report. With the deadline approaching, he filed a short place holder for an update in later editions:

Seattle police have launched a homicide investigation into the death of a pregnant woman, whose body was found Wednesday in an abandoned industrial area of the Port of Seattle. The unidentified woman died of an apparent gunshot wound. An autopsy will be performed.

That done, Jack Hoffman jogged to the hotel for his meeting with Tess Danton. A woman in her mid-thirties stood in the lobby, obviously waiting for someone. It was her. Her resemblance to her father seemed even stronger. As he approached, she smiled broadly. He couldn't remember ever having seen Alan Danton smile.

"Hello, Mr. Hoffman," she said, offering her hand in a businesslike way. "Thank you so much for agreeing to see me. I must be the last person in the world you expected to drop in like that."

"Stranger things have happened, but it's right up there," Hoffman said, grinning. "And it's 'Jack.'"

"And 'Tess' works for me. I should apologize for not contacting you earlier."

"It's quite alright. Let's get out of this hotel. I know a better place to talk."

They stepped out into a Pacific Northwest drizzle. He held his umbrella over her head for the short walk to an office tower where he had made reservations at a restaurant on the thirtieth floor. It afforded a fine view of the sound and, on a clear day, the Olympics, but the weather was not cooperating. The maître d' showed them to a table.

"So you're here for a law seminar," Hoffman said as the waitress handed them menus.

"Annual training. Session on official corruption."

"Plenty of that. What's your practice?"

"I'm a prosecutor with the US Department of Justice in Austin."

"Really."

"Really. Ten years."

"Your father would be proud of you."

"Think so?"

"Definitely."

"Tax law didn't interest me. I've been told I am combative."

"Anyone told you how much you resemble your father?"

"I don't have much contact with people who actually knew him, and that's the problem. They remember things about him, of course, but he's a puzzle to me. I have a lot of questions about him, the kind of man he was, and how he died."

"I see," Hoffman said. He had lain awake through the night thinking about what he was going to say to her: the usual banalities, what a high-performing officer he was, a certified hero, a patriot she could be proud of, all ostensibly true.

"So I'm thinking, perhaps you can help me with things that aren't on the record," Tess said.

"You know, Tess, I really didn't spend a lot of time with him. Our platoons operated alone most of the time—small units, guerilla tactics. We seldom spent any significant time back in base camp. So I never got very personal with your father, knew very little about his personal background."

"Did you know he'd already served four years in the Navy before he enlisted in the Army?"

"Now that you mention it, I do recall something about that. He was in his late twenties when I met him, older than most of us. Captain Northrup used to call him 'Swab.'"

"When he got out of the navy, he went to night school on the GI Bill, but Mother said he was restless. He was selling cars during the day and attending classes at night. She had a part-time waitressing job. They were just scraping by. That's what drove him to reenlist."

"Why not the Navy?"

"He would have liked to, but he couldn't qualify for officer candidate school because of the college degree requirement. The Army didn't care."

In Hoffman's infantry OCS class, there were mustangs, men who had come up through the enlisted ranks, and some green recruits with little or no college behind them. Late in the war, the pool of willing volunteers was shrinking. The gag was, if you could fog a mirror and sign your name on an enlistment form, you were qualified. At least a fourth of those admitted to OCS were either eliminated as unsuitable or dropped out before graduating.

Hoffman said, "Your father was as capable as any officer I knew over there, with or without a college degree." If killing enemy soldiers was the primary objective, this was true.

"I ask questions for a living, so excuse me if I seem pushy," she said. "I have a lot of questions. I've even written them down so I won't forget." She opened a small notebook. "I hope recalling those awful days isn't upsetting for you."

"I think about Vietnam almost every day. It's like a stone in your shoe. You learn to ignore it."

"So why don't you take off your shoe?"

"Not that easy."

"There's so much I'd like to learn about him; I don't even know where to start. What were your impressions of him, just as a human being, I mean?"

"He was respected by his superiors, a very gutsy guy. But our relationship was strictly professional. We went into the jungle alone, with our platoons, and seldom saw one another during normal operations. When we did stand-down back at the base camp, we stayed close to our platoons. Platoons were like family."

"I've been unable to find anyone in his platoon. Do you know where I might find someone who served under him?"

"Can't help you," Hoffman said. "When I got home, I just wanted to forget the whole damn thing, get on with my life."

"How strange that must have been. Isn't there anything you remember about him? Little things like his habits, his sense of humor, just anything."

"I do remember that when he had free time in the rear, which was seldom, he read. And he liked to play cards, poker." Hoffman was struggling. What do you say to the daughter of someone you so thoroughly disliked?

Tess Danton gazed pensively at office towers and the Space Needle outside. A gull flashed by the window. She said, "The army's version of Alan Danton," she shook her head, "is all so cold, so canned. I suppose I should be proud of him, but from my selfish point of view, I'd rather have a live father than a dead hero. He went to war when he didn't have to. I'll never understand it."

Hoffman desperately wanted to say something to comfort her. "I'm sorry," were the only words that came to mind.

"Well, I guess what I said was harsh," she said apologetically. "You went, too."

"We all had our own reasons, none of them very satisfying in retrospect. Do you have any memories of your father?"

"Just snapshots, like watching him shave, the pipes he smoked, the way he tucked me in at night. But sometimes, I'm not even sure I remember that. Maybe I just imagine things."

"Do you remember when your mother was informed of his death?"

"Just what she told me. Jim Northrup flew home with his body at my mother's request. Dad stipulated in his will that he be buried at sea, so the memorial service was held on a Coast Guard cutter out of Galveston, his hometown. I stayed with my grandparents for a few weeks. Mother told me Daddy wasn't coming home, but I didn't fully comprehend what she meant. I remember her crying a lot."

"I didn't know that Northrup accompanied the body. Not surprising, though. They had a friendship. Northrup had a very high opinion of him."

"Jim was a great support for Mom, helping make arrangements, holding her hand through it all. Over the years, he would drop by occasionally until Mom remarried; then that stopped."

"Northrup would be able to tell you more about your father than I can. You indicated you spoke with him?"

"I saw him last year in Atlanta when I was passing through. We had a nice visit. He talked in glowing terms about Dad as a soldier, a patriot, the kind of thing I'd heard a hundred times. He said Dad could be a real cutup and a lot of fun when he could get away from the job. They apparently took a three-day pass together on the coast, at a 'Trang' something."

"Nha Trang," Hoffman said.

"Yeah, that's it. He said they had a great time."

"Northrup was my first company commander but only for a few months. He got a transfer to a safe job in Long Binh, a big army post near Saigon. He wanted a career in the army. He'd be . . . let's see, sixty or so."

"He retired years ago. He said he got caught in the reduction in force after the war. Like my dad, he attended officer candidate school after prior service as a noncommissioned officer. When the Vietnam War ended, the army gave him a choice: leave or accept a demotion to his former rank of sergeant. He chose the latter, but I think he was pretty bitter about it."

Hoffman nodded. "That RIF started just as I was getting out. The Army's policy was to shrink the officer corps by demoting or separating out men considered inferior officer material. Often that meant no college background. Imagine that—qualified to lead men in combat but not in peacetime. It was a rotten deal."

Tess' eyes flashed with anger. "I suppose the same thing would have happened to Dad. Did anything good come of that war, anything at all? Oh, there I go, shooting off my mouth. You put your life on the line, and I shouldn't be saying things like that to you. I apologize."

Hoffman had seen those fiery eyes before, her father's, for sure. He said, "You can't say anything about that damn war that would offend me. But I don't think you should make assumptions about your father's future in the army. He had proven his worthiness."

Over lunch, she confided to Hoffman details of the years following her father's death. Her mother, Claudia, suffered from chronic depression. To anyone willing to listen, Claudia repeated the same stories, like tape recordings: how the two had been high school sweethearts, how upon graduation he had joined the Navy, how his ship had been sent to waters off Vietnam, how he had returned to civilian life and found it difficult to adjust, and how he had joined the Army against her wishes.

So absorbed was Claudia Danton in her own loss that she was incapable of recognizing the emotional price her daughter was paying. Tess recalled her mother finally saw a therapist.

"No one asked me how I felt about losing my father. I guess they assumed I was too young to understand; you know, the kid must be okay because she isn't making a fuss."

Early in her grieving, Claudia Danton would set out two cups of coffee every morning, one for Alan Danton and one for herself. When Tess asked her why she did it, she would only say it made her feel better.

“Scared the hell out of me,” Tess said. “I’ve often wondered whether Mother’s own guilt might have had something to do with it. She sometimes wondered whether she tried hard enough to stop him from joining the Army.”

As she matured from childhood to adolescence, it was easier for Tess to be angry than sad about her loss. She blamed the Army. Everything about it became repugnant: the flag that had draped his coffin and sat in a reliquary on the buffet, the shadow box containing his military decorations. They were merely stage props in a tragic play. She and her mother made several pilgrimages to the Vietnam Veterans Memorial in Washington, D.C., where Claudia Danton would run her fingers over Alan Danton’s name “as if she could bring him out of the stone, like a genie out of a bottle,” as Tess put it.

To support herself and her daughter, Claudia Danton took a job as a practical nurse at the hospital at Fort Benning and eventually returned to night school to become a registered nurse. The routine was exhausting, Tess said, but on the positive side, all-consuming. She was moving on. She was still young and attractive, and there was no scarcity of bachelors around Fort Benning. She started dating but found no one who measured up to Alan Danton.

With her mother’s rambling recollections and what childhood memories she retained, Tess imagined a man as she wanted him to have been: kind, gentle, and supportive. He would have understood her adolescent problems. He was handsome; she knew that from photos. She conversed with him mentally when she felt down and sometimes aloud when she was alone, even wishing him good night when she turned out the light. Her father's absence left a hole in her life, but one she learned to live with. Then everything abruptly changed.

"Mother came home one night and told me she was going to marry a man she had met at the hospital. He was an administrator, a colonel. She had known him only a few months, so it blew me away. After she became Mrs. Peter Rhodes, we moved into his house in Columbus. From then on, she rarely mentioned my father. All her grieving just stopped. It was as if she had amnesia. I was sixteen."

Fortunately, Tess said, Peter Rhodes was an easygoing, nonjudgmental presence in the house. Her mother was happy. She had found a good match for herself and a receptive, patient guardian for Tess. A stepbrother was soon on the way, and Tess embraced with alacrity the role of big sister. With both mother and father working during her teenage years, Tess took on much of the responsibility of caring for the child. She adored the boy, but she never felt like a member of this new family fully. She was still a Danton.

Growing up in Columbus as a "military brat" wasn't easy. During the war, Fort Benning "processed" thousands of men for service in Vietnam. Many were followed to Columbus by brides and girlfriends, away from home for the first time. The women spent lonely months waiting in cheap off-post apartment complexes, while their partners were confined to post in training. There the women met equally lonely young men, with predictable results.

The social turmoil surrounding the fort reflected the changing fortunes of the Army. With the withdrawal of the US troops, the fall of the Saigon government, and the end of the draft, the Army made a rocky adjustment to an all-volunteer force. Downsized and demoralized, it struggled to redefine itself. Standards for recruits dropped. Signing and retention bonuses were adopted to attract recruits and keep them. Drug use and disciplinary problems plagued the ranks. It was a dark time, and Tess couldn't wait to flee Columbus.

"When I graduated from high school and left town for the university, it was for good. No way I was ever going back," she told Hoffman.

Tess said that, as years passed, she became more keenly aware of how little she really knew about her father. Her mother's off-handed recollections failed to satisfy her. She had nowhere else to turn for information; her paternal grandparents had died when Alan Danton was a teenager. His surviving brother was a taciturn man, six years older than Alan. She learned not to press him because he grew impatient, as if he was embarrassed he had so little to say.

"I've never been particularly introspective," Tess said, "but there are a lot of things about myself I'd like to understand. Not having known my father is a little like taking up a book with pages missing. You must remember more than you've told me."

"He and I didn't make much small talk when we were together. It was all business." Memories of Alan Danton were flooding back, none of which Hoffman felt suitable to discuss with her. But Tess had found someone who actually spent time with her father, and she wasn't buying his reticence. Her prosecutor's antennae were up.

"Jack, this must be difficult for you, and I apologize. Captain Northrup says you were with him when he died. Let's start with that."

She opened her bag, removed an envelope, and handed it to him as if she was entering it into evidence in court. "I'd like you to look at this," she said.

Hoffman removed a document from the envelope. It read: General Orders Number 5421, HHC 24th Inf. Division, 27 May 1970. 1st Lt. Alan Danton distinguished himself by exceptionally valorous actions during the Cambodian Campaign on 10 May 1970. In a covert mission in enemy-occupied territory, his Reconnaissance Platoon came upon a large, heavily fortified enemy tunnel complex. The platoon observed the NVA's activity for several days, gathering valuable intelligence.

As the platoon withdrew, the enemy detected its presence and closed in pursuit. Badly outnumbered and under fire, the platoon was forced to run for cover. Realizing the platoon was about to be overtaken, Lt. Danton fell to the rear, took up a blocking position, and single-handedly held off the NVA until his men could take cover in a bomb crater. This unselfish act cost him his life.

For his heroism, 1st Lt. Alan Danton is awarded the Distinguished Service Cross. The gallant defense of his platoon that day was in keeping with the highest traditions of military service and reflects great credit upon himself, the United States Army, and a grateful nation.

My God, what a snow job, Hoffman thought. But so what? Tess Danton waited for his reaction. "Well, as far as I know, pretty accurate," he said, knowing how much of what happened that day was omitted.

She said, "I think there's more. Captain Northrup said you would know everything, what led up to Recon's encounter with the NVA and the firefight." Now she was holding something back, something Northrup told her.

He slipped the citation back into the envelope and returned it to her. He looked at his watch. "Tess, it's a long story, and I have to get back to the office. Can you break away from your seminar sometime tomorrow morning?"

"Anytime you say."

"Ten thirty, then."

Hoffman liked Tess Danton. He didn't want to disappoint her, but he couldn't figure out a way to give her what she wanted without either lying or hurting her deeply. The truth was an early victim of the war in Vietnam; one more lie wouldn't matter, would it? No, he was tired of the lies, but he couldn't bring himself to tell her everything he knew about her father and his final days. No way would he do that.

5
DEAR JOHN

It was a moonless clear summer night at La Push. A driftwood fire sent sparks dancing into a star-strewn sky. Hoffman and Clara Morris, with two additional couples, all close friends, lay on blankets around the fire, listening to the surf and singing, led by Hoffman and his guitar: "The answer, my friend, is blown in the wind . . ."

They had spent the day much as they had during summer breaks from school, sunbathing, body surfing, and tossing a football. But to Hoffman, this day felt very different. This would be their last time together before heading off in pursuit of graduate school and careers—everyone but him.

The other couples grew silent, disappearing beneath their blankets. He put his guitar back in its case. Clara snuggled close. "Fire's dying," he said.

"Let it die," she said, pressing her nose into his neck and pulling him down beside her. They lay together, looking up at more stars than Hoffman could recall seeing. The salty air, the smoke from the fire, the rush of the surf—this was home, the Olympic Peninsula. He had looked forward to being back permanently after graduating from Dartmouth.

Now it was not to be. He would be leaving again, not to return anytime soon. Maybe never. Had he made the right decision? He didn't know, but there was relief in having at last decided. Now he had to tell Clara.

They had met in high school. She attended the University of Washington while he went off to Dartmouth, but they had remained close, spending holidays and summers together. She flew to New Hampshire several times to visit. Their relationship was steady and comfortable, a few spats but no breakups. They were steadies so long and remained so close that their families and friends assumed they would eventually marry.

Hoffman was raised a Catholic but hadn't attended Mass in several years. Not that he rejected it, but it was like a shoe that had gotten too tight, all that sin stuff, so he just put it away for later consideration. Clara had no religious background at all, and the two of them agreed "commitment" should be the basis of a serious relationship. Their college years ended, and they began talking of marriage and they were having occasional sex. The timing was a subject Hoffman danced around, but the music was about to stop.

With a degree in political science and plans to apply for law school, Hoffman worked full time at his previous summer job as a deck hand on Puget Sound ferries. Clara, who had majored in business, found work at a bank. She shared an apartment with her girlfriend, Margaret, while Jack moved in with Margaret's significant other, Paul. Paul had been a classmate of Jack's at Dartmouth. When Margaret and Paul announced their engagement, the pressure was on Hoffman to make a move.

Clara had been a bridesmaid three times in the last year. They were invited to another wedding in the fall. Their friends were coupling up "like cats in heat," as one of Jack's buddies joked. Clara made it clear what she wanted. She was willing to pay the bills while he studied. Her father, a successful attorney, gave her a Volkswagen Beetle as a graduation gift. The two would marry, and he would pursue his law degree. The money would be tight for a while, but they could get by.

Their engagement seemed foreordained, except for one thing. During his senior year at Dartmouth, Hoffman had been carrying a stone in his gut, and it was getting heavier. With his student deferment gone, he would be 1-A, raw meat for the carnivores on the local draft board. Clara assumed he, like nearly all of their male friends, would avoid military service, claiming a deferment for law school, or escape some other way, legitimate or not. Her father offered to pull some strings with someone he knew on the draft board if it came to that.

The Hoffman men had a history of military service going back several generations. Andrew Hoffman, his father, was a navigator aboard a B-17 in World War II. Yet he viewed the current conflict with ambivalence. Although he didn't say much about it, by 1968, the lack of progress had him shaking his head. "A real mess," as he put it.

During Jack Hoffman's four years at Dartmouth, occasionally, a political science professor would bring up the war, but it wasn't a subject many of them felt comfortable discussing. There had been a few campus demonstrations calling for the abolishment of the ROTC Department, but like most of his fellow students, Hoffman was too busy with his books and sports to be distracted. When not in the library, he was training for cross country and track.

In his senior year, with the draft looming after graduation, the war was becoming personal and not just for him. Classmates were considering their options, too. The moral and political implications of the war became a subject of debate over beers. Something big was happening, one of those events that defined a generation, and it was dividing the nation. Hoffman's thesis for his degree was entitled "Vietnam, Nationalism in the Post-colonial Era." It argued that communism was a response to generations of colonial repression and economic exploitation.

On the Puget Sound ferries, he had worked alongside young men from blue-collar families, youths planning to follow their fathers as longshoremen or in the trades. In three successive summers, he arrived on the docks to find most of the previous year's deck crews gone, replaced by young men from the same working-class Seattle neighborhoods. The winnowing effect of the Selective Service System bothered him. Only those least able to avoid the draft were the ones ending up in uniform.

A friend who joined the National Guard offered to move Hoffman's name to the top of a two-year waiting list, guaranteeing him entry into the Guard within a month. He would not be drafted and still be able to serve in uniform. Chances that the unit would be called to active duty in Vietnam were practically nil. Clara urged him to take the offer. For two weeks, he agonized about it and, in the end, turned it down.

"Are you crazy, Hoffman?" his friend moaned. "You'd better get into something fast or head for Canada. They're drafting anyone who stands up to pee." The draft was barreling toward him like a funnel cloud, and it was time to evade it or get sucked up. Clara saw it coming, too. "Quit procrastinating," she insisted. "Get a deferment. Dad has connections. He can help you. What are you waiting for?"

Then the president, Lyndon Johnson, sat behind his desk in the Oval Office, his jowly, beleaguered face filling the TV screen. Finally surrendering to his own doubts about the war, he said he would not run again. The nation was weary of Vietnam and growing tired of him. Hoffman assumed the war couldn't go on much longer. But how would the next president end it?

Well, maybe he could get into a noncombat position. Maybe Clara would tolerate that. But the Air Force, Navy and Coast Guard had year-long waiting lists—too long with the draft nipping at his heels. There was no wait for the Army, and if he volunteered for the officer candidate school, the US' role in the war might be over by the time he graduated. He made an appointment with an Army recruiter and signed up. He didn't feel great about it, but at least the vacillating was over. The Army owned him.

He would be reporting for a physical exam in two weeks and leaving for training a few days later, assuming he passed. He had to tell Clara and she would be mad as hell, but proposing marriage now, even if she said yes, wouldn't be fair to her. Family and career would have to be put on hold. Would she wait for him? He couldn't ask her to do that. He wanted to be alone with her, away from family and friends, when he told her what he had done. He made a weekend reservation at a hotel on Orcas Island.

"You're awfully quiet," she said to him on the ferry, assuming he had asked her to come with something important on his mind.

"No, just tired," he said. "Been a long week."

"Jack, I know you better than that. What is it?"

"Just thinking about next year, about us. We have a lot to talk about."

"Yes, we do."

He knew what she was assuming, and he was ashamed. Over dinner, the two spoke idly about her work at the bank, where she was in training in the investment department, and gossiped about friends, their marriages, and those moving on to graduate school or finding jobs. He wanted to come clean with her but hesitated, holding his breath like a cliff diver gathering the courage to leap.

After dinner, they had a nightcap in the bar. It was nearly empty. A young woman in a mu-mu, her hair falling to her waist, sat in a corner softly playing guitar and singing folk songs: "If I had a hammer . . ." Hoffman screwed up his courage. They finished their drinks and retired to their room where they made love mechanically. Afterward, he lay on his back, staring at the ceiling, Clara asleep on his arm. He listened to her slow, deep breathing. The intimacy felt stolen. This was all wrong, and he cursed himself for deceiving her. Maybe I've made a big mistake. Canada is only two hours away. No, I've made my decision.

He woke to the cries of gulls and the sun beaming through the veranda's open door. Clara was gone from the room, probably fetching coffee in the lobby. Sweet of her to let him sleep. He sat up in bed and turned on the TV to catch the news. Martin Luther

King had been shot in Memphis. My God, what next? Hearing a tap on the door, he turned off the TV and let Clara in.

"Good morning, Gloomy," she said, carrying a tray of coffee and scones. She seemed in high spirits. "I was just out for a quick run on the shore. It's a gorgeous day. I'll shower while you get your butt out of bed."

"You mean you haven't heard?"

"Heard what?"

"Martin Luther King has been assassinated."

"Not funny."

"I'm serious."

"Has this country gone mad?"

"One wonders."

"Do they know who did it?"

"I think so. They have someone in custody."

She added milk and sugar to his coffee and handed him the cup. "I want to cry," she said, plopping down on the bed next to him. His plan to tell her of his decision seemed blown to bits. King was assassinated—and, oh, by the way, I'm joining the Army and going to Vietnam. Well, putting it off any longer won't make it go down any easier.

He said, "Clara, I've something to tell you."

She studied him. Now maybe she'd find out what was bothering him.

"I feel terrible about keeping this from you, but I've been struggling with it for a long time. I don't know how to break it to you, so I'll just spit it out. I've joined the Army."

"You what?" she shrieked.

"I did, Clara. I joined the Army, and I'll be leaving at the end of May."

"Goddamn you, Jack, were you drunk? How could you do such a stupid thing without discussing it with me first?"

"Look, I have to live with myself. I just couldn't take another deferment. If I don't go, someone else will go in my place."

"Oh, very noble of you, Jack. For this crazy war? It makes no sense. Our friends seem to have no qualms about their deferments. Paul's trick knee, for crying out loud, never stopped him from rock climbing."

"Everyone has to make his own decision. I've been terribly conflicted about it, Clara. I have trouble explaining it to myself, but it just didn't seem right, dodging it I mean. Rightly or wrongly, we're in this thing in Vietnam. I need to be there."

"What about us? How long will I have to wait for you?"

"Three years. I signed up for officer candidate school."

"So I'm going to sit here wondering every day whether you're dead or alive. Jack Hoffman, you did not have to do this."

Tears welled in her eyes. He reached for her hand, but she pulled away, burying her face in a pillow. He wanted to comfort her but was afraid to touch her. "You have every right to be angry," he said lamely.

The dogs of war had caught up with them. With one exception, a friend who joined the air force, the men in their gang weren't about to risk throwing their lives away in Vietnam. No one ever spoke of duty or patriotism with regard to that war, as if such sentiments didn't apply. To them, the war was like a bad flu epidemic, and it would pass. In any case, their social status rendered them immune.

Clara went to the window, her back to him, her arms crossed. She appeared so small and vulnerable. "What do you expect me to do while you're playing soldier?" she asked.

He would be locked up at some military outpost in training for a year, then be assigned to some dreary Army post before shipping out to Vietnam. That he might not come back was a reality he accepted, but why should she? He couldn't put her through that even if she was willing. He would not ask her to be Penelope to his Odysseus.

"Clara, I'm not asking you to wait for me. This was entirely my decision, and you're right. I didn't have to do it."

"Just great, Jack," she said, turning angrily toward him. "So you just disappear like nothing ever happened between you and me, forget everything. Did you have to surrender your brains when you signed up?"

Now she was angry. His heart was in his stomach. He wanted her to beat on him if it made her feel better. There was no way to make her understand.

"Clara, I love you, but this is something I've got to do."

She went to the mirror and brushed her hair. He saw in reflection that she was crying. "I'm a mess," she said, daubing her eyes with a tissue. "When did you say you were leaving?"

"My physical is a week from Monday. I'll be heading to basic training on the first of April."

"I hope you flunk."

"Not much chance of that."

"Maybe I should get a gun and shoot you in the leg. On second thought, I should aim a little below the belt."

"I wouldn't blame you."

"I just can't believe this is happening. I need some air."

She opened the door to the veranda and stood by the railing. The waters of the strait sparkled. The air smelled of fir and salt. A woman walked her dog along the shore. A sailboat exited the small harbor and made for open water. Hoffman approached her from behind and reached around her waist. She stiffened and pulled away.

"Let's get going," she said. "It's a beautiful, lousy, rotten day."

They packed their bags and loaded them into the car without a word to one another. On the ferry to Anacortes, they sat like strangers. He wanted to reach out to her, but it was as if he had left her standing alone on the ferry landing, receding from view. I've hurt her badly, he knew, but it's done, and there isn't a damn thing he could do about it.

On the day of his departure for Fort Dix, they met for lunch downtown. He planned to go directly from there to the induction center where he would take the oath with other draftees and recruits. A bus would transport the new batch of conscripts to SeaTac Airport. As instructed, he carried only a small handbag containing a change of underwear and a toilet bag.

"Aren't you going to eat?" she said when he told the waiter he wanted only coffee.

"Not hungry," he said.

"Nervous?"

"Nervous as hell."

"Did they tell you when you'd be able to come home for a visit?"

"When I asked, the sergeant at the induction center just smirked and said, 'At the convenience of Uncle Sam.'"

"And so it begins."

"Yeah."

They made small talk about her plans for the summer, some hikes she wanted to take in the Olympics. When the waiter brought the check, it had the finality of an arrest warrant. He would be hauled off soon and not see Clara again for months. He walked her back to the bank building.

"I hope you'll write," Hoffman said.

"Of course I will," she said. Her eyes filled with tears. "Sorry. I promised myself I wouldn't do this."

He embraced her. She trembled. He whispered, "I'm going to miss you terribly."

She kissed him on the cheek. "You're always late. You'd better get going."

He grinned. "Guess I'll have to break that habit pretty soon."

They stood for a moment, staring at one another. Someone had to move. "Well, goodbye, Jack. All the best," she said, turning away.

"See you by Christmas, I hope."

She turned and passed through the revolving glass doors, disappearing into the lobby without looking back. He felt as if he had just had the wind knocked out of him.

He and Clara corresponded by mail during the months of his training at Fort Dix, New Jersey. He kept his messages light about the men he met and the humorous aspects of army life. She sent news of friends and family, work, but conspicuously, nothing intimate. As the weeks passed, mail from her arrived less frequently.

He finished basic and advanced infantry training, then moved on to Georgia and Fort Benning for OCS. Several months of unanswered letters to Clara ensued, then finally, her neat cursive on an envelope at mail call. He carried it to his bunk in the barracks, hesitant to open it:

Dear Jack,

I'm sorry I haven't written much lately, but these past weeks have gone by in a blur. All is well here, and I hope it's the same with you.

As I write, I'm sitting in my apartment with a photo of you in front of me. If I said I wasn't sad, I'd be lying. You see, something unplanned has happened, something I never expected. I've met someone pretty wonderful, and we've been dating. I resisted seeing him for several months but then, why not? Right away, I told him all about you, of course. Well, to get to the point, I think I'm falling in love with him.

I'm not sure at this moment where my friendship with Mike is leading. You once said it would be unfair if you were to ask me to wait for you. As angry as I was with you, I still intended to wait. Honest, I did. My anger was selfish, and I see that now. I can't tell you how awful I feel, telling you this just as you are about to head into harm's way. All I can do is ask your forgiveness, and I hope you understand.

Please don't let us become strangers. I want to know how you are doing. I'm looking forward so much to seeing you when you get leave over the holidays.

Affectionately,

Clara

It was a classy "Dear John." From a mutual friend in Seattle, he learned Mike was an attorney in her father's law firm.

6
ASSUMING COMMAND

At twenty-three, Hoffman was "LT, the Old Man." Most of the men in his platoon were eighteen or nineteen, too young to vote, too young to buy liquor in most states. A few months earlier, they had nothing on their minds but fast girls, fast cars, and their blue-collar jobs. Most hadn't even begun to think seriously about what they wanted to do with their lives. They were easy marks for their local draft boards.

Yes, they were just kids, but as Hoffman observed them, they seemed much older. They were soldiers, no doubt about that. A phrase from his high school Latin class came to mind—*uri, vinciri, verberari, ferroque necari*—to endure, to be burned, to be bound, to be beaten, and to be killed. The gladiator's oath. Was it Homer? He couldn't remember.

To the grunts under his command, his leadership must have seemed as chancy as a lottery ticket. They had seen platoon leaders come and go, some good, some bad. He sensed their indifference. There was only one way to win their trust and respect, and that was in the boonies, in battle.

He had heard their last operation was a costly one. The executive officer who had assigned him to the platoon told him this much, that it took place in the Bu Prang Massif, a hellishly precipitous spine of mountains straddling the Cambodian border. These same mountains hid the Vietminh during their struggle against the French, and for months, enemy activity had been increasing there. The Third Battalion was sent to root them out.

The operation, deemed a success by senior commanders, did not end well from the platoon's perspective. With reticence about past operations typical of grunts, Galvin had said little about it, but it was important for Hoffman to know for his own edification. He pressed Galvin for details one night as the two sat in the flickering light of a candle in their bunker.

"Unnerfeld tells me you lost five, three KIA, two wounded," Hoffman prompted. "He said Second Platoon was in the lead when the company walked into that ambush."

"Yeah, shouldn't have happened," Galvin said as he sharpened his knife on a whetstone.

"How so?"

"This battalion rarely moves together, but for the Bu Prangs, togetherness is SOP. Every time we go in there, guaranteed to lose someone. Those mountains are crawling with NVA. A few months pass, and some new higher higher at division will get the itch to try it again—moth to a flame, the way it is."

Galvin explained that Delta Company was sent ahead of Alpha, Bravo, and Charlie up a ridge where infrared thermal imaging taken from an aircraft detected probable human presence the night before. Second Platoon was in the lead, and Danton put his men on a heavily trodden trail through wooded terrain.

"You could smell Dinks, feel their eyes watching, but you couldn't see 'em; the jungle was quiet like it was waiting for something. Walking that trail was suicide, and we all knew it. Sure enough, we came under machine gun and small arms fire from the front and both flanks. We lost three men in the first ten seconds."

Galvin slid the blade of the knife against the stone, lifting it now and then to test it with his thumb.

"A machine gun had us pinned down from a bunker less than twenty meters above us. We couldn't move without drawing fire, and our point was hit. His slack crawled up to get him, but he got hit, too."

"Slack?" It was grunt patois, among the many terms he had never encountered in training.

"Yeah, the second man in the file is supposed to back up the point. We just lay frozen behind trees, anywhere we could find cover. Danton shouts we should stay put. I see him crawl off and disappear into the brush. Then—*kaboom*—and the gun wasn't firing anymore. He tossed a frag in their hole."

"Courageous thing for him to do."

"We had no business on that trail. You walk a trail, and you get ambushed sooner or later. We were still taking fire and couldn't pull back. Alpha and Bravo moved forward and got stopped, too. Artillery support was coming over the top of us because we were in the shadow of a steep ridge. Firefight lasted all afternoon. Then, as they do, the bastards just slip away. I saw nothin' the whole time."

In several more contacts, the battalion was credited with twenty kills, but not a single NVA body was found, Galvin said. "The gooks always clean up their mess," as he put it. Delta

Company spent the next two days destroying empty bunkers and sealing tunnels, the ones they found. They knew the mountains hid many more.

If Hoffman had taken command of the platoon a week earlier, would he have walked his platoon on the trail? He couldn't help wondering.

In the morning, he was summoned to the company command post where Northrup informed him that the brigade commander was coming to award a Silver Star to Danton and Bronze Stars for valor to others who participated in the engagement on the trail. The company would stand in formation, and Hoffman would command the award ceremony. Captain Northrup would assist the general in the pinning.

Northrup said, "Have the men look as presentable as possible. I don't want to see any peace medallions, love beads, or that kind of garbage. Strictly regulation. Steel pots, pistol belts, and their weapons, that's all. And Unnerfeld, shave that damn mustache."

The highland dawn broke clear and cool as the company stood in formation near the airstrip, awaiting the arrival of the general's chopper. The bird was a half hour late when it made a low pass over the assembly. The polished skin of the helicopter glinted in the sun as it banked sharply and settled onto the runway. General Marshall Falconer stepped off a skid, while Captain Northrup ducked under the idling blades to greet him with a salute.

The general placed an avuncular hand on Northrup's shoulder as they approached the troop formation. Lieutenant Colonel James Standley, the Delta Devils' battalion commander, and several aides followed like ducklings. The glossy leather of their jungle boots, the starched fatigues, and the pristine helmet covers shouted REMF, rear echelon mother fucker, to the troops who hadn't seen a shower and a change of clothes in nearly a month.

Hoffman called the formation to attention as the general approached, his aides watching at a distance. The general was stocky with a leonine face and bushy eyebrows. Hoffman saluted and commanded the men in formation behind him to parade rest. With a Southern drawl, Falconer began:

"Gentlemen, your success in the Bu Prangs sent a clear message to the NVA that there will be no safe sanctuary for them as long as we are here. You no doubt have heard that a gradual drawdown of US forces in Vietnam is beginning. But make no mistake. Our mission is as vital now as it has ever been to stop the NVA movement through these mountains. We'll continue to hit them and hit them hard . . ."

It was a pep talk. He droned on about the need to keep up the pressure on the enemy. Hoffman didn't notice anything amiss until he heard a muffled voice in the formation behind him: "Man, a fool." Another voice responded, "Right on, bro." Hoffman broke into a cold sweat. He couldn't order it to stop without calling attention to it. Sweat trickled down his back. Did the general hear it? He seemed too absorbed in his soliloquy to notice.

"I'm here to recognize the courageous actions of these men," General Falconer said, nodding at the five men lined up in front of him, "and to honor those we lost," he added, glancing at three pairs of empty boots. "A grateful nation recognizes those who made the ultimate sacrifice. Their families will receive their

Bronze Stars for valor and Purple Hearts. Take some comfort in knowing you made the enemy pay a far greater price."

Again, the voice behind Hoffman mumbled, "Kiss my ass." The general twitched. Did he hear someone say something? Apparently, he wasn't sure. He approached the five awardees, followed by Northrup with a stack of blue boxes. General Falconer said a few words to each man as he pinned on the medals, shook hands, and exchanged a salute. That done, he paused for a moment of reflection over the empty boots while his Huey's engine accelerated, its blades thumping the air. Then the visitors climbed aboard and were gone.

Hoffman stood before his troops, astounded, angry, and relieved all at once. It took a lot of nerve to badger a general. Whether or not Falconer heard it didn't matter; it was insane. Hoffman didn't want to think what would have happened if the insults were overheard. Someone was damn lucky, and so was everyone else.

"Alright, who's the smart ass?" Hoffman demanded as the helicopter disappeared over the trees.

No one spoke.

"Indian, who was messing around behind me?"

"I didn't hear anything," Indian said.

"Squad leaders, who was it?"

No one responded.

"Okay, this is no joke. I want that man to fess up, now."

"You heard the lieutenant," Sergeant Galvin barked. "We'll just stand here if it takes all day."

"Oh, come on, Razor," said Specialist 4 Bart "Batman" Ludwik. "The general's full of shit. We got hurt bad in those mountains, and you know it."

"Ludwik, if I wanted your opinion, I'd ask for it. See me at my bunker and bring your entrenching tool."

The troops returned to their positions on the bunker line, jostling and laughing about Ludwik's audacity.

"Jesus, I hope Northrup didn't hear that," Hoffman said to Galvin.

"You'll be hearing from him soon, I reckon."

Sure enough, Hoffman received a summons to the company command post where he found the captain looking more serious than usual. Danton grinned with a cheek-load of chew.

"Well, well, well, young lieutenant, we need to have a talk," Northrup said. "You didn't perchance hear anything strange during the medal ceremony today, did you?"

"Nothing in particular, sir," Hoffman said.

"How about in general, then?"

"Possibly, sir."

"How about you, Lieutenant Danton? You hear anything unusual?'

"Matter of fact, I believe I did."

"Quite strange, wouldn't you say, Lieutenant Hoffman, that someone would sound off during a general's speech to his men? I mean, a serious lack of discipline, wouldn't you say?"

"Yes, sir," Hoffman said.

"Therefore, I think it demands a disciplinary response, don't you, Lieutenant Danton?"

"Oh, most affirmative, sir."

"Sound right to you, Lieutenant Hoffman?" Northrup asked.

"Yes, sir," Hoffman said. It was the only response prudently possible.

"Who was that comedian in the ranks? Or was there more than one?" Northrup asked.

"I don't know, sir." This was no lie since Ludwik never confessed.

"Then the whole company shall bear responsibility. Tomorrow at 0500, I want every swingin' dick in formation, bright-eyed and standing tall, for a little physical training. Lieutenant Danton here will lead the PT."

"Officers too," added Danton.

"And one more thing," Northrup said. "Every can of beer in this perimeter is to be collected and delivered to my bunker by 1800 hours. No more beer for the duration of our stay here. You roger that?"

"Yes, sir."

"Very well then. Carry on."

Hoffman left cursing under his breath. He headed for Lieutenant Unnerfeld's position on the bunker line to let off some steam. Unnerfeld sat atop his bunker in a chair built of sandbags, watching his men shore up the bunker below him. A marijuana cigarette smoldered between his fingertips. Frozen in that position, with his long face and jutting jaw, he might have been a Bill Mauldin parody of the Lincoln Memorial.

"About that award ceremony this morning, we've got a problem," Hoffman said, looking up at the soldier.

Unnerfeld, obviously stoned, drew deeply from his spliff and stared blankly at Hoffman. “Wassup, mon?”

“Someone was making editorial comments on the general’s speech. My pucker factor went to ten. Fortunately, the general apparently didn’t catch on, but Northrup and Danton did.”

Unnerfeld watched a mosquito draw blood from his arm and smacked it with his palm. “There’s only so much you can control, bro. It don’t mean nuthin.”

“Well, Northrup thinks it means something. He’s got a little attitude adjustment planned.”

“What this time?’

“Everyone in formation for PT tomorrow at 0500. And he wants all the beer turned in to the CP.”

“The dude got no sense of humor,” Unnerfeld said.

“Get serious, Todd; I don’t need any more grief from Northrup and Danton.”

Unnerfeld climbed down from his perch. “You know, Jack, there are a few things they didn’t tell you at Fort Benning about this here war. You’re going to have to chill, or you’ll go bat shit. Have a toke.”

“You going to remember anything I told you?” Hoffman asked, waving it away.

“Every word, bro, every word.”

“Do me a favor and make sure you collect any beer your platoon has left and get it over to the CP.”

“An issue of one lousy can of warm beer per day? Big fucking deal.”

“Never mind. Just do it, please.”

If Northrup intended that the innocent would hold the guilty accountable, he was wrong. The troops accepted their discipline with unanimity; the lifers giveth, the lifers taketh away. At dawn the next morning, Danton led the company in calisthenics, then double-timed them in formation three times around the airstrip:

I don't know, but it's been said,

Jody done took my girl to bed . . .

Sound off, one two . . .

Sound off, three four . . .

Bring it on down, one, two, three four, one, two, three four.

The hassles of life inside the wire notwithstanding, bunker guard duty brought respite from the unremitting demands of survival in the jungle. For Hoffman, it was fortuitous that the company was not on an operation when he arrived in the field, affording him the opportunity to get acquainted with his grunts. The men in the platoon seemed cohesive, just kids thrown together by fate, bonded by a common objective to survive. They knew the days left in their tours as well as any convict counting down his sentence. Of Hoffman, they were withholding judgment.

There were natural leaders like Sergeant Galvin and the squad leaders who had earned their positions by proving to be able and trustworthy in a fight. Most of the men were content to keep a low profile, to "skate," by doing only what was required of them and getting home. Knowing who was who would be important.

Racial relations in the company were less easy to discern. Out of the twenty to twenty-five men in the Second Platoon, there were six "soul brothers" and three Hispanics. The latter mingled with the whites when not in "the boonies," but the blacks tended to hang together, greeting one another with raised fists and baroque handshakes, killing time rapping about girls, music, and home.

The American Forces Viet Nam Network (AFVN) would broadcast music and news twenty-four hours a day from Saigon. A grunt could purchase a cheap transistor radio at the PX, tuck it in his ruck, and listen to music and news when not out on an operation in the jungle. The men relaxed with the latest rock-and-roll hits, sometimes singing along:

"Take another little piece of my heart now, baby! You know you got it if it makes you feel good."

Just before sunrise, a squad exited the barbed wire enclosure and conducted a sweep of the perimeter, expecting to find nothing but a few water buffaloes grazing in overgrown rice paddies. Daily "details" included incinerating excrement in "honey barrels," reinforcing bunkers, stringing coils of razor wire, and setting up trip flares. In the heat of the day, the troops were allowed a few hours to relax.

At night, each man pulled two one-hour stints of bunker watch. After a few months of this, he would develop a circadian rhythm of sleeping and waking. The arrival of a chaplain on Sunday to conduct a service was one of the few reminders his life had ever been otherwise. And so it went, days of "good time" credited toward a grunt's 365-day obligation to the USA.

For Hoffman, the luxury of observation would soon be over: he would have to prove himself to his men. How would he react under pressure? It was a question he would answer as much for himself as for them. He was green, a neophyte put in command of a seasoned platoon. His training prepared him for few of the practical aspects of everyday life in the jungle, like pitching a poncho shelter to stay dry at night, which C-rations were most coveted, or how to make a heat-tab stove of a tin can for brewing coffee or warming food, or how to rig a rucksack frame for humping a ninety-pound load of ammo and gear.

He would have to learn by experiencing the sights, sounds, and scents of the jungle. Moreover, he needed to be able to distinguish the distinctive reports of various types of weapons he couldn't see, to know the different sounds of incoming fire as opposed to outgoing, the age of a boot print or broken twig on a trail, the sooty smell of an enemy camp. On several successive nights, Hoffman heard a rumbling in the mountains to the west accompanied by flashes, which he mistook for an electrical storm.

"Oh, that's just arc lights," Galvin explained, "B-52s carpet bombing Cambodia. A couple of months ago, we were operating near the border and got word to dig in and get our heads down. We couldn't see the planes, but the ground shook like an earthquake. Kinda like fishing with dynamite. Drop a lighted stick in the water, and see what floats to the surface."

"I didn't think we were bombing in Cambodia," Hoffman said.

"Officially, we ain't," Galvin said.

Each morning a clutch of Vietnamese gathered at the perimeter gate, waiting to be checked in. Locals did house cleaning and laundry for the small air force detachment at the edge of the airstrip. What thoughts lay behind the obsequious expressions of these peasant people?

One of them, a wizened old man, carried on his back a stool, a bucket, and a large box. In minutes he set up an open-air barbershop. Grunts began to drift to him for haircuts and shaves. He worked fast, finishing off each customer with a shoulder massage and a neck pop. Hoffman hadn't seen a barber since before he left the States, so he decided to avail himself of the opportunity. The barber greeted him with a wide smile; his teeth were stained nearly black from chewing betel.

"How long you like?" the barber asked.

"Close on sides, short on top," Hoffman said, not sure he understood, but it made no difference anyway.

"Okay, GI, I give number one haircut."

The sun, the clicking scissors, and the soft falsetto humming of the barber were relaxing, and Hoffman began to nod off, but the old man kept talking.

"You got children, GI?" he inquired.

"No, no children," Hoffman said drowsily.

"No wife?"

"No, no wife."

"Maybe you like a number one girl tonight?" the old one giggled.

"No, not tonight, but thanks anyway, Papa San," Hoffman said.

"You have a big car in Merica, I think," the barber persisted.

"I have a car. Not big," Hoffman answered vaguely.

"I have a bicycle," the barber laughed.

"Someday, maybe you'll have a car," Hoffman said.

"No want car, want a scooter. You buy me a scooter?"

The two laughed together. Across the airstrip, the roar of a C-123 taking off saved Hoffman a reply. When it was airborne, the barber said, "Maybe you go home tomorrow and drive a car."

"No, not tomorrow," Hoffman said, sorry to be reminded. "A year, maybe."

"Ohhh, that long time. Know when I go home?" the old man asked.

"No. When do you go home, Papa San?" Hoffman asked, playing along.

"Tonight, six o'clock," the old man chortled.

The irony didn't escape Hoffman. Vietnam was a graveyard of invaders: the Chinese, the Japanese, the French, and now the Americans. The old man had no reason to believe the latest foreign intrusion would end any other way.

As per the TV news coverage back home, Hoffman expected to find Vietnam in ruins, but that was not the case. Occasional bullet-pocked or collapsed buildings along the roads testified to earlier battles and the destructive capability of American weaponry, but larger towns appeared unaffected. Children, wearing immaculate white shirts, walked hand in hand to school. Markets bustled with activity; roadside restaurants and street carts served up steaming bowls of Pho. Men and women in conical hats and black pajamas stooped in rice paddies from dawn to dusk, while their young perched like crows on the backs of water buffaloes. This was eternal, the war passing.

Not that life was as placid as it sometimes appeared. In the countryside, where 80 percent of the population resided, the VC were woven so tightly into village and hamlet life that it was impossible for outsiders to thread them out, let alone eliminate them. Meanwhile, the cities were filling up with the displaced. Drugs, prostitution, and stolen goods were plentiful in Saigon, Danang, Nha Trang, and other cities in the shadows of American military bases. The Americans brought both war and a thriving black market.

One evening Hoffman stood with Sergeant Galvin near the planked airstrip at dusk. Across the runway, there was a storage area. He noticed a frail little man lift a twelve-foot-long metal plank from a pile, shift it onto his back, and carry it away, his spindly legs pumping like shock absorbers.

"Look over there, Razor. That little guy is making off with a plank that's gotta weigh as much as he does," Hoffman said incredulously.

"Yeah, seen them scrawny little bastards carry some heavy shit. It's all in the technique."

"What's he going to do with it?"

"Maybe build him a bunker," Galvin said as he lifted his M-16 and took aim.

"You're not going to shoot the man, for God's sake," Hoffman blurted.

"Nah, just gonna make him piss his leg."

The shot ricocheted at the feet of the thief who dropped his burden and bounded behind a berm at the edge of the strip.

"Parasites steal anything ain't nailed down," Galvin said.

The VC were nothing if not ingenious. With supplies, ammunition, and weapons scarce or flat unavailable, they made do with whatever they could scrounge or capture. This would become abundantly clear to Hoffman over the next few days.

Every morning, pilots of three Loaches—tiny hummingbird-like light observation helicopters—checked out their machines in preparation for a day of low-level spotting of the enemy in the jungle so that heavily armed Cobra helicopters could attack them. The pilot of one of the Loaches happened to glance down at his feet. The pin of a Chicom grenade was rigged to explode upon the depression of one of the rudder pedals.

7
THE DECOY

Aircraft on night missions landed at Buon Binh to refuel. For security reasons, the Air Force kept the runway dark at night, activating lights only at the approach of an aircraft. Runway beacons had been disappearing for several months, presumably pilfered like everything else. No one thought much of it at first, but finally, the base commander asked Captain Northrup to start patrolling the runway at night. Good training for the new platoon leader, Northrup and Danton figured.

"We've got a problem, Hoffman," the captain said. "Someone's making off with runway lights, and the fly boys are getting damned tired of replacing them. So, here's what we're gonna do. I want you to take a squad to the end of the runway tonight and post yourself near those beacons. You detect anyone moving around, grab 'em, and if you can't grab 'em, convince 'em it's a very bad idea to be there."

Hoffman chose a squad leader, Juan Alvarez, and two others, Luke Foreman and Jake Miller, to accompany him. His RTO, Tom Sullivan, would hump the radio. The five slipped out of the perimeter at dusk with their weapons and a Starlight Scope.

The night was moonless—a tactical fact that Hoffman, with no field experience, hadn't considered. The patrol stumbled along in the blackness, at first trying to stay off the runway to avoid being detected. Finally, realizing that if he couldn't see anything, neither could anyone else, he rerouted his team to the runway's planking. As they reached the end of the strip, all they could do was hunker down for the night and listen for movement.

They lay like the spokes of a wheel in the inky darkness and tried to stay awake. An hour passed, then two, then three, with no sound but the croaking of the geckos. "Fuck you. Fuck you," they seemed to be saying, which the grunts took as an objection to their presence. Sullivan radioed negative situation reports hourly to the company command post.

Hoffman switched on the Starlight Scope and lifted the lens to his eye. It came to life with a high-pitched hum. The glowing green image projected by the device was too fuzzy to make out more than a few trees and shrubs at a range of about twenty meters. It was better than nothing, but barely.

At about 0235, the drone of an aircraft approaching from the south broke the silence. Seconds later, in the direction of the inbound plane, green tracers arced skyward, accompanied by the crackle of small arms fire. Hoffman and his men, too far from the action to be of any assistance, watched helplessly until the runway lights snapped on and the darkened figure of an AC-47 Spooky gunship roared over them, clawing for altitude.

Sullivan handed Hoffman the radio handset. It was Danton. "Two six, Five. What the hell's going on out there?"

"Firing to the south, directed at an aircraft on approach."

"That's obvious, goddamn it. Did you hear or see anything?"

"Just tracers. Firing, maybe a klick from our location."

"Okay. Stand by."

A baffled air strip controller told Danton what he knew. The Spooky pilots had made the usual steep approach to Buon Binh airstrip. As the aircraft descended, they saw runway lights partially obscured by a thin patchy fog. It wasn't until the plane was about to touch down that the pilots realized there was no runway beneath them, but a swidden patch of jungle cleared for planting. They applied power and pulled up, pursued by glowing tracer rounds.

"I guess we know where those stolen beacons ended up," Danton radioed Hoffman. "The pilot says the fake runway was due south, a couple of klicks. Get moving, and see what you can find."

"They'll be long gone by the time we get there in this dark," Hoffman objected.

"Don't argue with me. Get moving."

It would be nearly impossible to move two kilometers over rough terrain in near-total darkness and find anything before morning, but reasoning with Danton was futile. The grunts were equally skeptical.

"No fuckin' way, LT. We can't see shit," objected Alvarez.

"Then it won't matter, will it? We have our orders. You lead, and I'll keep you on a compass heading. Everyone stay close."

The luminous dial of the compass rocked to magnetic north, and Hoffman pointed the arrow to 180 degrees. He put his hand on Alvarez's shoulder to orient him and gave him a nudge. A miserable night Hoffman had spent in a Panamanian jungle during escape and evasion training came to mind. Five hours of wandering through the thick jungle left him at first light only a few meters from where he started. Somehow, he had walked in circles.

Now the five grunts moved laboriously through palm and bamboo. Detours around fallen trees and impassable thickets made holding a heading nearly impossible. Hoffman concluded only dumb luck would bring them anywhere near the ersatz airstrip. He was also concerned about who might hear them or what kind of trouble they might blindly walk into.

The team had been walking more than two hours when they halted for a rest, and Miller had some bad news: "LT, I think we lost Foreman."

"Shit. I told you to stay in close," Hoffman said, exasperated.

"I swear he was here a minute ago, right behind me, but now he ain't."

"Okay, he can't be far. You men wait here. I'll go back and look for him."

He used his compass to backtrack, hoping Foreman had the sense to stay put. Hearing movement in the undergrowth to his left, he paused. Was it an animal? He raised his weapon, clicked off the safety, and whispered, "Foreman, that you?" It felt like shouting in a library.

"Yeah, over here."

"I'll tap my pot, and you move toward the sound."

Hoffman tapped his helmet with a magazine, and Foreman began pushing through the dense foliage. Hoffman could hear him coming only a few steps away. "More to your right, then straight."

Foreman's toothy grin was visible in the dark. "Found you. You're it," he cracked.

"Damn it, Foreman. How the hell did you fall behind?"

"Stopped to take a leak."

"Wet yourself if you have to, damn it, but at least let us know."

The five regrouped and moved out again, making halting progress until the jungle gave way to relatively open ground. Hoffman had no way of accurately estimating how far they had actually progressed or whether they were anywhere near the trap that had been set. It was 0430, and he owed Northrup and Danton a situation report.

Hoffman scanned 360 degrees with the Starlight Scope. The aqueous green image confirmed that, yes, they were definitely in a relatively open area. Was this the one they were looking for? Hoffman reported to Danton that he might be in the vicinity of the ambush, but it would be impossible to know until daylight. Danton insisted that Hoffman keep moving, keep looking.

With darkness lifting in an hour or so, it made no sense to wander around aimlessly. "We've gone far enough," Hoffman told his men. "We wait here 'til we get some daylight."

"I like your style, LT," Sullivan agreed, and the five crawled into some low palm, figuring it would hide them well enough. They became very still, and Hoffman knew they were dozing. He let them sleep while he monitored the radio.

He tried to occupy his mind with something pleasant, anything that would keep him awake, and with the usual heartache, it was Clara. There was that last day together on the beach, Clara in her bikini, bounding like a deer into the surf after a frisbee and laughing as a wave swept her off her feet. She'd be coming home from work about now, and he wondered what she would be doing that night, whether she'd be going out, whether she even gave him a thought. Forget her, dude, he rebuked himself. It's over, and it was my doing.

The nocturnal mutterings of the jungle began to fade with the approach of dawn. A thirsty mosquito probed Hoffman's ear. Grunt myth had it that Vietnam's mosquitoes were the size of dragonflies. It was only a slight exaggeration. He reapplied a coating of Army-issue repellent to his neck and face. It was bitter, foul-smelling stuff. After a few days of use, it had scored the face of his watch, which made him wonder what it was doing to his skin. Still, it seemed to keep the insects away from his ears.

At 0530, he woke his men. They could now see that they were at the edge of a clearing. A Montagnard swidden slash-and-burn meant there was a village nearby. The five watched for any movement, any indication of human presence, as the murky darkness receded. Detecting none, Hoffman sent Alvarez and Foreman to check the open area. The two men slank off across the field and, on reaching the far side, waved for the others to follow.

As Hoffman approached, he sensed something was wrong. Alvarez was frozen in place and looking at his feet, while Foreman was standing behind a tree and talking to Alvarez. The two seemed quite anxious about something.

"Stay back," Foreman shouted as the others closed in.

"Tripwire," cried Alvarez. "Over my right foot."

"Freeze," Hoffman ordered.

"Jesus, whaddya think I'm doing?"

Hoffman saw the grunt was on a footpath across which stretched a black-coated communication wire. It lay taut against the toe of his jungle boot and stretched into the undergrowth on both sides of the trail.

"You men take cover," Hoffman instructed. "Juan, I'm going to hold this thing tight with the barrel of my weapon while you remove your foot, real slow. Then you to get back behind the trees with the others."

"Then what?" asked Alvarez.

"Never mind. Just do as I say."

Alvarez hesitated, and Hoffman added, "Now."

The lieutenant held the wire snug with the flash suppressor of his M-16, while Alvarez gingerly withdrew his foot and stepped back. The wire didn't move. So far, so good. Alvarez joined the others, prostrate with their heads down. Hoffman let go of his rifle and dove away from the path, fully expecting to catch a load of shrapnel.

It's not courage that motivates a man to do such things. Courage implies some degree of forethought, and this was a reflex, not unlike snatching a small child off the window sill of a ten-story apartment. Hoffman lay still for a moment, thinking explosives might be on some sort of fuse. Nothing happened, but his heart was pounding.

Alvarez stood over him, offering a hand up. "Thanks, LT, but it's not a booby trap."

"Apparently not," Hoffman said sheepishly.

There were smiles all around as Sullivan handed Hoffman his M-16 and his steel pot, which had gone flying. Well, the lieutenant thought, no style points, but perhaps I just passed my preliminaries.

"We see a lot of this stuff in the boonies, LT," Miller said. "Commo wire. The Dinks leave it on all over the place and never pick it up when they're done with it. Hard to say whether it's connected to anything, but it serves other purposes."

"Well, let's follow it and see," Hoffman said.

The wire led them through the forest to a clearing larger than the first, planted with pineapple. Jackpot. There, mounted on a stump, was a runway beacon. Twenty meters away, another connected by a wire in what the men surmised was a circuit. The enemy had devised a clever ruse to lure an aircraft into an ambush. It was simple and deadly, and it nearly worked.

Hoffman reported the discovery to Danton and Northrup on his radio. They wanted more information to send to a curious chain of command. Danton would arrive within the hour with reinforcements to secure the area. In the meantime, Hoffman would conduct a sweep.

Footpaths and cultivated fields meant a village nearby. That he and his team hadn't seen a soul perplexed Hoffman, but he didn't have to wait long for an explanation. From the jungle to the north came the cough of a mortar tube and, seconds later, the hiss and crump of an incoming projectile. The men hit the ground. The first attempt was wide left, sending up a geyser of dirt. They knew their attackers would adjust their aim, walking the next ones closer.

Hoffman now knew what it was like to be mortared. What to do now? Run like hell out of the beaten zone. "Head for the tree line," Hoffman yelled to his companions, and they ran as fast as their legs could carry them.

Hoffman felt oddly detached as he ran, as if he was merely an observer, curious about whether he and his men would reach the concealment of the trees ahead of the mortars. He heard a cry behind him and, glancing back, saw Foreman on the ground. The others saw him, too, and stopped to help him.

"No," Hoffman shouted. "Miller, you come with me. The rest of you keep moving to the tree line."

Now the enemy was bracketing their target, left, right, closer and closer. A mortar arrived at a high angle with a *pffffft* and a bang, allowing no time to react. A round thumped into the earth no more than five meters from Hoffman and stuck in the soft red dirt like a dart. It didn't explode, a dud, but he didn't have time to consider his luck.

When the two reached the wounded man, they found him in the fetal position, holding a blood-soaked left leg.

"You hit anywhere else?" Hoffman asked.

"No. Just the leg. I think the bone is broken."

"Can you stand?"

"No fucking way."

"I'll carry him," Miller volunteered. "Help get him up on my back."

Miller wasn't a big man, but he was well built. Hoffman pulled Foreman up, laid him across Miller's shoulders, and the three struck out for the cover of the forest, stepping over rows of pineapple. Spouts of dirt from exploding mortars and buzzing shrapnel followed them. Foreman, bouncing on Miller's back like a sack of potatoes, began to laugh.

"Think this is funny, Foreman?" Miller huffed.

"Million-dollar wound, man; I'm goin' home."

"You ain't there yet, bro."

The green curtain of the jungle was a mere ten steps away when Miller fell, Foreman landing on top of him cheek-to-cheek.

"Kiss me, you fool," Foreman giggled.

"Fucking queer," Miller said angrily, rolling him off.

Hoffman, just behind them, said to Miller, "Grab an arm, and we'll drag him."

The three managed to duck into the forest just as their antagonists zeroed in, dropping a round on the spot they had just vacated. They took cover with their companions among the roots of a banyan tree and waited for the enemy mortar crew to grow weary of its sport. Several more rounds dropped through the treetops but wide of the mark, then silence.

Foreman was bleeding profusely from his left thigh. Alvarez cut the soldier's bloody fatigues, exposing an ugly wound near the groin. He pulled a field dressing from his pocket and pushed it into the hole, then tore strips from a shoulder towel to make a tourniquet.

"Never a doc when you need one," he grumbled.

"Jesus, not so tight," Foreman groaned, arching his back.

"Shut up and hold still, you pussy," Alvarez admonished. "Two inches to the right, and you'd be carrying your balls home in a jar."

Hoffman was on the radio with Danton who was patronizing as usual, inserting himself into the situation. "Mortars, huh? Any small arms fire? Over."

"Some. Over."

"Can you tell where they are coming from?"

"Other side of the clearing."

"Are you still taking fire?"

"Negative. What is this, 21 Questions? I'm busy here."

"Listen up, Ivy, and maybe you'll learn something. Give me your coordinates, and I'll get a medevac out to you. But I don't want to send a medevac until you secure an LZ. And what about those lights? Have you swept the area? Over."

Hoffman was irritated. "Look, it's a large area, there's only five of us, and we've got a wounded man. Just get us some help and send the medevac."

"Help's on the way, but I want you to sweep now. Get me a few of those lights and anything else you can turn up. You copy, Two Six?"

Hoffman cursed under his breath. Someone would have to guard Foreman, and there was only one radio. Foreman could be left with a guard and the radio, but the remaining three would be without communication if they ran into trouble. The math just didn't work. Hoffman rolled his eyes. "You're breaking up, Five. Got to go. Out."

He returned the handset to Sullivan who smirked and held it in the air as Danton ranted, "I say again: conduct a sweep immediately. You don't run away from mortars; damn it, you run toward them."

Hoffman fired a flare skyward to guide the First Platoon, as well as the rest of his own Second Platoon, to the fake airstrip. Hoffman was glad to see Lieutenant Unnerfeld emerge from the surrounding jungle.

"You missed the party, Todd."

"So I heard. They must have prepared a welcome."

"No shit. Caught us in the open."

"How's Foreman?"

"Million-dollar wound. Well, half a million, but his war is over."

"Did you see them?"

"Hell no. Mortars and small arms from the woods over there." He pointed to the far side of the clearing.

"We'll go check it out."

First Platoon left to circle the clearing. In trees to the north, they found AK-47 shell casings and the probable location of the mortar tube. It would have taken no more than three or four men to pull off the ambush.

A medevac helicopter arrived for Foreman. He waved farewell to his buddies from a stretcher as the chopper rose. Among those below, there was no regret, only longing; Foreman was returning to The World.

Hoffman felt he got off easy with his first enemy contact. He had found the runway lights and had escaped a mortar attack with only one WIA. It could have been much worse. Most of all, he was amazed at the ingenuity of the enemy. The lights were wired in a crude circuit. But where was the power source? It had to be nearby.

“Ever heard of anything like this?” Hoffman asked Unnerfeld when he returned from his sweep.

The more experienced soldier lit a Lucky Strike with his Zippo. “This is why we’re losing this war, bro. We got airplanes and bombs; they got duct tape and baling wire. They are clever and very patient.”

“And inventive to think of something like this. Had to be a local, someone familiar with the procedures on the airstrip,” Hoffman conjectured.

“Matchbook engineers. I’ll bet everyone in Buon Binh knows exactly who done it, but they ain’t sayin’. Someone’s kid or brother-in-law. These people just want us to leave ’em alone. Which, damn it, is what we want, too.”

The two followed the wire to a shallow bunker containing two dozen vehicle batteries wired in series. The Air Force detachment at Buon Binh later confirmed that batteries had been stolen from Jeeps over the past year, an annoyance but nothing arousing suspicion.

Sullivan came running with word that Colonel Standley and General Taggart, division commander, were on their way. The area would have to be secured prior to their arrival. The novelty of the fake runway captured the attention of the brass all the way up the chain of command from division to MACV headquarters at Tan Son Nhut where the staff read a report about it over a breakfast of steak and eggs and wanted to know how it had happened.

Anticipating the arrival of the curious higher highers, Northrup and Danton headed out to make sure there were no screwups. They arrived by chopper a half hour ahead of Taggart and conducted a quick inspection of the site. Danton called Hoffman aside and demanded an explanation of what had happened that night.

"I told you what happened," Hoffman replied. "We were in the open, taking fire."

"Don't give me that crap, Ivy League. You ran away."

"Correction. We ran for cover."

"And that almost got you killed, so listen up. The Dinks don't set up their mortars and stay put the way we do. If you move toward them, you make them move. The more they move, the less they can fire and the worse their accuracy. You ran the wrong way."

In theory, it sounded reasonable, but what if he had run into an ambush with no backup? What about the wounded man? Danton wasted no opportunity to criticize, and there was nothing to be gained by engaging him in a debate about tactics.

Danton turned his head and spat tobacco juice. "You know, Hoffman, you might think I'm picking on you, but you don't know shit. You think you do, but you don't." They both turned and walked away.

Hoffman was pissed. Danton is a pompous ass. Yes, he had a Silver Star. His superiors lavished praise on him for the enemy bodies credited to his account. He would be promoted to captain soon. And yet, his men hated him for the risks he took with their lives. To him, their losses were unfortunate but unavoidable.

Division Commander General Taggart, along with General Marshal Falconer, the brigade commander, and several aides arrived in the general's chopper. A grunt, arms upstretched, guided it to a landing in the clearing where Northrup and

Danton waited. Colonel Standley, battalion commander, landed in another chopper just behind Taggart's. A Cobra gunship circled above like a hawk, ready to dive in defense if things below got hot.

Captain Northrup proudly led his superiors along the wire connecting the beacons and the power source, housed in a trench concealed with freshly cut tree limbs. Hoffman's platoon provided security. The general squatted and peered inside the enclosure. "Flashlight," he said to one of his aides. He shined it on the batteries inside. "So simple but so damn clever," he said. A soldier traveling with him started taking photos, intending to write a story for *Stars and Stripes*. The click and whine of the Nikon turned the general's head.

"Put that damn thing away," Taggart ordered. "Imagine what the civilian press would do with this if they caught wind of it. Makes us look like damn fools."

General Falconer nodded. Colonel Standley blanched. Captain Northrup's sphincter rattled. They hadn't anticipated this reaction by the general. That hungry predator, Blame, was looking for someone to devour, and it was working its way down the chain of command. Captain Northrup was a low man.

Well Captain, I'd like to know what the hell you were thinking when those lights went missing. This should never have happened."

"You're absolutely right, sir, and it won't happen again," Northrup said. "We'll work with the district officials here to track down those responsible."

"Damn right you will. Wasn't it your company's responsibility to patrol this airstrip?"

"Yes, sir, which we do daily," Northrup said defensively.

"Apparently, not well enough. We almost lost an airplane and crew. I expect better security here from now on. Is that clear?"

Hoffman had never witnessed such a dressing down by a general. In fact, in his two years in the army, he had never exchanged more than a salute with a general.

Northrup said, sweat beading on his forehead, "We'll double our sweeps."

Taggart said, "And listening posts at both ends."

"Yes, sir. In fact, we had one out last night. Lieutenant Hoffman was with the LP at the south end of the strip."

Oh shit, Hoffman feared, my turn.

"Did you see or hear anything, lieutenant?" the general asked.

"We heard the aircraft approach. We heard small arms and saw the tracers going up."

"How far from your position?"

"Several hundred meters, hard to say exactly. We moved in that direction immediately but couldn't find this place until morning. Then we started taking mortar fire."

"From which direction?"

"Just to the north of this clearing." Hoffman wondered where he was going with this.

"Then what?"

"We took cover in the tree line."

Taggart rubbed his smooth chin reflectively. His nails were manicured, and his grooming was impeccable. A small nick was the only blemish on his closely shaved face.

"You didn't engage them?" Taggart asked.

"No, sir. We got caught in the open, and a man went down with a leg wound."

Hoffman noticed Danton standing behind the general, grinning smugly.

Taggart looked at his watch and said impatiently, "Well, I've got to get going. Three congressmen due at base camp at 1500 hours. I want the company here replaced as soon as possible. And keep this quiet. Damn embarrassing."

8
SAME OLD SHIT

Rumors of imminent troop withdrawals spread through the Twenty-fourth Division's ranks. When word came that a division to the south had struck its colors and was headed back to the States, the men of Delta Company dared to think that maybe, just maybe, they would be next. Then troops from that division began showing up as replacements.—So much for an early return to The World.

The drawdown meant the division would be spread thin in III Corps, a tactical area comprising a huge swath of the country's Central Highlands. The Twenty-fourth Division shouldered primary responsibility for denying the enemy free passage from the Cambodian border to the populated area on the South China Sea's coastal plain, and they would do so at half strength. Platoons, often fewer than twenty men, played hide and seek with the NVA in a trackless wilderness. It was classic jungle warfare.

Days at Buon Binh gave Hoffman the opportunity to get his boots on the ground with his men before leading them on his first mission. There were no college diplomas in the platoon. All hailed from blue-collar families, most never having crossed a county line. Without complaint, they suffered the indignities of an Asian jungle, hammered by the sun in the dry season, never dry during the monsoon, and teeth-chattering cold during highland nights. They humped ninety-pound packs in terrain that would challenge a mountain goat, hacking a path with machetes.

When he took command, his platoon had been in the jungle for over a month, subsisting on "C-rats," government-issued canned food delivered by chopper once a week, weather, terrain, and tactical conditions permitting. They warmed their "Ham and Motherfuckers" (ham and lima beans), "Beanie Weenies" (Frankfurter chunks in tomato sauce), and "Beef and Shrapnel" (beef, potatoes, and gravy) over heat tabs—when they had heat tabs. If not, one could always filch a pinch of plastic explosive from the innards of a Claymore mine or from a stick of C-4. Lit gingerly with a match, it burned white hot.

Hoffman's training had not acquainted him with C-rations. Now, consuming them for the first time, he found them bland and greasy, meals by the low bidder. It was up to Sergeant Galvin to distribute the contents of each resupply even handedly. Then the bartering began, everyone looking to trade for "units" he liked better. Peaches and pound cake, Hoffman found, would swap for almost anything else. And even the worst fare could be improved by adding chili or Tabasco sauce sent from home. The Escoffier in the platoon, a short-order cook back in the States, taught the others ways to combine rations to make them more palatable.

Hoffman noticed that virtually all of his charges suffered from maladies inflicted by the jungle. The medic treated any infection with hydrogen peroxide, including that festering skin infection the grunts called "jungle rot." Everyone had it, along with ring-worm in the dark places, and chronic dysentery. It had been over a month since the men had an opportunity to wash the filth from their bodies. Laundered jungle fatigues stuffed in bags without regard to size came by resupply chopper every few weeks, again, weather and other circumstances permitting. It didn't matter because, in two days, they would be infused with sweat, blood, excrement, and jungle muck.

These indignities the grunts accepted without complaint, but the hubris and incompetence of senior commanders was another matter. "If a soldier ain't bitching, he ain't happy," the saying went, but Hoffman overheard a lot of grumbling that went far beyond mere cynical opinions. Nothing was being accomplished in the highlands, and no one knew that better than the grunt. At this point in the war, he was fighting to stay alive, period.

However, as much as Hoffman's men ridiculed the competence of their leaders, they respected that of their adversaries. Galvin spoke of the VC and NVA with grudging admiration. Charlie knew the terrain. He could strike and vanish preternaturally. The NVA were fearless fighters who seemed to anticipate every move of the US units. So the grunts stalked the enemy in the jungle as one would a tiger, as both the hunter and the hunted.

Hoffman saw ARVN troops loitering on the other side of the airstrip. Dressed in tailored skin-tight fatigues, they waited to catch the daily flight to the coast, to Saigon or Hue. Mostly they remained immured in their nearby camp, letting the Americans do the dirty work. The vast majority of the South's fighters were lowlanders for whom the jungle was an inhospitable, forbidding place. They had no stomach for the fight in the highlands and just wanted to get home. Desertions were common.

The grunts had no faith in the ARVN's ability to hold the highlands. The Northerners had entirely different expectations than their Southern cousins: the long trek from the north of the country to the South was a one-way journey, and they were fighting to the last man, victory or death. By 1969, Communist leaders in Hanoi were playing a waiting game. In due time, their forces would cross the border as they had before but this time with no American opposition. North to South, they would roll up the ARVN like a cheap rug.

The US' strategy of "Vietnamization" was not going to work. The grunts knew it, and so did the NVA. So why suffer heavy casualties in battle for no purpose? The Communist strategy shifted from large-scale attacks on American and South Vietnamese installations to guerilla warfare. In response, the Americans sent half a platoon into the jungle to hunt the NVA and the VC. The two sides pummeled one another in firefights and ambushes like exhausted boxers, neither able to land a knockout blow.

Hoffman learned these facts by listening to his men during his stay at the airstrip at Buon Binh. Soon he would see for himself, because the guard duty at the airstrip was ending.

"Gentlemen, our light duty here is over," Captain Northrup announced in the morning briefing of his platoon leaders. "The choppers arrive at 1100 hours to take us north. We're headed to a former ARVN firebase in Happy Valley. Unfortunate name for that place, as some of you know from our unhappy visit in June. Well, the NVA are back, if they ever left, so back we go too."

Those grunts who were there at the time recalled the Se Son River as a swift stream cutting a serpentine path through narrow canyons until widening on the coastal plain. Trails along its banks were pipelines for NVA troops and weapons. Jungle-covered ridges hid caves and bunker complexes. US troops and the enemy met like street gangs and slugged it out until the enemy melted into jungle redoubts to fight another day.

Northrup continued, "The ARVN went in and, as usual, got smoked. They're pulling out for, shall we say, lighter duty."

Delta would chopper into the ARVN's former landing zones, or LZs, which sat atop a mountain above the river; the rest of the battalion would follow, along with a battery of 105-mm howitzers. Four-deuce mortars (4.2-inch-diameter tubes) and 81-mm mortars would also deploy. Per standard operating procedure, line platoons would be assigned grid squares on a topographical map in which to search for and engage the enemy.

The diary of an infantryman fighting in the highlands would follow his journey from one LZ to the next. The term "LZ" generally applied to a patch of ground large enough for a helicopter to land but also to small portable fire support bases hacked from the jungle. Given the fact that the territory captured was almost never held, these remote bases were repeatedly abandoned and reoccupied over the years. LZ Intrepid and LZ Marilyn Monroe, both bitterly contested and overrun by the enemy at some point, were infamous. The names of most, however, were remembered only by the men who once occupied them.

Northrup said the former ARVN LZ would be rechristened LZ Daring. For the grunts, it was back to business as usual and, for Hoffman, his first opportunity to lead a platoon on an operation involving the entire battalion. Northrup had another announcement to make:

"You'll be disappointed, I know, but I won't be moving out with you. My request for transfer to Signal Corps came through. I'll be off to Tan Son Nhut tomorrow."

The news elicited no regrets from the grunts who rarely saw him anyway. He stayed low during firefights, playing it safe. This was his second one-year tour in Vietnam, and risking his life in the bush served no career purpose. A transfer to Long Binh in a noncombat role afforded him a far safer career track.

To the four platoon leaders, his departure meant little from a practical standpoint because they operated in platoon strength anyway, out of the direct control of Northrup who monitored their movements by radio from a bunker on an LZ. As Unnerfeld put it, "That tailbone, Northrup, is my kind of company commander—useless."

Northrup continued his farewell: "You'll be happy to know I leave you in the very capable hands of Lieutenant Danton who will assume command of the company as of 0800 hours tomorrow."

Northrup paused to enjoy their reaction, which they denied him the pleasure of seeing. The news wasn't all bad. Danton would command the company only temporarily until Lieutenant Julius Gilman, who was leading the Recon Platoon, returned from R&R to replace him. Danton would trade positions with Gilman at Recon.

"I know it disappoints you that you can't keep Lieutenant Danton," Northrup said sardonically. "I pressed Colonel Standley to give command of the company to Lieutenant Danton, but

Gilman is a few months senior and will be promoted to captain when he returns. So the company is his. He's a good man. Alan will be very successful in Recon, I'm sure, and eventually will get his own company to command."

The officers knew Julius Gilman only by reputation. His record with Recon was a modest one, with a few successful ambushes, nothing spectacular in the way of body count. He was a graduate of West Point, a rarity in the boonies. The troops of Delta Company rarely crossed paths with those of Recon, so they had little gossip to go on in assessing his leadership style. Anyone would be preferable to Danton. Gilman was short in stature with a boyish appearance.

Preparations for the operation proceeded in earnest. Every man would receive a five-day supply of C-rations. Sergeants distributed Atabrine tablets to prevent malaria and purification tablets to drop into canteens refilled with groundwater. By evening, weapons were cleaned, ammo meted out, and rucksacks packed and ready for inspection the following morning.

Hoffman watched Galvin assemble his gear and followed suit. The grunts never traveled light. Unlike their adversaries, who cached their supplies in the jungle, the Americans "humped" everything they might need. They normally started a new operation with eighty to one hundred pounds of supplies and equipment on their backs. Over the years, they devised ways to attach a prodigious amount of baggage on a pack frame.

It was dusk when Hoffman was summoned to the company command post. The first guards of the night were watching the perimeter from sandbagged parapets atop the bunkers, positions that gave them a better view than the firing slits in the walls. Others conversed quietly inside, wrote letters home, or played poker by candlelight. From one of the bunkers, a radio blasted, "We gotta get out of this place if it's the last thing we ever do . . ." It was their theme song, and they sang along. They were savoring the company's last night at the airstrip, the end of light duty.

Hoffman pushed back the tarp at the entrance of Northrup's bunker. A propane lantern hanging from the ceiling hissed. Northrup, sitting on a cot, paged through a *Penthouse* magazine, while Danton reclined on an air mattress, a half-empty bottle of Old Overholt within reach.

"There you are, Hoffman," he said. "We're celebrating tonight. Please join us in a small libation. Alan, don't hog that bottle."

Hoffman reluctantly sat next to Northrup on the cot, the only seat available. Northrup's breath was flammable. What were these two up to now? Celebrating Northrup's escape from combat duty? The captain reached into his breast pocket and removed an object.

"I'm tying up some administrative loose ends before I jump on that chopper and unass this AO tomorrow," he said. "I'm having orders cut awarding you the Combat Infantry Badge."

It was the furthest thing from Hoffman's mind. He'd been in the field only a few weeks and hadn't even taken his platoon out on an operation. The CIB was the symbol of an infantryman's rite of passage, of his initiation into a blooded brotherhood, awarded for engaging enemy troops in active combat. If this was one of their jokes, it was a cheap one.

"No thanks," Hoffman said.

"What?"

"I said no thanks. I'll get it when I've earned it."

"Technically, you have, in that airstrip attack the other day. You'll get one sooner or later, anyway. Humor me."

"I've done enough of that."

"Oh, I believe we've offended the young lieutenant, Alan," Northrup said.

"Apparently so," Danton said, "but I happen to agree with him. He doesn't deserve a CIB."

"Well, have it your way, you two," Northrup said.

9
THE SEARCH FOR A FATHER

Of her father, Tess Danton had the fragmented recollections of a very young child, blowing out the match he used to light a cigarette, watching him shave in the morning, coming home at night with some small gift. She had taken a few old photos of him with her when she had left home for the university in Austin: a smiling, youthful Danton in cap and gown as a high school graduate; a slender teenage Danton leaning on the fender of his 1957 Chevy; a fresh-faced sailor in a Crackerjack uniform and Dixie Cup hat; a young man about her age in a Hawaiian shirt, a lei on his shoulders.

Her paternal uncle, her father's only surviving sibling, lived in Chicago. He was ten years older than her father. Tess rarely saw him and found him disinterested in discussing his younger brother. A dozen photos of Lieutenant Alan Danton's R&R in Hawaii survived: Tess playing in the sand and a young couple in bathing suits on a lanai, deeply tanned, smiling, drinks in hand. Were they as happy as that? she wondered.

Tess could see some facial resemblance to her father, but what other similarities were there? His personality was a mystery. Was he an introvert like her? No, her mother would say, he was no introvert. Did he have a sense of humor? He laughed a lot. Was he intelligent? Very. Was he kind, gentle, or sensitive? He was a good man. The piano in the living room—did he play it often? Yes, by ear; he couldn't read a note.

That he was an avid reader with an interest in military history she knew from the books in cardboard boxes in her mother's apartment. The boxes moved with them several times until Claudia remarried, and then they went to a used bookstore. Tess missed them when they were gone. They were the last tangible evidence of his existence.

Of all the mysteries surrounding him, the final months of his life in Vietnam loomed the largest. What could the men who served with him tell her? She had the name of one person who served with her father in Vietnam: Jim Northrup. An address on his last Christmas card was no longer current, but a prosecutor skilled at locating the indisposed easily tracked him down: he retired from the Army at Fort Ord, California, in 1980 and moved to Phoenix.

When she phoned, he seemed pleased to hear from her. Yes, he often wondered about her and her mother, should have stayed in contact, apologized, was glad to know they were fine and that Claudia was in good health. Such fond memories of her father, so long ago now, but would never forget him. Didn't travel much himself, but of course, he would love a visit when she passed through Phoenix.

On the airplane, she prepared as if for a deposition, questions jotted on a legal pad. It was 11:00 a.m. when the cab pulled up in front of Northrup's suburban bungalow. A portly man in his mid-sixties, avuncular, graying, not at all the trim young soldier in photos taken at her father's burial, greeted her at the top of the steps. They stood facing one another for a moment, his warm hands heavy on her shoulders. "You are definitely Alan Danton's daughter," he said. "The last time I saw you, you were, what, about five?"

"Yes, when Dad's remains were brought home. I don't remember much about it. How have you been, Captain Northrup?"

"Please, it's just Jim these days. Insults of age, but the VA takes pretty good care of me. Two new hips. For my addled brain, they have no replacement."

The two sat on the porch in wicker chairs, a small table and a pitcher of iced tea between them. It was a quiet neighborhood of modest homes, of the type preferred by retirees in Sun City, a yard landscaped with ornamental rock and an assortment of cacti, euphorbia, and other succulents, maintained as if prepared for an IG inspection at any moment. Northrup filled two glasses. Ice cubes rattled. A dog yipped somewhere inside the house. Tess assumed Mrs. Northrup was there.

Northrup said, "So, how's your mother?"

"Doing well. She sends her love."

Northrup smiled. "Fine lady. Happily married and all, you said. I'm glad she has a good life. Give her my regards."

"I will. She deeply appreciated your bringing my father home."

"It was an honor. I just wish he'd have made it home alive. It hurt."

"Yes. You two were friends. I know that from his letters."

They sat reflectively for a moment. Northrup said, "So, what have you been doing with yourself?"

"I work in the federal attorney's office in Austin."

"A lawyer?"

"Umm hmm."

"Well, that's just great. I'm not surprised. Your dad was a smart guy, and your mom is, too. You started your own family?"

"No. Single."

"Goodness. Attractive young lady like you?"

"Thanks, but that's not sufficient grounds for a decision to marry."

"Spoken like an attorney," he laughed.

"You're probably wondering why I looked you up, Captain Northrup—Jim. It's wonderful to meet you, but I confess I have something on my mind, something I hope you can help me with."

"Of course. What is it?"

"I have questions about Dad and about what happened to him. I hope you don't mind."

"Of course not."

"For starters, you two became friends. I'm interested in your impressions of him."

"Well, I was his company commander, but we hit it off right away. We were about the same age, and we enjoyed one another's company whenever we had the opportunity. I admired him. He was very committed to his job and good at it."

"But what was he like, as a human being I mean? Start at the beginning when you met."

A pack of cigarettes lay on the table near a full ashtray. "Mind if I smoke?"

"Not at all."

"Your dad smoked," Northrup said wistfully, "but mostly he chewed. Beechnut, Army issue. Yeah. I used to give him a bad time about it." Northrup lit up. Smoke hung like cotton in the still desert air. "We were in a forward position east of Pleiku. He joined the company as a replacement, a second lieutenant a few months out of officer candidate school. Because he was older than most OCS graduates, I figured he probably had prior service."

"Mother said he was so proud when she pinned the gold bars on his shoulders at Fort Benning. You can see it in the photo. She was smiling, too, but really, frightened by what he was doing."

"Typical wife of an infantryman, then. He reminded me of myself on my first tour in Vietnam, right out of OCS, full of piss and vinegar. We were going over there to prove ourselves and win some decorations for our uniforms. Couldn't wait to get into combat."

Yes, he had the medals, and all Tess had was a folded flag in a display box. She said, "He must have considered the possibility he wouldn't come back. Did you?"

"I'd be lying if I didn't admit it crossed my mind. But you can't let that fear take over, or you can't function. It's always there, in the background, though, kind of like a stray dog that follows you around. You chase it away, but it keeps coming back."

Northrup snuffed out his cigarette as if to expunge a lamentable fact.

"I was on my second tour in Nam, and I figured I'd tempted fate enough. I managed to get a position in the rear and left Alan in the boonies. He'd done his six months in the field and was due a promotion to captain and a staff job in the rear. I was confident he'd move on."

"Why didn't he?"

"He was a star in our outfit, leading one of the only line platoons that was generating any significant enemy contact. The battalion commander wanted him to lead Recon for a couple of months. Promised him any position he wanted after that."

"If only he had."

"He didn't want to disappoint his superiors, I guess. After I transferred out of the division, I lost contact with him. As close as men got in that pressure cooker, they vanished like steam when they left. I learned of his passing when I got word that he was KIA. Your mother wanted me to escort his remains back to the States."

"Did you hear anything about how he died?"

"Mostly what others told me and what I read in reports."

"I have official records. They don't really say much about the circumstances. In the national archives, I found the names of other men that got medals. I was able to locate one of them in Texas, a small town near Lubbock. I called him on the phone, but he said he didn't know anything about it. If he did, he obviously wasn't interested in talking."

It was noon, and the temperature was rising. A small lizard scurried across the porch and disappeared beneath the steps. Tess said, "I know he was determined to succeed, like you said, to make the Army a career. Mother said that was his plan. I just wish he had found some other way to provide for us. It seems so . . . well, desperate."

"He didn't see it that way. He often talked about you two, about what he was going to do for you when he got home. He wanted to settle into his next assignment and buy a house. He was going to have a new car waiting for him when he arrived. He had a plan." Northrup looked at his watch. "But it's time for lunch. I hope you'll stay." He turned toward the door and shouted, "June, come meet Tess Danton."

A matronly woman with a florid face appeared at the door. "Oh, Tess Danton," she said warmly. "You were just a baby when I saw you last. My, you are the image of your father. Isn't she, Jim? Don't you see it?"

"Yes, dear, I do. Already told her so," he said.

"Come and eat, you two."

The conversation over tuna sandwiches stayed clear of Vietnam and the final days of Alan Danton's life. They spoke, instead, of subsequent years, of Jim Northrup's military assignments, the four Northrup children. Tess answered questions about her mother and her adjustments to life without Alan.

June said as she cleared the table, "Your poor mother. I can't imagine what I would have done if I had lost Jim. I lived with my heart in my mouth those two years he was gone."

Jim Northrup said, "Let's go into the living room. It's cooler there. Another iced tea?"

"I'm fine, thanks."

Tess sank into a large overstuffed couch. A grandfather clock stood in a corner. Jim Northrup sat in a leather recliner. Framed prints of desert landscapes hung on the walls. Family photos cluttered tabletops. Tess saw no mementos of Northrup's military service. She said, "I've been told about my dad as a soldier, so little about him as a human being. I mean, what were your impressions of him?"

"Well, he was ambitious, demanding of his men, what we would call a hard charger, but he had a soft side too."

"How so? What do you remember?"

Northrup smiled. "I recall one operation when we had set up a defensive perimeter near a large Montagnard village, and every morning a gaggle of them, mostly women and children, came to beg for cigarettes and C-rations. Made me damn nervous, but your dad liked 'em. Even visited them in their village and drank some of that awful rice wine they fermented. It made him sick and me nervous."

"Mother said he loved to party."

"That he did, but I preferred not to encourage the Yards to hang around. Alan felt differently. There was a wild-eyed elder, a fellow in a loincloth and a fancy woven shirt, a lot of amulets around his neck, likely a medicine man. He showed up every morning, babbling incoherently. The troops started calling him Old Crazy. Well, he had a nasty-looking infection in his calf, maybe a punji wound. It was deep and looked gangrenous. Damned if Alan didn't tell a medic to clean and treat it."

"Of course, why wouldn't he?"

"Well, we weren't a civil affairs unit. We were there to fight. As callous as it sounds, there wasn't a damn thing we could do to improve their lives anyway. The Vietnamese abused them, and we would soon abandon them. They would suffer like they always had."

"How sad," Tess said.

"Collateral damage, as they say. Anyway, Old Crazy came back several days later, and his wound was nearly healed. Antibiotics worked fast on people never exposed to them, I guess. He brought several villagers with him, all of them with infections of some kind. Your dad set up a makeshift clinic that kept our medics busy until we pulled out."

Northrup leaned back in his chair and closed his eyes. Dishes rattled in the kitchen. The pendulum clock chimed twice.

Tess said, "Mother told me he was kind. What did you two talk about when you were alone?"

"Oh, we talked about operations, the Army, our future in it. He was actually glad to be in Vietnam. I never heard him express a moment's regret about joining the Army. I really believed he had a career ahead of him and he was trying to prove himself. I had the same hope for myself, but it didn't work out as I planned."

"You had a career."

"Yes, but not the one I wanted. Not long after I returned to the States, the army pulled the rug out from under men like me, those of us who came up through the enlisted ranks. There was a big reduction in force, and I was given a choice. In order to stay on active duty, I had to give up my commission and return to my previous rank as a noncommissioned officer. One day I was a captain, the next a sergeant."

"You chose to stay."

"Yeah, I stayed. The Army was all I knew. My two tours in Vietnam and officer efficiency reports might as well have been a clerical error. Sorry, Tess, you didn't come to hear me complain. I was disappointed, but I don't regret my years in the Army."

Tess said, "I hated the Army growing up." It was an awkward moment. Had her father died in vain, hoping for a military career? The clock chimed, and she looked at her watch. "I have to get to the airport. You've given me a lot to think about. Mother told me to be sure to thank you for being there for her when she needed you." She rose from her chair. "Let's talk again, stay in touch."

He stood and embraced her. "I certainly will. I apologize for letting so many years pass without writing. Your dad was a fine officer and a good man. I'll never forget him."

Northrup called for a cab and walked with her to the street. "You know, I'm recalling there might have been another young officer with him when he died. And a Montagnard woman."

"A woman? How strange."

"Apparently they found her near the NVA camp and wanted to bring her back for questioning. Of course, these are just things I heard from others, and I can't vouch for them."

"If accurate, why wasn't this in the official reports?"

"Probably considered unimportant," Northrup said. "Those reports were sketchy at best anyway."

10
JUST DON'T ASK

Huey helicopters lifted Delta Company from the airstrip at Buon Binh and took it to the former ARVN fire support base in Happy Valley where it would await the arrival of a convoy of the rest of the battalion. The choppers flew high over Route 19, a narrow road connecting Qui Nohn, a port on the coastal plain, with Pleiku on the plateau. Supplies moved from the coast to the bases in the highlands on this artery. It was notorious for ambushes.

Several tanks and armored personnel carriers sat in a circle above the road. Their crews, lounging on aluminum folding chairs beside their vehicles, looked up at the helicopters. The armor was positioned to roll into action if called upon by convoys traveling a narrow pass just to the west. Razor Galvin tapped Hoffman on the shoulder and shouted over the din of blade and turbine, "Mang Yang Pass." It was here that a Vietminh force had slaughtered the lead element of a French convoy, the final blow of the First Indochina War. The helicopter passed low over rows of white patches, mostly obscured by brush. "French graves," Galvin shouted.

Like a flock of mechanical geese, the helicopters flew over the pass and continued west, passing several small villages before turning away from the paved highway at its junction with a dirt road heading into the hills to the north. The road petered out in a small valley drained by a serpentine river. The valley floor was a savanna of lush elephant grass and scattered palm and bamboo groves. From the air, the valley resembled the tropical depictions of a biblical Eden Hoffman recalled from his catechism. As he would soon learn, on the ground, it was no Eden.

Near the center of the valley, a hummock rose, and on its crest sat the recently vacated fire support base. South Vietnamese forces, which periodically operated here, had left the hill a few days earlier to be relieved by the Desert Devils. Communist forces passed through the valley and the hills surrounding it on their way to the coast, a route dating back to the First Indochina War. The ARVN had sustained heavy losses here in recent months.

As the helicopters pivoted over this rise in the valley floor, those aboard saw nothing remarkable, just a firebase like dozens of others on tonsured peaks throughout the highlands. Delta Company's orders were to secure the vacated position in preparation for the arrival of an artillery battery and the battalion headquarters, which would come by convoy. The LZ would be called Fire Support Base Luck. Of course, the grunts immediately replaced "Luck" with "Fucked."

Slicks carrying the First Platoon touched down first. From his chopper, Hoffman watched Unnerfeld's grunts scurrying over the hill like fleas, checking bunkers for any unpleasant surprises. Having confirmed that the base was as abandoned as it appeared to be, Unnerfeld gave the all-clear for the rest of the advance party to land and take up positions on the perimeter.

The condition of LZ Luck only amplified the grunts' disdain for their predecessors. Soaked and rotting sacks of rice, empty tins of fish, scattered shell casings, discarded clothing, and untended latrines littered the hill. Black flies swarmed over the filth.

"This place is a garbage dump," Hoffman said. "Why would anyone want to live like this?"

"Pigs," spat Galvin.

"Well, Danton wants the place ready for inspection before the colonel arrives tomorrow," Hoffman said.

"Tall order. The sump is full, and we don't have time to bury all this garbage."

"What do you suggest?"

"Police it up as best we can in sandbags and pile them at the base of the hill. The engineers will push them in when they blow a pit."

The men worked fast to clean out the bunkers before nightfall. Meanwhile, Unnerfeld's First Platoon conducted a sweep of the jungle below, looking for any sign of recent enemy presence. By evening most of the detritus had been removed from the hilltop, leaving a sour stench inside the damp bunkers.

The sun set behind the lumpy hills to the west, painting the horizon in pastels of red and purple. With just enough light to see where they were going, Hoffman left the perimeter with the two men he selected to establish an LP, a listening post. Spending the night alone outside the wire ranked high among the infantry's standard issue of miseries. Every nocturnal sound worked on a man's mind in terrifying ways. In an attack, LPs often found themselves cut off from friendly lines and subject to both enemy and friendly fire.

Hoffman led the two men down the hill, about fifty meters, to a patch of elephant grass near a trail, a likely avenue of enemy approach. Here the LPs would remain hidden with a radio, responsible for alerting those on the hill at the approach of anyone on the trail.

Hoffman said, "Stay awake, no talking. We'll be calling you for a situation report every half hour. If your situation is negative, break squelch twice."

He needn't have instructed them. They had done this frightening job many times, and they were no happier about it now. They spread a poncho on the ground and sat on it, back to back, and there they would remain for the night, like scared children abandoned in the wilderness. Hoffman regretted having to leave them there.

Meanwhile, back in the perimeter, the grunts drew straws for shifts of the night watch. Uninterrupted sleep was a thing of the past. They napped like cats when and where they could. On guard at night in the jungle, it was the responsibility of each man to make sure his successor was on his feet and alert. Failure to do so would leave his sleeping buddies unguarded.

Bunkers on forward firebases were hastily dug holes. The grunts filled sandbags with dirt and stacked them like bricks around the holes. Engineer stakes served as rafters, upon which more sandbags were stacked for overhead. The bunkers provided ample protection against shrapnel and bullets but less if hit by a mortar or rocket. Specialist 4 Sullivan was on guard atop the bunker where most of the men sat for a 180-degree view of what lay before them.

"All cool, Sully?" Hoffman asked the RTO.

"Groovy. You run into Danton?"

"No. Why?"

"He's snoopin' around. Was just here."

"What'd he want?"

"Looking for someone to write up for sleeping on duty."

"Well, if he comes back, come and get me."

Hoffman looked at the luminous dial of his watch: 2300. He was dead tired. He crawled inside the bunker and turned on his flashlight. Sergeant Galvin was rolled in his poncho liner, head covered, feet hanging out the other end, looking like a fat cigar. He was sleeping soundly. Hoffman spread his flat air mattress on the dirt floor; he didn't have the energy to inflate it. The bunker smelled vaguely of urine. He laid his weapon at his side, covered himself with his nylon liner, and closed his eyes.

Sleep wouldn't come. His mind raced. Three weeks in-country and finally leading his platoon in combat. After all his training, just those few short weeks proved to him he didn't know squat. Twenty-four men relied on him for their lives. How would he measure up? Well, he got lucky with Sergeant Galvin. Then he did something he hadn't done in years—he prayed.

He was dozing off when he felt a strange sensation, like a tennis ball rolling down his side and onto his boots. Dismissing it as overstimulation, he pulled his poncho liner over his head. When it happened again, he had no doubt—something had moved along his body and was resting on his boot. He reached for his flashlight and cast a beam at his feet where two small red eyes met his. "What the hell," he shouted, kicking it away.

"Something wrong, LT?" Galvin mumbled.

"There are rats in this goddamn hole," Hoffman blurted.

"Yeah, heard them squealin' earlier. They're tunneled into this bunker, and they're hungry. But don't worry; you ain't on their menu."

Following Galvin's example, Hoffman rolled himself in his poncho liner, covering his head. The next thing of which he was aware was a tapping on his back. It was Sullivan. "LT, wake up. Your shift of guard."

"Okay, just a minute," Hoffman said groggily. He rose to his knees, groped for his M-16, and crawled out into a moonless, starlit night. He shuddered in the highland chill. After the heat of the previous day, how could it be this cold? "Don't shoot me, Sully," Hoffman said, "Have to take a leak." He felt his way to the crest of the hill and pissed into a coil of concertina wire. Sullivan was waiting with the radio when he returned.

"The LPs okay?" Hoffman asked.

"Due a sitrep now. Want me to do it?"

"No, I'll do it. Get some rest."

The RTO handed Hoffman his radio and disappeared into the bunker. Hoffman whispered into the handset: "Wide Eyes, Wide Eyes, this is Two Six. Sitrep negative break squelch twice. Over." The static cleared twice in response. And so it went for the rest of the night as Hoffman, Sullivan, and Galvin rotated on guard, manning the radio.

At dawn, word came that the battalion commander and a battery of 105-mm howitzers would arrive by convoy before noon. The Third Platoon walked the dirt road with a metal detector to check for mines or boobytraps and found none. By 0900, Sullivan heard on the battalion frequency that a “Shit Hook,” the grunts’ appellation of a Chinook helicopter, was coming in.

The distinctive whomping of the big bird’s twin rotors announced its approach with a sling load the size of a Volkswagen dangling from its undercarriage. A soldier dropped a canister of green smoke on a level patch of ground. Struggling to keep his feet under the furious buffeting of blade wash, he guided the chopper down with upraised arms. When the cargo came to rest, he clambered to the top of the bundle and released the cable. Hoffman admired his agility.

The Chinook flew half a dozen sorties in the following hours, keeping the artillerymen and the grunts of Delta Company busy storing equipment in bunkers and preparing the LZ for an operation of several weeks. The convoy arrived at noon, led by an armored deuce-and-a-half

truck with a fifty-caliber machine gun mounted in its bed. A buxom bikini-clad girl and the words “Highland dreamin’” adorned the steel plate shielding the rear of the truck.

Soon LZ Luck was bustling with activity. Three 105-mm howitzers were sited in and prepared to fire, while Hueys ferried Bravo and Charlie companies to their respective areas of operation in the hills surrounding the valley. Delta would remain on the LZ, defending the hill and patrolling the valley itself.

An abandoned Montagnard village was known to be located four kilometers to the north. The residents of the village had been relocated to a resettlement camp more than a year before when the area became subject to random harassment and interdiction barrages by long-range artillery. But aerial reconnaissance indicated recent activity in the area, and Danton, acting company commander, dispatched Hoffman's Second Platoon on a three-day mission to investigate.

"And oh," Danton said offhandedly as he dismissed Hoffman, "I'm advised by G-2 that there might be Cidges operating here, so make sure you don't light up any friendlies."

"Cidges? Hoffman asked.

"Yeah, Civilian Indigenous Defense Group, villagers trained to defend themselves. They operate out of villages along the highway."

"What the hell? Can't their presence be confirmed?"

"That's all I can tell you, Ivy League. I'll alert you if I get anything further."

When Hoffman briefed Galvin on the mission, the normally sedate sergeant looked irritated. "What are you thinking, Razor?" Hoffman wondered.

"Fucked up, LT. These dudes wear black pajamas and carry weapons, same-same VC. So do we ask for ID before we waste 'em?"

"I don't like it either, but it is what it is. Get everyone ready to move out."

Hoffman was glad to leave the LZ under any circumstances. The jungle would be more hospitable than that crowded, filthy hill. His map told him the river meandered through the valley in wide hairpin turns over its entire course. There were swampy areas. Mountains and ridges rose sharply from the lowland.

The twenty-three grunts of the Second Platoon left the perimeter in a single file and descended the hill into the valley. Specialist 4 Ludwik was on point, followed by his "slack," Specialist 4 Pepe Armijo. Hoffman elected to walk third with his compass to guide Ludwik, while Armijo—"Army Joe"—kept a pace count to get a rough idea of the distance traveled. Sullivan was in the fourth position with the radio.

They progressed easily at first, but as the ground fell toward the stream, the jungle put up more resistance. Finally, Ludwik halted before a dense wall of elephant grass. Knowing from experience what was in store, he turned questioningly to Hoffman who nodded to proceed. The grunt pulled a machete from a sheath tied to his ruck and went to battle with the razor-sharp grass.

As the sun climbed higher, the men found themselves submerged in a sea of grass with nothing to guide them but a compass heading. The line of men made slow progress, halting while the point hacked a path. An hour of labor in suffocating heat had gained them less than thirty meters. Hoffman wondered how far they would have to go to break out. There was no way to know, yet he was reluctant to give up the progress that had been so dearly gained.

The grunts stooped sullenly under the weight of their rucks, uncomplaining. Some lessons have to be learned the hard way, lest there be repetition. Sergeant Galvin remained silent until Hoffman sought his counsel.

"So what do you recommend, Razor?"

Galvin wiped the sweat from his face with his shoulder towel. "Shade and a cold beer."

"No, seriously."

"Seriously? Sometimes the shortest distance between two points ain't a straight line, LT."

"Point taken. Let's turn around."

The platoon reversed its course and followed the path it had hacked out of the grass. Hoffman consulted his map and mentally charted a more circuitous route to the village, avoiding low ground. It was longer but easier humping. He reckoned the abandoned village would be easy to find once the platoon forded the stream. Armijo spelled Ludwik on point, and the platoon picked up the pace toward a grove of trees, promise of shade, and a short rest.

As the platoon approached the copse, Armijo stopped and took a knee. The men behind him followed suit. Hoffman moved forward and joined him.

"What?" Hoffman whispered.

"Movement," the point replied.

Hoffman saw nothing but a glade surrounded by palms and small trees, as still as a photograph. A shrill chorus of insects pulsated in the still, humid air. Then, there was movement of something, barely visible behind the screen of trees. Whatever it was, it was large. Armijo put his hand on Hoffman's arm and pointed. "There—did you see that?"

"Yeah. But what is it?"

"Could be water buffalo," Armijo said.

"Okay," Hoffman whispered. "Move up but go slow."

The file advanced cautiously, maintaining a generous separation. Armijo raised an arm and halted again, turning to Hoffman. "VC elephant," he said, grinning.

Tethered in the trees was a juvenile elephant, about six feet tall at the shoulders. It eyed them indifferently as they passed and continued to strip leaves from the trees with its trunk and push them into its mouth. Where there's a young elephant on a tether, there must be a keeper, and that concerned Hoffman.

Exhausted from the morning's hump under a tyrannical sun, the men dropped to the ground in the shade of the trees, removed their helmets, and sat in them, topside down. Hoffman consulted with Lieutenant Danton on the radio. An elephant, Danton mused, was interesting, but he still could provide no information on civilians in the area. Keep moving toward the village.

Hoffman went over his map with Galvin. Deep in the valley, they had no prominent terrain features on which to take a bearing. The two agreed they must still be several hundred meters from the objective, but considering the battle with the wall of grass and the detour, this was just a guess. By continuing west, they would have to cross the stream sooner or later, and the village would be on the other side. If they could reach it before dusk, they would spend the night there.

The platoon moved out again. Hoffman felt he might have been at sea with no stars to guide him. What if he needed artillery support? What if he never found that damn village? What if he got lost on his first mission? Of course, he could always rely on Galvin to rescue him, humbling but comforting nonetheless.

Another fifty meters brought the point man to the muddy bank of the stream, confirming that at least the platoon was headed in the right direction. Now they would have to cross it. Water, the color of chocolate, hid the channel's depth. Ludwik tied the climbing rope around his waist and waded in, holding his rifle over his head. The water filled his ruck and reached his armpits before he scrambled up the slippery bank on the other side.

With the rope tied to trees on both banks as a handhold, the grunts waded in like a raft of ducks. Galvin went with the first squad to secure the opposite bank. That accomplished, Hoffman waded in. The water rose to his knees and crept past his groin. The mud sucked at his boots, and he nearly lost his balance but was able to pull himself upright with the rope. When he felt himself going over again, there was no averting it. As he went under, someone pulled him to the surface by his ruck frame. It was Sullivan.

"Grab the rope, LT," Sullivan shouted.

Hoffman held his rifle with his right hand and reached for the rope with his left. "Jesus," he said, embarrassed, as he struggled to regain his footing, "I stepped into a damn hole."

"No sweat, LT," Sullivan said. "You aren't the first or the last."

Hoffman realized he had lost his steel pot. He probed the bottom with his foot, but it was hopeless, and he was holding up the crossing. In his ruck, he had an Australian bush hat he had purchased from local peddlers at the airstrip. It would keep the sun off his head until he could replace his helmet back on the LZ. His pride would be more difficult to recover.

The platoon completed the crossing with no further mishaps and reassembled in a grassy area above the streambank. The sun would dry their fatigues in minutes, but their water-filled boots were another matter. Once a new pair were laced on, they might as well have been grafted to their feet. Immersion and trench foot were common.

As the platoon reassembled on the streambank, the Green Monster added another ingredient to the gooey muck that caked their boots and legs. "Fucking leeches," someone shouted. The grunts leaped to their feet, cursing and stomping on the attacking horde. Hoffman felt a tickle on his forearm where a fat leach sucked ecstatically. He reflexively slapped it with his hand, and it burst like a balloon, spattering his arm with blood.

"Everybody, cool it," Galvin commanded. "Get your rucks on and let's move away from this stream."

Hoffman worried about a far greater threat, that of an enemy attack while his men were preoccupied with the leeches. He thanked God for that sergeant as the men fell back into a single file and resumed their hump into the forest.

It wasn't long before the platoon came upon fallow agricultural plots. An overgrown footpath led them to the abandoned village. It was a typical Montagnard settlement, longhouses elevated on posts, walls of tightly woven bamboo, and thatched roofs. All of the buildings, a dozen or so, were dilapidated, some with collapsed roofs. The platoon moved through the cluster in a skirmish line, peering into each building and finding only bats and lizards.

The platoon pulled back from the hooches into a draw for the night. It was dusk when Hoffman sent squads out to look for any signs of human company. They found none. Peppers in a neglected garden spiced their C-rations, welcome spoils of war. The grunts strung trip flares around their night lager. Nightfall came, and a few hours of sleep after a long day of struggle with the Green Monster.

Given the possibility that friendlies might be somewhere in the area, Hoffman opted not to call the artillerymen on the LZ for marking rounds, points from which he could quickly adjust fire if needed. He encrypted his position and called it in. Office work done, he rolled into his poncho liner. It had been an eventful day. One down, an eternity remaining, but the journey had begun.

He lay on the ground listening to the jungle's nocturnal choir, eerie, haunting, foreign to his ears. His thoughts turned again to Clara. The luminous dial of his watch told him it was 1042 hours in Vietnam, so early morning in Seattle and she would be preparing to go to work, putting on her makeup and deciding what clothes to wear. He visualized her sitting at her vanity, brushing her waist-length hair. She was beautiful, and it hurt to think about her.

Sleep came, interrupted by a hand on his shoulder and someone whispering, "LT, LT." He opened his eyes and saw Sergeant Galvin's face above his. Was it already his shift monitoring the radio?

"We've got movement," Galvin said under his breath.

"Where?"

"There," Galvin said, pointing into the darkness.

Yes, Hoffman heard it now, a shuffling sound, but darkness denied him a view of anything but a blur of trees about one hundred meters from their position. The rest of the platoon heard the sounds, too, and everyone was alert, listening, watching, their weapons at the ready.

"There it is again. Hear that?" Galvin said.

"Yeah. Didn't we sweep those trees?"

"Ludwik told me he went that way and didn't see anything."

"Well, make sure no one gets trigger-happy," Hoffman said. "No firing unless I say so."

While Galvin passed the word, Hoffman took up the radio handset to report the situation to Danton at the company command post on the LZ but better judgment dictated that he wait and see what developed.

In the next several hours, the sounds continued randomly, unassignable to any human activity. Then Hoffman remembered the juvenile elephant the platoon had come across earlier. Galvin was thinking the same thing. "Where there's a baby, there's a family somewhere," the sergeant said.

Jungle Operations School in Panama covered jungle survival techniques, but dealing with elephants wasn't in the curriculum. If a herd was moving in his direction, what would he do? How would the big animals react if they caught the scent of the grunts? He had visions of the beasts charging into his defenseless platoon. M-16 fire would only anger them.

The men spent a wakeful night on alert, but the animals kept their distance. At first light, Galvin led a squad to investigate. Sure enough, four adult elephants were tethered to stakes just beyond the stand of trees at the edge of a freshly logged ridge. "Lot of timber on the ground," Galvin reported back to Hoffman on the radio. "Looks like the elephants are pulling logs out of the woods."

Hoffman's map showed no road but the one the battalion came in on. He reported the find to Danton and asked again about civilian activity in the area. Danton still had nothing to tell him. He would press the battalion for better intelligence from the Vietnamese provincial authorities. He cautioned Hoffman to stay away from the animals and refrain from confronting any loggers who might return.

It was 0630 when the jungle's nocturnal sighs gave way to the din of day. The air was cool, and the scene surrounding the vacant village was still. The grunts smoked and chatted quietly while brewing powdered coffee over heat tabs. Hoffman plotted a course for the day on his map. His instructions were to reconnoiter upstream, which he pondered reluctantly. The channel meandered severely through a quagmire of swamp and elephant grass.

At 0730, Hoffman gave the order to saddle up. Hoffman's map told him a turn to the west would keep them on higher ground. Reconnoitering the valley floor as ordered was a fool's errand. He knew the enemy would not be there because no rational human beings would willingly subject themselves to its abuse. If Danton insisted otherwise, to hell with him. To the relief of his men, Hoffman chose an azimuth that would take the platoon to higher ground.

By noon the grunts had moved easily through low-growing palm and pomelo. In the forested fringe of the valley, the grunts found welcome shade. Hoffman gave his men a rest break, and they circled around a large tree with roots like the arms of an octopus. The men sat silently, communicating with hand gestures.

At that moment, they heard a rustling sound like that of wind rushing through the leaves of trees, but there was no wind. A cloud of black winged insects darkened the sky.

"My God, butterflies—there must be thousands of them," Hoffman said in awe.

"Yeah, butterflies aren't supposed to be black," Galvin said. "Every time I saw 'em, something bad happened."

"You superstitious, Razor?"

"Maybe, but somethin' like that, man, you better pay attention."

Grunts wore various talisman around their necks: rosaries, peace medals, black crosses woven of bootlaces, Montagnard amulets. The distinction between faith and superstition was blurred where their survival was concerned.

"Omen or not, we've got to get to some potable water soon," Hoffman said.

Hoffman pondered how far to push before stopping for the night. The logging operation made him uneasy, but they had encountered no other indications of human activity. What precisely was his objective? He didn't know. The platoon was running low on water, an issue he never dreamed he would deal with in the jungle. His map showed a small creek flowing from higher ground a few hundred meters to the northwest. It would be cleaner than the muddy river.

With Ludwik on point, the platoon passed through rolling, relatively open terrain until it came upon a wide trail that dropped precipitously to a stream. Suddenly, a man wearing nothing but a loin cloth bolted from the dense foliage along the bank with his hands in the air, bellowing in Vietnamese. The grunts aimed their weapons at him.

"Hold your fire; he's unarmed," Hoffman shouted.

That the man's life didn't end in a fusillade was his sheer good fortune. The fellow's ribs stood out like xylophone keys; he appeared starved. Just then, Ludwik called out, "There's another one just ran up the bank on the other side."

The two apparently were equally surprised by the appearance of the grunts. Perhaps the first was trying to distract the platoon and facilitate the second's escape. Were there more of them in the riparian foliage? Ludwik grabbed the man's boney arm and twisted it behind him, prompting him to object loudly.

"Shut the fuck up," Ludwik growled. "We ain't gonna hurt you."

To Lieutenant Hoffman, the fellow seemed more defiant than fearful. Was he merely a poor peasant harvesting some greens for his pho? Or was he VC, or both? If only there were better intelligence about civilians in the area, or any at all. The officer wished he had a translator. Emaciated, naked except for the filthy rag covering his groin, he was a pitiful specimen, hardly a threat. A grunt tied his hands and feet with bootlaces and sat him under a tree, while Hoffman pondered what to do with him.

"Delta Six, this is Two Six," Hoffman said into the handset. "We've got one Vietnamese male, unarmed, apparently harvesting greens in a creek. It's about a klick northwest of that abandoned Montagnard village. Another one got away. Please advise. Over."

"Two Six, Delta Six. Hold him, and I'll get back to you. We may want to fly him back for interrogation."

Hoffman returned the handset to Sullivan and shook his head in frustration.

"What?" Galvin asked.

"They might want to send a chopper for him."

Galvin put out security on the trail while the platoon waited. Danton responded in ten minutes: "It's getting late, and there are no birds available. Our Vietnamese counterparts have no confirmation of any friendlies in the area."

"So what am I supposed to do with this guy?" Hoffman protested.

"Use your imagination, Ivy League."

Hoffman looked quizzically at Galvin. "He said no chopper and still no information on friendlies."

"So what about our little friend here?"

"Danton says, 'use your imagination.'"

"I was afraid of that."

"So what do you suggest, Razor?"

"Your call, LT. Rank has its privileges."

The sun was on the way down, but it was still hot. The officer paused to mop his face with his shoulder towel as if it might also clear his mind. "Okay, cut him loose."

"You sure?"

"No, but do it anyway."

The Vietnamese stood up on spindly legs, resembling a featherless hatchling. "Di di, you piece of shit," Ludwik snarled, giving the fellow a poke with the barrel of his rifle. The man slowly backed away, his eyes wide, apparently thinking he was about to be shot, then turned and bound like a deer down the stream-bank, splashed through the shallow stream, and disappeared into a dense green wall of palm.

Now Hoffman had another decision to make: track him deeper into the surrounding foothills or continue to sweep down the valley. Hoffman's instructions were to avoid civilians, and if the man was VC, following him could lead to an ambush. The grunts filled their canteens in the stream and continued their sweep.

They progressed less than fifty meters when two hisses followed by the *crump-crump* of exploding mortars cleared up the ambiguity. The rounds were off target, dropping wide left, their shrapnel absorbed by heavy vegetation. Recalling Danton's admonishment concerning mortars, Hoffman directed Ludwik to cross the stream and move toward the source of the fire.

The point man ascended cautiously to higher ground. Three more rounds fell harmlessly behind the platoon, then the firing ceased, and the jungle grew ominously quiet. It was the kind of silence that made a grunt's skin crawl. Hoffman called his platoon to a halt and summoned Galvin from his position in the rear.

"What do you think, Razor?"

"I got really bad vibes, LT."

"Me too. Those two Dinks weren't boy scouts."

"Got to be more of 'em up here somewhere, and they'll be waiting for us."

Hoffman had to decide whether to press ahead and risk walking into an ambush or return to lower ground and the muck near the river. As unfriendly as the latter course was, it was better than walking into a trap.

"Okay, we're turning back."

"Roger that. It's dark soon and no sense in asking for trouble," Galvin said, returning to his position. "And LT, for what it's worth, on my first tour, those two Dinks would never have left that stream alive."

The comment stung. Hoffman wondered, Did I screw up, put my men at risk by releasing the little guy? But what if those two had been civilians? There was no good answer.

The platoon formed a perimeter in a stand of bamboo. It had been an eventful day. With a green second lieutenant in command, the platoon labored through a nearly impassable jungle, camped near a herd of elephants, let two VC run free, narrowly escaped a mortar attack, and likely avoided a firefight. He didn't know about his men's opinion, but he gave his performance low marks.

Hoffman lay awake most of the night, monitoring the radio and pondering the platoon's next move. The VC were active in the area, and they were aware of the platoon's presence. Who would be quicker, smarter, or luckier? By 0630, the grunts were awake and moving around, answering nature's call, heating powdered coffee, and, if they were very lucky with the draw of rations, eating canned fruit cocktail and peaches.

Hoffman turned to his map to chart a course, but with no destination in mind, any course would do. What did the contour lines suggest, if anything? Ahead, another stream entered the valley, a likely place to find a trail. The platoon would sweep fairly level ground toward the head of the valley in the morning, set up an ambush on any trail it came across, then return to the fire support base the following day. He felt some comfort in having a plan rather than bouncing around a grid square like a pinball.

The point man clung tenuously to a course that led to an area where mountains closed in on the valley and the forest grew taller. In the gothic gloom of triple canopy, mosquitoes sang in the grunts' ears, but at least the air was temperate and the forest floor relatively free of knee-whacking bush and wait-a-minute vines. After battling the nearly impenetrable jungle for days, this was an easy walk.

The sound of rushing water told them the map had not let them down, and they found a crystal-clear stream rushing over a bed of gravel. They approached it cautiously, thinking about fresh water for their canteens; they were less sanguine about the trail on the other side. Galvin and a squad waded across.

"Looks like a major highway, lots of use," Galvin reported after taking a closer look.

"Damn, I wish we had some confirmation that there are no civilians wandering around there," Hoffman fretted. "That logging operation—why didn't someone know about that? This is all very strange."

"We've been mortared."

"So what? What does that prove?"

"All the proof you're gonna get, LT."

Hoffman looked across the stream. The platoon's position provided good cover and afforded a clear view of a stretch of trail as it skirted the stream on the opposite side. Damn, he realized, this is a great place for us to set up an ambush. While he still didn't have confirmation of the absence of civilian forces in the area, and this bothered him greatly, he was sent out into the bush to reconnoiter. No way could he walk away from a fat trail like this.

"Okay, set up here, get out the Claymore mines, and let's see what materializes," he directed Galvin.

The platoon was well concealed in the undergrowth. Hoffman would detonate one of the Claymores as the signal to open fire. The mine would spray more than a thousand steel balls across the creek. He had seen one demonstrated at Fort Benning, and he knew what it could do. While Galvin positioned the gunners and riflemen, Hoffman reported the platoon's coordinates to the artillery battery for quick fire support if necessary.

When everyone was in position, Hoffman crept down the firing line to make sure it was understood no one was to fire until he detonated one of the mines. This was his first ambush, and he didn't want any screwups. Satisfied that everyone was ready, he joined Galvin behind a tree with a good view of the trail in both directions.

"Look okay?" Galvin asked.

"By the book," Hoffman answered.

"You can throw that away, LT," the sergeant said.

Hoffman clicked the safety selector of his M-16 to semi-automatic and sighted in on the trail. It was damn close, about the distance from the pitcher's mound to home plate. There was nothing to do now but wait.

The stream murmured. Rivulets sparkled in the sun.

Such a stream would have trout back home. The soft, spongy ground on which he lay exhaled a sweet fecundity. It was such a peaceful place to do such a deadly thing, nothing like the night in rural Quitman County, Georgia, where in training at Fort Benning, he lay freezing in the rain, waiting for mock "aggressors" to come down a road.

The men lay motionless behind their weapons, resisting the narcotic effect of the maundering stream and buzz of insects. An hour passed, then two, then nearly three. Hoffman's wristwatch nagged him. The evening was approaching, and he had a decision to make: should the platoon stay put or pull back for the night? Then he heard something strange.

Music, voices, and laughter came from his right, the source not yet in sight. He held his breath and picked up the Claymore detonator. The grunts gingerly lifted their weapons and pressed the stocks to their cheeks. A young man in the baggy black attire of the Vietnamese peasant was the first to appear, the transistor radio he carried blaring Vietnamese music.

Hoffman got a good look at him as he passed. He appeared to be in his early twenties, with sharp cheekbones and a fuzzy goatee. Six men dressed the same way followed him, five porting heavy bamboo logs on their shoulders, and the sixth carried a rifle. It wasn't an AK-47 but of a type Hoffman couldn't identify. They appeared to be as carefree as a little band of woodsmen returning home after a day's work.

Like sprinters listening for the report of a starter's pistol, the grunts held their fire, waiting for Hoffman to blow a Claymore. No one blinked, and no one moved a muscle as their targets passed by in plain view: one, two, three, four, five, six, seven. But the deafening explosion, the signal to open fire, didn't come. Galvin, who lay next to Hoffman, glanced quizzically at him.

The ambushers watched the seven Vietnamese vanish around a bend in the trail. Perhaps more would follow, but none did. What the hell was the LT thinking? Galvin rose to his knees and said, "Looked like VC to me, LT."

"How the hell can we be sure?" Hoffman objected.

"One of them was carrying a weapon."

"Yeah, so what?"

"Well, you see these VC carrying old French and Russian stuff."

"And so do the local indigenous fighters."

"I don't think so. They're VC, and those logs are for bunkers. About as sure as you're ever gonna be, LT."

"I'll be damned if I'm going to waste some civilians," Hoffman fumed, angry at the lack of intelligence from his commanders that put the platoon in this predicament. "Saddle up, and let's get out of here."

"Yes, sir."

Hoffman felt like an executioner unable to close the circuit. But what if the accused were innocent? He kept turning it over in his mind, looking for an answer. As the first armed man on the trail came into view, he tightened his fingers on the detonator, felt it move ever so slightly, then loosened his grip. A vision accosted him: the flash of an explosion, a back blast from the mine, the deafening clatter of machine guns and M-16s on full automatic, human beings ripped limb from limb in a maelstrom of bullets and balls.

The following day, the platoon returned to LZ Luck. Hoffman was mad as hell, at himself, at the highers running things from their bunkers in the rear, at the whole damn situation.

11
DEAD RECKONING

Back on LZ Luck, the Second Platoon returned to the bunker line on guard duty. The enemy made its presence known at night with a few rockets fired at the hilltop, provoking a furious response by the battalion's artillery. And every day at about 1330 hours, a sniper hiding somewhere in the forest below emptied a magazine at the troops on the hill and ran. Return fire fell into the jungle like pebbles cast into the sea. The grunts named their antagonist "Charlie One Thirty."

For Delta Company, days on the LZ fell into a grinding routine. Combat engineers blew a sump with a shaped charge, creating a repository for the garbage left by the ARVN troops. An unidentified white powder sprinkled around the bunkers did little to repel the rodent population. When troops weren't incinerating excrement or filling sandbags, they were patrolling the perimeter. The only casualty occurred when an artilleryman accidentally shot himself through his jaw while cleaning a pistol.

The heat of the day gave way to a teeth-chattering chill at night. Fog covered the hill, reducing visibility to a few meters. The troops watching the perimeter wrapped themselves in their poncho liners and tried to stay awake. Weariness dissolves fear and, combined with cold temperatures and blinding fog, makes sleep irresistible. It was the responsibility of the night duty officer to make sure someone at each bunker was awake and alert. Hoffman's turn in the rotation of platoon leaders meant he would get little, if any, sleep this night.

A single circuit of the defensive perimeter required a good hour of stumbling and groping from bunker to bunker in the dark with no flashlight. Having been advised by Galvin that guards suddenly aroused from sleep were known to fire on a duty officer, he approached positions cautiously. As he neared a bunker near the chopper pad, he noticed a blue glow at the entrance.

"New York," he said, from behind a stack of pallets, hoping the guard remembered the password for the night.

"Giants," came the response. "Who goes there?"

"LT Hoffman, duty officer."

"Advance and be recognized."

The rubric reminded Hoffman of the give-and-take between a priest and an altar boy at the foot of the altar. He stepped out into the open and approached the bunker where the guard squatted over a burning heat tab.

"Just in time, LT. Coffee's ready."

"You're supposed to be watching the wire, soldier," Hoffman said.

"I have been watchin'. In this fog, can't see shit."

"All the more reason to plant your butt at your post."

"Roger that, LT, with sumpin' hot. Helps me stay awake. Join me?"

Hoffman recognized him as Reardon, Third Platoon. Reardon was popular among the blacks, and Hoffman rarely got an opportunity to rap with men in other platoons. "Just a taste, but I need you back on guard in that bunker," Hoffman said. Reardon poured two sacks of powdered coffee into the cup he held over a heat tab and stirred it with a plastic spoon.

"Got some of that nasty creamer and sugar. You want?" Reardon, the good host, asked.

"Any way you like it is fine."

"Black then, like me," Reardon chuckled.

The title of a book Hoffman had read in school, written by a white man about what it was like to be black. What would the author have written about being black in this crazy war?

The two climbed onto the top of the bunker where they took turns sipping from the canteen cup. The coffee was lukewarm and tasted metallic. Hoffman decided to ask him about something that was going on in the rear. "Help me out, Reardon. I've seen you and the other brothers raising a fist. And someone's been passing around leaflets saying you should lay down your weapons. What the hell's going on?"

"Well, the way most of us feel, no VC ever call us nigger, LT. I ain't got nothin' against no VC; I just want to get my black hiney back to the States."

Hoffman said, "I see how you can feel that way, but you're here now. I hope the brothers don't make things worse for themselves."

"Worse? What's worse? Know what I was doin' before the army? Tryin' to burn down Newark. Got caught makin' off with a TV, and the judge says jail or join. So I joined. Figured it would be better than jail, but I was wrong."

The correct response was to assure him that he did the right thing. But correctness died a long time ago in Nam. "I'm sorry it worked out that way," he said.

"Is what it is, man."

The two sat at the edge of the chasm that separated them. Hoffman said, "Thanks for the coffee, Reardon. You stay out of trouble, hear?"

"Roger that, LT. Sixty-four and a wakeup. I'm too short to fuck up now."

A parachute flare swished like a Roman candle into the blackness over the LZ, bathing the fog-enshrouded hill in a chalky light. It was then that Hoffman saw Lieutenant Danton standing next to the bunker.

"You boys enjoying yourselves?" Danton said.

"Is there a problem, Danton?" Hoffman countered.

"Damn straight, there's a problem, Ivy League," Danton bellowed into Hoffman's face. "I just found a bunker in the Third Platoon's sector with all four of those punks having wet dreams."

"Give me a break. I was there less than half an hour ago, and it was guarded. I can't be everywhere at once."

Danton shouted at Hoffman, close enough to spray him with spittle, "But you got time to chit-chat over coffee, Ivy League? I want you on the move from bunker to bunker all night, and I better not find anyone sleeping on guard again."

With that, Danton disappeared into the fog in the direction of the company command post higher on the hill. Reardon, who was listening from his perch atop the bunker, said, "That mutherfucker gonna get his one day. Be glad when he does."

Several more uneventful days passed on the fire support base before Captain Gilman arrived. The troops tended to give everyone a handle, and due to his short stature, Gilman became "Captain Stretch." Delta's platoon leaders, all four OCS types, greeted the change of command with ambivalence. In the entire battalion, there were only two West Pointers in combat positions. The rest were OCS graduates, save one product of ROTC. This was not unusual; OCS provided the vast majority of commissioned bullet stoppers. The platoon leaders wondered what sort of officer Gilman would be, though anyone would be better than Danton. They didn't have to wonder long.

"Gentlemen, I have a few observations," Gilman said in his introductory briefing. "Some of the men are hacking off the sleeves of their fatigues. That's destroying government property, and I want it to stop. I also want you to tape down the spoons of your grenades, as directed by division. There have been some accidents due to carelessness with grenades. I have friction tape here. See that it's done A-S-A-P."

Okay, a by-the-book type. In ensuing days, he would also make it clear he had no intention of going home in a refrigerated box, the ultimate career spoiler. Credit him on that score because no one else did either. He would be around a few months to get his ticket punched as a company commander, then go to safer duty in the rear. As it happened, his first task would be supervising the dismantling of LZ Luck.

Three weeks of fruitless searching for a spectral enemy amounted to another frustrating tactical failure. To the troops, though, little enemy contact and few friendly casualties meant LZ

Luck proved to be lucky after all. Delta Company spent two days collapsing the bunkers they had just laboriously improved, rolling up concertina wire, loading supplies on trucks for the convoy back to the base camp, and leaving nothing behind on the hill, which they returned to the rats.

In its next operation, the battalion would air assault from the base camp to an area about a klick from the Cambodian border. It would operate from a "hip shoot," a small fire support base carved out of the jungle, armed with a single 105-mm howitzer and three 81-mm mortars. The hip shoot would provide close fire support for the battalion and perhaps invite attack by the NVA—an unspoken hope of the highers who had conceived of the operation.

"Recon went in yesterday and has had enemy contact," Gilman told his assembled company as it waited on the chopper pad for a lift into the new area of operation. "Three NVA dead so far."

Obviously, Danton was back in his element, leading Recon to body counts far greater than those accomplished by the line platoons. If Gilman envied Danton's success with his former platoon, he didn't show it. He was relieved to be quit of Recon and elevated to the command of a company.

Delta's grunts stooped under full rucks, shifting from leg to leg, smoking cigarettes and saying little. An impending combat assault was no time for joking. The LZ might be just a cool glade or a smoking caldron, a hot bath of bullets. They didn't dwell on it; they felt it mindlessly in their bones. Then, from a few soul brothers in the Second Platoon came voices in perfect harmony.

"I've got sunshine on a cloudy day.

When it's cold outside, I've got the month of May.

I guess you'd say
What can make me feel this way?
My girl, talkin' bout my girl . . ."

There, on a hilltop in Southeast Asia, was the sweet sound of home. The *whump-whump-whump* of choppers high over the mountains roused the men from their reverie. Hoffman's Second Platoon lined up, ready to board the lead sortie. The first slick's skids touched the ground, and Hoffman's eyes met those of the pilot. The face in the flight helmet was as expressionless as a bus driver's. Seven men scrambled aboard, and the chopper slowly rose and slung itself forward over the valley.

The pilots, both warrant officers, looked too young to vote. On the back of one's helmet was a decal of Yosemite Sam holding two smoking pistols, on the other's a skull-and-crossbones. The port-side door gunner, a black soldier, rested his muscular sleeveless arms nonchalantly on his weapon. On the starboard side, a soldier with a wispy blonde mustache had a cigarette hanging from his lips. His sleeves were also hacked off at the shoulder, exposing his right bicep with a tattoo of a heart and the name "Francine."

Hoffman's bird flapped along beneath puffy clouds, accompanied by two more choppers carrying the balance of the platoon. At several thousand feet, the flight seemed pleasant, safe, and well out of range of small arms and rockets. To the east was the blue haze of the South China Sea, to the west the rolling hills of Cambodia. The pilots chatted over their intercom, but the whine of the jet engine and beating of the blades made conversation by the passengers impossible. They sat cross-legged on the deck, resting against their rucks, some lost in thought, others appearing to be dozing.

They were airborne for half an hour when the changing tone of the engine and blades signaled the start of a gradual descent. Hoffman saw a clearing below that appeared no larger than a postage stamp. The chopper made a steep, tight turn around it and dropped to treetop level for an approach. Treetops whizzed by below. Suddenly the clearing reappeared. The door gunners, now standing behind their M-60s, opened fire into the wood line. Was it a precaution, or had the helicopter taken fire? Hoffman could hear nothing but the screaming jet engine, the pounding blades, and the syncopated rhythm of the machine guns.

The slick came to an abrupt stop, rearing up like a horse on its hind legs, then leveled and hovered. The grunts groped for the skids with their boots. Below them, deep grass rolled in waves. The distance to the ground was impossible to judge. The copilot turned his head and nodded, making it clear this was as low as he was going to descend. Hoffman knew the drop always looked higher from above, but this was crazy. He saw the others slip out of their shoulder straps, toss their rucks to the ground, and surrender themselves to gravity. He struggled to remove his ruck, but the chopper was beginning to move forward, so he abandoned the effort and stepped from the skid.

The bone-jarring collision with the ground that followed left him dazed. Only once in his life had he been knocked unconscious, when he had taken a hit to the head during puggle stick training at Fort Dix. He had assumed that seeing stars was a comic book invention, but no, he saw them now. He rolled to his knees and tried to clear his head. Sullivan was crawling toward him with the radio.

"LT, Gilman on the horn," the RTO said.

"Okay, where's Razor?" Hoffman asked.

"Over there," he said, pointing to the tree line.

The grass was nearly waist high in a field littered with stumps. Hoffman saw the sergeant running through the grass, gathering the platoon. The officer's ears were ringing, but he heard no small arms fire, only the shouts of men trying to locate one another.

"Delta Six, Two Six. Over," he said into the radio handset, trying to sound calm.

He heard Gilman's voice. "Two Six, we're circling. Have you secured the LZ? Over."

"Not yet. Working on it."

"Have you got incoming?"

"Not that I've heard."

"Good. We're coming in."

Galvin was in the process of reassembling the platoon at the edge of the landing zone, where it took up defensive positions. Smoke grenades marked a part of the clearing free of stumps and fallen timber where helicopters could safely plant their skids on the ground, and the rest of the company arrived without incident.

Delta Company's first task was to quickly construct a fire support base. The grunts commenced clearing elephant grass and undergrowth with machetes. Soon a Chinook arrived with supplies and equipment. Shirtless men toiled with entrenching tools, filling and stacking sandbags. A single artillery piece and three 81-mm mortars were in position by nightfall.

Meanwhile, Recon hunted to the south, tracking the enemy. Alpha, Bravo, and Charlie companies explored the surrounding ridges and peaks. Contacts were light, sniper attacks and firefights that ended quickly with no body count. But high-speed trails and recently constructed bunkers said the NVA were there, recently, but how many?

After his first patrol and the problem of identifying civilians, Hoffman was relieved that none resided in this wilderness. From the air, peaks bearing the remnants of old fire support bases constituted an archaeological history of the war. Time and again, American military units returned to the area to intercept NVA troops trickling from Laos and Cambodia through the deep gorges and escarpments of the Annamite Mountains.

The enemy trekked at night on trails they could walk blindfolded, while the troops of the Twenty-fourth Division slashed through dense jungle in daylight, generally avoiding trails except to ambush them. Rarely now did the NVA mass their forces for major attacks, and only to prove they still could. The NVA were waging a grinding war of attrition against a demoralized retreating enemy. This was a hybrid war, part insurgency, part civil war, quite different strategically than the one Hoffman had expected. The new LZ was christened "Louisiana" by Division Commander General Taggart who hailed from that state. On day three of the operation, Captain Gilman sent two platoons to push toward Recon, which had drawn first blood. Unnerfeld's First and Hoffman's Second left the perimeter late in the evening carrying Claymore mines, grenades, and plenty of ammo. They proceeded together several hundred meters to the top of a ridge and found a high-speed trail.

"Major highway," Unnerfeld said, noting layers of fresh prints in the soft red clay, some made by boots, others by Ho Chi Minh sandals. "It rained yesterday, so these are very fresh. The bastards are up in these hills somewhere, and not far, I'll wager."

"Must be dozens of 'em," Hoffman concluded from the prints.

"This trail probably leads to an unpleasant surprise," Unnerfeld opined.

"We made a racket coming in. They have to know we're here," Hoffman said.

"Think so?" Unnerfeld said, pulling a pack of cigarettes from his breast pocket. "Fag?"

Camels were not Hoffman's brand, but a smoke seemed called for. Unnerfeld lit their cigarettes with a Zippo. Was the normally cool officer's hand shaking?

"We'd better report this to Gilman," Hoffman said.

Unnerfeld took a drag of his smoke. "Really think so?"

"Don't you?"

"I think what we have here is a judgment call. Why bother him with it? Unless, of course, you're dying of curiosity and want to barge on up this trail."

"I like the way you think."

"Elementary, my dear Watson."

With Armijo on point, the Second Platoon took the lead, bypassing the trail and pushing on an azimuth toward Recon's last position. Snipers were Hoffman's chief concern as his platoon proceeded, halting now and again to search the upper story of foliage, looking for any sign of the enemy. Armijo walked cat like for about three hundred meters when, at a small opening in the forest, he took a knee. Those behind him did likewise, alternately facing left and right.

The grunts stared into the forest looking for movement and listening for any clues in the pulsating hum of the jungle. Armijo fixed his eyes on something ahead of him, the butt of his weapon pressed against his shoulder. Hoffman joined him. "Whaddya got?" he whispered.

"Some kind of a hooch up there."

"Any movement?"

"None I can see."

Now Galvin came forward from his position at the rear of the file. "Smell that?"

Therc was something, the faint odor of charcoal. "I do now," Hoffman said.

"Dink smell," Galvin said. "Nuoc mom, rice, maybe a little Mary Jane in there, too."

Hoffman said, "Razor, take four men and check it out."

Galvin, Armijo, and three riflemen dropped their rucks and slipped forward, darting from tree to tree. They quickly covered the forty meters to a small thatched hooch perched on four posts. Galvin approached a small portal accessed by a notched log. He peered inside and then motioned to the others to advance. They stood guard, while he examined the entrance for booby traps and, finding none, entered.

Hoffman watched Galvin disappear inside the hooch and emerge moments later carrying something. He motioned for the rest to move forward, and the two platoons took up positions around the small shelter.

"Someone's home away from home, really cozy," Galvin reported to Hoffman. He handed the lieutenant some maps, a notebook, and some photos. "These might be interesting to the assholes in the rear."

Hoffman crawled into the hooch where he found radio batteries, toilet articles, a small book with Ho Chi Minh's picture on the cover, and some maps. NVA khakis with officer's insignia were folded neatly on a shelf beside a straw sleeping mat. Also on the shelf were a sack of rice and several tins of fish. Unnerfeld's platoon checked the immediate area and found rows of benches and a speaker's platform, a crude classroom with enough seating for thirty to forty men.

NVA conscripts moved on foot hundreds of miles from home in the north, stopping along the way for indoctrination and training. While American troops spent a year thrashing around aimlessly in a hostile environment, the men from the north lived symbiotically in the jungle. To them, the jungle wasn't a monster but a friendly giant they had tamed to help them subdue another giant many times their size and strength.

The officer who sheltered in this hooch obviously spent a lot of time there. Who was he? Where was he? In a box by a sleeping mat, Hoffman found a plastic bag containing a small packet of photos, images of an elderly couple, a young woman, and several children. Obviously, these were people dear to this man, the photos a window into his life. They made Hoffman uncomfortable. He returned them to the box.

Captain Gilman radioed instructions to remove the contents of the hooch and torch it. The two platoons continued their sweep toward Recon, leaving the hooch behind them in flames. Tactically, it was a futile gesture. The grunts took no satisfaction in it.

Now the enemy's presence was palpable. Somewhere ahead, Recon was waiting in a blocking position. If the NVA were lurking somewhere between the two converging US elements, the squeeze should precipitate a collision. Three muffled booms in quick succession, followed by the stutter of M-60 machine guns and the furious stutter of automatic weapons ahead, told Hoffman Recon had made contact.

Sullivan rolled the radio dials to the battalion frequency and handed the handset to Hoffman. The anxious voice he heard was Danton's, shouting over the fusillade: "Contact. NVA, bunker complex. Need artillery, air support, whatever you can get me."

Had Danton, this time, bit off more than he could chew? An artillery round swished overhead and crumped on the ridge above the two platoons. Yes, that would be Recon's last reported position, Hoffman concluded. Captain Gilman was on the radio at the hip shoot LZ, trying to get a situation report.

Gilman said to Hoffman, "How far are you from Recon? Over."

Hoffman replied, "Maybe half a klick."

"Get up there as fast as you can, but make sure you stay in radio contact with Recon and fire support. I don't want any friendly fire problems."

The jungle was thick, and the climb steep as Unnerfeld and Hoffman pushed their platoons toward the firefight. They halted on yet another trail, this one appearing to lead up the ridge. Progress was so slow that Hoffman considered using it. Unnerfeld reluctantly agreed. Before he could give the order to move up the trail, three NVA in pith helmets and carrying AK-47s rounded a bend, moving quickly in the platoon's direction.

Armijo was the first to collect his wits and open fire. One of the NVA fell. The other two disappeared into the jungle in a hail of bullets. Hoffman shouted for a ceasefire, and the jungle fell quiet, save the metallic clack of reloaded magazines and bolts charging forward. Then, chillingly, from the NVA soldier sprawled on the trail came a keening complaint like that of a suffering child. Several shots rang out from Hoffman's right, and the crying ceased.

Hoffman had the disturbing realization that he was completely unmoved by what had just happened, but with Danton waiting for reinforcements, this was no time to indulge in moral quandaries. His immediate concern was that more NVA might be coming down the trail or waiting just ahead. He and Unnerfeld agreed it would be best to scale the hill separately. That way, when either platoon made enemy contact, the other could maneuver.

The two platoons split up and moved forward. As Hoffman passed the dead NVA, he saw the body of a young boy, appearing to be maybe fifteen or sixteen. This, he regretted, is what we are up against.

Foliage tugged at the grunts' shoulders and rucks as they made their way up the gradual incline. There were blood smears on leaves and droplets on the ground, leading to another fallen NVA trooper, this one badly wounded but conscious. He was older than the first, handsome with chiseled features and thick black hair. His boots were clean, as was his uniform. He wore a red bandana around his neck. He gazed up at the grunts, his eyes wide with fear.

With no time to waste, Hoffman called for his medic who found that a round had struck him in the back and exited from his chest. His breathing was labored, and blood bubbled from his mouth. Knowing his survival was unlikely, Hoffman ordered morphine for him. While the medic was digging into his bag to retrieve the drug, Armijo searched through the young trooper's pockets and removed a wallet containing a spindled photograph of a youthful man and a pretty woman in a white ao dai.

"Hey, look at this," Armijo said. "Souvenir."

"You gonna steal a dying man's family photo?" Galvin growled. "Put it back."

"Geez, take it easy, Razor. It don't mean nothin'," said Armijo, returning the wallet.

The medic pushed the syrette into the man's arm, and the platoon continued toward the sporadic exchanges of rifle fire and the thump of grenades. As they pushed ahead, Hoffman monitored radio transmissions between Danton and the battalion's tactical operations center. The hip-shoot howitzer was now pouring fire onto the ridgeline, and helicopter gunships were en route.

Unnerfeld's First Platoon reached Recon's position first and engaged the bunkers, allowing Recon to pull back. Hoffman's Second closed on the battle shortly thereafter under occasional sniper fire. The three platoons set up a defensive position. Charging the bunkers was exactly what the enemy hoped their opponents would do and pay a heavy price. It was going to take air support to blast the bunkers and drive the enemy out of their holes.

Two Cobra gunships arrived and unleashed rockets on the bunkers, with Danton coolly directing their assault. The ground shook. Geysers of flame and debris rose from the jungle floor in an awesome display of firepower. How can anyone survive that? Hoffman wondered. And yet, the embattled enemy continued to return fire with small arms and rocket-propelled grenades. The battle continued another half hour and then gradually diminished under the pressure of the Cobras' miniguns.

"I think they're running," Danton announced. "Recon, move forward online."

Recon's grunts advanced, covering one another with rifle fire and tossing frags into the apertures of the bunkers. Hoffman admired the moxie of Recon's grunts. They knew the drill, and they seemed fearless.

The enemy had slipped back into the jungle, as they always eventually did. They left behind eight bodies in the bunkers, and they undoubtedly carried more dead and wounded with them. With two enemy KIA credited to Hoffman's platoon, the body count was a confirmed ten. The bodies lay in a line on the trail like a catch of fish. Danton was snapping photos of them with an Instamatic camera.

"You got here late, Ivy League," Danton said. "You missed most of the fun."

"This your idea of fun, Danton?"

"Sure as hell beats the alternative," Danton replied. Flies were already beginning to swarm on the corpses.

"What's the plan for these bodies?"

Danton was preoccupied with a close-up. "Plan?"

"Yeah, plan."

"Oh, their brethren will return for the disposal. Of course, if you'd like to bury them . . ."

Hoffman was disgusted. "You want to pose with your body count?" He held out his hand for the camera.

"Getting a little squeamish, aren't you, Ivy?"

"They're human beings, for god's sake," Hoffman said.

"We're all human beings, Hoffman. You know, I'm beginning to think you don't have the stomach for this. That's the difference between you and me. I'll still be eating C-rats in the rain when you're fucking your secretary after a two-martini lunch."

Hoffman wanted to tell him to go to fuck himself, but he held back. Sullivan approached, holding the handset to his ear. "It's Gilman. He wants us to move out ASAP."

Gilman's instruction was brief and, as usual, included no explanation. Choppers would arrive to move the platoon to a point five klicks to the west. Its task would be to patrol that map grid. The company's other platoons searched the adjoining grid squares and were moved like pawns on a chessboard.

Danton was kneeling over one of the NVA bodies, his back turned, busy with something. "What the hell is he doing?" Hoffman said, returning the handset to his RTO.

"Stay back, LT," Sullivan warned. "He's booby trapping that gook body with a frag."

Danton pulled the pin and placed a grenade under the body, careful not to release the spoon. He shouted, "Fire in the hole," and darted behind a tree. One thousand one, one thousand two, one thousand three, one thousand four, one thousand five—no explosion. The trap was set.

"Little surprise for our friends when they come back to police up the bodies," he said.

12
GOODWILL TO MEN

Christmas drew near, and so did the three-month mark of Hoffman's tour of duty in Vietnam. It seemed he'd been there half a lifetime. Delta Company continued its search of jungle ridges and ravines, finding recently used trails and fresh bunkers, but enemy contact was light and spotty. Even Recon was having trouble hunting down prey. Hoffman wondered whether the enemy had, for some reason, simply gone to ground in Cambodia and Laos.

But Galvin opined, "Don't bet on it, LT. They pull back to rest and resupply. They're like snakes. You don't see 'em 'til you step in a nest.

Declaration of a twenty-four-hour "Christmas truce" buoyed spirits. It seemed too good to be true. Dinks didn't celebrate Christmas, did they? All the units in the field were directed to move inside defensive positions when possible and stand down. Led by Lieutenant Danton, Recon's men emerged from the bush looking like heavily armed elves. Shaving cream beards and red stocking caps someone received from home seemed to satirize Christmas in the jungle, but everyone got a good laugh.

A resupply chopper with a door gunner dressed as Santa landed with packages mailed from the States: sardines, smoked oysters, salami, fruitcake, crackers, and other edibles selected to survive transport and Southeast Asian heat without spoiling. A few cases of beer would be distributed, one can per man, by Captain Gilman. There would be a Yuletide feast, ceasefire or not.

As Christmas Eve approached, the grunts gathered with buddies to talk of home, bet their pay at poker, prepare a meal of C-rations, and feast on packages of holiday food from home. No one paid much attention to another helicopter landing in a cloud of green smoke. Then, shouts from those closest to the pad announced the arrival of three attractive showgirls in white go-go boots and miniskirts. The grunts gaped in disbelief as the women leaped from the bird, their long blonde hair flying in the blade wash.

Colonel Standley escorted the women and their agent off the pad to a growing gathering of grunts jostling for a better look. Their agent introduced them and said their stop would be brief as they were hopping from one fire support base to the next to wish everyone a Merry Christmas. Instamatic cameras clicked as the girls waded into the crowd of grunts, laughing and hugging, and quite comfortable with the exuberant reception the men were giving them.

"Hey, soldier, where you from?" one of the girls asked.

"Chicago."

"Wow, I love Chicago."

"Where you from, darlin'?" the tall grunt asked.

"Saint Louis," the woman said.

"Never been there, but I love Saint Louis. Give me your number, and I'll visit you when I get home."

Hoffman and Unnerfeld watched the grunts enjoy playful innocence with pretty young women, the first American civilians many of them had seen in nearly a year. After the group posed for the cameras, the visitors retreated to their chopper and were gone. They had been on the ground for exactly twenty minutes.

"They should get hazardous duty pay for this," Hoffman said.

"Wouldn't want my sister out here, but God bless 'em," Unnerfeld said.

At dusk, a mellow spirit pervaded the LZ. Candles flickered in the gloom of the bunkers, and here and there, around the perimeter, clutches of grunts did their best to sing a few Christmas carols on key. The ceasefire seemed to be holding for the birthday of the Prince of Peace, and Hoffman wondered what concessions were made to convince the Communists to agree to it. It was just another paradox in a senseless war.

Captain Gilman called his platoon leaders to his command post to arrange security for the night. "We are going to need double guard duty at the bunkers, and the battalion headquarters wants to make sure we have listening posts outside the wire tonight, ceasefire or not."

The platoon leaders groaned. "Some ceasefire," Unnerfeld said. "The men are going to love this."

Gilman said, "How it has to be. Jesus' birthday don't mean nothin' to the NVA."

Choosing which two men he would send outside the wire was a task Hoffman normally laid off on Galvin, but it was a lousy thing to do on Christmas eve, so he would do it himself. It wouldn't go down easy with the chosen.

No official protocols governed many of the grunts' ad hoc practices, one of which was expecting the greenest troops to do the most undesirable jobs. Everyone had to pay their dues. Two replacements had arrived less than a month earlier, and one of them, Louis Pardin, was next in line for LP. But putting two inexperienced men together for a night alone in the jungle was a bad idea. Pardin was in Ludwik's squad, so the veteran grunt Ludwik would have to go with him.

"Get Ludwik and Pardin over here, and I'll break the news," Hoffman directed Galvin.

"Ludwik ain't gonna like it. He's got no use for Pardin," Galvin noted.

Pardin had established a reputation as a whiner, constantly looking for an excuse to get out of the field and back to the relative comforts of the rear. Grunts can smell fear, and Pardin wreaked of it. Galvin found Specialist 4 Bart Ludwik in his bunker with a mouthful of cookies from home. "Lieutenant wants to see you," Galvin said.

"What for?" Ludwik asked suspiciously.

"Never mind. Just get over there and don't give me any shit. Bring Pardin with you."

The two arrived expecting an order to do something they wouldn't like. "Get your ponchos, bandoliers, and a couple of frags," Hoffman ordered. "You two are pulling LP tonight."

"It's fucking Christmas Eve, sir," Ludwik shot back.

"Yes, and there's still a war going on. So get your gear."

"Okay, but not with this guy. Give me someone else, Alvarez or Miller, anyone."

"I'm not interviewing candidates for this job, Ludwik. Get your gear, both of you, and report back here immediately to pick up a radio."

Pardin's eyes were the size of golf balls. "Don't make me, LT. Lud is right. I ain't no good for this."

"Got that right," Ludwik said.

Hoffman said, "You're going, both of you. Go get ready."

"Merry fucking Christmas," Ludwik muttered as he stomped off toward his bunker, with Pardin following at his heels like a puppy. "You goddamn better do exactly what I tell you, Pardin," Ludwik scowled, "or I'll kick your sorry ass."

The radio was a lifeline to the perimeter. Ludwik tied it to his pack frame. Hoffman led the two past their celebrating counterparts through a break in the wire to a copse about fifty meters outside the wire. He watched the men spread their ponchos at the trunk of a large tree and sit back-to-back, their weapons in their laps, frags close at hand.

Hoffman's final instructions were more for Pardin's benefit than Ludwik's who knew what to do: "If you have movement, get back to the perimeter as soon as you can. But be sure to tell us you're coming in. If you're cut off, hunker down and wait. Our mortars know your position, and they won't drop any rounds on you. Don't fire your weapons and give yourselves away. Use frags if you have to."

A scowling Ludwik added, "And no matter what, don't move unless I say, and keep your big fat mouth shut."

Hoffman left the two men and made his way back to the perimeter in the dark. He felt sympathy for the LPs. It was terrifying duty, but everyone had to pull it sooner or later. Back at the bunker, Galvin handed him a hip flask filled with J&B. "Merry Christmas, LT. Make the Yuletide gay."

"What, no chestnuts, Razor?" Hoffman said, sipping from the flask.

Sullivan, who was manning the radio, said, "Got some sardines and crackers from my sister. Here—help yourselves."

The three, warmed by the Scotch, talked of what their families would be doing right now and snacked on that day's delivery of crumbled cookies and stale fruitcake. In all the bunkers along the small perimeter, others were doing the same, visiting, enjoying as best they could a brief respite from war in a place even Santa Claus couldn't find on a map.

As midnight approached, the merriment on the LZ slackened, and the troops retired to their bunkers to converse quietly, play poker, and write letters by candlelight. News came by radio from the division headquarters that the ceasefire was holding throughout Central Vietnam.

Hoffman told his RTO, Sullivan, to get some sleep and relieved him at the radio. He would get situation reports from the two LPs every half hour. Sleep in combat came in amounts barely sufficient to avoid physical collapse, and Hoffman would get little this night. He found it useful to do mind exercises, solve math problems in his head, conjugate as many Latin verbs as he could remember, recite poetry. A poem he was required to learn verbatim in a high school English class seemed particularly appropriate at that moment:

"Deep into that darkness, peering, long I stood there wondering, fearing,

Doubting, dreaming dreams no mortal ever dared to dream before;

But the silence was unbroken, and the stillness gave no token . . ."

He crawled out of his bunker and inhaled the cool night air. He promised himself that, if and when he returned to civilian life, he would sleep for a month. In the moonlight, he could see obscurely the black curtain of the jungle where the LPs were hiding. Their last situation report was negative, with no movement or suspicious sounds detected. He looked at his watch. It was nearly time to ask them for another sitrep. He took up the handset, but before he could do so, he heard the static interrupted by frantic keying. He answered, "Wide Eyes, Wide Eyes, if you've got movement, break squelch three times. Over."

Three breaks in the static came, then a pause, and three more. "Okay, I read you've got movement. Stay put until I tell you to get back into the perimeter."

The bunker line would have to be alerted that the LPs would be reentering the wire. He slipped inside the bunker and woke Galvin. "Razor, the LPs have movement."

The sergeant said groggily, "Huh? Say what?"

"Ludwik's detected something out on LP."

"Give me the horn," he said, yawning. "Wide Eyes, can you talk? What's going on out there? Over."

A panicked whisper from Pardin came in response: "Razor, I seen 'em. They run right past us, and they're butt nekkid. Over."

Then Ludwik's muffled voice came: "Four Dinks just walked by us with satchel charges. Over."

Galvin radioed an alert to the battalion command post, which informed the rest of the bunker line that there was movement, there would be friendlies coming in, and everyone was to hold their fire. Hoffman grabbed his M-16 and stepped outside the bunker. Several flares swished skyward and popped like flash-bulbs, bathing the jungle in an eerie white light. Galvin fired a parachute flare to help guide the LPs. It oscillated lazily, casting long, shifting shadows. As its light faded, Hoffman saw the two LPs running into the perimeter.

"How many?" Galvin asked before the two could catch their breath.

"Maybe a dozen," Ludwik panted. "Too dark."

"They almost step on us, Razor," Pardin added, his voice trembling. "Them mofuckers got nothin' on, swear to God."

Ludwik gave him a shove that sent him staggering. "You yellow bastard. You coulda' got us greased out there, cryin' like a fucking baby. Hey, where's the radio?"

Pardin looked blankly at the three men standing around him and said nothing.

"I said, where's the goddamn radio?" Ludwik yelled angrily.

"Back there," Pardin said sheepishly, pointing outside the wire.

"Are you crazy? I told you to carry the radio. Go back and get it, you idiot."

"No way," Pardin whimpered.

Galvin said, "Take it easy, Lud." Then turning to Pardin, he asked, "Where did you leave it?"

"How do I know?" Pardin said. "I was runnin'; next thing I know, it's gone. I musta' dropped it."

Galvin grabbed him by the shirt and shook him. "You carry a radio, you guard it with your life. Do I make myself clear?"

"I ain't cut out for this, Razor. Honest to God, I ain't," Pardin pleaded. "Court-martial me. Just get me out of here."

"I'm gonna kick your sorry ass outa here," Ludwik fumed, leaping on Pardin.

Hoffman grabbed him and pulled him off of the cowering Pardin. "Return to your bunkers, both of you, and we'll settle this later."

Captain Gilman was not pleased, worrying about how he was going to explain it to the battalion commander. Hopefully, the sappers wouldn't stumble onto the radio in the dark. Flares sporadically lit the perimeter in frozen light as the troops tried to push back the night. There was nothing for the LZ's two hundred defenders to do but wait.

Minutes passed in ominous silence, save the swish and pop of flares and occasional rounds fired into the darkness by edgy grunts. Hoffman knelt under the low ceiling of his bunker, resting the barrel of his M-16 on the firing aperture in the wall. Sullivan sat beside him, monitoring the tense voices on his radio:

"Delta Four Six, Delta Six. Was that one of your men just emptied a magazine?"

"Delta Six, Four Six. Roger that. Came from one of my bunkers."

"See anything?"

"Negative."

"Well, have 'em hold their fire until they're sure."

Where were the bastards? Should he doubt his LPs? Were they figments of Pardin's imagination? No, Ludwik saw them, too, and he was as reliable as they come. Confirmation came in the form of several rocket-propelled grenades and a stream of green tracers emanating from the tree line. Return fire burst from the bunkers, punctuated by the drumbeat of the LZ's fifty-caliber machine gun.

The mortar platoon fired an illumination round into the air over the LZ, bathing the perimeter in about thirty seconds of light. Hoffman held his hand over one eye to maintain night vision and searched the wire for attackers. He saw none. Then, mysteriously, the muzzle flashes from the surrounding jungle ceased.

The grunts reloaded and braced for whatever came next. Minutes passed with more flares, but oddly, no ground assault and no indication of what the enemy had in mind. The hiatus ended when a barrage of AK-47 fire erupted on the side of the perimeter opposite Hoffman's, which was Unnerfeld's section.

Before he could get a status report from Captain Gilman on the radio, two deafening explosions shook the bunker. Hoffman felt claustrophobic in the cave-like pile of sandbags, unable to observe what was happening around him. He crawled out the door and stood just as an explosion occurred in the direction of the artillery position. A concussive blast of air hit him, and shrapnel zipped over his head.

He ducked back into the bunker. "Dinks inside the wire," he shouted to Sullivan.

"I know," Sullivan said. "Six, on the horn for you."

Gilman shouted over the clatter of rifle fire, "They hit the Red Leg position. Get a squad over there."

"How many sappers?" Hoffman blurted, realizing the question was ridiculous as soon as he asked it.

"How the hell do I know? Just get men over there and secure the position."

Hoffman felt useless inside the bunker. He decided to lead the fire team himself. With three of his men, he ran toward the gun pit, ignoring the small arms fire snapping by his ears. Flares burst over a frozen tableau, gradually fading to black and then lighting again like a change of scene in a movie. As they made their way past bunkers and scattered stockpiles of supplies and equipment, Hoffman saw something that stopped him in his tracks.

There, in the midst of the chaos, sat the shadowy figure of a grunt sitting on a makeshift latrine. Hoffman was struck by the white skin of his butt and legs, which were almost phosphorescent in the light of the flares. Hoffman recognized him as a rifleman in the First Platoon.

"What do you think you're doing, soldier?" Hoffman demanded in disbelief.

"Got the shits, sir," the grunt said.

"For Chrissake, there are gooks in the wire."

"I saw 'em. They run right by me."

"Where's your weapon?"

"In the bunker."

"Get your sorry ass back to your bunker and pick up your weapon. Do it now."

If there is a providence that protects idiots, drunkards, children, and the United States of America, this was the time to invoke it. Hoffman found himself asking for Divine intervention as he continued toward the artillery pit, setting a course by the light of flares. The four were near their destination when another blast forced them to the ground, this one much closer, and Hoffman feared the sappers had hit the battalion tactical operations center. Well, it was someone else's problem; his orders were to secure the Red Leg.

He and his men arrived to find the artillery piece tipped onto its side, one of its tires smoldering and several artillerymen attempting to right it. Acrid smoke and the smell of sulfur rose from the gun. While his squad took up positions behind sandbags around the pit, Hoffman went to the fire direction center's bunker to find the officer in charge. He pulled back a tarp covering the door and found a medic holding up an I-V sack and working on two wounded men. Two bodies lay on the floor, covered by ponchos.

"I need the CO," Hoffman said. "Where is he?"

"The one on the left," he answered, nodding toward the bodies.

"Who's in command?"

"Sergeant Maxwell, over at the howitzer."

Hoffman returned to the canon where a heavy-set soldier was barking orders to several others trying to lever the canon upright with engineer stakes while other another man heaved on a rope tied to the barrel. Hoffman joined them, and after several attempts, the gun rolled back onto its carriage. It was in bad shape.

"Are you Sergeant Maxwell?" he asked the big fellow who was inspecting the breach for damage.

"Yeah," he said, occupied by his attempt to manipulate the breech block. "The barrel looks okay. I think we can fire a beehive if we have to." Spraying the LZ with a round containing eight thousand flechettes was the last resort; no one in its range, friend or foe, would escape the blast.

Hoffman used the Red Leg's radio to report to Captain Gilman who now had another concern: guards on the Second Platoon's sector of the perimeter had fired on NVA sappers attempting to slip through the wire. Fearing an imminent ground assault, Gilman ordered Hoffman to return to his platoon. Hoffman wished Sergeant Maxwell luck and started back.

If more sappers were hiding somewhere inside the perimeter, the defense of every bunker would be a 360-degree proposition. Anyone moving outside the bunkers risked being hit by friendly fire, a fact of which Hoffman was acutely aware. As he approached the bunker line, he encountered Ludwick. "Just looking for you," the soldier said. "Trouble over in my bunker. You'd better come."

"What kind of trouble?"

"That shithead Pardin's gone dinky dow, screamin' and firin' his weapon. We had to take it away from him, and then he starts bashin' his head into an engineer stake."

"Okay, I'm coming," Hoffman said.

As he approached the bunker, he heard plaintive cries inside: "Oh sweet Jesus, get me out of here. This ain't my war. I don't wanna die."

"Settle down, or I'll grease you myself," shouted someone else.

In the darkness of the bunker, Hoffman made out three men struggling to hold down a fourth. "Goddamn it, he bit me," one of the restrainers yowled.

"Pin his shoulders," cried another.

"Shit, I'm tryin'," said a grunt as Pardin arched his back and tried to buck him off.

"Them nekked bastards is comin'," Pardin bellowed. "I saw 'em. I can't take it no mo'. Call a chopper. Get me out of here. I wanna go home."

"Hold still, Pardin, or I'm going to kick you in the balls," said a soldier gripping his legs.

The threats proved ineffective. "Ohhhh Lawd, have mercy. I gonna die."

Hoffman knelt over Pardin and grabbed a handful of his hair. It was slick with blood from lacerations. "Listen to me, soldier, you're not going to die. Settle down, or we'll have to tie you. You hear me?"

Pardin wasn't responding. "I wanna go home. Oh, mamma, please, get me home," he continued to plead.

Hoffman said, "Okay, tie his hands and feet with his bootlaces. And if you have to, gag him."

Outside the bunker, tracers ricocheted across the LZ. Whether it was better to run or walk through a rainstorm crossed Hoffman's mind as he took off running. It was a fifty-meter dash to his bunker where Sullivan and Galvin huddled over the radio. Galvin said, "There you are, LT. Where the hell were you? We were getting worried."

"Ludwik's bunker. Pardin freaked out and completely lost it. Lud had to take his weapon from him, and the damn fool started smashing his head against an engineer stake," Hoffman said.

"That guy has been looking for a ticket to the rear since he got here," Sullivan said.

"Put the yellow bastard on point with a gun to his back," Galvin said.

"Don't tempt me," Hoffman said. "Any situation report from Gilman or battalion?"

"Circular shooting gallery out there," Galvin said. "No one seems to know what's going on. Heard from First Platoon more gooks trying to sneak through the wire."

Hoffman's neck was bleeding from a spot below his right ear. He had forgotten about the sting he felt earlier, but treating the wound would have to wait.

Sullivan, holding the radio handset to his year, said, "Battalion must still be up and running because they're trying to get some artillery support. What about our arty?"

"Sappers got to it. Salvage," Hoffman said.

"Some Christmas ceasefire," Galvin said.

"I guess the sappers didn't get the word," Hoffman said.

Fire support from a 155-mm howitzer battery somewhere to the west arrived, sending shrapnel shrieking over the LZ and suppressing the fire of the attackers. Gradually, the firing ceased, and with the approach of dawn, it became apparent that the enemy had withdrawn. Like a developing Polaroid photo, the surrounding jungle came into focus, and grunts crawled like groundhogs out of their sandbagged holes.

At the artillery pit, the canon listed on its carriage like a broken toy. The bodies of three sappers lay nearby, crediting the dead artillery lieutenant. Two more NVA had fallen in a wall of gunfire near the tactical operations center before they could properly deliver their Christmas packages. Six were found dead in the wire, and blood trails were found in the surrounding jungle. The cost: two Americans KIA, seven wounded.

A chopper arrived to carry the bodies of the two artillerymen back to Graves Registration at the base camp. Hoffman refused medevac and was treated on the LZ for a puncture wound on his neck. Years later, he experienced neck pain, and an X-ray revealed a sliver of shrapnel the size of a grain of rice lodged near a cervical vertebra.

Colonel Standley's report to the division described an intense night-long battle in which the small LZ was overrun by elements of a sapper battalion. His troops repulsed the attack in close combat, forcing the enemy to leave behind eleven dead. Evidence of additional dead or wounded was found outside the wire.

13
ESCAPE DOWN UNDER

A resupply helicopter carefully descended through a small opening in the jungle canopy near the Cambodian border, hovered low, and First Lieutenant Hoffman scrambled aboard. As relieved as he was to be finally escaping on R&R, he felt a stab of guilt as his men watched him climb away. They looked orphaned, or so it seemed to him. He took some consolation in the fact that he was leaving them in Sergeant Galvin's capable hands.

His R&R arrived at the six-month mark of his tour of combat duty, a welcome milestone. Airliners packed with ebullient young men shuttled daily between South Vietnam and destinations such as Hong Kong, Bangkok, and Taiwan. Accounts of high living and sexual frolicking in Asian fleshpots did not attract him. He wanted peace and quiet in a place as far removed physically and mentally from the war as possible. Sydney would fit the bill, and he hoped he could get a seat on an airplane. He did.

He dug through his duffel bag at the base camp and pulled out some civilian underwear. He hadn't worn boxer shorts in six months. He had lost three inches at the waist and had to borrow a pair of Levis from the battalion clerk. A polo shirt and a windbreaker would get him to Sydney where he could purchase anything else he might need. Six hours later, his chartered jet was climbing over the aquamarine South China Sea, leaving the white ribbon of Vietnam's shoreline behind. With every foot of altitude gained, the tensions of combat seemed to ease.

The route took him over the jungle-covered island of Borneo, finally reaching the Australian coast and Darwin where the plane refueled. It immediately took off again for the traverse of the Australian continent. Occasional dirt roads stretched endlessly to the horizons, but otherwise, there was no hint of human presence, just endless miles of dry scrubland. After several hours in the air, the visits in the aisles diminished. Some of the men read magazines and newspapers provided by the attendants, and a few played cards. Hoffman tried to read a paperback copy of *The Godfather* he had purchased at the PX before leaving but couldn't keep his eyes open. Sitting in his seat, eyes closed, ears filled with the rush of jet engines, he slept more soundly than he had in months.

It was morning in Sydney when a voice on the intercom woke him with instructions to prepare for landing. The aircraft banked over the downtown area, the Harbour Bridge, and the unfinished opera house. Sailboats and ferries crept across the blue water of the bay. The windows of tall office buildings flashed like mirrors in the morning sun, and lush tree-shaded residential areas hugged numerous bays and inlets.

The slow flow of rush-hour traffic on the arterials below bespoke a normality that seemed distant to Hoffman now. The plane might have been circling Seattle, The World he knew, but this was Sydney, a place he had never dreamed of visiting. What awaited him down there? What would he do? It was too much to contemplate. Some good food and sightseeing—that would be enough. Cheers erupted in the cabin when the plane's wheels chirped on the runway.

Buses waited to take the men to a reception center in the city where the visiting soldiers received a briefing on appropriate behavior in a host country: "Remember, you are guests. Any reported trouble will put you on the next plane back to Vietnam. Be back at this location in one week, or you're AWOL."

Two hundred men squirmed in their seats: Okay, okay, cut the bullshit and let us out of here. They burst through the doors like cattle from a barn and rushed to the taxis and buses queued up outside. Hoffman stepped into the cool morning air and took a deep breath. When he exhaled, it was as if the humidity and foul odors of the jungle oozed from every pore in his body. He threw his dopp kit into the back seat of a cab and climbed in. Back in Camp Farrell, he had made a reservation from a list of hotels provided there. "The Grand," Hoffman said.

The cab pulled into traffic. "Welcome to Sydney, mate. Where in the States?"

"Seattle."

"Got a cousin there. Been meaning to visit, but you know, a far piece," he chuckled.

The two made small talk about things to see and do in Sydney. Hoffman had the impression the driver shuttled many soldiers over the years; he seemed to know places frequented by men looking for "fun," strip clubs, and the like, in which Hoffman had no interest. The cab pulled up in front of the Grand Hotel. It was an older building with no doorman. Hoffman checked in and asked for a quiet room off the street. He got one on the sixth floor with a view of a ventilation shaft.

The first order of business was a hot shower, and he stood under the clean, steaming water for twenty minutes washing Vietnam from his body. His mind would not be so easily cleansed, knowing his grunts would be somewhere in the jungle, searching for the enemy and hoping they didn't find him. You've got to put them out of your mind if you're going to get any rest, he insisted to himself.

He stepped from the shower, dried himself, and stood in front of a mirror for the first time in six months. He had lost a lot of weight. His eyes were dark and recessed and his cheeks sunken. Angry red patches of jungle rot infected his forearms and shins. My lord, he thought, the price of glory.

He put on the Levis he had borrowed back at the base camp. Two inches of slack around the waist required tightening his belt two notches. With a good meal in mind, he headed for the lobby. The elevator stopped on the fourth floor, and a young couple got on. He nodded, and they nodded back but said nothing. He felt their eyes on him. Did they suspect who he was? No, he was just Jack Hoffman visiting from Seattle.

He stepped through the revolving door into dazzling sunlight. The air was fresh and cool, the contrasts sharper and brighter, shockingly so. It was as if a film had been wiped from his eyes. He paused and inhaled a breeze rising from the harbor. The sounds of traffic and pedestrians' footsteps were familiar and comforting. The concierge made a reservation for him that evening at "one of the best seafood restaurants in Sydney," so he had several hours to kill. He turned left and joined the flow of pedestrians.

After months in jungle boots, the penny loafers he had rescued from his duffel bag back at the base camp felt odd on his feet. He passed a men's store where he supplied himself with some underwear, three pair of socks, chinos that fit his waist—three inches smaller than when he had arrived in Vietnam—and two polo shirts. That should get him by, he guessed.

As he walked on among Sydneysiders, a term he had heard the cab driver use, he felt safe. No need to look behind me, he told himself. He passed a park where children were playing, watched by their nannies or maybe their mothers. The kids were plump, scrubbed, and well dressed. Their voices were like music. He sat on a bench and listened until other children, those with distended bellies, arms outstretched, begging for C-rations from a passing convoy, came to mind.

It was nearly seven when he hailed a cab and headed east toward Watsons Bay. For company, he brought a paperback he had bought at the airport. He didn't like to eat alone, but real food was his primary objective. The cab driver knew the place, located in a park-like setting overlooking the bay. Upscale homes climbed the surrounding hills, reminding him of the hills of Seattle rising from Puget Sound. He felt good and safe, if a bit truant. It would pass. He was not "LT," just John Hoffman in, of all places, Sydney, Australia. He tipped the driver, and the cab pulled away.

A hostess greeted him at the door. Yes, he was dining alone. She seated him at a small table in the corner and handed him a menu. He couldn't help noticing the waitress serving nearby tables. She was attractive, very much so, but it was her graceful confidence that fascinated him, the warm way she spoke to her patrons. There was something about her. He hoped she would wait at his table.

She was still helping other customers when she glanced in his direction, and their eyes met. He didn't want her to think he was staring at her and quickly looked down at his book. When he looked again, she was gone, and her disappearance disappointed him. Dude, you are really horny, he said to himself. There must be a million attractive women in Sydney, and if you're going to go gaga over all of them, it's going to be a frustrating week.

He tried to read but couldn't concentrate, so he laid out a plan for the week, intending to make good use of every minute. He would take a bus tour of the city, visit some museums, and visit the opera house. He heard there was surfing at Bondi Beach. Evenings would be for food and entertainment. With any luck, he'd meet some locals. What he wouldn't do is waste time and money in bars.

He returned to the book and didn't see her approach from behind. "Good book?" she said, standing over him.

"Not sure yet. I brought it along for the company. No fun to eat alone."

"Hmmm, that's a little gloomy. Perhaps a drink will brighten things up."

"Just what I was thinking. Bushmills on the rocks, please."

He watched her walk toward the bar. Her name tag said "Susan." She didn't seem to have an Australian accent, but he couldn't be sure. She returned with his drink and asked if he was ready to order. He wanted to hear her speak. It had been more than six months since he last heard a woman's voice. "Everything looks so good. What do you recommend?"

"The barramundi is the chef's special tonight. It's always excellent," she said.

"Okay, I'll have that," he said, although he had no idea what this fish was and decided not to ask.

"By the way, you're not Australian."

"What makes you think so?"

"If you are Australian, you've mastered a darn good American accent."

"I'm not sure that's a compliment. I'm Canadian."

"Where in Canada?"

"Vancouver."

"We're neighbors. Seattle's my home."

"Small world. Excuse me; I have to run." Someone at a nearby table was motioning for her.

Hoffman liked her. He would like her anywhere, anytime, here or at home. She wore no ring. When she returned with his meal, he said, "So, neighbor, allow me to introduce myself. I'm Jack Hoffman."

"Pleased to meet you, Jack Hoffman. I'm Susan Lazard," she said and left again to wait at the next table.

Hoffman was ravenous, but he ate slowly, in no rush to return to his hotel room, and this Susan was changing his mind about the possibility of female companionship. He finished the main course and ordered a flan, which he ate while sipping two cognacs. As the dinner crowd thinned, he decided he wasn't leaving until he had a chance to speak with Susan for more than a few seconds, so he ordered coffee and buried his nose in his book.

The night lights of the city blinked around the bay. An unsettling, surreal feeling came over him. Perhaps Vietnam was the reality and this was all a dream, and at any moment, he would awaken, soaked and shivering under a poncho.

The last of the patrons got up to leave, and Susan began resetting tables. She glanced at him but said nothing. Was she expecting him to leave? He looked at his watch. The leather band was rotting, and the crystal was so etched by insect repellent it was difficult to read. It was nine eighteen, past closing time when she returned to his table.

"We can make a bed for you here if you want to spend the night," she grinned. Sarcastic. He liked it.

"I've slept in worse places."

"I imagine you have. My guess is you are a soldier on R&R."

"What gave me away?"

"The haircut. We see a lot of you fellas in here."

"So you know what brought me to Australia; what about you?"

"Needed a change, I guess. School teacher, taking a year off for travel. But who knows, it might be longer. When did you arrive?"

"Just today."

"Any plans?"

"Not really. A little sightseeing, relaxing."

"If you'd like to meet some Australians, you're invited to my place. It's Anzac Day tomorrow, and we're having a few friends over to celebrate. Oh, and there will be some North Americans too."

"You sure you want me to crash your party?"

"Don't be silly; I'm inviting you."

"Then I'd love to. Can I bring anything?'

"Just yourself. Be there at sevenish. And oh, it also happens to be my birthday, but it's not a birthday party. Most of them don't know, and I don't want a fuss."

He couldn't believe his luck. He had come with modest expectations of a change of scenery and some rest, but after only a few hours, this Susan was opening the door to him he would never have anticipated. Susan said the party was to celebrate Anzac Day, similar to Veterans Day back home. Was the invitation merely an act of kindness to a lonely soldier on Anzac Day? Of course it was, but it didn't matter.

He returned to his room at the hotel dead tired, stripped, and crawled into bed. The sheets were crisp and clean. A bed never felt so good. He lay in the dark, eyes open, jet-lagged and amped up. His day had begun in the Central Highlands of Vietnam and ended in Sydney, Australia, a world away. It was hard to fathom. And then meeting this angel of mercy, this Susan . . . He fell asleep thinking of her.

He rose at 9:00 a.m., stood in a steaming shower for twenty minutes, and just because he could, ordered breakfast brought to his room: an omelet, orange juice, and toast. He took his time dressing, rode a crowded elevator to the lobby, and found it filled with tourists dressed in Bermuda shorts, carrying cameras and wearing belly packs. He heard the concierge say the parade would pass the hotel in two hours. Good. He'd have time to purchase a gift for Susan before the sidewalks got too crowded.

He walked toward the city center and found a department store open. What does one give to a lady he doesn't know? Perfume. Perhaps a nice bottle of Chanel No. 5. Clara wore it. Well, so what? He had it gift wrapped and returned to the street, now lined with spectators.

He turned off Market Street to escape the throng and slipped into a small pub. It was crowded, but there was a free stool at the bar. He ordered a Fosters, the only brand he recognized, and reverently put it to his lips. Beer never tasted this good. A couple of dozen middle-aged and older men were smoking and drinking. A few glanced at him when he entered. He wasn't averse to some conversation, but no one seemed interested until he noticed a pair of eyes studying him in the mirror behind the bar. They belonged to the elderly gentleman at his left elbow.

"Been in Sydney long, Yank?" the old fellow asked without turning.

"Got in yesterday," Hoffman said, having somehow blown his cover. He noticed several medals pinned on the fellow's sport coat.

"R&R, then."

"Yeah."

"Welcome, mate. We see a lot of you chaps these days, and better for it." Turning to the others at the bar, he shouted, "Hey, blokes, the Yank here is just in from Vee-et-Naam."

Many of the men in the pub were veterans in town for Anzac Day festivities. Several approached to shake his hand. One, who said he had a son with Aussie forces in Danang, asked if he had come across any Diggers. No, they were on the coast; Hoffman's unit was in the highlands. The men at the bar thanked him for what he was doing. Before he could finish his pint, two more appeared on the bar in front of him. Hoffman couldn't help noting the unlikelihood of such a reception back in the States where war protests were tearing the country apart. He had a long day ahead, and fearing their generosity was limitless, he began to plot a polite escape.

"Well, gents, thanks for the hospitality," he said, "but I have to run. I have a date with a young lady this evening and some things to do before then."

"Found you a Sheila already, have you?" a gentleman with medals pinned on his sport coat shouted. He raised a glass. "Hear that, boys? Here's to the young Yank's luck tonight."

"Here, here," a male chorus sang out as Hoffman slid off his stool and ran a gauntlet of well-wishers to the door and out into the bright sunlight. He decided he would have to avoid pubs.

The sound of drums and bagpipes echoed through a canyon of buildings. Applause and cheers greeted khaki-clad soldiers in cargo shorts, shirts, and Australian bush hats. They marched along at a brisk pace that belied their aging bodies. Their banner identified them as veterans of World War I. They were followed by two Cadillac convertibles transporting men unable to walk. Veterans of World War II and the Korean War followed, among them members of a Sydney post of the American Veterans of Foreign Wars.

Hoffman spent the rest of the day sightseeing and shopping for gifts to send home. By a quarter to six, he had showered, shaved, and dressed in new chinos, a polo shirt, and deck shoes. Satisfied he was reasonably presentable for Susan's party, he hailed a cab. The address took him to a neighborhood of large homes somewhere on the outskirts of Sydney. The driver pulled up in front of a colonial with a wide porch. He paid the driver, climbed the steps, and rang the bell. Susan opened the door. Last seen in waitress attire, now she appeared in a blue cashmere sweater and black leather pants. Her copious auburn hair fell nearly to her waist. He had to catch his breath. "I found you," he stammered.

"I'm glad," she said, giving him a quick hug. "Follow me. Most of the gang is here."

"Something for you," he said, handing her the gift-wrapped Chanel. He almost forgot it was in his hand. "Happy birthday."

"How nice of you, Jack, but you shouldn't have. Thank you."

"It's nothing. You were kind to invite me."

"Forgive me, but I've forgotten your surname. I was so busy last night."

"Hoffman."

"Oh, of course. I'll introduce you to my roommates and friends; then, I have to get back to the kitchen. You'll be in good hands. They're all friendly people."

She led him from the kitchen down to a recreation room in the basement where a dozen twenty-somethings chatted amiably over drinks. A Ray Conniff album played softly on a phonograph. His entrance drew a few glances, but no one seemed surprised or discomfited by the appearance of this stranger. Susan must have warned them.

"Can I have your attention for a moment?" she said, holding his arm. "I'd like you to meet Jack Hoffman. I met him last night in the restaurant, just arrived from Vietnam. He's from Seattle. Please introduce yourselves."

Short and sweet—no further explanation necessary. Her composure made him feel comfortable in what might have been an awkward situation. She invited him to help himself at a well-stocked wet bar, excused herself, and went to the kitchen to tend to the food. It was her birthday, but she was definitely the host.

Tom and Liz Lafferty promptly engaged Hoffman in conversation. Tom said his brother was in the Australian forces in Vietnam, involved in civil affairs. They agreed that the war had gone on too long and needed to end. The Laffertys offered to show him around Sydney, go to Hyde Park for a picnic, visit the zoo, and have dinner. They agreed on Wednesday, Tom's day off from work, and exchanged contact information.

The Laffertys were renting in the neighborhood; all of the guests either lived nearby or were Susan's roommates. Hoffman gathered that all were young professionals. One was an assistant conductor of the Sydney orchestra. Of the eighteen guests, men and women in equal number, three of the men were North Americans. Their accents and the fact that they were discussing their recreational baseball team's record made them easy to spot.

Susan spent most of the next hour running up and down the stairs with plates of finger food. Hoffman caught her on one of her trips with a tray and whispered, "You're working awfully hard on your birthday."

"It's Anzac Day. My birthday is coincidental."

"Well, happy birthday anyway."

"Thanks. You enjoying yourself?"

"Very. I like your friends."

"I knew you would. The chili and salad are almost ready; then I can join you."

When the last of the food was served, the guests sat in small groups, chatting and eating. Hoffman and Susan joined the Laffertys on the sofa. Hoffman had a third helping of the chili and cornbread. Susan noticed. "They starve you over there?"

"If you only knew," Hoffman said.

Susan didn't stay long. She was up and down the stairs again, this time with cake and ice cream—but not a birthday cake. Hoffman wished he could hold her attention. The meal finished, chairs and tables were pulled back, and someone put a Four Tops album on the turntable. The lights went down. "Can't help myself . . ." Guests coupled up and took to the floor.

But Susan disappeared again. Hoffman noticed a young lady standing alone near the bar, watching the dancers. He had spoken with her briefly earlier. Her name was Valerie, and she was finishing her nursing studies. Hoffman asked her to dance, and they joined the others.

"So you're going to be a nurse," he said as they danced.

"Yes. I should graduate in the spring."

"And then?"

"And then work in a hospital. So you're from Seattle."

"Born and raised."

"Is the army your career?"

Hoffman laughed. "Far from it. I'll be a civilian again when I finish my obligation next year, then probably law school."

"It must be good to get away from that war, even for a few days," she said. "I hope you have a good time in Sydney."

"I already am," he said. "Any recommendations, places to go, things to do, people to get to know? Especially the latter." It was oblique, but she got his drift.

"I just might."

The album ended, and another dropped onto the turntable: "Ah, now I hardly know her, but I think I could love her, Crimson and Clover . . ."

She pulled herself closer to him. He could feel her breath in his ear. The lights were low. Then he heard Susan's voice: "Cutting, Val."

Valerie stepped away. Hoffman said to Susan, "I was beginning to think you forgot about me."

"Sorry. I won't leave you again."

"You're working way too hard on your birthday. What can I do to help? I mean it."

"Don't worry; I have plans for you."

"Such as . . ."

"Stick around after the guests leave."

It sounded like an order. "Yes, ma'am."

She moved close and lay her head on his shoulder. The Chanel—she must have applied it when she was upstairs—made his head spin. Jesus, can this really be happening?

The party broke up just after midnight and the guests headed for the door, while Hoffman and Susan carried dishes, unfinished food, empty bottles, and glasses up to the kitchen. When the room was cleared and the furniture back in place, she said, “Let’s walk. I need some fresh air.”

The night was warm and moonlit. Susan took his arm, and they strolled through a sleeping neighborhood of stately homes, down the hill to the seawall. They spoke of their families, their plans for the future, and their interests. She intended to spend one year in Sydney, maybe two, then return to teaching in Vancouver. Yes, she had a significant other there, but she wasn’t sure about him. He told her about Clara and how their relationship ended. He really wasn’t sure what career he would pursue when he completed military duty. They were comfortable with each other, shared their life stories freely, and seemed to have much in common.

It was 2:00 a.m. when they returned to the house and sat on the front steps, waiting for his cab to arrive. Hoffman wanted to see her again. He had only a week, but he would gladly have spent every moment with her. It was presumptuous of him to even think that way, but he had so little time. “I don’t know how to thank you for tonight,” he said.

“It’s nothing. I’m glad we met.”

“What would you say if I asked to see you again?”

“Try me.”

“Okay, what are you doing tomorrow?”

“Call me in the morning.”

The cab rolled up, and he got in. “Susan, I hope you don’t think I’m being pushy, but—”

She placed a finger on his lips. “It’s okay, soldier. Go to your hotel and get some rest.”

14
TERROR AND TEARS

Hoffman's week in Sydney was the stuff dreams are made of. Susan took a few days off work to spend time with him at the beach, and he hung around the restaurant every evening until it closed and they could spend a few hours together. The Laffertys, on holiday, showed him around the city. All too soon, he was back in Vietnam, rejoining his platoon. He felt as if he had known Susan for years, and returning to Southeast Asia was like running a film backwards. All he had left of their meeting was the heartache of leaving her, and not knowing whether he would ever see her again. It was back to business as usual.

A grunt never knew where he was, where he was going, or why. This time, though, there seemed to be a clear objective. A VC defector had provided information indicating males in a Montagnard village were working with the NVA. It was the last remaining village in the area. Vietnamese authorities would hold and interrogate the tribesmen captured there, and US helicopters would evacuate the entire population to a resettlement compound in Pleiku.

Standley gathered his company commanders around a topographical map spread on a folding table. He placed the tip of a rifle cleaning rod on the map, Sheet 6436, with a scale of 1:50000 (or 1 cm = 500 m). Widely spaced contour lines meant relatively level terrain. A major river cut across a corner of the map like a question mark. The village lay near the river.

"This area was supposedly cleared of locals last year," Standley explained, "but this village, for some reason, was missed. We have intelligence indicating the males may be assisting the NVA, willingly or unwillingly. Our objective is to move in quickly at night, cordon off the village, and hold everyone for evacuation. If the tribesmen have turned against us, they may try to run, so we'll have to move fast."

"How many folks are we talking about?" Gilman wondered.

"Last anyone knew, less than fifty. At one time, there were several large tribal enclaves in this area. From the air, we see people moving around, livestock, water buffalo."

One of the other company commanders pointed at the map. "So we're here, and they're there. How are we going to get to 'em without scattering 'em?"

"I'm coming to that," said Standley. "There's a trail to the village here." He traced a line on the map with the cleaning rod. "Recon has scouted this trail and will lead Alpha, Bravo, and Delta companies to the village under cover of darkness. Charlie will remain on the LZ."

"At night?" Gilman asked skeptically.

"You heard me right, captain," Standley said. "Not my idea. Orders from division, so it's up to us to figure out how to do it, which is exactly what we will do. Is that clear?"

The four captains nodded, but to them, it was just another whacky scheme dreamed up by people who spent zero time in the jungle. Night movement was difficult for twenty- to twenty-five-man platoons, and three companies and nearly three hundred troops on a jungle trail at night was, well, the makings of a clusterfuck.

Standley continued, "So we jump off tomorrow night at 0200 hours. Recon will be in the lead, followed by Delta, Bravo, and Alpha, in that order."

He sketched out the operation on the map with a grease pencil as if he was drawing up a football play. The task force would arrive at the village before first light. Alpha and Bravo would split off to the left and right, leaving Delta to fill in any middle gap when the net was joined on the other side of the village. Men would be stationed along the way, near enough to detect and prevent anyone inside from escaping.

"Once the net is in place, Recon will wait until dawn to launch a sweep through the hooches and clear them of anyone left inside. Captain Gilman, one of your platoons will back up Recon, holding men, women, and children here, in the center of the village. This part of the operation has to be done quickly because a chopper is scheduled to arrive at 0800 with a translator and a Vietnamese district official. They will conduct interrogations and explain to the villagers what will happen next, which is the transport of the entire population by helicopter to a resettlement area in Pleiku."

Gilman asked the question on everyone's minds: "What if we take fire from the village?"

"Glad you asked. This My Lai thing has everyone on edge. Hear me loud and clear. Return fire only, and only if you have a sure target. No exceptions. You company commanders will be held responsible for any unnecessary casualties."

The officers listened uncomfortably. Noncombatants getting caught in a firefight—not uncommon in the heavily populated lowlands, but in the sparsely inhabited Central Highlands, grunts seldom encountered civilians. How would their men react if fired upon from the village? To the company commanders, it seemed Standley was covering his own ass: "Shoot up any civilians, and it's on the company commanders."

The four company commanders returned to their charges to break the news. Gilman wasn't surprised by the reactions of his platoon leaders. Lieutenant Hank Gildersleeve, First Platoon, said, "Danton is going to take the lead? He couldn't find his butt with both hands in the dark."

Unnerfeld said, "Three companies in single file, huh? We'll be strung out from here to Saigon."

"Never mind. Just make sure your troops stay together," Gilman said. "Hoffman, your platoon will back up Recon. It will be your job to assist in the sweep of the village at first light. Get with Danton and coordinate."

Hoffman said, "Sleeve, there's a fifth of Old Grand Dad in it for you if you back up Recon."

"No deal, Jack," said Gildersleeve. "I want nothing to do with that asshole."

Gilman barked, "Knock it off. It's you, Hoffman. Galvin and several of your people have experience clearing villages. I don't want any trigger-happy people going in there. No civilian casualties, no matter what. Make that abundantly clear to your men."

Hoffman's grunts received the order as skeptically as their officers, no one more than Razor Galvin. "Three companies in a night march? Someone up the chain of command has shit for brains, LT."

Specialist 4 Ludwik added, "Yeah, and even if we make it to the village without getting lost or ambushed, for what? We cleared a village just before you got here, and I hated it. The big losers are these poor Yards. Take 'em away and lock 'em in a lousy compound. Leave 'em in the boonies, and they slave for the gooks or get hit by our artillery."

As night fell, Hoffman met Danton outside the bunker serving as the battalion command post to coordinate their respective roles. "Well, hot shot, it seems you and I are responsible for sweeping the village in the morning," Danton said. "I wanted someone else, but your Captain Gilman didn't agree."

"What a coincidence, Danton. I made the same request."

"So it would seem we're stuck with one another. Sure you're up to it?"

"Get off my back. I've got nothing to prove to you."

"You ain't shown me shit yet."

Hoffman wanted to tell him to fuck off but held back. "Look; I've got a lot to do before dark. Let's get this over with."

The two agreed that, once there was enough daylight, Recon would move into the village and drive the residents out of their longhouses. Hoffman's platoon would follow close behind, checking the hooches for weapons, rounding up the Montagnards, and holding them in a field just outside the village.

At 0130 hours, the two companies and Recon silently assembled at the north end of the LZ in preparation to exit the perimeter. At precisely 0200, Recon's point man stepped through the wire, and 325 men filed into the jungle. Clouds blocked the light of a waning moon, limiting visibility to a few meters. Danton picked up the trail leading to the village easily enough, but staying on the right path with many intersecting trails would be another matter.

The men hadn't gone far when the file succumbed to the law of elasticity, stretching and snapping back as Recon's point man struggled to follow the trail. Grunts trotted to keep up one minute and stepped on one another's heels the next. They tripped and fell; foliage slapped and vines grabbed. Cursing and giggling at the absurdity of it all spread down the line.

About an hour into the march, the file came to an abrupt halt. The men stood, waiting for it to move again. Minutes passed. Galvin, walking some thirty meters from the front, became impatient and moved forward to find out what was holding things up.

"Has Recon reached the village?" he asked Hoffman.

"Don't know. Tried to reach Danton on the radio but got no response."

"Bet he's lost."

"Better not be."

"He could lose his way in a chow line."

The point man had taken the wrong fork in the trail. An "about face" made its way down the file, received with whispered groans and epithets. Like a train switching tracks, the men backtracked twenty meters, bumping and jostling, before resuming forward progress. Another half hour of stumbling through the undergrowth and another halt, this time with word that Recon had reached the village.

Hoffman moved up and found Danton prone in the wood line, peering through a Starlight Scope, so absorbed by what he saw that he didn't acknowledge Hoffman's presence. The village seemed somnolent, with no fires or lamps, no sounds except the incessant yelping of dogs and a strange rhythmic swishing, like the sweeping of a broom.

Hoffman whispered, "They're awake, but what the hell is that whisking sound?"

"Never mind. Just move everyone up on the double."

The companies quickly moved forward, splitting off left and right. Thrashing noisily through the forest, they took up positions around the village, closing the loop on the far side. It became obvious to the grunts that anyone in the village who wanted to slip away in the dark could easily have done so. Nothing to do now but wait for dawn. Hoffman checked his watch, and at 0447, as if on cue, a rooster declared a new day.

A scene worthy of a spread in *National Geographic* gradually came into view: a cluster of thatched longhouses mounted on posts, water buffaloes tethered beneath them, chickens and potbellied pigs foraging, ceramic pots stacked near a kiln, a village garden. One longhouse lay in ruins beside a crater, apparently the victim of random artillery fire.

Women squatted on the stoops of several of the longhouses, tossing and catching rice in shallow baskets, swish, swish, swish in the dark. There was nothing to be gained by charging in. A few women emerged from the longhouses to light cooking fires and drew water from a cistern. They went about their morning chores as usual. Several elderly men joined the women. A dozen youths and small children appeared. The young tribesmen that the senior commanders hoped to capture made no appearance.

At about 0600, Danton gave his men the order to sweep through the village. Recon's grunts formed a skirmish line and moved forward apprehensively, knowing a peaceful scene could suddenly shatter in gunfire. As the grunts approached the longhouses, the villagers stood motionless, like wax figures in a museum. The women, some bare breasted and nursing infants slung from their shoulders, appeared miniature beside the advancing American giants who commenced to search the longhouses and remove anyone remaining inside.

As instructed by Danton, Hoffman and his platoon followed, the grunts shouting and brandishing their weapons to herd the villagers into a holding area. Some of the women objected shrilly in a tongue the grunts understood without translation. Pandemonium ensued as villagers scattered, not knowing what was asked of them. The Americans brandished the stocks of their weapons to herd them together like cattle, shouting in the few words of Vietnamese they knew:

"Come here, den day, mama san, and don't give me any shit."

"You heard me, di di, move it, move it, move it."

Gradually the villagers gathered in a field that would later serve as a landing zone for the helicopters taking them to Pleiku. They spoke little, their expressions a combination of fear and puzzlement. All morning, the piercing cry of a frightened adolescent boy rose like an indictment. “In the name of God,” Hoffman muttered, “what are we doing?”

But this was no time for moralizing. All he could do now was make sure no one got hurt, and as chaotic as it was, so far, the operation had progressed without violence. Then, what he most feared, happened: six shots behind one of the longhouses. He ran toward the building, while others scrambled for cover. He heard someone yell, “Look out; he’s trying to get up,” and two more shots rang out.

Hoffman arrived to find two grunts standing over a massive twitching water buffalo on its side. They aimed their rifles at its head. One of them fired another round, and the animal lay still.

“Who told you to do that?” Hoffman demanded.

“The damn thing charged us,” one of the men explained. “We kept shooting, but it kept coming.”

If there was one Asian animal the grunts feared more than the Asian tiger and the bamboo viper, it was two thousand pounds of angry ox. “Who cut it loose?” Hoffman asked.

“Nobody. It broke loose as we were walking by,” one of the men explained.

It took about nearly an hour to clear the village of some sixty residents. None of the young men the higher highers hoped to capture were among them. They had escaped in the night if they were ever there in the first place. As the morning progressed, the villagers squatted under a pounding sun, under guard. Listless kids clung to their mothers. What could these people be thinking? Hoffman often wondered. To the ethnic Vietnamese, they were a lower life form, dispensable. To the Americans, they were reminiscent of Indian tribes back home, driven from their lands into reservations, often pathetic recipients of sympathy. Their peaceful tribal existence was coming to an end, and they seemed to sense it.

A few grunts passed the time searching buildings for souvenirs. The troops knew that Remington Raiders, the typewriter jockeys in the rear, would pay top dollar for hooked knives, crossbows, and brass bracelets, souvenirs from a jungle into which they seldom ventured, like tourists in a wildlife park. One of the soldiers emerged from a longhouse holding a ceremonial drum. "Dude, look, a fucking drum," he called happily to another grunt who had collected a crossbow and several clay pots.

Hoffman spotted them. "You men, what the hell are you doing?" he bellowed.

"Souvenirs, sir," one of them responded sheepishly.

"Put them back."

"Why?"

"Because they're not yours, that's why."

"Aw, come on, LT. We gonna torch this ville anyway," said the other.

"You heard me. Return that stuff, and get back to your positions."

As the afternoon wore on, the keening of the boy was the only violation of the village's silence; no one made any effort to comfort him. Hoffman, Danton, and several company commanders stood near the gathering of villagers, waiting for word of the arrival of helicopters. An attractive young woman stood up and walked toward them.

It was difficult to discern the ages of the women, as life in the mountainous jungle was hard and short, but this woman stood out. Her appearance and the deference the other villagers afforded her suggested she held authority in the village. She was dressed elegantly in a woven black and orange jacket and skirt. Her heavy dark hair was coiled behind her head, and her skin was smooth. She appeared to be pregnant. A guard stopped her, but Hoffman shouted to let her pass.

"What do you want, mama san?" Danton said impatiently. "We're busy."

"Que voulez vous avec nou?" she responded defiantly.

"Oh, a Frenchie," Danton said caustically. Some of the Montagnards spoke broken French, which they learned working on plantations carved from the jungle by French settlers. "Speak English, mama san. Tell us where the men went."

"No Englais," she said.

"Let me try," Hoffman said. "Où sont les hommes?"

"Ils sont partis," she answered.

"What did she say?" Danton asked.

"She said they're gone."

"We can see that, goddamn it. Ask her where they've gone."

"Où sont-ils allés?"

"Je ne sais pas."

"She doesn't know," Hoffman said.

"Bullshit," Danton bellowed.

This she understood but didn't flinch.

"Leave her alone," Hoffman objected. "We can't force her to talk."

"She's lying, Hoffman. Ask her when they left."

"Quand ont-ils quitte'?"

"Trois jours," she responded.

"Three days," Hoffman said.

"I ain't buyin' it," Danton scoffed. "Anyway, the Vietnamese police will make her talk, one way or another. I've been watching her give orders to these people all morning, and they do what she says. Tell her helicopters are on their way, and we're moving everyone to Pleiku."

Hoffman did his best with his high school French to explain what was about to happen to them. A Vietnamese district official and a translator would arrive soon to coordinate the evacuation.

The village women squatted submissively under a despotic sun, draping blankets over their heads to protect themselves, chewing betel, and waiting for whatever fate would deliver. Children huddled listlessly at their mothers' sides, while feeble old men leaned on their staffs and smoked pipes. They spoke little.

Sensing the injustice of this, the grunts guarding them were like kids ordered to do something that didn't seem right. But the line between right and wrong in this war had become so blurred that it was often impossible to find it. Dispossessed of their land and herded into fortified compounds, the mountain tribes gained nothing from the war but misery, no matter which of the opposing forces eventually prevailed.

Finally, a slick carrying Colonel Standley, two of his staff, a Vietnamese district official, and a Montagnard interpreter landed at the village. The latter addressed the villagers, telling them the village was to be evacuated and everyone taken to a resettlement village in Pleiku. The anxious eyes of the villagers told Hoffman this was incomprehensible to them. They were inseparable from the jungle. It was as vital to their existence as their beating hearts.

The district official relied on the interpreter, who spoke the Malayo-Polynesian dialect of the tribe, to question the young woman. Standley and his officers stood by, hoping to learn where the NVA might be moving. The woman identified herself as the daughter of the tribe's chief who had disappeared with the other tribesmen taken by the NVA. Through the questioning, the woman glared defiantly at the Vietnamese official. It was obvious he was getting nowhere with her.

"She says she does not know where men have gone; only NVA take somewhere. That's all," the interpreter said.

"She's lying," the official angrily asserted and raised his hand to strike her, but Standley grabbed his wrist.

"What the hell's wrong with you?" he growled. "She's pregnant, for chrissake. I'll handle this."

The Vietnamese official stepped back petulantly. The woman turned to her protector and said through the translator that the tribesmen would return soon. She pleaded that everyone be allowed to remain in the village until the families could be reunited.

Standley answered, "Take a look at that longhouse over there, blown to splinters. Tell her this is a free-fire zone, and it's not safe. They have nothing to fear. They'll have everything they need, a much better life. They have to go."

The woman responded in a tone that didn't sound compliant. The translator said to her something equally insistent. The two argued briefly, then the interpreter shook his head and translated for Standley: "Woman says, you take other people now; she waits here for men."

"No," Standley said, frustrated with the process. He was not a civil affairs officer; he was infantry, and his job was done. "She goes, too. Those are my orders."

Danton, taking in the conversation, said, "Sir, can I have a word with you?"

"Yes, what is it?" he said peevishly.

"Out of her hearing, sir. I'm not sure how much she understands."

The two stepped away. Danton said, "Her father and the father of that child she's carrying aren't going to leave her alone. I suspect they'll show up soon. Let her stay until they do."

"Just how would we know that, lieutenant?"

"Recon will disappear with the rest of you and do what we do best, which is hide. She won't know we're watching. Anyway, it's worth a try. She's worthless to us back in Pleiku."

Standley paused to think about it. Leaving a pregnant woman alone in a free-fire zone offended his sense of noblesse oblige, but there was no harm in letting Danton try. Standley had hoped to round up collaborators, at the very least gather some intelligence, but the net cast around the village had caught no fish.

Standley said, "I have my doubts, but okay. I'll have to go higher to get authorization."

The translator explained to the woman she could remain in the village for one week, but she must wait for the men there. She agreed, then explained to the villagers that she would bring the men to Pleiku when they returned. The women chattered, the old men listened, and the children clung wide-eyed to their mothers.

Hoffman was glad she wasn't going back, at least not right away. She was quite capable of taking care of herself in the jungle. In Pleiku, she would be caged like an animal and likely subject to rough treatment by the Vietnamese. He had seen where the villagers were going, a large impoundment like a dusty trailer park on the road between the division base camp and the city of Pleiku. Its clapboard hooches sat on stubby pilings, mocking the hand-crafted bamboo and thatch longhouses of their villages. The residents, no longer sustained by the jungle, wandered listlessly or sat idly on the porches of the hooches.

The unavailability of big Chinook helicopters meant Hueys would ferry the villagers out in sorties, bird by bird. The women and old men were allowed back into their longhouses to retrieve a few belongings, and they emerged like pack animals, weighed down with baskets and slings bulging with pots and urns, roots and gourds, pipes, knives, machetes, family keepsakes, as much as they could carry.

Three grunts were tasked with reducing their baggage to an armful. A wizened grandmother approached with a large sack on her shoulder and a live hen, its legs tied, hanging on her waist. One of the grunts stopped her and ordered her to drop the sack. Perplexed, she tried to walk past him. He grabbed the sack, and a tug of war ensued. The bird squawked and flailed, and the sack burst. Pipes, tobacco, brass jewelry and beads, a few pieces of pottery, and a small box of French coins flew through the air.

The woman fell on her knees, sobbing and frantically gathering up her treasures.

Observing the commotion, the young woman rushed to her assistance, calming her with soothing words. The grunt had made his point. One by one, the villagers dropped everything but a few clothes and personal items and trudged off to await the helicopters.

Several hours passed before the first sortie of three Hueys circled over the village. The Montagnards had no doubt observed airborne helicopters many times in this long war but never on the ground, up close, and they fell back, cowering as if threatened by some strange malevolent beasts. As soldiers divided the villagers into parties of eight for boarding, a screaming boy of about ten broke from his group and ran to a woman in another group, clinging to her leg, refusing to let go when a grunt attempted to separate them.

"What the hell are you doing?" Hoffman shouted at the grunt over the whine of engines and thump of blades.

"This kid ran from his group," the soldier answered.

"So let him go with his mother, for god's sake," Hoffman yelled.

Glaring at the officer, the soldier released the boy.

The villagers huddled on the open deck of the chopper, embracing one another for dear life as it rose from the earth. Hoffman was struck by the incongruity of what he was seeing, an indigenous people lifted from a primitive existence in a jungle wilderness in a twentieth-century contraption, a virtual time machine. The chopper hovered for a moment as if to give them a last look at a way of life they might lose forever.

"Can you believe this shit?" Hoffman asked Galvin.

"Seen it before, LT, so I guess I have to believe it."

"Sorry situation."

"These people are screwed any way you look at it."

"Think that young lady knows where the males are?"

"Damn sure she does."

She was expendable, a pretty butterfly caught in the iron web of war. The evacuation of the villagers proceeded through the afternoon, and hunter-gatherers were removed from the forest to an existence of dependency and despair. Gradually the gaggle waiting for transport shrank. Whatever agonizing feelings the young woman had as she watched her way of life taken away, she betrayed none of them.

The last sortie rose from the village and beat off toward Pleiku, leaving her alone with the Americans. The village assumed the empty look of abandonment, like a town vacated in the path of a plague. Animals, tools, cooking pots, sacks of rice, the objects of everyday life, remained in place. The pervasive odor of charcoal fires remained, and the livestock, but not for long. The order was issued to dispose of anything of value to the enemy, first the animals, then the dwellings and storage buildings.

Two men were detailed to slaughter the animals. Several shots were required to drop the remaining water buffalo where it was hobbled. The pigs and chickens were not as handily dispatched. The first shots sent them scurrying for their lives with the grunts in pursuit, laughing at the sport of it. A carelessly fired round raised a puff of dust near Captain Gilman's boot, prompting him to call a halt to the fun.

Then the torching commenced. With a few strikes of the Zippo, flames soon roared through the thatched roofs of the longhouses, and the grunts had to pull back from the heat. A small hooch in the village garden was preserved to provide shelter for the woman. Inside, the grunts deposited a basket of rice, some papayas, and a few C-rations.

15
THE CHASE

It was evening when Bravo and Delta companies formed columns for the walk back to the LZ, expecting to cover the distance in a fraction of the time it took the previous night. As Hoffman entered the curtain of jungle surrounding the smoldering village, he glanced back at the solitary figure of the pregnant Montagnard woman, frozen like Lot's wife, gazing at the ruins of her village. He admired her for defying the command to leave but couldn't help fearing for her safety. That her fate was in Danton's hands gave him pause.

Well out of sight of the burned-out village, Recon broke off from the main force and took up a position in a shallow ravine. From this location, two grunts would slip back in shifts to observe, from hiding, the woman's movements. As night fell, she remained near the hooch, leaving only briefly to harvest cassava in a garden. At dusk, she built a fire and prepared a meal.

A sliver of moon offered little light, and Danton worried that she might slip away in the dark. But why would she bother to travel at night unless she suspected she was being watched? She sat in the flickering light of the fire, passing the time by weaving something of bamboo. After several hours, she let the fire die and entered the hooch. So far, so good.

Dawn brought Danton hope that his plan was working. The woman emerged from the hooch and filled a sling with a few items from the hooch. It appeared she was preparing to leave, but this wasn't the case. She sat meditatively at the entrance of the little shelter through the morning, moving little, then took up weaving again. Was she really waiting for the men to return, as she said she would? At nightfall, she retired to the hooch where she spent another night.

The second morning was like the first. The woman rose at dawn and resumed her routine. As the sun climbed, she poked through the ashes of the longhouses. What was she looking for? Still, she stayed put, and no one joined her. Danton was getting impatient. He reported the situation to Colonel Standley and proposed to give her another day. They agreed that, if the status quo prevailed, Danton was to call in a chopper and have her transported to Pleiku.

A rooster announced day three, and the watchers reported the woman had not emerged from the hooch. They moved in to check, and as Danton feared, she had slipped away in the dark. But he had no intention of letting her story end there. He radioed Standley: "Well, she must have someplace to go, pregnant and all. My hunch is she's headed west, toward the border. We'll need a dog to track her. Over."

Standley was dubious. "She's got a good lead on you. If she crosses into Cambodia, you'll have to give it up. Over."

"Roger, but still, I'd like to keep going. Over."

"Okay, we'll send a dog and handler within the hour. Keep me advised."

A slick brought a German Shepherd named Boogaloo, Boog for short, and Specialist 4 Pete Lucas, its handler. Like all dogs and their handlers, Boog and Lucas were fast friends. They bonded during training eight months before shipping out to Vietnam and hadn't spent a day apart since. Lucas gave the animal a good sniff of the interior of the hooch and a few items left behind by the Montagnard woman, then turned the dog loose to pick up a scent.

Boog trotted nose down through the burned-out buildings, disinterested until it reached the garden where the woman had harvested roots. There it paused, then ambled off in the direction of a high green wall of foliage, an impenetrable snarl of bush and vine. The dog found an opening large enough to allow a small animal to enter, or a human on hands and knees. Lucas leashed the dog and held it back, fearing a boobytrap.

"What are you waiting for, Lucas? Get your ass on in there with that dog," Danton ordered.

"No fucking way. Tunnels are not our specialty."

"Jesus Christ," Danton said, disgusted. "Jackson, get over here, on the double."

There was, of course, no such military occupational specialty. Specialist 4 Calvin Jackson was the platoon's frequent point and occasional tunnel rat. Most men wouldn't—or couldn't—crawl into a dark hole with nothing but a flashlight and a pistol. Jackson, a black, was of medium height with the physique of an hourglass. He was tough and didn't seem to mind crawling into holes with nothing but a .45 pistol. He dropped his ruck and disappeared into the opening. Moments later, he popped out, grinning.

"This here's the entrance to a . . . a . . . like a room hacked out of the brush, man," he said. "And there's a hooch in there, full of rice, some mortars, AK ammo, rolls of commo wire, that kind of shit. But no one home."

Danton said, "I'm going in for a look."

The interior was as Jackson described. Another passage in the undergrowth opened onto a trail. Lucas gave Boog a treat from his pack, and the dog surged down the path, which eventually took the platoon from a mature forest into a savanna-like woodland. The platoon moved quickly in pursuit. From time to time, the big dog paused on the trail, nose to the ground as if sniffing for truffles, then pulled at the leash and trotted on.

It was a windless day with suffocating humidity, and as noon approached, the heat weighed heavily on both dog and man. Boog panted and frequently stopped to lap water from Lucas' helmet, which he filled from a blivet he carried. The grunts' fatigues were drenched in sweat and their steel helmets radiated heat like convection ovens, but Danton drove them on relentlessly, pausing only briefly to check his map.

The trail made a sharp turn to the north and entered a cathedral-like stand of giant trees with pillared trunks supporting a vaulted ceiling of limbs and leaves. Here and there, shafts of light reached the jungle floor as if through clerestory windows. The usual thrum of the jungle's biota faded, leaving a foreboding stillness. Boog trotted along on a relatively clear carpet of decaying vegetation, unimpeded by aerial roots that hung like thick ropes from the upper story.

Lucas called for a break to water his dog. Little remained of the ten-quart supply hanging on his ruck frame. As the dog lapped noisily from his helmet, the grunts gratefully dropped to the ground, leaned back against their rucks, and drank from their canteens. The shade of the trees brought welcome relief from the pounding sun, but everyone was getting low on water. Recon's NCO, Sergeant First Class Conner Flannigan, wondered how far the lieutenant intended to push before dark. The Cambodian border had to be nearby, and depending on the woman's lead, she might already have crossed it. In any case, it was unlikely the grunts would overtake her before dark.

Sergeant Flannigan was thirty-eight years old and on his third tour in Vietnam. From a blue-collar family in Philadelphia, he was too young to serve in World War II but old enough to court the favors of lonely women left behind by those who did. Dressed in a zoot suit, he had looked older than his fifteen years and enjoyed the favors of women much older. He supported himself by collecting money for a bookie, and when the war ended, aimlessly facing the grim realities of life on the streets, he wandered into a recruiting station.

As an E-7 sergeant, Flannigan might have had a job in the rear but hated garrison life. He volunteered to go forward and serve with Recon. In the short time Danton led the platoon, Flannigan found himself frequently questioning the officer's judgment. He had served under many junior officers who respected his experience and listened to his informed opinions. Danton was the rare exception, and Flannigan had little use for him. He approached the officer, map in hand. "It's getting dark soon, and we need water. If we continue west, we should cross a blue line, this one, in an hour or two. This would be a good place to stop for the night."

"Not yet. We've still got some daylight, and we're making good time," Danton said.

With Lucas and the dog forging ahead, the platoon followed the trail into an area of sparser trees, bamboo, and palm, making good time. It must have been the smell of water that caused the dog to pull hard on the leash with Lucas in tow. Jackson, who was walking just behind him in second position, warned the handler to slow down, but the thirsty animal bolted forward, pulling Lucas around a bend in the trail.

"Luke, you crazy motherfucker, get yo ass back here," Jackson growled and pursued him into a maze of towering bamboos as straight as organ pipes. In a crouch, his weapon pressed to his shoulder, Jackson crept down the narrow footpath through a corridor of bamboo to the grassy bank of a streambed. He stopped and took a knee but saw nothing and heard nothing but the murmuring of the creek. There was no sign of Lucas. Where could he be? His muted call for him got no response.

He turned and began to retreat back up the trail when he heard something that sent a chill down his spine. From a point near the stream, he heard, feeble but clear, "Ohhh. Ohhhhh. Hail Mary full of grace . . ." His legs wanted to run, but he hesitated in that zone every grunt knew, somewhere between paralyzing fear and absolute necessity. Again, he heard a faint voice, very nearby. "Uhhhh, sweet Jesus, help me." He saw nothing; the prayer seemed to rise out of thin air.

Jackson's groin puckered as he forced himself to move toward the voice, his M-16 raised and ready to fire. He scanned the jungle for any telltale sign of human presence, and step by careful step, he proceeded until he felt the ground sag beneath his left boot. He froze. Now he knew: the missing man had fallen into a punji pit trap, and he was one step from joining him.

A blanket of bamboo matting, camouflaged by soil and foliage, covered the pit. Jackson saw the gap Lucas and Boog had made falling through. He dropped to his knees and peered in. It was dark, but he reckoned it was about eight feet deep and he knew the floor would be a nail bed of stiletto-sharp punji sticks. The pit was large enough to trap a large animal, a tiger, a monkey, a deer . . . or a man. Montagnards used them, and the woman would have known it was there.

"Luke, you hear me?" Jackson asked.

"Ahhhh, hurry. I can't move," Lucas groaned.

"Hold on, bro. We'll get you out of there."

Jackson ran back some twenty meters to the platoon.

"What the hell is going on?" Danton demanded. "Where's Lucas?"

"Luke and the dog fell into a pit trap . . ." Jackson said breathlessly.

"What the hell?" Danton said.

"I told him to slow down, but him and that dog just bolted."

The platoon moved up and secured the pit, but with nightfall near, there wasn't much time to extricate the handler. Flannigan approached with a climbing rope coiled over his shoulder and stood over the pit. "Lucas, can you move?"

Lucas just moaned.

"Stand up, Lucas. Can you stand up?"

"I can't. There's a punji through my thigh, another in my side. I can't move."

He was pinned like an insect specimen, and there was only one thing to do: drop someone into the hole to extricate him. Flannigan lowered himself with the platoon's climbing rope and carefully squeezed through a maze of split bamboo stakes, sharp, flexible, and deadly. He found the handler near the wall. The dog lay a few feet away, impaled and not moving. The sergeant felt Lucas' sticky, blood-soaked fatigues when he pushed his hands under him and hoisted him off the stakes. The soldier let out a scream, but he was freed.

Flannigan carried Lucas through the stakes to the wall, tied the rope under the wounded man's arms, and told the troops above to pull. When the sergeant returned to the surface, he noticed a stake had torn the skin of his calf. It would have to be cleaned, quickly.

The medic went to work on Lucas, deploying an IV. Flannigan poured hydrogen peroxide from a bottle on his own wound. He was lucky. It hadn't penetrated to the bone, but he would have to have the gash opened up and properly cleaned in the rear—standard procedure to prevent infection. Punji stakes were frequently smeared with feces. He was more worried about Lucas who was losing blood and might have internal injuries. Lucas, however, was more worried about his dog.

"Where's Boog?" the handler whimpered.

No one answered.

"Did you get Boog?" he demanded.

Still, no one dared tell him.

"Answer me, damn it," Lucas said.

"He's gone," Flannigan confessed.

Lucas wept convulsively. "It's my fault."

Flannigan said, "Negative. If it hadn't been you and the dog, it would have been one of us."

Tears left trails in the red dirt on Lucas' face. No one tried to console him. Flannigan only said, "We'll get you out of here, Luke."

With darkness setting in, a medevac would have to wait until morning. Recon prepared for another long night in NVA country. The grunts silently conducted their evening routine, deploying trip flares and listening devices on the trail and positioning Claymore mines. When everyone was in position for the night, Danton took up the radio handset and issued a report to the battalion.

All was quiet, save the trickling of the nearby stream and the whispering of the bamboo. Danton weighed his options for the coming day. The dog was gone, so Recon would have to track the woman without it. And now he had the wounded man to deal with. Finding a suitable LZ for the medevac would consume valuable time. Alternatively, Lucas could be lifted in a basket to a hovering chopper. In either case, the arrival of a helicopter would give away the platoon's location. No, I will not compromise the mission, Danton decided. Doc stopped the bleeding, and Lucas is doing okay. I need one more day, maybe two.

The night passed uneventfully. In the morning, Danton informed the men of his decision to continue the chase, carrying Lucas. Lucas had lost a lot of blood, and the medic warned of shock and blood poisoning. But Danton was obdurate: the border was only a klick away. The wounded man could be carried that far, and if the chase ended there, Lucas could be medevaced then.

For some time, Flannigan had been concerned about the platoon's location. The triple canopy did not allow obtaining a compass fix from prominent terrain features, and a trail that wound through hilly terrain rendered pace counts, to estimate the distance traveled, virtually useless. Even so, multiple tours in Vietnam gave him a feel for distance, and the Cambodian border had to be close. That being the case, Recon was in danger of inadvertently crossing it.

Danton's approach to land navigation seemed to be that he would determine his location when he got where he wanted to go. Until then, don't worry about it. Flannigan found it prudent to challenge his judgment in this regard frequently. "I figure we're about here," the sergeant said, showing Danton a point on his map less than a hundred meters from the border.

Danton pointed to the coordinates of a ridgeline well northeast of Flannigan's estimate. "That last ridgeline we crossed was the highest yet, highest by far. And this little blue line is the one we're on now. We're at least five hundred meters from the border as the crow flies."

This wasn't a minor difference. Flannigan rubbed his square jaw pensively. Neither man could defend his guess, but there was a way. Though they couldn't see any prominent terrain features, they could summons artillery to fire two rounds at designated points on their map. Though they couldn't see the shells splash, they could use a compass to take back azimuths from the sounds of the impacts and triangulate. This would give them a rough idea of where they stood.

"Not necessary," Danton said. "We should be able to get a better view from the higher ground just ahead."

"It would be nice to have a better fix now, lieutenant. We could be moving out of range of our artillery."

"Look, I know what I'm doing. I don't want the gooks to detect we're anywhere in the neighborhood, and making a lot of noise defeats our purpose."

Well, that was that. Flannigan folded his map and directed that a poncho stretcher be fashioned for Lucas. "Keep me briefed on him. If he gets any worse, we'll call for a medevac," Flannigan promised the medic.

"He needs one now," the medic insisted.

"I know," Flannigan said resignedly.

Without the dog, the trail was all Danton had to guide him, but Boog's nose had indicated the woman had stayed on the trail and she was definitely making for the border. The platoon resumed its pursuit, carrying the badly wounded Lucas on an improvised stretcher. The file proceeded up a gentle incline to a fork in the trail, one branch narrow but well worn, the other less used, heading south. But with a visibility of only a few meters, one couldn't be sure. Danton, never distressed by topographical ambiguity, was uncharacteristically cautious.

He consulted with Flannigan.

"Damned if I know," the sergeant said. "Anyway, we're so close to the border that woman has to be in Cambodia by now."

Danton removed his steel pot and wiped the sweat from his eyes with his shoulder towel. He was thinking. When he plopped his helmet back on his head, he smiled thinly. "You see any signs saying, 'Entering Cambodia,' Flannigan?'"

"No, sir."

"Neither do I. Let's drive on that way."

The platoon, Jackson on point, continued to the west on the high-speed trail. The division routinely operated along the border but was not authorized to cross it, even in pursuit. But in the jungle wilderness, borders meant little. The Air Force secretly bombed Cambodia nearly every night. Why should we, Danton reasoned, observe a ridiculous policy others violated with impunity? If we have to go in, we will, and get out again with no one back at division headquarters the wiser.

The grunts, issued no maps or compasses, were beginning to wonder where they were. Land navigation was solely their leaders' responsibility, and Danton's weak map reading was worrisome. Jackson walked point under the triple canopy until he came to a steep drop into a narrow canyon. Through the trees, he saw a patch of corn planted in rows on the opposite slope. Thin smoke filtered through trees far below. Danton raised his binoculars for a closer look but saw only dense forest.

A narrow gorge appeared nowhere on the map on either side of the border. "Probably just too narrow to chart on a map of this scale, LT," Sergeant Flannigan opined. "Either that, or we have no idea where we are."

"Negative, sarge. I know exactly where we are," Danton grumbled. "We're going down there. I want to get a closer look."

"What if we need artillery or air support? Let's get a better fix on our position first."

"For chrissake, are you losing your nerve, Flannigan? Probably just some Yards in that canyon, roasting monkey meat for lunch."

Flannigan's face reddened. "My nerve is fine. We don't want to get trapped down there with no air or fire support. And what about Lucas?"

Danton softened. "Take it easy, Top. We're just going for a look-see. But if you're so goddamn worried about it, take a scouting party and check it out first."

Flannigan didn't need another reason to dislike this man, but they kept coming. He grabbed a radio and chose two grunts to accompany him. They would avoid the trail, sliding down the canyon wall on their butts until they had a clear view through the trees. The men used tree branches as handholds, digging in their heels as brakes. Occasionally a dislodged rock bounded down the slope, and all they could do was pray it didn't give them away.

As they neared the bottom, they heard falling water and got whiffs of the "Dink smell," the distinctive odor of charcoal fires, canned fish, rice, and nuoc mam. They advanced from tree to tree until they came to a rock shelf clear of vegetation. They crawled out and peered over the edge, gaining a clear, though constricted, view of the canyon floor.

The scene was worthy of a picture postcard. On the canyon rim and slopes, the limbs of enormous trees arched over the gorge, blocking surveillance from the air. Artillery shells would strike the walls or pass over harmlessly. A waterfall drained into a pool in a small grotto. Three Montagnard-style hooches stood on poles nearby. Tents were pitched along the streambank, and hammocks hung like cocoons from the trees. Two Montagnard women prepared food at a fire pit. And though Flannigan couldn't be sure, his binoculars told him one of them might be the woman they were following.

While the grunts watched, mesmerized, two naked Vietnamese men emerged from one of the hooches with towels, laughing and jostling as they headed for the pool to bathe. Five in NVA uniforms sat at a table smoking cigarettes and chatting while they cleaned AK-47s. Flannigan counted nine Vietnamese and two male Montagnards. Judging from the number of tents and hammocks, there were more somewhere nearby.

Flannigan was reluctant to move any closer, so they lay still, watching. Another trail was visible on the opposite flank of the canyon, and four more soldiers, armed and wearing pith helmets, arrived on it. The men at the table greeted them. Three Montagnard tribesmen, stooping under large bundles on their backs, followed the soldiers. One of the NVA troops growled a command at them. The tribesmen dropped their burdens and retreated to the fire where they squatted with the women.

Flannigan took the radio handset and whispered to Danton: "NVA, about a dozen I can see, maybe more. And a few Yards."

"Hot shit, I knew it," Danton said. "Can you get a better view?"

"No, can't move any closer."

"Okay. Observe another half hour, then get back up here."

The NVA appeared to be doing what soldiers do when standing down: eating, grooming, cleaning equipment, conversing, and relaxing. Occasionally they shouted orders at the Montagnards who seemed to be doing menial tasks around the camp. Perhaps the young Montagnard woman was truthful when she implied the tribesmen were forced to leave the village. The encampment was apparently some kind of sanctuary or staging area. But where was it? With the border so near, its precise location was a guess. And how many more NVA were down there? These questions plagued Flannigan as he made his way back to rejoin the platoon.

"There's a little Shangri-La down there," he reported to Danton, "a pretty little waterfall, a pool, hooches, some kind of R&R, maybe even a hospital. A few Montagnards, apparently porters, some women doing the cooking."

"Did you see our Montagnard woman?"

"One that looked like her, but couldn't be sure."

Danton could barely contain himself. "I knew it. I knew it. She was going to lead us to the NVA. How many do you think?"

"I already told you, LT; we couldn't get a good count. About a dozen, give or take, but there's a trail on the other side, and some were coming and going. Could be boo-coo more."

"Can we get a good field of fire from above?"

"And take 'em on ourselves?"

"We've got the drop on 'em, don't we? They don't know how many we are. They'll never know what hit 'em. Why not?"

"I can think of a dozen reasons. For starters, we aren't sure where the hell we are and whether we have artillery support. We could be on the wrong side of the border. We could get flanked and cut off from above. And what about Lucas if we have to run?"

"So what do you suggest, just walk away?"

"I'm pretty sure we're inside Cambodia. Let's pass this along to battalion and let them deal with it."

"An opportunity like this doesn't come along every day. They've been playing cat and mouse with us for months. I think we can handle this ourselves. I'd rather ask for forgiveness than permission." To Danton, withdrawing from a fight was coitus interruptus. "Besides, who's gonna bitch if we made a small miscalculation?" He took out his map and marked the coordinates. "I have us about here, just inside the border. Get this back to the battalion on the horn, and tell them to have fire support ready."

The wounded Lucas was left near the canyon rim with a guard and a radio. With Flannigan leading the way, the platoon descended a slope so steep, in some places they had to use the rope to let themselves down. At a point just above the ledge, they stopped, and Danton crawled out for a look. What lay about seventy-five meters below mesmerized him. He had never encountered so many NVA troops gathered in one place. It would be a shooting gallery.

The grunts crawled forward and took up positions on the ledge. Danton would fire the first shot. He glanced at his watch: just past noon, with sufficient daylight remaining to climb out of the canyon and find an LZ. As he watched for the most productive moment to open fire, something fortuitous happened. The NVA troops, bowls in hand, formed a chow line and began to file by the Montagnard women who dispensed whatever they had been preparing. This time, Danton swore, we are going to really waste them.

The grunts watched the NVA assemble, receive their rations, and squat in small circles to eat. Others entered the hooches with their meal. A dozen Montagnard tribesmen sat apart from the soldiers, listlessly smoking pipes and waiting for the soldiers to finish. The NVA troops took their time eating, conversing, laughing and enjoying themselves. Flannigan wondered what Danton was waiting for.

The sun stood directly overhead when Danton tapped the men to his left and right, who nudged the men next to them; on down the line, the grunts sighted in on targets. Danton aimed at one of the four men sitting at a table, playing some kind of card game and laughing. He took a deep breath and squeezed the trigger. His shot broke the silence like a firecracker, echoing off the canyon walls. Before the NVA soldier's face hit the table, Recon was raining bullets on the hapless enemy troops below.

Automatic weapons, machine guns, and grenade launchers all firing at once echoed through the canyon. The two grenadiers launched high-arching rounds at those fleeing for cover in rocks and trees. There was no place for the hapless men below to hide. The two M-60 machine gunners sawed away at the hooches. In seconds, the buildings were burning, and bodies lay on the canyon floor.

Danton called for a ceasefire. The grunts froze, hearts pounding, watching for any movement below. The barrels of their weapons were smoking hot. Empty magazines and shell casings lay around them. As far as anyone knew, only a few shots had been fired in return. As they surveyed the carnage, they had no sense of accomplishment. It had been too easy.

"Did anyone see the woman?" Danton asked those nearest him.

"I saw her duck down behind some rocks," someone offered.

"Damn good thing she wasn't near the hooches," said another.

The men watched as the walls of the buildings collapsed in flames, lit by tracers. Ammunition stored in one hooch began to cook off. Danton counted the bodies he could see. It was payday. They added up to twenty-one, but there had to be more. So he estimated twenty-five, not to be greedy.

A few feet away, a grunt rose to his knees, pulled a Kodak from an ammo pouch, and snapped several photos. Flannigan pulled him down by the pistol belt. "Get your skinny ass down before you get it blown off," the sergeant demanded. "Look over there." The words barely left his mouth when the first shot rang out from their right. Men in green uniforms swarmed through the trees like a pack of wolves toward the platoon's position.

"Everybody up. Let's get outta here," Danton shouted, and the chase was on. The platoon clambered back to their starting point and picked up Lucas on his stretcher. Figuring the NVA would be waiting for them on the trail, Danton took the platoon through heavy jungle. The grunts ran as fast as they could, carrying the stretcher as bullets spat errantly into the trees overhead.

Flannigan, who was in the rear guard of the file, glimpsed the NVA less than hundred meters behind and moving up. And yet, their fire dwindled to a few random shots. The NVA had no reason to break off the chase, and when automatic weapons fire opened up from close range on his right flank, he wasn't surprised. Bullets whittled away at a tree near his head, one of them striking his left earlobe just beneath his helmet. He looked desperately for cover and crawled to a large fallen tree where he found the medic, Jackson, and Lucas, the latter on morphine and semiconscious.

Jackson blindly traded bursts of fire with the hidden enemy gunner, while Flannigan looked for his radio operator. He saw the grunt's legs protruding from a clump of rattan about ten meters away, and they weren't moving. The sergeant's shouts went unanswered. He knew he had to go to him and retrieve the radio. It wasn't heroism that drove him but naked necessity: without the radio, he had no way of communicating with Danton at the front of the file.

"Cover me," the sergeant shouted to Jackson, and he threw himself over the log and low-crawled toward the RTO. Bullets passed so near his head he was sure he felt their wind. He found his radio operator face down, motionless and bleeding from the mouth. He lifted the RTO's head and saw a small entrance hole in the man's neck. There was no pulse. In neither shock nor grief, he single-mindedly removed the radio from the pack frame and bolted back to the cover of the log, somehow evading the bullets that followed him.

Hearing the heavy fire to his rear and fearing he had lost contact with Flannigan, Danton halted the platoon to regroup. With communication restored, he learned that the sergeant was cut off from the rest of the platoon and pinned down. Moreover, with the loss of the RTO, he had one each, killed and wounded, to deal with. As Flannigan had foreseen, Recon had kicked a hornets' nest and was now paying for it.

Danton realized he had no choice but to regroup and fight his way back to Flannigan. Shoulder to shoulder, the platoon advanced through the trees toward enemy fire, discharging their weapons on automatic and shouting at the tops of their lungs. It was an old trick, a desperate attempt to make the enemy think they were facing more troops than there actually were and forcing them to pull back, at least temporarily.

The mad minute of fire held the enemy down long enough for the line to reach Flannigan and those with him. The enemy wouldn't stay fooled for long, and Danton knew it. His platoon was outnumbered and trapped far from reinforcements. His only recourse now was to form a defensive position as best he could and wait for air support to arrive.

Danton kept busy on the radio, while Flannigan took a nose count: one KIA, four wounded but mobile, and Lucas. Flannigan's RTO was a sweet nineteen-year-old from Omaha, only two months in-country. He had begged to hump the radio when Flannigan's regular radio operator had gone to the rear with malaria. Now he was dead. Flannigan felt blood on his neck and shoulder. He felt his ear. A piece of his earlobe was gone. Well, he didn't need it anyway.

The platoon was surrounded, mooting any possibility of a hasty retreat. Danton was finally able to make a weak connection with the battalion headquarters and report the platoon's location—or what he speculated it was. He was desperate for fire support, artillery, air, whatever he could get. The grunts lay prone, trying to scrape out a few precious inches of defilade with their entrenching tools. A 175-mm howitzer, the longest-range canon in the arsenal, positioned just over the border in Vietnam's Kontum Province, was the first to answer the call. The swish of the first shell passing over their heads encouraged the men of Recon, but when it splashed down, its crump was barely audible.

"What the hell is Danton doing?" Jackson wondered aloud. "Is he in the same fucking firefight as we are?"

"The LT is reading his map upside down again," said the grunt lying next to him.

Danton called in adjustments and walked the rounds closer, still posing little threat to the attackers. He had to adjust carefully; any mistake could strike his own position. The men worried when the fifth round landed in trees about fifty meters from Recon's defensive perimeter. "Close enough, LT," someone shouted, and Danton told the artillerymen to "fire for effect."

Back in the battalion tactical operations center at Camp Farrell, Colonel Standley was monitoring the situation on the company frequency. The good news was that Recon had apparently encountered a sizable concentration of NVA, ending a long drought. Word of the engagement traveled from battalion to brigade to division, and Recon was headed for top billing in the evening commanders' briefings.

Standley had to think his own stock was rising, and he could barely contain his excitement. "That bobcat Danton has cornered the bastards, and now we're going to hammer them," he said to his executive officer. "Get me a helicopter. I want to get out there for a look."

"Not a good idea, sir," the XO said sheepishly.

"Why the hell not?"

"Well, sir, the Red Leg just informed me that, based on where he is adjusting his artillery fire, his position appears to be about two hundred meters inside Cambodia."

"Can't be."

"That's what they say."

"Are they sure?"

The XO gave Standley the map coordinates. Standley went to the wall map. His heart sank. A moment earlier, he was sure he had impressed the higher-ups, and now he had a problem on his hands: one of his platoons was trapped in Cambodia where it wasn't supposed to be. It would be difficult to get them out and even harder to explain. He ordered that a company be moved immediately to an LZ on the border, but there was no way it would arrive in time to help Recon.

"Get that helicopter warmed up and ready to leave as soon as I get to the strip," he directed, ignoring his XO's advice, "and a couple of gunships. I'm going out there."

At that moment, Lieutenant Danton lay behind a tree, studying his map, his radio handset glued to his ear. Now he was pretty sure he had crossed the border. He would need air support and a lot of it. The platoon would have to hold out until it arrived, then make a run for the border with the dead and wounded. He calculated it wasn't far if they could only get some air support.

Standley's helicopter beat through the air at top speed to the invisible line defining the two countries. That damn border was the best thing the NVA had going for them. We nibble at it when we should be crashing through. The inviolability of the border and the vastness of the highland jungle had been the Americans' bane from the day they arrived. Two Cobra gunships flew beside the colonel's chopper, heading west. Mountains and ridges rolled beneath them like a green sea, nothing distinguishing one from the next, no signs of human presence. The enemy troops swam invisibly beneath the treetops like schools of fish.

Meanwhile, Flannigan crawled to Recon's four fighting positions with instructions to conserve what little ammo remained. When he heard the two Cobras circling above, he pulled the ring on a smoke grenade. The helicopters banked sharply and dove in, miniguns snarling, rockets swishing from tubes. A hail of bullets and flechettes shredded the surrounding jungle. Every time he saw this, Flannigan wondered how any living thing could escape the hell pouring from the sky, but somehow, they always did.

Colonel Standley circled in his slick high above the strafing Cobras, monitoring the situation by radio. After several runs by the gunships, Danton judged the moment had arrived for Recon to break out of the encirclement. Two of the larger men took turns carrying Lucas, now unconscious, on their shoulders. Two more dragged the body of the RTO wrapped like a mummy in a couple of ponchos. Danton took the lead, keeping Recon moving in an easterly direction, while Flannigan covered the rear.

They were moving as fast as they could, relying on the low-flying Cobras to hold back the NVA. Standley watched with binoculars through the open door of the chopper, catching glimpses of the grunts moving like a column of ants through trees. He desperately wanted to help them, but what could he do? Perhaps he could find an opening in the canopy large enough for extraction. If Recon could hold out there long enough for relief to arrive . . . And he might even be able to land and take aboard the dead and wounded. The risk to himself didn't bother him. In fact, that was the point. He welcomed it.

He saw a clearing on a ridge some fifty meters southeast of Recon. Would it accommodate a landing? He directed his pilot to descend for a closer look. The chopper made a quick pass. The pilot advised that he couldn't land because of the severity of the grade, but he might be able to set one skid down and still avoid a blade strike on the high side. Standley gave Danton a direction that would take him to the clearing.

The NVA's firing had dwindled under the pressure of the Cobras. The grunts knew a pause in the pursuit meant nothing; the enemy liked to play a shell game, breaking contact in one place while massing out of view in another. Guided from above by Standley, the platoon ascended the ridge and found the clearing. Thirsty and exhausted, they assumed defensive positions. Now they could look down on the wilderness they had crossed in pursuit of the Montagnard woman. Where was the border? It was anyone's guess.

Out of nowhere, a Phantom jet screamed in over the platoon and released two bombs below them. A fiery orange and black ball mushroomed from the trees. Jackson drifted down to Flannigan's position. "Sweet smell of napalm," he said. "If we get outta Cambodia alive, no credit to that crazy motherfucker Danton."

"And what makes you think we're in Cambodia?" Flannigan said, knowing Jackson was probably right.

"Don't bullshit me, Top. The NVA was on R&R down there. Damn straight, we're over the border."

"You just mind your own business," he admonished the grunt.

"I'm makin' it my business. Lucas ain't lookin' good. That asshole wouldn't dust off his own mother. One of these days, we just might dust him off."

"That's crazy talk. Get your butt back up to your position."

A grunt popped smoke to mark the spot for Standley's helicopter to attempt a landing. Lucas, the other wounded, and the KIA lay beside the clearing. The Huey hovered like a hummingbird as the pilot deftly held the aircraft level, his gloved hand tweaking the cyclic stick, his eyes focused on the tips of the spinning blades and nothing else. The pilot slowly brought the chopper down but had to hover a few feet above the slope. Colonel Standley jumped out.

In the racket of the engine and blades, he didn't hear the shots fired from the top of the hill. Several rounds struck the tail and engine housing of the aircraft as Standley's feet hit the ground. He felt a blow to his shoulder, staggering him. The grunts opened up on the sniper above them while the dead and wounded were hastily lifted on board. A door gunner pulled Standley back inside as the helicopter rose, wheeled, and accelerated down the slope, skimming the treetops.

Parched and exhausted, the grunts of Recon prepared to link up with Alpha Company, which had secured a clearing on the Vietnamese side of the border. A Chinook circled high overhead, waiting to carry the platoon back to the base camp. As if on order, a rolling rumble announced the arrival of a squall, and in minutes, a deluge roared through the jungle canopy, providing cover for their escape.

Standley's helicopter landed on the airstrip at Camp Farrell, leaking fuel. The battalion surgeon removed a flattened bullet, probably ricochet, from his shoulder, and he returned to duty with his arm in a sling. The medal machine cranked. In addition to a Purple Heart, Standley's actions earned him a Bronze Star for valor. Lucas was not so fortunate. The delay in getting him treatment for the punji wounds caused septic shock, and he succumbed to his wounds. He was posthumously awarded a Purple Heart and a Bronze Star for valor. On the airplane carrying his body back to the States was the body of Flannigan's RTO.

The after-action report of the "enemy contact," the Army's fits-all-sizes euphemism for a firefight, mentioned nothing of Cambodia, only that it had occurred "near the border, west of Plei Doch." Sins of omission were easily ignored, and no one in the chain of command demanded an explanation, let alone contrition. Among the battalion's grunts, however, Danton's gamble and the contact inside Cambodia was another reason not to trust him.

16
STAND DOWN

The battalion returned to Camp Farrell to rest and reequip after more than two months of nonstop humping. A tent city, already occupied by the rest of the brigade, awaited it. For the entire brigade to stand down simultaneously was odd, a fact of only passing curiosity to soldiers accustomed to the inexplicable.

A few days to clean up, sleep in a dry tent, and eat mess hall food were a welcome relief from a primitive existence in the jungle. Card sharks would win their buddies of enough cash to make down payments on new cars waiting for them back home. *Patton* was showing nightly on an outdoor movie screen. The post exchange sold liquor by the imperial quart, and stoners found a ready supply of weed available from the "clerks and jerks." Officers and enlisted men socialized separately in their respective quarters and clubs. As long as the troops behaved, the officers cut them some slack.

In a camp with no plumbing, a warm shower was a luxury, and Hoffman knew where to find one. The engineers would not be denied any creature comfort that could be obtained with a little American ingenuity and available materials. They salvaged a tank from a wrecked water truck, mounted it on a scaffold, and filled it with water warmed by immersion heaters.

It was a half-mile walk across the post to the engineers' barrack. Hoffman set out on foot. Along the way, he passed scores of vacant boarded-up buildings. The Sixth Air Cavalry Division had built the camp and airfield years earlier to serve its huge squadron of helicopters. Keeping the birds flying and the troops supplied required a huge logistical operation. Now, the much leaner Twenty-fourth Division, which was more foot-mobile than airmobile, occupied only about half of the camp's footprint. Whole sections of unoccupied buildings gave some areas the appearance of abandonment.

Hoffman encountered a few soldiers in the engineers' area and went straight to the shower stalls, hoping to slip in and out unnoticed. He quickly stripped and opened a valve. The water flowed cool at first, then warm and plentiful, far preferable to the trickle from the canvas shower buckets back in the company area. He lathered with a bar of Palmolive Gold from a sundry pack and savored the first real bath he'd had since his R&R.

It was getting dark when he returned to his platoon's tent where a few soldiers rapped quietly; others played poker. Since his return from Australia, Hoffman had scribbled one brief letter to Susan, which he had handed to a door gunner on a resupply chopper for mailing. Now, the weight of combat lifted, she was all he could think about. Clara was lost to him, and it was as if Susan had stepped into the empty space. He began to write:

Dearest Susan,

It has been only a month since we met so unexpectedly. The short week we spent together was one of the happiest of my life, and

I miss you so much it hurts. Here I am, just trying to get out of this place alive. Maybe my feelings for you are not to be trusted. I know this sounds crazy, but I think I'm falling in love with you . . ."

Yes, it did sound crazy, boocoo dinky dow. Here was a guy she hardly knew, someone she might never see again, coming on to her. How did he expect her to respond to an emotional outburst like that? He tore up the letter and started over:

Dear Susan,

I am in the base camp now, washing the jungle from my body and enjoying a few days of leisure. We are preparing for a new mission. No one knows what it will be, but something big, we think. Pray that all goes well.

I can't tell you what a pleasure it was meeting you. Our week together was wonderful and so unexpected. I find myself wanting to see you as soon as my tour of duty here ends. Would you mind if I paid you a visit in October? I'm pretty sure I can catch a flight directly from Cam Ranh Bay to Sydney. You promised to show me Canberra, and I'll take you up on that, assuming you are still willing. If that is inconvenient or not possible, I won't be offended.

Affectionately,

Jack

Sufficiently anodyne. He dropped the letter in the mailbox at the battalion headquarters and headed for the officers' club, a repurposed storage building furnished with a bar and tables. It was packed, standing room only. Company grade officers, all newly returned from operations throughout the Central Highlands, shouted to be heard over their own voices and music played on a reel-to-reel tape deck:

Don't go around tonight
Well, it's bound to take your life,
There's a bad moon on the rise.

Two tiny Vietnamese bar girls dressed in colorful ao dai maneuvered through the crowd of giants, deftly carrying trays of drinks over their heads. Hoffman pushed his way to a bar. On the wall behind it hung the coat of arms of every regiment that operated from the camp in its six years of existence. Prominently displayed above them hung a photo of the commander-in-chief whose thin smile seemed as false as his plan to end the war. He ordered a beer and searched through a haze of cigarette smoke for someone he knew.

He felt one of the bar girls tapping him on the back. She pointed to a table on the other side of the room, where Todd Unnerfeld sat with two men, both pale faced and wearing newly issued jungle fatigues. Replacements, and Todd is no doubt scaring the shit out of them, Hoffman assumed. Beer in hand, he made his way to them. Five empty shot glasses were lined up in front of his friend. They told Hoffman all he needed to know about Unnerfeld's condition.

"Gentlemen," Unnerfeld slurred to the two others at the table, "this here's the officer with the highest IQ in the whole battalion, Lieutenant Jack Hoffman. Hell, maybe the whole damn army."

Hoffman said, "Thanks, Todd, but that's the liquor talking."

"In vino veritas, bro. Meet my new drinkin' buddies. These fine young officers arrived yesterday, highly trained killers, ready for ac-she-own. This here is, ah, ah . . . Damn, help me out, bro."

"Sarkowski, Roy Sarkowski," said one. His head was shaved close. Round, Army-issue glasses magnified his eyes and made him appear froglike.

"Okay, Ski then," Unnerfeld said. "And this here is ah, ah . . . No hints now . . ."

"Ben LoSalvo," the other interjected. He had a bad case of acne and could have passed for eighteen.

"Sal, thass right. All present and accounted for, sir," Unnerfeld said, saluting. "I was just telling these two heroes they'll soon be saving starving peasants from communism. Like those nice villagers we put on a chopper to Pleiku—lucky them. Right before we burned their village. Right, Jack?"

"Lighten up, Todd," Hoffman said. "Where you boys from?"

Sarkowski said, "Louisville."

LoSalvo said, "Gary, near Chicago."

"Jack knows where Gary is," Unnerfeld said. "He's Ivy League."

"Oh, what school?" Sarkowski asked.

"Dartmouth," Hoffman said.

"ROTC, then," Sarkowski assumed.

"OCS," Hoffman said.

"Us too, graduated together at Benning School for Boys," LoSalvo said.

"Fully qualified to eat from a can, sleep on the ground, and shit in a hole," Unnerfeld said.

"Any West Point and ROTC in the battalion?" Sarkowski asked.

"Not many. Allergic to bullets," Unnerfeld said.

"So how does someone with a degree from Dartmouth end up here?" LoSalvo asked.

"Ran out of deferments," Hoffman said.

"So he joins up, a bona fide fucking patriot, protecting our great country from enemies, foreign and domestic," Unnerfeld deadpanned. "Hoorah."

"What about you two?" Hoffman wondered, ignoring Unnerfeld's sarcasm.

Sarkowski said, "Was at the University of Kentucky, which I couldn't afford. Dropped out and went to work in construction. The draft board got on my case. Figured, what the hell, I'll finish up on the GI Bill."

"What about you, Sal?" Unnerfeld said. "What's your excuse?"

"Got married. Only lasted two years, and my ex turned me in. They told me I scored high on that test they gave at the induction center. Applied for OCS and got in. What about you, Unnerfeld?"

"Your turn, Unnerfeld," Sarkowski said. "Why are you here?"

"I wanted to come. Military service is a rite of passage where I come from in Alabama. Is it too late to change my mind?"

The four laughed. The conversation drifted to recent operations and what the veterans knew about the drawdown of troops. "The news back home is all about pulling out," LoSalvo noted. "Any chance we're next?" There was hopefulness in his voice.

"Just rumors," Hoffman said. "Besides, even if this division is next, don't count on going home with it. You'll just end up a replacement in a unit that's staying behind. But don't worry about being the last man to die in Vietnam. Be more worried about who's next."

"Well, I've got a candidate for that one," Unnerfeld said. "That crazy mutherfucker, Danton. After that last mission, he should face a court-martial, but they'll probably pin another medal on him."

"If crossing the border into Cambodia and almost getting his platoon wiped out makes him a hero," Hoffman said.

"Cambodia? Since when are we operating in Cambodia?" Sarkowski asked.

"Damn good question," Unnerfeld said.

"Strayed in, I'll wager," Hoffman said. "It happens."

"Give me a break," Unnerfeld guffawed. "The guy's a glory hound. Lost two good men so he could hang a few more hides on the wall. His ditty boppers hate him. I hate him."

"Maybe so, but Recon gets more Dink body count than the rest of us combined," Hoffman said.

"And more of ours delivered home in a refrigerator," Unnerfeld added.

The new men looked at one another as if none of this was to be taken seriously. They would soon find out. They were cherry boys, soon to be deflowered.

"Got your assignments yet?" Hoffman asked.

"Bravo Company," LoSalvo said. "We take command of our platoons tomorrow."

"Captain Shandly's outfit. Good man," Hoffman said. He finished his beer. "I've got a few things to do before I crash. See you back in the company area, Todd." He will probably be on his hands and knees, but why not? Tying one on was his way of escape.

Hoffman stepped out of the smokey air of the club into a clear, starry highland night. It was the dry season, cool and fresh. It felt good. He fell in with a rowdy gaggle of men heading for the evening's entertainment, a band brought in by the USO. A Jeep passed from behind, gunning its motor to clear a path, and lurched to a stop. "Need a lift, soldier?"

"Hey, Sleeve, how's it hangin'?" Hoffman said. It was Gildersleeve, First Platoon leader, night duty officer.

"Off to a shitty start, dude. Hop in." Hoffman hopped into the back seat, and the driver proceeded in low gear.

"Of all nights to draw duty officer. Starts with a battle royale at the EM Club," Gildersleeve said. "Took one kid to the infirmary with a mangled arm from a broken bottle. Another idiot dislocated his knuckles beating on someone's head. Lunatics."

"What started it?"

"The usual nonsense, some special forces cat questioning the manhood of one of our guys. Are these guys fighting the same war? Why me, Lord?"

"Sibling rivalry, Todd. They're just letting off some steam."

"Yeah, but do they have to kill one another? And now I have this damn concert to contend with. How 'bout hanging with me, pal? Might need some help."

"Okay, but only if Hope brought Welch."

"In your dreams, pal. The USO doesn't carry enough insurance. I think it's one of those Filipino garage bands."

The Jeep pulled up beside a makeshift stage. About a hundred troops stood in the dark below the platform, waiting for the show to begin. A generator hummed, powering the stage lights. A rowdy group of heavy drinkers gathered in front of the stage, while four musicians did a sound check with their instruments. They looked young enough to need parental permission to be there, but then, so did many in the audience.

The band opened with a song that rattled two huge speakers mounted on poles. It was a number the testosterone-soaked audience recognized from the first few chords, and they whistled their approval of what they saw next: two girls in miniskirts and knee-high boots prancing across the stage to take up their mics.

"You've been messin' where you shouldn't have been messin'
And now someone else is getting all your best

These boots are made for walkin'

And that's just what they'll do . . ."

The Filipino kids came prepared to play songs from the Top 20 in the States. It was anyone's guess whether they understood the words, but it didn't matter: the sound of home filled a big hole in carefree young lives interrupted by the war. The two officers watched with growing concern as the behavior of the crowd nearest the front grew more raucous with each song. Then, as Gildersleeve feared, a grunt vaulted onto the stage and commenced to bump and grind with one of the girls. Fueled by liquor and encouraged by the cheers and laughter of the audience, several more leaped onto the platform and joined in. In seconds, half a dozen sweaty, sotted young men surrounded the terrified girls.

“Okay, Jack, I’ve seen enough,” Gildersleeve said. “Follow me.” The two went to the generator behind the stage. “I’m going to open the breaker and cut the power to the lights,” Gildersleeve said. “Count to twenty and close it.”

The lights went out, the music abruptly stopped, and more than a hundred men stood in darkness. When the light was restored, the band and dancers were gone, and the miscreants were scrambling off the stage, leaving Lieutenant Gildersleeve at a microphone.

“Alright, gentlemen, the show’s over,” he shouted. “Return to your company areas on the double.” Scattered boos and objections rose from the troops, but Gildersleeve was adamant: “No. You’ve had your fun, the band is gone, and they aren’t coming back. You will vacate the area in good order, and you will do it now.”

Four MPs arrived in two Jeeps and parked near the stage, aiming their high beams at the crowd. But their intervention was unnecessary. Most of the audience had begun to comply, and the troublemakers joined them.

“Band wasn’t worth a damn anyway,” someone grumbled.

“Yeah, but better than nothin’. Fucking lifers spoil all the fun,” his buddy said.

Hoffman had to admire Gildersleeve’s grit. “Good command presence up there, Sleeve,” he said. “You have a future in this man’s army.”

“Yeah, I’d eat a pound of C-4 and become a human Claymore mine before I re-upped. Can I give you a lift someplace?”

“No, rather walk. Think I’ll head back to the tent and write some letters.” Hoffman owed his parents an update. He never had much to say but felt he needed to tell them he was okay. The paperback copy of *The Electric Kool-Aid Acid Test* he had purchased at the PX was waiting for him, too.

It was a moonless night, and there were few road lamps along the way. At first, he didn't recognize the black soldier who approached him, asking for a light for his cigarette. Hoffman flipped the lid on his Zippo. The flame exposed the face of Specialist 4 Calvin Jackson, Recon Platoon. Before volunteering for Recon, Jackson had been in Delta Company. He was known to question orders, but he could be counted on under fire. He was tough, an alpha male among his peers, white and black. Hoffman liked him.

"What's up, Jackson? Staying out of trouble?" Hoffman asked.

"Never make no trouble, LT."

"Sure, Jackson," Hoffman said. "Heard Recon had quite a contact last week."

"We was in Cambodia, LT. Had no business bein' there. Lieutenant Danton was goin' too far chasin' after that woman, but he kept pushin'. We lost that dog handler, Lucas, for no good reason."

"No one's fault. It happens, Jackson. You know that."

"Didn't have to. Danton killed him."

"Come on, Jackson; you don't mean that."

"Damn straight I do. Lucas should a' been dusted off. We dragged him along, watchin' him bleed to death, man. Danton, he don't listen to no one. One of these days . . ."

Jackson was angry and grieving. Blame the lifers; blame men like Danton. It helped to have someone to blame.

Hoffman said, "I'm sure Danton didn't want that man to die."

"He knows what he doin', crazy motherfucker," Jackson snapped.

"You volunteered for Recon. You knew what you were getting into."

"Didn't volunteer for this kind of bullshit."

"Then request a transfer back to a line platoon. No one is making you stay."

Jackson scoffed, "Danton would. Besides, I don't cut and run on my bros."

"Well, you shouldn't be wandering around in the dark by yourself. Go chill with your brothers and get a good night's sleep. You'll feel better about things in the morning."

Jackson stared at his boots, thinking. He took a long drag on his cigarette, dropped it, and stepped on it. "Anyway, thanks for the light, LT," he said, turning away.

"Any time," Hoffman said.

"And LT, sixty-two and a wakeup."

There were more soldiers like him now, men who had had enough killing and dying. Time was both their ally and their enemy. Eventually it would all be over, one way or another.

The sounds of the camp suffused the still highland night air, a diesel truck idling somewhere, small generators humming, the burst of a flare over the bunker line, and the muted voices of men moving about in the dark. The oiled dirt road took Hoffman past the airconditioned trailers of brigade headquarters. As he approached, a door flew open, and half a dozen figures burst out, sprinting to a large heavily sandbagged bunker across the road. "Incoming," one of them shouted as he passed.

A moat of bunkers and barbed wire surrounded the huge camp. Beyond that, an apron of the defoliated jungle. Nothing, however, could prevent the VC from dropping mortars and rockets into the perimeter. Hoffman didn't hear the first projectiles strike; they must have landed some distance away, perhaps over by the airstrip. The artillery battery's response was full throated. A siren began to wail.

Hoffman broke into a run and took a shortcut through an area of abandoned storage buildings. Alone now, he ran along, listening to the tit-for-tat firing of incoming and outgoing. He wasn't too concerned until a rocket struck some Conex containers a few dozen meters to his left. Spotting what appeared to be a fighting position behind a wall of sandbags, he leaped into it.

"Hey, dickhead, this ain't no Motel 6," growled someone in the hole. "Find your own goddamn accommodations."

"It's dickhead, *sir*," Hoffman snapped.

"Oh, was I insubordinate, *sir*? I apologize; I really do."

Hoffman couldn't see his face in the dark, but he knew the voice. "Danton?"

"None other, Ivy League."

"You're a real comedian, you know that?"

"Have you no sense of humor, Ivy?"

"Obviously, this hole's not big enough for both of us," Hoffman said. He tried to get up, but Danton grabbed him by the arm.

"Get down, numb nuts, before Charlie gets a Bingo," Danton said. "Under the circumstances, you can stay."

"I'll take my chances," Hoffman said, freeing his arm from Danton's grip and getting to his feet.

"Awe, come on, Ivy; be a sport and join me for a little nip. Besides, there's something I've been meanin' to ask you."

A rocket exploded somewhere off to their right, and Hoffman reflexively dropped to the ground. The two men lay side by side, listening to the camp siren's mournful moan. Danton said with disgust, "A few rice eaters with a piece of fucking pipe have the whole goddamn division crawling around like earthworms." He sat up, belched, and thrust a bottle of Hiram Walker at Hoffman. "Here, this will settle your nerves." His breath could have fueled a blow torch.

"No thanks. My nerves are fine," Hoffman said.

"Oh, come on, Ivy; don't be an arrogant bastard. I may be a redneck, but I'm not a bad sort. I've read a few books, too. And I can be downright charmin'."

"Charming as a scorpion," Hoffman said.

"So I've given you a hard time. It's for your own damn good. Besides, you can help me with something that's been bothering me. It's important."

Another of Danton's entertainments? Perhaps not. Something in his voice made Hoffman curious. Danton was known to be a heavy drinker, and it was probably just the liquor loosening his tongue. Hoffman took the bottle and swallowed hard. The whiskey burned going down. "Okay, Danton, I'm listening."

Flares lit the sky like distant lightning. Skittish clerks and cooks on the bunker line fired at shadows. Danton belched loudly. "'Scuse me, Ivy. You're probably thinkin' I was raised in a trailer park. Ain't so. But unlike you, I wasn't born with a silver spoon in my mouth."

"You don't know anything about me."

"I know this much: you wouldn't have set foot in my world a few years ago. And I'd have been a turd in the punch bowl in yours. But here we are, hunkered down in the same filthy hole in this God-forsaken place. Ironic, ain't it?"

"Feeling sorry for yourself, Danton?" Hoffman said, taking another pull from the bottle and handing it back.

"No regrets, Ivy. I'm going to make the most of it, grab for the brass ring, as they say. This is my destiny. I'm not just Christmas help like you are."

"I didn't have to come. I volunteered, just like you did," Hoffman said. He took another drink and looked up at the stars. The sky rotated ten degrees to the right, then swung back.

"I guess you wouldn't understand, Ivy," Danton said. The bottle sloshed. "Put it this way. I'm here to stay. When you have your two-Martini lunch on Wall Street, I'll be eatin' C-rations in the jungle or someplace else. Maybe the desert next time."

"Very dramatic, Danton."

"No, just reality. I know what I'm doing here, but what about you? Last time I checked, we were here to kill slopes. The more, the better. You seem to have a problem with that."

"It's not that simple."

"It *is* that simple. Take notes, Ivy League. We hammer 'em until they got no choice but to lay down their weapons and go back to planting rice. It doesn't take no sheepskin to understand that."

"Really think we can kill our way out of this?"

"We aren't paid to think."

"About the ones going home in a body bag?"

"This is war, man. People die in wars. What we have here is a test of wills. Can't you see that? The sooner we break theirs, the sooner it's over. Dig it."

"Looks to me like it's our wills getting broken."

"Only if we let them, Hoffman, and that's exactly what you and your type are doing."

"What are you talking about?"

"Oh, come on, Hoffman. Our orders are clear: find the enemy and kill him. But you avoid contact. You aren't the only one; the whole goddamn bunch of you do it. That's a dereliction of duty at best, at worse, cowardice. No doubt in my military mind."

"This is taking us nowhere," Hoffman said, getting up to leave. "Thanks for the drink."

"What's the matter? Can't take the truth? I haven't even asked my question yet."

"You know everything, don't you?"

"Don't be an asshole. Sit down and explain something to me. Is it the killing that bothers you? You don't seem to have the stomach for it."

"Of course, it bothers me," Hoffman said. "I mean you'd have to be psycho if it didn't."

"Oh, excuse me, your holiness. What do you think those crossed rifles on your lapel mean, membership in a gun club? You missed your call. You should be a fucking priest."

"Do you really think more killing is going to end this war?" Hoffman rejoined.

"I've already made myself clear on that issue. Besides, I'm the one asking the question," Danton said.

"You apparently don't ask enough questions," Hoffman countered.

"As few as possible. Hesitate in this business, and you can end up with your mug in the hometown newspaper, framed in black."

Glass shattered somewhere outside the hole where Danton tossed the empty bottle. For the first time, Hoffman pitied him. Three or four years ago, when victory was believed possible, the risks he took would have been expected, even lauded. But he arrived on the stage late, and the tragedy was in its final act. Only he benefitted from his small bloody victories.

There had been no firing for five minutes; the camp's artillery seemed to be standing down. "This war is over, Danton," Hoffman said.

"Hell, I know that, Ivy," Danton said.

17
LAST CHANCE GLORY

The company grade officers converged on the battalion headquarters for the briefing. Colonel Standley leaned against a podium, chatting with the other battalion commanders and staff. Hoffman couldn't help noticing their close shaves, fresh haircuts, starched jungle fatigues, and glossy jungle boots. These guys slept in clean sheets behind a mosquito net, sipped Cutty Sark, and dined on T-bone steaks.

An easel held a large board covered by a drape, raising the curiosity of those assembled. The volume of conversation rose as more officers converged for the briefing. The purpose of the rush back to the base camp had been tightly held, the subject of much speculation. Many of the battalion's company grade officers had never met prior to the standdown, having gone directly to their assigned units in the jungle upon arrival.

Someone shouted, "Tensh hut," and the door to an adjoining office swung open. The officers stood as the brigade commander, General Falconer, walked briskly to the dais. Now it was obvious that, whatever brought them together, it must be big. "Take your seats, gentlemen," Falconer said crisply.

He was a short, wiry man with a voice that belonged to a much larger body. A hooked nose gave him a birdlike appearance. His jungle fatigues were tailored to fit, not too tight, not too loose. Master jump wings, Ranger tab, and a Combat Infantry Badge with a star demanded obeisance. A holstered pearl-handled Colt .45 service pistol hung on a belt. The podium was made ready for him with a box to stand on, but he stood clear of it for what he had to say:

"Gentlemen, four days ago, elements of three divisions of the US Army, along with several ARVN divisions, crossed into Cambodia from Three Corps and commenced operations. As I speak, these units are sweeping into staging areas of the North Vietnamese Army and encountering stiff resistance."

He had the full attention of his audience. The US did not openly operate in Cambodia. To be sure, in recent months, a nightly rumble to the west betrayed carpet bombing, but enemy sanctuaries in Cambodia were malignant tumors that had been spreading into Vietnam for years. They should have been rooted out on the ground much earlier, denied a chance to metastasize. Well, it has finally come to this, but to what purpose? Another futile show of force? Another threat to escalate? But why the withdrawal of troops if that were the case?

The general turned to the draped easel. "Colonel Standley, please."

Standley tugged on the drape, and it dropped, revealing a map of the border of Vietnam with Laos and Cambodia stretching from the DMZ to the Mekong Delta. The officers leaned forward to see dozens of small flagged pins representing US forces in operational areas west of Saigon, in the Mekong Delta and inside

Cambodia. A low rumble of voices filled the room as the men began to comprehend what they were looking at.

"Tomorrow, beginning at 0900 hours, you will convoy to Plei Mrong here." He tapped the map west of Pleiku with a pointer. "It's 1500 now, so you don't have a lot of time to get ready to move out. You won't be getting much sleep tonight. You will spend tomorrow night bivouacked at Plei Mrong. It's the site of an old Special Forces camp. You will combat assault into Cambodia in the morning."

Hoffman had heard stories about the camp, LZ Mirage. Green Berets there had provided training and support for local Montagnard fighters, but it was too remote to be adequately defended. Villages in the area were relocated, and the camp was abandoned. A dirt airstrip was all that remained.

"You will establish two fire support bases in Cambodia, each with a battery of 105 howitzers. You will have all the gunship support you need from base camp, fixed-wing from Phu Cat. Your battalion commanders will fill you in on details, where your companies will be positioned, and what you are to do when you arrive."

Intelligence reports, he continued, indicated the existence of weapons and rice caches, as well as training facilities for green NVA troops heading south. All materials captured would either be removed or destroyed in place. The headquarters of a sapper battalion was recently detected in the area and a bonus if found and engaged.

The operation had been kept under tight wraps, he said, and had been announced only the day before to the American people on TV by the president. "Our objectives are limited: hit fast, deprive the enemy of food and weapons caches, then withdraw. Search and destroy. I don't expect we'll be in Cambodia for more than a few weeks, a month at most, but events will dictate the length of our stay."

The officers peered at the map. The terrain to the west of the Annamese Range was a plateau, much flatter, rolling. There was no indication of villages. Several blue lines meandered west from the highlands, emptying into the Mekong. General Falconer said aerial surveillance found crude dirt roads through the brigade's prospective area of operation, some having been improved in recent months.

"We've been able to detect movements of enemy forces through this area, here, here, and here. It's possible you will encounter rolling stock: trucks, heavy equipment, and possibly personnel carriers and even a few Russian tanks."

He tapped the map with the pointer. His West Point class ring looked too large for his small hand. "Understand this. The war you find over there may not be the one you know, the sudden ambushes and quick firefights. Battles with large contingents of NVA could extend over hours or even days. Do not, and I repeat, do not pause in the middle of the fight to recover your KIAs. It will only expose you to more casualties. The dead will be recovered as battlefield conditions permit."

Hoffman wondered how the others were reacting, but he resisted the urge to look around. The general's voice rose: "Gentlemen, the success of this operation is essential if we are going to pass the baton to the South Vietnamese forces. The enemy must not be allowed to build strength along the border, then launch an attack when we leave. But this is personal. We've been fighting with one hand tied behind our backs for years. Let's kick some butt, take names, and leave with our heads high. Godspeed, and I'll see you on Cambodian soil."

The officers responded with "Hoorahs." It was the liturgically correct response to the high priest's benediction, but it lacked enthusiasm. After years of war, Vietnam was a battlefield they knew—this was a strike into the unknown, the heart of darkness.

Hoffman left the room pondering what would come next. Heads held high, the general said, or a last desperate attempt to prove we really didn't have to leave at all. The US had invaded Vietnam expecting a speedy victory and exit, but Vietnam was like the fairytale tar baby. Every blow struck seemed to require another, to no effect except to trap the US forces in an unwinnable war. The North had outlasted its opponents, as it had the French. No one, from the lowest private to the generals in the Joint Chiefs of Staff, really believed the ARVN could hold out for long against the northern forces. "Vietnamization" of the war was less a strategy than an expediency and a fig leaf.

Hoffman joined a somber Captain Gilman and the other platoon leaders for the walk back to the company area. The oiled clay road took them near the San Son River, a sluggish stream that cut through the north end of the base camp. Deuce-and-a-half trucks were parked wheel-deep in the river while their drivers bathed them, dousing them with buckets of water as if they were elephants.

Unnerfeld said, "I suspected something was up when they yanked us out of the boonies like a bad tooth, but nothing like this."

Gilman said, "Hell, I only learned of it just before the general's briefing when the XO distributed maps."

Hoffman said, "And yet, the operation began two days ago down south, and the folks back home saw it on TV before we knew about it. So much for the element of surprise."

Gilman said, "Well, better late than never. It's about time we hunted them down in Cambodia. Brief your men and get them supplied by 1800 hours, every weapon cleaned and inspected, and extra magazines and ammo for everyone. We'll hump with five days' rations. Make sure every swinging dick gets to the water trailer."

The troops took the news as they did every order from on high, with sober resignation. There was nothing they could do about it, so they concentrated on the little things that could become big things, cleaning their weapons and supplying themselves with ammo and equipment. Fully loaded, they would shoulder up to one hundred pounds of ammunition, gear and water. They had to hurry to preserve enough time before dark to write letters. Some took time out to attend religious services offered by the brigade's Catholic and Protestant "sky pilots."

Gilman convened his platoon leaders to brief them on the order of march. The Third Platoon would board choppers first and assault a predetermined LZ. The rest of the company would follow and immediately secure the LZ as the site of the fire support base. It would be called "LZ California" for a reason no one knew. The rest of the battalion, its artillery, mortars, and staff, would follow. Except for the location, it seemed routine.

The next morning, the battalion ate a tepid breakfast ladled from marmite containers. The powdered eggs were "OD" (olive drab), the pancakes rubbery as tire patches, and the ham tough as shoe leather, but they ate as if the meal was their last. Delta Company had ten minutes to wolf it down, collect its gear, and move to a line of deuce-and-a-half trucks. Bumper to bumper, it seemed to stretch a mile.

Platoon leaders took a nose count. There was none of the usual joking to break the tension before an assault. Delta Company waited for the rest of the incursion force to board the trucks. Finally, the line of vehicles came to life, and the convoy rumbled out the main gate, heading west on a paved road. It passed through several small villages where naked young children with distended bellies pleaded with outstretched arms for C-rations. Several years earlier, the sides of the road had been sprayed with Agent Orange, leaving skeletal trees.

An hour and a half later, the convoy arrived at a hastily prepared bivouac in an open field near LZ Mirage, the abandoned special forces camp less than a kilometer from the border. There the troops would spend the night camped on a field stripped of all vegetation. Every passing vehicle raised choking clouds of red dust. The men dug shallow slit trenches and cursed the powdery airborne dust that filled their noses and coated their sweaty bodies.

The unusually large movement of troops could not escape the notice of the omnipresent camp followers. They descended like locusts on the bivouac area, arriving on foot, bicycle, and motor scooter with an assortment of iced soft drinks, pornographic post-cards, love beads, peace medallions, knockoff Rolex watches, bush hats—anything that might attract the fancy of young soldiers. And that included prostitutes. Pimps had already pitched small tents in the brush near the road.

At dusk, Hoffman gazed across an open area larger than two football fields dotted by poncho shelters. It reminded him of old photos of Civil War encampments. Evening meals of C-rations were warming over heat tabs. Men fussed with their gear, spoke little, and milled about listlessly. The impending assault weighed heavily on everyone's minds. Years earlier, their predecessors may have operated together in such numbers, but this was new. If they ran into enemy forces of similar strength, they fully expected a major battle. Some would not leave Cambodia alive.

At 1900 hours, the presence of every grunt was required in his own platoon's area for the night. Galvin checked the roster and reported to Hoffman that one man, Armijo, was missing. "Last time anyone saw Armijo, he was headed up the road alone," Galvin said.

"For Chrissake, for some tail? Here?"

"He told his friends he didn't want to die a virgin. There was a long line over at those tents."

"Incredible. How many virgins do we have in this outfit, anyway?"

"State of mind, LT."

"Well, find him and see that no one else sneaks out."

"Yes, sir."

A half hour later, Galvin returned with Armijo in tow, looking like a whipped dog. “Found him over at the aid station,” Galvin said.

Hoffman said, “You were AWOL, soldier, and for that filthy business? I hope it was worth it. You should get an Article 15, but I’ll let you off this time. Just don’t ever pull that stunt again.”

“Yes, sir,” Armijo said, turning away sheepishly.

“Tell him why you went to visit the doc, Armijo,” Galvin prompted.

“Awe, Razor, do I hafta?”

“You heard me.”

“Well, sir, I think I got VD. I wanted a shot.”

“What would your mother say about this?”

Armijo just looked sorrowfully at his boots. Hoffman said, “Okay, get your sorry ass over to the water trailer and clean up. I hope you learned a lesson.”

Galvin shook his head as the miscreant slank off. “Nasty business. The doc gave him an injection. I’ve told them a hundred times to stay clear of the whores.”

“Not our job to raise ’em, Razor, just keep ’em alive. I’ll take the first watch. Why don’t you try to bag some z’s?”

“No, you go ahead, LT. Don’t feel much like sleeping anyway.”

Hoffman had noticed a subtle change in Galvin lately. He was normally a cool head, never rattled, but he was taciturn and seemed distracted. He often had that thousand-yard stare. With only three weeks separating him from his freedom bird, a case of short-timer’s nerves was understandable. Maybe the Cambodian thing had him worried.

"Something bothering you, Razor? I mean you've seemed a little down lately."

"It's nothing."

"Come on, sergeant. Level with me."

"Just damn tired, LT. Spent. I have some bad feelings about this operation. On top of that, things aren't going well at home."

"Want to talk about it?"

"Well, it's about my lady."

The younger men often spoke of their sexual exploits back in the States, real and no doubt imagined. Sex was constantly on their minds. But Galvin never spoke about the special woman in his life. Judging from the letters the sergeant received, there was one, but Hoffman didn't want to pry.

"You two been together long?" Hoffman asked, easing into the subject.

"Couple of years." He paused. "Three if this one counts."

"It does," Hoffman said.

"Haven't had a letter from her in over a month."

"A month, huh?"

"Yeah. We were serious. Asked her to marry me and she said yes, soon as I got home. It wasn't exactly the engagement she was looking for, but we were really happy. Least, I was."

"Razor, look, I'm sure there's a good reason you haven't heard from her. You'll be able to iron things out when you get back to The World."

"If she's found someone else, so be it. Can't blame her. Anyway, I'm done with this man's army. No reenlistment. When I get home, I'm going back to work at the paper mill. If I get home, that is."

"What do you mean, 'if'? You shouldn't be thinking that way. You know that."

In two tours in the Nam, Galvin had had two Purple Hearts, several Bronze Stars, and one Silver Star. He'd humped in the Iron Triangle and the Central Highlands and seen it all. To the kids in the platoon, he was preternatural, but the man speaking now was a mere mortal. Hoffman was worried about him.

"Look, Razor, if you're in a bad place, I'll gin up some excuse to send you to the rear. I can make it happen with the captain."

"Thanks, LT, but that's a big negative. I can't dash on these kids now. I wouldn't be able to live with myself."

"Razor, trust me; we'll be okay without you. You'll be on that Freedom Bird in a few weeks, and this will be history."

"No, I'm stayin'. You get some rest; I'll make the rounds and make sure everything's cool."

Hoffman lay under his poncho shelter surrounded by shuffling boots and muted voices of restless men. As he did every night since his R&R, he sought an escape in dreams about Susan. One week, one beautiful week, was all they had together. He desperately wanted to be with her again. Was he making too much of their relationship? Did her embraces mean anything more than sympathy for a lonely soldier?

He was getting a letter from her every week now. They might have been written by any friend—chatty and news about her adjustments to life in Sydney. She was thinking about renting her own apartment; she planned to seek certification to teach, and she was taking piano lessons. In his letters, he related little of what he was doing, just that he was on an operation and he was okay. He dwelt instead on his plans post-Vietnam: a new car, a sailboat, and law school on the GI Bill.

But would she be part of his plan? He didn't dare suggest it. What he really wanted to say had to wait until he could return to Sydney, but approval of a second R&R was highly unlikely. With the withdrawal of troops underway, combat officers were in short supply. He promised he would come as soon as he completed his tour of duty. He wrote how grateful he was for the time they had together, that he missed her terribly. She wrote she missed him, too, and was praying for his safety. Nothing passionate, no commitments.

But she was filling Hoffman's deep need for something to hold on to in a time of existential uncertainty. He had arrived in Vietnam accepting that he might not get home alive. Certainly, he wanted to survive, but she gave him a reason to live he never expected. They were strangers, brought together by fate, sharing the most intimate details of their lives. He sifted his memory for every moment they spent together: their evening strolls by the harbor, her talk about growing up in Vancouver, and a relationship there that was ending. He shared with her details about his life in Seattle, about Dartmouth and about Clara.

Preparations in the encampment for the incursion continued through the night. It was a huge logistical effort to move a brigade so quickly. Hoffman tried to catch an hour or so of sleep, while engineers and support personnel readied supplies and equipment for the airlift. The noise didn't bother him; he was constantly exhausted and had conditioned himself to sleep under the barrels of firing howitzers. He had just dozed off when he felt a nudge on his boot. It was Sergeant Galvin: "Showtime, LT."

He looked bleary-eyed at the iridescent hands of his watch. It was 0430. He crawled out from under his shelter. Everywhere in the clearing, men were breaking camp in the murky pre-dawn darkness, silently rolling up their ponchos, cinching their rucks, and checking their weapons. "On the double, Second Platoon," Galvin prodded, pacing among the men. "Top off your canteens if you haven't. We're due on the pad in thirty minutes, so get your shit together."

Hoffman grabbed his ruck and his M-16. When everyone was ready, he led them across the bivouac area to the field where the battalion would stand for a final inspection. Six hundred shadowy figures scuffled out of the night and lined up in rows at arm's length. As the last of them took their positions, brush strokes of magenta and cyan streaked the horizon.

The taking of roll call filled the morning silence with shouted names: Italian, German, and Polish names; English, Scandinavian, and Hispanic names; and American names. Company commanders conducted a walk-through inspection of the troops. With all present and accounted for, shouted commands echoed down the long chain of platoons, and the battalion marched to the airstrip where the first flight of Huey slicks was waiting.

A morning dew settled the dust raised by the frenetic arrival of the brigade the previous day. As the sun broke over the Annamites, the helicopters woke like dragonflies. Delta Company, the first in the battalion to board, loped to its assigned aircraft.

One by one, the choppers lifted off with their grim-faced passengers, their legs hanging from the doors.

Would the LZ be hot? It was supposed to have been scouted, but one just never knew. He was concerned about Razor Galvin's mood but not in the least worried about whether the sergeant would come through if the NVA were waiting. Hoffman would ride the first of the platoon's three birds, Galvin the last. As Hoffman climbed aboard his chopper, he shouted to Galvin, "Breakfast in Cambodia." Galvin managed a smile.

It was a fine morning for an invasion. The helicopter climbed to two thousand feet and sailed serenely in the still, cool air, its companion birds sailing along on the right and left. The grunts pulled in their legs and rested against their rucks, cradling their M-16s and machine guns on their laps. Hoffman had known these guys only a matter of months, and yet he cared about them like brothers. He had given up any pursuit of holiness in high school, but a Hail Mary came unsummoned.

A vast trackless wilderness stretched placidly beneath the chopper. A silver thread of river wound through the forest toward the edge of a cliff, where it fell into a cloud of mist. This was the densely forested landscape of Ratanakiri Province, the sanctuary of the NVA. Scattered patches of cleared land appeared here and there, but Hoffman saw no other indications of human presence and no hint of the bitter struggle everyone aboard the helicopters fully expected. Hoffman figured they were well inside Cambodia now. The LZ couldn't be much farther.

Neither of the warrant officers at the helicopter's controls appeared old enough to purchase a legal beer in Washington

State. The copilot occasionally glanced at an open map on his lap, his lips occasionally moving against his headset's microphone. By evening, the fliers would return to Camp Farrell for beer and pizza, or not. They were vulnerable targets on a hot LZ with no place to hide. The grunts didn't envy them.

The platoon had been airborne only about ten minutes when a quilt of slash-and-burn clearings appeared below. Rice and cassava, Hoffman speculated, food for the villagers and the NVA. The slick began a rapid ear-popping descent, and the door gunners got to their feet and made sure the ammunition belts were properly lined up in the receivers of their M-60s.

The chopper banked steeply, affording Hoffman a full view of a field of high grass. The grunts on board scooted to the doors and reached for the skids with their boots. The chopper's downwash spread the grass below, exposing the ground a good eight feet below. The bird hovered, and the copilot turned, looking expectantly at the men behind him. He wasn't going to land.

"Not again," Hoffman muttered. He stood beside Sullivan, gathering courage for what he knew would be a jarring collision with the ground. Sullivan's eyes reflected his own reluctance to jump. The RTO slipped out of his ruck, radio attached, and dropped it into the grass. Hoffman quickly slid out of his ruck, too, and they both stepped into thin air.

Hoffman's legs buckled, and his right knee slammed into his chin. He staggered to his feet like a boxer after a ten count and retrieved his weapon and steel pot, which lay near his ruck in the thick grass. Gathering his men was the first order of business, and he called out for his RTO Sullivan and the radio as his helicopter skimmed away over the treetops. Only after the chopper's departure did the firing of AK-47s become audible.

Hoffman wondered why the LZ was undefended by the Third Platoon, which was supposed to secure the LZ. Where the hell were they? The incoming fire seemed to be coming from the tree line to the north. He rolled behind a large stump, shouting for his RTO. He tasted blood, and only then realized that he bit his tongue in his collision with the earth.

"Over here, LT," Sullivan yelled from the thick brush a few meters away.

"Come to me. I need that radio."

Sullivan's head popped up, drawing several shots that missed high. He low-crawled to Hoffman.

"Third Platoon was coming in first," the RTO complained. "Don't see 'em, and can't raise 'em on the horn."

"Because they aren't here," said Hoffman. "Give me that handset."

Several attempts to contact the Third Platoon's Lieutenant Gildersleeve went unanswered. Captain Gilman wasn't responding either. The battalion frequency was a bedlam of back and forth as units landed and tried to assemble. No help there, Hoffman concluded as shots whizzed from the tree line. "Where the hell is Razor?" he cried out to no one in particular.

"Saw two birds hover south of ours," Sullivan said. "One must have taken some hits 'cause it was spillin' fuel when it passed over us."

Hoffman keyed the handset and repeated Galvin's call sign. Hearing the sergeant's voice was an immense relief. "Your chopper put you down north of mine. I've got most of the men here with me," Galvin said.

"Fire a flare, and we'll come to you," Hoffman said.

"No, stay put. I saw where you landed. Better I come and lead you back."

The high grass, brush, and woody debris denied the platoon's attackers clear shots but also hindered Hoffman's assessment of his platoon's situation. Standing upright and exposing one's self was risky. A fine mess we're in now, he thought. Just then, Galvin appeared, dodging like a deer through the tall grass and fallen timber. Hoffman watched in admiration as Galvin defied the enemy's fire.

"Most of the small arms fire is coming from those trees east of us," the sergeant confirmed, panting from his dash. "I've found a little cover in a dry creek bed. Follow me; just keep your heads down."

Hoffman and the others from his bird followed Galvin through the chest-high grass to the brushy swale where the rest of the platoon had taken cover and was setting up a defensive perimeter. Hoffman wanted to know if anyone was hit in the landing. "Three. Doc is working on 'em," Galvin said.

Hoffman weighed his options. He feared more casualties if the platoon tried to move, but staying put didn't seem like a good idea either. How many NVA were in that tree line? Where was the Third Platoon, the rest of the company? Obviously, something had gone haywire with the landing.

"Delta Six, Two Six. Do you read me? Over," Hoffman voiced as calmly as he could into the horn. "Delta Six, this is Two Six. Give me your location. Over."

"Just landed," Gilman responded. "Your birds must have set you down in the wrong place. I hear firing. Over."

"Hot LZ. This location was supposed to be secured."

"No problems where we are. Judging from the firing I can hear, we're probably about a klick east of your position. Can you move?"

"Negative. Pinned down. Over."

"Can you estimate how many NVA? Over."

"Hard to say, maybe a dozen. They're firing from the tree line to my north. Over."

"Stand by. I'll send Tiger Six to help and get a gunship headed your way."

"Roger. Make it fast."

Hoffman pulled his map from his hip pocket. It wasn't any help, showing little contour and no prominent terrain features he could use to pinpoint his position.

Galvin joined Hoffman after checking the defensive perimeter. Hoffman said, "You won't believe this, but the rest of the company is a klick east of here. They dropped us in the wrong place."

"You're shitting me."

"Shit you not."

The firing was coming now from several directions. The attackers were spreading out, trying to put the platoon in the crossfire. The medic was frantically working on one of the wounded.

"How bad is he, Razor?"

"Bad. Sucking chest wound. Junior was hit in the hand. Hammer took one in the thigh."

Slow down and think, Hoffman urged himself. The enemy fire seemed to be getting heavier. Were more enemy troops joining the fight? He desperately needed that gunship Gilman had promised. The battalion's artillery wasn't set up and ready to fire, but there were some long guns, 155-mm and 175-mm canons, on the border. They were within range.

Just when things couldn't get much worse, there was no mistaking the *shhhhhhht crump, shhhhhht crump* of incoming shells.

"Mortars," Galvin shouted. "Get your heads down."

"Dig in," Hoffman yelled, but it was too late for that. The enemy's mortars walked within a few meters of the perimeter. Shrapnel buzzed over the men's heads. Sullivan spun the radio dial to the Red Legs frequency, and Hoffman called for a fire mission. A response came from a mobile 175-mm unit stationed near the border, about twenty miles away. The long gun wasn't very precise, but its 174-pound projectile would make a big impression on the attackers.

Because he couldn't be sure of his position, prudence dictated that he call for a marking round and adjust from there. He shouted map coordinates into the handset, and the artilleryman in the fire direction center repeated them slowly and calmly as if he was preparing to solve a math problem.

"Heads down, here it comes," Hoffman shouted to his platoon.

The round made a vicious ripping noise as it spun overhead and exploded about one hundred meters to the north. "Right on, baby." Hoffman began adjusting fire on the enemy in the tree line. Grunts under siege hear no sound more gratifying than that of heavy artillery falling on attackers. It had the desired effect when the incoming rifle and machine gun fire waned, and the grunts could take a breather.

Alvarez looked at Ron Becklin, "the professor," and laughed.

"What's so goddamn funny?" Becklin protested.

"I always said you were an airhead. Check out your steel pot."

Becklin removed his helmet and saw a small perforation dead center but no exit hole. He felt his head for blood. Finding none, he removed the helmet liner and found a deformed slug where it had lodged between the steel shell and the fiber liner. He kissed it and dropped it into his ammo pouch. "Thanks for the souvenir, assholes," he said.

No one believed for a second that the fight was over. The NVA expected heavy bombardment and adapted to it, changing positions or retreating to bunkers. They moved unseen and so fast that sometimes it was impossible to tell how many there actually were. The assumption around the hastily formed perimeter was that the attack would resume.

Suddenly a cry of "Frag" went up from the position to Hoffman's right. He turned and spotted a Chicom grenade, which resembled a potato masher, lying about two meters behind him. He knew brave men covered live grenades with their bodies, men braver than he. He hugged the ground and prepared to take the blast. But the frag lay inert, a dud.

Chicom stick grenades were notoriously unreliable, and the platoon got lucky with this one. It was followed by a burst of AK fire that came from bushes less than a horseshoe lob from the platoon's perimeter. Several NVA had managed to slither through the high grass, intending to escape the artillery fire and attack from close range. The grunts answered by tossing made-in-America frags that rarely failed, and the firing ceased.

Hoffman could think of only two options: stay put and wait for reinforcements, or retreat to the jungle on the far side of the LZ. Neither was good, but the first was becoming untenable. If they fought their way out of the clearing, they would almost certainly sustain more casualties. They would have to carry their wounded, one of whom badly needed a medevac helicopter.

As if on cue, not one but two Huey gunships circled high above like hawks. Sullivan poked Hoffman with the handset. "LT, I've got gunships on the horn. They want us to pop smoke." Galvin pulled a smoke grenade from his webbing and flipped it out in front of the platoon's position. A green cotton-like cloud rose in the dead air. "Easy Rider," hovering above, confirmed he saw green smoke. He also reported that about twenty NVA troops were moving through the grass in the platoon's direction.

With the wounded to think about, Hoffman decided to stay put for now. The arrival of the gunships gave him hope that the enemy would break off their attack. He watched an awesome display of firepower as the gunships began to strafe the closing enemy troops. The choppers passed low overhead, wheeled sharply, and disappeared behind the trees surrounding the field. They reappeared over the treetops, rockets swishing, miniguns groaning. After several passes, "Easy Rider" radioed that the helicopters were returning to the base to reload, but they'd be back. What he didn't say was both birds had taken hits and one crew member was wounded, a fact that Hoffman would learn a week later.

Hoffman checked his watch. Less than an hour had elapsed since the platoon had set boots on the ground in Cambodia. The insertion had gone wrong, men were wounded, and he wanted to know why. The wounded Hans Miller, known as "Kraut," had been in Vietnam for six months. Born in Germany and holding a green card, he had been drafted even though he wasn't a citizen. Now he desperately needed a medevac. Galvin said, "You'd better go check the wounded. Kraut's in bad shape, and Doc is freaking out."

The bullet had entered to the right of Kraut's sternum and exited from his left side. It didn't look good, but in the field, appearances were deceiving. Seemingly minor wounds were sometimes killers, ugly ones survivable; you just couldn't tell what damage was done inside. Kraut was a tough kid. The medic, new in the country, was treating his first chest wound. One man held an IV over Kraut's body while the medic, "Doc," worked on the wound. Kraut's lips were blue, his face the color of wet cement. His eyes were open but unseeing.

"His heart is stopping," the medic said as he frantically performed CPR. "Come on, Kraut; don't bug out on me." Blood frothed from Kraut's mouth.

Hoffman felt the wounded grunt's neck for a pulse and said, "Doc, he's gone."

The medic glanced at Hoffman questioningly and continued pumping. "Come on, Kraut. Breathe, goddamn it, breathe," he sobbed.

"Doc, you've done all you can," Hoffman said, pulling him to his feet. The young medic gazed blankly at Kraut's body, hesitantly, as if he had forgotten something else he might try to revive the man, then turned and walked away. Galvin covered the corpse with a poncho.

Meanwhile, Recon was moving to link up with the Second Platoon. The enemy seemed to have broken contact, but the silence that follows a firefight can be as sudden and unnerving as the havoc with which it begins. The men remained on alert lest the enemy resume attack, listening to the pulsating din of the jungle chant a requiem for Kraut.

Half an hour had passed when Hoffman heard Danton's voice on the radio, asking for a flare to guide Recon to the Second Platoon's position. Moments later, Recon's point man emerged from a screen of heavy vegetation, and the two platoons linked up. Hoffman was angry. "What the hell, Danton? You were supposed to scout this area."

"Calm down, Ivy League. You are in the wrong damn place. Murphy's law—anything that can go wrong will go wrong. Ol' Murphy must have been in the infantry."

"Yeah, well, I lost a man because someone fucked up."

Danton grinned. "So what? How this happened is irrelevant. You just had a hell of a firefight, and that hero just gave his life for his country. What are you complaining about?"

"You're nuts, man."

"Arguably, but we're wasting time talking. Let's see how many of the bastards you bagged."

The two platoons, minus a squad guarding the dead and wounded, crept online across the clearing and into the surrounding jungle where they found blast craters, splintered trees, and blood trails but no bodies. The firepower inflicted on the NVA troops had forced them to withdraw, leaving behind a bunker complex.

In the eyes of senior command, the Second Platoon's firefight was a win. That the platoon had been inserted in the wrong place, near a previously undetected enemy bunker complex, wouldn't even merit a footnote in the record. But to every grunt on the ground, it was a tragic mistake, one that had cost them a brother.

18
UNDER THE DEADLINE

It was nearly midnight when the garage door rattled shut. The cat stood up in its basket on the workbench and stretched. After Susan's death, Hoffman had banished the tabby to the garage where it could come and go as it pleased through its own little door. He had no affinity for cats, and LuLu sensed his indifference. He gave the animal a perfunctory scratch between the ears as he passed.

He went to the kitchen. A week's worth of dirty dishes was piled in the sink. The housekeeper would come on Saturday and take care of them. He dropped three ice cubes in a glass and filled it with Scotch. On his way to the bedroom, his phone rang. At this hour, it could mean only one thing. "It just never stops," he mumbled and picked up the receiver.

"Jack, sorry I didn't catch you before you left." It was the night city editor. "Just got a report of a shooting in the MacArthur District. Apparently several homicides involved. See what you can find out and get back to me within half an hour. I might be able to squeeze something into the first edition."

Hoffman called the dispatcher at Central Precinct, who confirmed the report but gave no details. He tried the number of the detective on duty that night and got a leave-a-message recording. Well, there wouldn't be time to file a story before the deadline. He resisted the temptation to call the newsroom, tell them he'd get to it in the morning, and hit the sack. But what the heck; he wasn't sleeping well anyway.

He left the Scotch on the counter and went to the closet for a jacket. It was a cool night, and he'd likely see the sunrise before he was able to crawl into bed. This wasn't the first time he'd chased a story all night, getting right on it while mouths that closed in the light of day were still open. His car seat was still warm when he turned the key in the ignition.

Aside from a few cabs trolling for nighthawks, the streets were empty. He slowed at red lights, then sped on through canyons of darkened office towers. He saw the usual dark figures lurking in doorways or huddled under tarps on steam grates. He assumed the shooting was gang related; there had been more of them lately.

He knew a pot of stale coffee awaited him at the station as he punched the code into the door lock. At the front desk, he found Sergeant Mallory in the process of fingerprinting three young Asian males. They appeared to be in their late teens or early twenties. Two uniformed jail guards stood by.

"Just can't stay away, can you, Hoffman?" Mallory quipped.

"If you boys cleaned up this city, maybe I could get some sleep," Hoffman countered.

"Take a sleeping pill 'cause it ain't gonna happen," Mallory advised.

"So what's this about some trouble over in MacArthur?"

"OK Corral more like it."

The sergeant pressed the fingers of one of the arrested men on an ink pad. The other two, cuffed and ankle-chained, sullenly waited their turn. When Mallory was finished with the booking, the guards marched the three off to the elevator and holding cells on the fifth floor.

"So what can you disclose?" Hoffman said.

"Looks like gang bangers in a shootout. Don't have an official count, but several wounded taken to Saint Joseph Hospital and two on their way to the morgue."

Hoffman whistled. "Where'd it go down?"

"132nd and Beach. Asian nightclub."

"Those three involved?" Hoffman nodded toward the elevator.

"Maybe."

Several drive-by shootings had occurred in the neighborhood in recent months. It was hard to get anyone in the Asian community to talk, but the word on the street was that gangs, which had originated in the Bay Area, were moving up Interstate 5 as far as Vancouver, BC, looking to expand their operations. Asian communities gave them the cover they needed to trade in stolen property, drugs, and prostitution.

"Which bar?" Hoffman asked.

"Uhhh, the My Song, something like that."

"I know the place," Hoffman said. "What time did it happen?"

"Just after midnight."

Hoffman drove south on the interstate, exiting into a neighborhood of modest bungalows. In the exodus following the fall of Saigon, the area had become an enclave of Southeast Asian settlers. Over the years, he had written about the plight of the boat people, their efforts to reunify their families and their integration into American society. It was a special interest of his. During his tour of duty in Vietnam, he found the Vietnamese people able to make do with little and as far as he could observe, to continue their daily routines as if the war was merely an inconvenience.

Their smiling obsequiousness gave the impression of cooperation. But behind those masks, something different was going on. The immigrants had no need for masks. They worked hard, established small businesses, and purchased homes in ethnic neighborhoods, just as their predecessors from other migrations had done. The first generation remained largely insular, patriarchal, and enigmatic. Some never learned to speak English well, if at all. Their kids, on the other hand, navigated a cultural maze, pressured by their parents to adhere to the old ways while trying to fit in socially with their peers. Most transitioned successfully into American life, but a few got lost.

As he drove, Hoffman wondered whether there was any connection between the young woman slain earlier and the shooting tonight. It was 1:35 a.m. when he arrived at the My Song. The bar and restaurant were on the first floor of a dingy two-story brick building in a block of small shops. Half a dozen squad cars, their lights flashing blue and red, blocked street access to the bar. A fire and rescue truck was leaving as Hoffman parked his car a block away. A gaggle of onlookers huddled quietly under dripping umbrellas in the glare of a street lamp.

Hoffman ducked under the yellow tape at the building's entrance and approached a cop at the door. He was a patrol officer

Hoffman didn't recognize. "Sorry; you can't go in there," the officer said.

"Press," Hoffman replied.

"My orders are no one goes in."

"Who's in charge?"

"Lieutenant O'Brian."

"I'd like a word with him."

"He's busy."

"Will you get word to him Hoffman's outside?"

"Look, he's questioning witnesses right now and doesn't want to be interrupted," the cop said, sounding exasperated.

"I heard two dead," Hoffman persisted.

"Can't confirm that."

Hoffman called what few facts he had in to the city desk in time for a placeholder in the morning edition. A fuller story would have to wait for the next day's street edition. For now, all he could do was hang around and hope to intercept the detective working the case. O'Brian was a combat veteran, having served with the 1st Marines in Vietnam. He made a relatively soft landing back in civilian life by joining the police force and found he liked it. Hoffman knew this because he and Barry O'Brian burnished their military bona fides over beers, the way veterans do. Hoffman could get helpful information from him, even if off the record.

The onlookers behind the yellow tape all appeared to be Vietnamese who lived nearby. What motivated them to stand in the cold drizzle after midnight? Did they know the people in that club? They could tell him a lot, but he had no expectation they would. It wasn't in their DNA. Hoffman identified himself and inquired whether anyone witnessed anything before or after the shooting. Did they know anyone in the bar? The same inscrutable faces he had encountered decades earlier in Vietnam greeted his questions. Back then, you knew there were bad actors among the villagers, husbands, brothers, sisters, and cousins. But who would betray them? The VC among them were like the biblical tares in a field of wheat: you couldn't pull them out without uprooting the grain.

The newspaper's photographer arrived, but she had nothing to shoot. Rain glinted in the light of the street lamp. Hoffman and the photographer stood under his umbrella and made small talk, their feet getting wet. At about 4:00 a.m., the coroner's staff wheeled out two bodies and loaded them into panel trucks. The photographer's camera whined. Bodies on gurneys were not very sexy, but the paper might use a photo to fill space. Hoffman intercepted O'Brian as he walked briskly from the building and headed for his car.

"Barry, a couple of questions."

"Can't tell you much at this point, Jack."

"Gang related?"

"Apparently so."

"Any idea which gangs?"

"Think so, but can't talk about that now."

"Fatalities?"

"Two. Three in critical condition at Saint Joseph's."

"What the hell happened in there?"

"You'll have to wait for a statement from the DA."

"Help me out, O'Brian. I've got a deadline."

"Can't."

"Off the record."

O'Brian hesitated. "I can confirm what witnesses told me, that there were three attackers. But there may have been more involved. The rest has to be strictly off the record."

"You got it."

"You know what happens. You get as many versions of events as there are witnesses. It was dark in there. They agree that three gunmen burst in with stockings pulled over their faces. Seemed to know their targets."

"Motive?" Hoffman asked.

"Just a theory right now. It could be someone new in town, maybe settling a score. You know these gangs. Sometimes it just comes down to who's the baddest ass."

"What weapons are involved?"

"Shell casings from 9-mm handgun and at least one long gun, an AR-15. We'll have to do the forensics."

"Was there return fire?"

"Possibly, but we'll have to do the forensics."

"Kind of unusual for our local types to have that much firepower."

"This was pretty slick, out of character. We found a blood trail outside under the awning, so another victim or one of the attackers might have been wounded."

"Witnesses give you any leads?"

"Weren't many witnesses still here when we arrived. Patrons scattered, and the staff said they were too busy hiding and ducking to get a good look at the attackers. No one is ready to talk. Too scared."

Hoffman dictated a lead to the city desk and returned to the front door of the club, hoping to collar an employee, but he was stopped again by a uniformed officer.

"Can't go in there, sir," the officer said.

The door opened, and two women, perhaps employees, exited covering their faces with their purses. Hoffman asked them if they were inside when the shooting started. They ignored him and left on foot, disappearing down the block.

Well, nothing to be gained by standing here in the rain, he decided. He drove to the newsroom where he phoned the hospital for the status of the wounded. All were in serious condition. He would have to make some phone calls, but it was hard to concentrate; he was dead tired. Coffee and cigarettes would keep him going.

Some months earlier, he had done an in-depth series on the rise of Asian gangs, but scores of interviews produced no clear answers. Many of these young men, and some women, had escaped Vietnam as children, boat people, separated from their families. They survived resettlement camps and ended up living with relatives or being placed in foster homes. Family disruptions and the trauma of war certainly affected them, and though resettlement agencies did their best, no one really understood the scars they were living with.

To all outward appearances, here was an immigrant population trying to preserve its cultural roots while striving to climb into the American middle class. They were hardworking, highly motivated to succeed, and ingenious. They opened restaurants where they simmered pho into small fortunes. The first generation might have had trouble learning English, but they insisted their kids excel in school and earn college degrees. The second generation was on a fast track to doing that, but a few jumped the rails.

As his deadline for the next edition approached, the police had not yet held their press briefing. Hoffman would have to go with what he had, padding the story with background information. He called the hospital for a report on the wounded, who were still alive but critical. Smoking a cigarette and sipping bad coffee from the vending machine, he started typing:

Three gunmen burst into a Vietnamese restaurant in the Macarthur District late Monday night and opened fire, leaving two dead and three critically wounded. The shooting, believed by police to involve gangs, was the most violent in the city in nearly 20 years.

The trouble broke out at the My Song Social Club just before midnight, according to police. Witnesses reported the masked gunmen walked in and abruptly opened fire, then ran. The wounded were taken to St. Joseph Hospital. Police are withholding identities of the dead and wounded pending notification of next of kin.

The motive for the shooting is unknown at this time. Two men are being held for questioning, and the police have launched an investigation. As reported last March in the series "Street war in Little Saigon," the incidence of gang violence in the area has escalated dramatically in the past two years. Burglary, auto theft, and other property-related crimes have increased by 20 percent.

It was a little before 9:00 a.m. when Hoffman hit the Send key on his computer and filed his story, which would be updated for later editions. It ran on page one above the fold, jumping to a story in the metro section in which Hoffman recapped gang trouble in recent months. The city editor called Hoffman to the desk, glanced from his screen, and said, "You look like death warmed over, Jack. Go home and bag some z's. I'll get someone else to cover the police briefing."

The briefing he could do without, but he was too wired to sleep. He learned a long time ago in Nam that you could write off a sleep deficit like a bad debt: it weighed on you but you could never make it up anyway, so you might as well keep going until you caught a second breath.. Tess wanted to speak with him again soon, but both were busy and they had left it up in the air. He tried the cell number she gave him, and she answered.

"Oh, Jack, I got your message. Are you still at the office?"

"I just filed. Long night. We can meet if you like."

"Sure, but shouldn't you rather get some sleep?"

"I'll get to bed early," he said. "The weather's good and I need to get out of here. Why don't we have breakfast, then take a little ride in the car? We can talk. Can you skip out on the seminar again?"

"Give me twenty minutes, and I'll meet you in the lobby."

He liked this young woman, so different in temperament than her father. He wanted to help her, but how? By telling her the truth? He took the elevator to the basement where his car was parked but decided to leave it there. Walking the six blocks to the hotel would do him good. He found Tess sitting in the lobby, reading the newspaper. She glanced up, seeming genuinely glad to see him.

"Good morning, Clark Kent," she said warmly, rising to give him an embrace he received stiffly.

"Hey, careful. The man of steel needs a shower," Hoffman said.

"I read your story. Awful."

"Not pretty. Some of these kids . . . I don't know."

"Wars end for everyone but the survivors, I guess," Tess said.

"So it would seem. Let's have breakfast here. I need a cup of good coffee, pronto," he said.

Men in business suits filled the hotel dining room. Tess turned heads en route to a table. Hoffman wondered what they were thinking, old man, beautiful young woman—business associate, of course. She ordered fruit and yogurt, and he opted for a salmon hash with eggs over easy. A sleepless night ends hungrily, and he wolfed down his meal while she watched in mild amusement.

"You were up all night. You must be famished," she said indulgently.

"Pardon my manners," he said, slightly embarrassed. "Guess I've gotten used to dining with the cat."

"The cat?"

"My wife's cat. Poor thing has been moping around since Susan died."

"Your daughter's not around?"

"During school breaks, just passing through even then."

"So you're alone? No significant other, I mean?"

Hoffman shifted in his chair. "If you mean a romantic relationship, no."

"Okay, I'm prying," she said unapologetically.

"It's quite alright. You and my daughter. She's always pestering me about being a hermit."

"Susan must have been a wonderful woman, but your daughter is right. I'm sure Susan wouldn't want you to be lonely."

"Funny thing is, I'm not. I just haven't decided what I want to do next," he said, drawing circles in the tablecloth with a spoon. "Susan and I had a great life together. This is a big change."

Tess watched him, waiting for him to say more, but he was reticent. "Was her illness long?" she prompted.

"About a year. It was hard."

"And still is, I'm sure."

"Yes, in a different way. Now it's all about me. I admit it."

"You're entitled to some self-pampering."

Hoffman grinned. "That's a nice way of putting it."

"You're obviously a kind, attractive man. I'm sure you'd have no trouble finding companionship. You should give it a try. But then, I'm the last one to be giving you advice in that regard."

"Perhaps I should," he said dismissively, "but it's low on my list of priorities. Actually, I don't have a list. The newspaper is struggling to hold subscribers, and I may have to find another way to make a living. Everything is up in the air right now."

"There must be something you'd like to do."

"Maybe I'll spend a few years with Mother Teresa."

"Sainthood then?" she laughed.

"I'm serious. A second career doesn't interest me. At my age, I don't have much slack left in my rope. Besides, I wouldn't know where to start. A Starbucks franchise? No thanks."

"You're a writer, so write. Get going on a book."

Hoffman rolled his eyes. "There are at least half a dozen manuscripts cooking in the newsroom right now, and I wouldn't bet on any of them."

"Oh, come on, Jack Hoffman. This is too dark. You're still young. Get your chin off the floor."

Tess Danton was direct, like her father, but sympathetic. When she gently chided him, he could hear her father's voice: "Quit making excuses and get your butt moving, Ivy."

"You know, Tess, when I got back from Nam, every nerve in my body was raw. I didn't want to talk about what I was feeling. Hell, I didn't know what was wrong with me. And Susan had no way of understanding what was going on in my head, let alone what to do about it. I don't know how she put up with me in those early years . . . No, I can't imagine living with anyone else."

"I think you're a little hard on yourself," Tess said, reaching over the table and squeezing his hand. "Of course, you can't replace her, but you can begin again."

"Too much involved in that, and I'm just not there yet. But you didn't track me down to listen to my sad story," he said.

"Oh, don't worry. Just being with you makes me feel close to my father. I mean I hope he was like you. Does that sound strange?"

Hoffman could in no way entertain an illusion that he resembled Alan Danton, but that his daughter might foster an emotional connection to him because he was present when her father died, he was prepared to accept. “Well, that’s very flattering, but don’t take it too far. You don’t really know me.”

“I guess I know more about you than I do him, just in a few days. What were your impressions of him, as a person I mean?”

She was a good interlocutor, quick to seize on an opportunity to draw him back to that subject, the one he didn’t know how to handle. “Let’s get going,” Hoffman said preemptively, “and we can talk about that later. There’s a beautiful day waiting outside.”

19
GHOSTS

Captain Gilman's Delta Company swept to the north with Lieutenant Unnerfeld's First Platoon in the lead. Cambodia's red clay radiated heat like a stovetop as the company moved in a column of two through an area of small trees, huge anthills, and naked red clay. The air was still and stifling, as if the earth was holding its breath. Hoffman was sure he could hear himself sweat.

Upon reentering the forest, the column came upon numerous compacted footpaths and a network of them. The grunts treaded carefully ahead, anticipating that at any moment they would walk into a volley of automatic weapons fire. It was obvious the area was populated, but by whom? Enemy troops would enjoy the advantage they always did, a familiarity with the terrain. If they attacked, it would be at a time and place of their choosing.

Unnerfeld halted the column and sent word back down the file that hooches lay dead ahead. The company double-timed to take positions around a village of thirty or so buildings elevated on posts. Cooking pots hung over cold fire pits, but the sticky-sweet scent of charcoal, boiled rice, and nuoc mam colored the air. A few chickens and pot-bellied pigs also evidenced that the village was occupied, but there was nary a soul to be seen. Zero. The buildings and animals could have been props for a movie set.

A search of the buildings turned up a single occupant, an old woman too feeble to take more than a few steps unassisted. Petrified at the sight of the soldiers, she had nothing to say to the interpreter about the rest of the villagers. Gilman directed that she be left alone in her hooch.

The village's appearance suggested it was Khmer Loeu, the indigenous hill tribes of Cambodia. But were these people in league with the NVA? Just outside the cluster of buildings, the grunts found three buildings holding a large supply of rice along with a cache of a dozen AK-47 rifles, a few RPGs, and a stack of mortar shells. Willingly or unwillingly, the villagers appeared to be storing food and equipment for the NVA trekking south through the wilderness.

Gilman reported the discovery to battalion headquarters, and the company pressed on to the northwest. It came upon numerous trails, which it avoided walking out of concern about booby-traps and ambushes. Cleared areas in various stages of cultivation would have required the care of a large number of indigenous laborers, but where were they? Three hundred meters brought the company to another village about the size of the first. The grunts quickly took up positions around the buildings, but again the village appeared to have been abandoned in haste. Food lay uneaten in bowls, cooking fires smoldered, and NVA uniforms hung on lines to dry.

Word came by radio that Charlie Company had found a larger settlement in a similar condition, apparently vacated earlier that morning when the battalion's fleet of helicopters arrived in the area with the stealth of a brass band. Could it be that the trails connected a cluster of villages, scattered to limit the damage of aerial bombardment? Had everyone cleared out using predetermined escape routes? Was the enemy hiding and waiting to pounce? Aerial surveillance offered no clue. An eerie silence enveloped the villages.

Delta Company continued its search. If the local population was not there to receive them, Cambodian insects gave the Americans their own rude welcome: mosquitoes, the men swore to be as big as house flies, attacked unfazed by the bitter repellent the Army provided; swarms of fire ants, appropriately named for their red color and the burn of their bites, leaped on the men from trees; killer ants in their zillions flowed in rivulets over the baked earth. Adding misery to insult, there was no water to fill rapidly emptied canteens; the blue lines on the map proved to be dry.

Day three of the invasion brought the same conditions, the same strange absence of villagers and the enemy, and the same feelings of foreboding. Unnerfeld's platoon again took the lead. The map indicated a stream some five hundred meters ahead, but was it, like others, an empty promise? There was only one way to find out. In a single file, the company wound down a steep rocky slope. Tangled brush grabbed at boots and ripped at arms and legs. Suddenly, the point man turned and ran shrieking past Unnerfeld, followed by a black swarm of angry wasps.

A cloud of insects swarmed on the panicking grunts who cast aside their weapons and dropped their rucks, furiously attempting to beat off their attackers. But the flailing seemed only to further infuriate the wasps. Training suggested to even the most cynical of the soldiers that their officer might know what to do when no one else does. Unnerfeld found himself mobbed by shrieking men. Would smoke grenades deter the insects? He pulled the pins on every one he possessed, but the colorful cloud did nothing to discourage the winged attackers.

The swarm of wasps moved down the file toward Hoffman and his men, wreaking havoc along the way. The insects reached the middle of the column somewhat diminished, but their onslaught was still fierce enough to cause the men to forget how vulnerable they were to a human attack. Captain Gilman, who was at the rear of the column, called for the lead elements to retreat and form a defensive perimeter, but no one was listening.

Hoffman ran up the line of troops trying to restore tactical discipline, shouting at the men to hold on to their weapons. The stings felt like hot nails in his face and neck, but adrenalin and concern that the NVA might take advantage of the situation kept him focused on restoring order. At the front of the column, he found Unnerfeld with a towel wrapped around his nose and mouth, eyes nearly swollen shut. Wounded men lay around him on the ground, groaning.

"My point man stepped on a nest," Unnerfeld said as if some explanation was needed.

"You got security on your flanks?" Hoffman asked.

"Kiss my ass, Jack. Look at these men. I ain't got shit."

"Okay, let's get everybody up and pull back into a defensive perimeter before something worse happens."

The two platoon leaders exhorted their charges to collect their weapons and gear and prepare to move. Some of the men had been stung inside their mouths and noses and were gasping for air. Medics, victims themselves, did what they could to treat the wounds with salve and hydrogen peroxide and get everyone on their feet. The less afflicted assisted those in worse shape to safer ground where the moaning grunts formed a defensive position and licked their wounds. Gradually, the intensity of the attack diminished until only a few stragglers zipped triumphantly overhead as if to assess the agony they had caused.

"You get the feeling we aren't welcome here?" Hoffman said to Galvin.

"Giant hornets," Galvin said. "Happened on my first tour. They're the largest hornet, and their venom can kill you. Their stinger is a quarter-inch long. Some of these guys are having trouble breathing. We could use a dustoff, pronto." It took nearly half an hour for a medevac chopper to arrive. The six worst cases climbed aboard, leaving the rest to cope. "Todd, you look like you went ten rounds with Muhammad Ali," Hoffman said. Galvin had walnut size lumps on his forehead and cheeks.

"I'm alright. But right now, thirst is the problem. By the way, you aren't a candidate for a recruiting poster yourself, LT." Hoffman's nose was swollen shut, and his lower lip had ballooned. He had been stung on the back through his shirt and on both arms.

The company badly needed to replenish its water supply. With the Third Platoon in the lead now, the men headed for a solid blue line on the map, signifying a year-round flow. But with the grim resignation of men accustomed to disappointment, the grunts found a streambed of putrid muck. The next blue line was nearly two hundred meters north through the heavy jungle. It was getting late, and the captain didn't want to blunder into an ambush at dusk. He consulted with his platoon leaders who agreed that pushing the men any farther made little sense; if the stream proved to be dry, they'd be in worse shape than if they stayed put.

Of all the miseries inflicted by the Green Monster, thirst ranked near the top. The grunts were weak and dehydrated after the encounter with the wasps. As night fell, the little remaining water in canteens was rationed, the haves sharing with the have-nots, the fit foregoing for the afflicted, a swallow at a time. There was no anxiety about the morrow; just getting through the night was worry enough.

Sometime after midnight, distant flashes appeared in the sky to the west, followed by thunder. Was it an Arc Light, a B-52 bombing run? Or could they allow themselves the hope that a cloudburst was headed their way? It was the dry season, but downpours were not unusual. The distant night sky lit up like a Japanese lantern, on and off, on and off. They counted the seconds between the flashes and the thunder, and the storm seemed to be moving closer.

A flash of lightning and a clap of thunder announced the arrival of a zephyr, cool and refreshing. The grunts knew exactly what to do. They quickly tied their ponchos to trees to provide shelter and to funnel rain from the cloudburst into their steel pots. Then they crawled under their flimsy shelters and, like fishermen with nets out, hoped for a good catch. They didn't have to wait long. Like the approach of a train from a blind curve, they could hear it coming until, suddenly, wind-driven rain roared through the treetops.

The downpour ripped at the ponchos, rendering them useless as shelters. Abandoning any attempt to stay dry, the grunts crawled out from under them, removed their shirts, and bathed their aching, swollen bodies in nature's cool beneficence. Then, something happened they never expected after the day's sweltering heat. It began to hail. They caught the icy rain in their hands and rubbed it on their lumpy faces. The dry stream bed began to fill, and they rushed to catch as much as they could in their canteens.

The storm ended as abruptly as it began, leaving the battalion's supply of water replenished and the grunts refreshed. They resumed the night watch listening to dripping trees, croaking lizards, and myriad of nameless utterings. The rain left the earth sweetly fecund, its thirst slaked.

The remainder of the night passed uneventfully. At first light, the men began to move about, digging their cat holes and preparing a grunt's breakfast of powdered coffee, canned fruit, crackers, peanut butter, and jam. Their swollen welts still throbbed, but such discomforts in the jungle must be borne with indifference. The company saddled up and resumed its sweep to the northwest, now with Hoffman's platoon rotating into the lead.

The company moved through a relatively open forest. It had not gone far when the point man came upon something the grunts had never encountered in Vietnam's highland wilderness: a dirt road. "It's well concealed under the trees and just wide enough for a single vehicle to pass," Hoffman radioed Gilman. "Deep wheel ruts." The captain came forward to see for himself.

Hoffman knew from intelligence reports there could be roads in the area and other units along the border had found them, so its existence came as no surprise. Still, seeing it on the ground was sobering; the enemy obviously had established a crude but an effective logistical system. But where was the enemy? If they were nearby, they apparently weren't aching for a fight, at least not yet. Other companies reported much the same conditions on the ground: roads, foot trails, clusters of hooches, stock-piles of rice, and caches of weapons and ammunition, with no human presence.

Several days passed. The hastily abandoned buildings and supplies suggested a rest and training area for troops making their way south. Hoffman's hot reception upon landing in Cambodia testified to the enemy's presence hours, even minutes, before the battalion arrived. General Taggart repeatedly asked for authorization to push his battalions deeper into Cambodia, but his requests were denied by the chain of command. He was to penetrate Cambodia no deeper than thirty kilometers, and that was firm.

As a young captain in Korea, Taggart had led a rifle company of the First Cavalry Division ashore at Pohang-dong. That war had ended indecisively at the 38th parallel, and this one seemed destined to conclude in a similar fashion. He often argued that the enemy should be denied sanctuary in Cambodia and Laos. "You don't enter wars, damn it, to settle for a stalemate. American forces should secure the northern and western borders and commit to the preservation of a free South Vietnam, no matter how long it takes." But the nation's will to continue had collapsed under the weight of time, casualties, and the belief that the war was unwinnable.

More than forty thousand American lives had been lost so far. In his military mind, slinking away like a cowed dog was a mistake, and he was far from the only senior officer who felt that way. They lamented the situation privately over Scotch and cigars and were skeptical that the South Vietnamese could hold off the North. As his career was nearing an end, he had hoped to retire with pride in what he had accomplished in this, his final, combat tour. Giving the enemy a bloody nose in Cambodia would at least demonstrate that the grunts had been fighting with one hand tied behind their backs.

The air conditioner at the division headquarters died that morning, and the double-wide trailer serving as the operations center was a sauna. Sweat beaded on Taggart's forehead and blotched his starched jungle fatigues. He snapped at an aide, "Lieutenant, is someone going to fix that damn air conditioner today, or do we wait for the second coming?"

"Yes, sir. They just got here, and they're going to replace—"

"Hell, not now, not yet," Taggart objected, cutting off the lieutenant, and he wasn't referring to the air conditioner. An order had just come to him from MACV headquarters to commence withdrawing his troops from Cambodia immediately. His men had been chasing ghosts. Meanwhile, the US and South Vietnamese forces west of Saigon were grappling with an NVA division. Did the enemy in his sector turn tail and run?

He mopped his face with a towel and studied the topographical map on the wall. An aide was adjusting marker pins on coordinates as reports of unit positions came in by radio from the field. The division had pushed westward to the line set for it, and Taggart was fuming under strict instructions to advance no further. They had pulled back for some reason, and Taggart wanted to know why.

If Taggart was frustrated, his troops were not. The grunts were surprised that the operation had been cut short, but they were far from demoralized. The enemy's presence somewhere nearby was palpable, but after nearly a week of combing the area of operation, they had nothing to show for it but thirst, filth, insect bites, and raw nerves. Compared to this place, Vietnam's mountainous jungle was Shangri-La. In an abandoned Cambodian village several kilometers from the LZ, some Hawaiian soldiers in Charlie Company prepared a luau of a captured pot-bellied pig and a few chickens roasted in a fire pit. Those who partook of the feast left Cambodia with hookworms.

Delta Company, meanwhile, dug in for the night near a plot of manioc and ate what was left of their C-rations. The men could only speculate about the decision to withdraw from Cambodia after a stay of only a week, but a grunt lives in the moment, and at this moment, fate seemed to be smiling at them. The scattered companies of the battalion were to reassemble on LZ California for transport by Chinook helicopter back to the staging area inside Vietnam. From there, they would resume search and ambush operations in the highlands.

Back at the base camp, General Taggart figured the enemy would pour back into its enclaves as soon as his forces withdrew, and he had a reception planned for them. He would withdraw all of his troops, save a small reconnaissance platoon covertly left behind. The platoon would pinpoint enemy positions and direct air strikes. It would be under strict orders to remain hidden and not engage the NVA.

He discussed his plan with his highers at MACV. He didn't minimize the risk to the Recon platoon but reasoned that the mission was no different than others these crack troops conducted routinely inside Vietnam. They would be operating just over that invisible line separating the two countries, and if engaged by the enemy, they could be quickly reinforced by troops standing by just over the border.

All morning, Chinooks were lumbering in and out of LZ California, nibbling away at what was left of the camp in Cambodia. At the old special forces airstrip across the border in Vietnam, activity was frenetic as the big birds arrived with troops and cargoes yanked out of Cambodia. Deuce-and-a-half trucks stood in line, engines grumbling, to remove troops and materials from the airstrip and carry them back to base camp Farrell where a hot meal, a good night's sleep in a field tent, and maybe even a warm beer or two awaited them.

It was mid-afternoon when the Chinook carrying Hoffman's Second Platoon, Delta Company, rose from Cambodian soil. The helicopter made a wide turn to the east, gaining altitude. From the cabin window, Hoffman saw the grunts of Charlie Company below, the last remaining troops, boarding the Chinook that would take them back across the border. Three helicopter gunships circled to provide security. If the operation had ended there, it would not have merited more than a few sentences in the archival record of the Cambodian campaign.

As the sound of the last Chinook's big blades faded in the distance, a haunting silence settled on that cleared patch of earth that was LZ California. At that moment, the troops of Recon, their faces blackened, waited clandestinely in the heavily wooded forest about two hundred meters to the north.

20
IT SHOULD HAVE BEEN ME

Troops sat elbow to elbow in the sling seats along the bulkheads of the Chinook. More sat "elbow to asshole" on the deck. When the chopper hovered for a landing at the staging area at the old special forces camp in Vietnam, its passengers sat stone-faced. Whether in Cambodia or Vietnam, victory looked like survival, and the grunts were returning from the heart of darkness to the ugly war they knew.

When the airship paused in its descent and crept lower, they anticipated the gentle bump of wheels on the ground. But the Chinook didn't land. It rose again, engines screaming, blades raising a windstorm of dust. The windows went dark, and a fine red powder hissed like sleet against the chopper's skin. Again, the pilot attempted to set the helicopter down, but it jerked and swayed like an amusement park ride. The grunts on board gripped anything within reach.

Hoffman peered out the porthole-like window of the Chinook. He could see nothing but roiling dust and surmised the pilots were struggling to find the ground in the brownout. He glanced at Galvin sitting on the sling opposite him. The sergeant's expression was blank, his eyes frozen. The big helicopter swung abruptly to the right, throwing the men sitting on the deck toward

Hoffman. He felt the bird's rear wheels strike hard and bounce before coming to rest.

The blades continued to spin as the tail ramp dropped, and the grunts scrambled out into suffocating dust. They stood near the rear of the aircraft for a moment, bewildered. Where were they to assemble? A deuce-and-a-half raced across the airstrip, heading in their direction, arriving just as the Chinook's twin rotors accelerated for takeoff. In seconds, the truck bed filled with men anxious to escape the dust storm on the airstrip.

As the Chinook rose and sailed away, another one approached, hovering down the airstrip on a pillow of dust. Hoffman heard someone shout his name. It was Sergeant Galvin, sitting on the truck bed near the tailgate. "LT, take my place; I'll wait for the next truck."

"No, you get the hell out of here. I'll wait here with the rest of the men," Hoffman shouted. Before the day was over, Galvin, a survivor of multiple tours of combat duty, would be back at Camp Farrell where he'd process out of Vietnam for his return to Fort Lewis, Washington, and pending separation from military service. He was way too short to spend a minute longer than necessary on the miserable airstrip.

Galvin cracked a grin, the first Hoffman had seen him manage in a month. The truck's gears engaged with a grind but too late to avoid the blinding dust raised by the approaching Chinook. "Damn," Hoffman grumbled, "here it comes again." He and a gaggle of others standing near the parked truck turned their backs and covered their eyes and noses with their shoulder towels.

The big machine's twin engines screamed as it hovered nearer, sliding left and right, searching for clear air, until Hoffman was sure it was nearly overhead. Something was wrong. He realized the pilot was struggling with the same conditions that threatened his chopper's landing, and he forced himself to open his eyes and take a look.

What he observed was surreal. A steel cargo container at the edge of the strip had snared the rear right wheel of the big chopper, causing it to list to the left. "Climb, you bastard," Hoffman shouted, but it was too late for that. As the helicopter began to roll, he could think of nothing but escape. He turned to those standing nearby and shouted, "Run; it's going down."

With the dust at their backs, they had taken only a few steps when they heard the groan of a dying beast. Something struck Hoffman's legs. He realized the sound he was hearing was that of spinning blades striking the ground and disintegrating. The grunts dropped and low-crawled as fast as their arms and legs could propel them away from the crash. Shards of the blades skittered past them as they crawled.

The helicopter's struggle ended abruptly, followed by silence. Hoffman lay still, trying to comprehend what had happened. When he gathered the courage to look, he saw something that appeared impossible. The helicopter, all thirty-three thousand pounds of it, rested on its side, squarely on the bed of the truck. A few bodies, rucksacks, weapons, and debris lay scattered around the wreckage, and flames licked from a fuel tank on the fuselage. The Chinook was a firebomb with a lit fuse.

Hoffman knew he had to do something fast, but what? He took three hesitant steps toward the wreck, then broke into a dead run, followed by several others intent on helping survivors. The tail ramp had fallen partially open, and grunts were tumbling out, the able-bodied assisting the injured. Hoffman's attention turned to those trapped beneath the helicopter in the bed of the truck. Oh my God, he anguished, Galvin is under that wreckage.

He approached it, nauseated by what he might find. Moans and cries for help came from the narrow gap between the chopper's skin and the truck bed. He forced himself to look. A grotesque tangle of heads, torsos, limbs, weapons, and equipment was compressed in a space no deeper than twelve to fourteen inches. Distinguishing anyone was impossible. He ran to the tailgate where Razor Galvin had been sitting, and his heart sank. That area, unsupported by the cab of the truck, was narrower than the rest of the bed. He shouted the sergeant's name but got no response.

That Galvin lay under that helicopter was simply unacceptable; he was the indestructible one, too smart to die in this way. Perhaps he leaped off the truck in time. Hoffman saw no way to rescue anyone from the truck bed, and he could think of nothing comforting to say to those who might be able to hear him. He turned away to see what he could do for those who lay in the dust near the truck, cut down by spinning blades.

He recognized one of them, a baby-faced grunt in Bravo Company. The kid was gray, unconscious, his shirt torn, and his pants ripped off and wrapped around his ankles. Hoffman noticed, oddly, a release of semen. He knelt over the boy and felt for a pulse. There was none. Another body lay a few meters away, so Hoffman moved to it. It was a lieutenant in Charlie Company, a man Hoffman met on arriving in-country. He hadn't seen him since and couldn't remember his name.

There are certain things a soldier just doesn't need to witness, the kind of things that imprint indelibly in memory, and they are never good. Hoffman was collecting them, and here was one more. The helicopter's blade had struck the lieutenant below the waist, removing both legs at the hips. The officer's face was frozen in wide-eyed horror. Had he retained consciousness long enough to see what had just happened to him? Hoffman pulled a poncho from the man's rucksack and covered the body with it.

He spotted Alvarez, one of his squad leaders, supine near the front of the truck. His eyes were half open, and he was semiconscious. "Can you hear me, Alvarez?" Hoffman said, kneeling over the injured man.

"I hear you, LT, but I can't move."

"Okay, hang in there; you're going to be okay. We'll get you a medevac."

He glanced up at the flames fed by the fuel from a ruptured tank. Two grunts were fighting them with small fire extinguishers removed from the truck's cab. It seemed a fool's errand, but they were doing what they could. Fearing an explosion, he pulled Alvarez a safe distance from the wreckage and waved down a stretcher Jeep speeding in his direction. The Jeep sped off with the soldier on board. It would be the last time he would ever see Alvarez.

Another deuce-and-a-half barreled onto the airstrip, and Todd Unnerfeld jumped from the cab. He spotted Hoffman and came running. Gaping at the wreckage, he said, "Jesus, is anyone inside that shit hook?"

"No, they're all out; it's the guys under it I'm worried about," Hoffman said.

"I don't even what to think about it," Unnerfeld said, glancing at the wreckage. "Any of your guys?"

"Yeah. Razor for one."

"God, I'm sorry, Jack. But there's nothin' you can do. It's gonna take a crane to lift that thing. Get on the truck, and let's go."

"I'm not leavin' without Razor." He could barely say the sergeant's name without losing control.

Unnerfeld reached into his thigh pocket for a mutilated pack of cigarettes and shook one out. Like everything else, it was stained by red dust. He lit it and gave it to Hoffman who took it with a shaking hand. A Jeep throwing up a rooster tail of dust raced in their direction and skidded to a stop. It carried Captain Gilman. "Everyone back to the assembly area. I want every swingin' dick accounted for." Then he sped off.

The two platoon leaders joined haggard grunts collecting on the bed of the waiting truck. They were somber, having trouble believing what had just happened. Hoffman held on to a thread of hope that Sergeant Galvin survived under that helicopter. Several hours passed at the assembly area with no word until Captain Gilman summoned Hoffman to the command post.

Gilman was pacing, chewing on a cigar. "Jack, I just got word that the men injured in that crash are on the way to the hospital at Qui Nohn. Twenty-five of the injured were trapped under the Chinook, and eight more were standing near the truck. Five dead. At least that's the latest count."

Hoffman held his breath. Gilman hesitated, looking at a list of names his RTO had just handed him. "I've confirmed that the four unaccounted for in your platoon were on or near that truck. Three were injured, Boyce, Dillingham, and Alvarez. One killed." He looked up. "It was Sergeant Galvin."

The two officers faced one another, wordless. That was no way for a man like Razor Galvin to die. Gilman finally said, "I'm sorry, Jack. It's a damn shame. Everyone respected Razor. He was one hell of a soldier. I can get his next of kin's address if you'd like to write them."

On the way back to his platoon's bivouac, Hoffman tried to make sense of Galvin's loss. In two tours of combat in Vietnam, Galvin had survived dozens of firefights. He was a certified hero. Once back at Camp Farrell, he would have showered, shaved, shouldered his duffle bag, and caught the next flight to Cam Ranh Bay and his Freedom Bird. A sixteen-ounce T-bone steak with all the trimmings was waiting for him at McChord Air Force Base near Tacoma. And there was that girl back home.

Razor Galvin had a premonition about Cambodia. When he landed back in Vietnam and climbed aboard that deuce-and-a-half, he must have believed he had it made home. But anyone who thinks soldiers have illusions of immortality was never in the infantry. As every grunt knew, fate would have the final say.

"Damn it," Hoffman lamented, "it should have been me on that truck."

21
THE TIGER'S LAIR

"This is bullshit, pure, steamin' bullshit," griped Lieutenant Gildersleeve upon leaving Captain Gilman's platoon leaders' briefing.

"Yeah, butt fucked again," Lieutenant Unnerfeld agreed.

"Why us? Always us," remarked Lieutenant Marcinovich.

Delta Company was not returning to Camp Farrell with the rest of the battalion for a stand-down but would remain right where it was, digging in, building bunkers, and patrolling in the vicinity of the airstrip. It was a head fake that General Taggart hoped would fool the communist forces back into their redoubts along the border and a trap. Recon would clandestinely watch for the NVA's return, pinpoint their positions, and call for air strikes. Delta would be a quick reaction force, ready to assault back into Cambodia to assist Recon in the event Lieutenant Danton and his men ran into trouble.

Gildersleeve said, "Be just like Danton to get in hot water and pull the rest of us in with him. Those villages were heavily populated hours, maybe minutes, before we got there. Hell, for all we know, we were standing right on top of 'em, in tunnels."

In several villages, the grunts puzzled over holes in the earth, each about two inches in diameter. Could they be providing ventilation for tunnels? A search for entrances turned up nothing, so they dismissed them as just another enigma in this mysterious place.

Delta Company's grunts were exhausted, hungry, and suffering from jungle rot. That they had to remain in miserable conditions on the border while the rest of the battalion was standing down with showers and hot food at the base camp was galling, to say the least.

Days of unrelenting heat and the movement of men and equipment churned the clay in the vicinity of the airstrip to the consistency of talcum powder. The cursed dust coated everything, weapons, clothing, food, skin. It penetrated every bodily orifice. But the weather had one more trick to play on the grunts. Just before midnight, another squall blew in from the South China Sea, filling bunkers and turning the chalky earth to paste.

Morning brought a slick to the airstrip with supplies and a mailbag. It had been two weeks since the last mail delivery, and Hoffman received a letter from Susan. She had quit waitressing, having found a temporary job teaching. She might stay in Australia for at least a year. She was happy there, hoped he was okay, and looked forward to seeing him again soon.

He held the letter to his nose, but there was no scent. He desperately wanted to be with her again but cautioned himself against imagining a future with her on so little evidence. She had a life to live and couldn't count on him ever returning. No, he should be grateful for the fantastic time they had together, and if he never saw her again, it was enough. He burned the letter, standard procedure lest it fall into the hands of the enemy.

While Delta Company sat near the border, Recon was in a night lager twenty kilometers to the west on a small rise that afforded a view of the Me San River as it flowed toward its confluence with the Me Cong. Somewhere in the hilly, forested landscape below lurked the NVA, but where? The enemy was the proverbial needle in a haystack, but Recon was a needle, too. Danton had bow hunted deer and wild hogs in Texas. He would sit for hours in hiding, waiting for an animal to walk into the range of his arrow. An impatient man, he could be patient when required.

Meanwhile, back in The World, the US Senate was considering a bill that would deny funding for operations in Cambodia, Thailand, and Laos. An estimated hundred thousand demonstrators gathered on the Capitol Mall to protest the "Cambodian Invasion," and the Ohio National Guard, hours before, had opened fire on students demonstrating at Kent State University.

Danton and the grunts of Recon, of course, were unaware of the demonstrations and bloodshed back in The World. Even if they had known, it would have made no difference whatsoever to them. If discovered by the enemy, their chances of avoiding annihilation were slim at best. Their survival concerned them, nothing else. Their orders to locate and direct air strikes on the enemy were simple enough, but every man knew a mission rarely went according to the script.

The eighteen young men of Recon, the most skilled and motivated fighters in the battalion, moved furtively through the jungle in solemn silence, communicating by hand signals, foregoing use of the machete. They had meticulously cleaned and oiled their weapons, checked their magazines, and packed their gear to prevent the slightest metallic click. They inserted foliage into the camouflage covers of their helmets, and with the camouflage fatigues issued especially for them, they blended into the flora like chameleons. Danton conferred with his platoon sergeant, Conner Flannigan, on the map coordinates of a high-speed trail they had come across earlier, one that seemed to meander west. “This looks promising,” he whispered. “Let’s see where it takes us.”

Specialist 4 Jackson was on the point, where Danton assigned him as the man with the most skill and experience. He followed the trail to the southwest into a triple canopy. They treaded cautiously in the arboreal gloom. Thick vines hung rope-like from high above, but there was little undergrowth to impede their progress.

They proceeded slowly nonetheless, alert to any movement ahead of them or to their flanks. There was no wind, the silence of the forest punctuated only by the screech of a bird, the croaking of lizards, and the high-pitched whine of mosquitoes in their ears. From tree limbs, several monkeys watched the procession pass. It was quiet, too quiet, and by some atavistic instinct, the hunters sensed the nearness of the hunted.

The trail eventually ended in a spongy blanket of duff on the forest floor. Trails often ended that way when the terrain no longer made them necessary. Danton shot an azimuth with his compass and pointed Jackson in the same general direction. Jackson took a few steps and stopped, having spotted something often encountered on the Vietnamese side of the border: strands of insulated wire. Several wires seemed to stretch haphazardly in different directions. Did the wire provide command-and-control communication between enemy camps?

The Vietnamese are lowland people, growers of rice on fertile coastal plains. The wilderness of the Annamite Cordillera and the upland plateau were as foreign as the Himalayas. But out of necessity, the Northerners had learned to use it for their insurgency. Danton halted the platoon in a stand of kapok trees, giants with fluted trunks nearly the girth of sequoias. From there, three-man teams would strike out in a cloverleaf pattern to search for signs of the enemy.

Sergeant Flannigan led one team to the north, following a strand of commo wire. It took them to what appeared to be a trail through the forest, and to another narrow dirt road similar to those discovered earlier in the area, barely wide enough for a single vehicle and rutted by truck tires. As before, the NVA had concealed the road under the dense triple canopy. The team hurried back to report to Danton.

"Could you tell how fresh the tracks are?" Danton asked Flannigan.

"Made since the rain last night."

"Footprints?"

"Yeah, lots of 'em."

Recon took up concealed positions from which the road could be observed. Danton stressed to his grunts they were not to fire their weapons, no matter how tempting the targets were. He needn't have. Somewhere nearby lurked a large NVA force. Every man knew that, if Recon's presence was detected, it would have little chance of escaping death or capture.

About three hours passed with no movement on the road, no sound but the wind's susurrous caress of the trees, the shrieks of birds, and the omnipresent chorus of insects. Noon came and went, and still, Danton kept his platoon waiting. How long would he hold this position? Occasionally the grunts glanced at him for a clue, but he lay stone still, his eyes focused on the road.

At about 1500 hours, Danton finally gave the order to pull back. Like a fisher having no luck, he decided to try another hole, but before anyone could shoulder their rucks, they heard voices, out of sight up the road but drawing nearer. The grunts quickly resumed their positions.

Six Montagnards—four men and two women—appeared on the road. The men wore the loin cloths and black shirts of tribesmen; the women, skirts, nothing covering their breasts. One of the women carried an infant in a sling and managed to balance a large basket of papaya and other fruits on her head. The men carried large bundles suspended from poles. Just behind the tribal people, a number of NVA soldiers came into view.

The NVA troops were young, perhaps in their teens. Their boots, green uniforms, pith helmets, and red scarves suggested they were conscripts newly sent from the North. They were laughing and chattering like carefree schoolboys. Danton took this as a sign the ruse had worked: the NVA obviously were not concerned about any Americans remaining on the Cambodian side of the border.

The NVA passed casually through the grunts' line of fire, as if on a Sunday hike. The watchers counted: three, four, five, eight, twelve, a total of eighteen. Where were they going? If there were that many, likely many more were somewhere very close by.

Medals aren't awarded for counting live NVA, only dead ones. Danton was already thinking about how he might engage the enemy and get away with it. His orders were to avoid detection, but what if he was unable to avoid it? At that moment, he couldn't imagine how that might happen, but he wouldn't be disappointed if it did. He had his Silver Star, but why not a Distinguished Service Cross, and maybe . . .? Wouldn't a Medal of Honor recipient have a lock on a career?

The party of NVA continued up the road, out of sight, and Danton motioned to his men to return to the kapok grove where he conferred with Sergeant Flannigan about the next move.

"It's a fucking freeway," Danton said. "Ever seen so many Dinks at one time?"

"Yeah," Flannigan said, "and regretted it. What do you have in mind?"

"Follow 'em; what else?"

"That road is headed west, and we're already as far as we're authorized to go," Flannigan said. "I'll radio for instructions."

"The hell you will. We don't know what's up that road. Who's going to quibble over a few meters if we locate the bastards?"

"Maybe so, but I don't like it."

This irritated Danton. "Look, sergeant, I don't give a damn what you like. I need you with me on this. Is that clear?"

"Yes, sir," Flannigan answered, swallowing his anger.

The platoon pressed on. Jackson was due to be relieved on point, but Danton ordered him to continue. Jackson, who was equally defiant of authority and savvy in battle, made no secret of his dislike of Danton, often questioning his tactical decisions. He considered the lieutenant a feckless idiot, a would-be lifer who cared more about promotions and medals than the lives of his men. Danton was well aware of the soldier's disdain for him but tolerated his insubordination as long as he remained useful.

Nearly a kilometer of slow, cautious movement took the platoon to an area recently carpet-bombed. Trees stripped of their limbs by the blast lay like toothpicks—a devastating display of American firepower. But the NVA supply routes were like ant trails, easily rerouted. The platoon skirted the blast area and picked up the road where it ascended a ridge in virgin forest. Jackson raised a fist and took a knee. Danton, fourth in the file, joined him.

"Hear that?" Jackson whispered.

Danton heard nothing but the unidentifiable screech of an unseen animal and the pulsating thrum of the jungle's insects.

"There it is again," Jackson said.

"I'll be damned if that isn't a chainsaw," Danton said, "somewhere up on that ridge."

Flannigan came forward in a crouch. Danton said, "They're up this road and not far. Let's take cover in that last bomb crater we passed and work from there."

Just then, two trucks appeared on the road, crawling in low gear up the grade with cargoes of ammo crates stacked high in the beds. Four NVA soldiers lolled atop the crates. The grunts lay low in the trees, watching. "Special delivery from Hanoi," Danton whispered to Flannigan. "All that ammo—there's something big going on up there."

The platoon doubled back to the crater, a pit gouged from the earth by a one-thousand-pound bomb. It was large enough to swallow a school bus. Danton and Flannigan sat at the bottom of the crater, poring over a map. Danton estimated the platoon was about twelve hundred meters northwest of where it had spent the night. "That would put us here, at the base of this ridge," he said with more certitude than warranted, pressing a black dot onto the map with a grease pencil.

The road climbed a forested ridge in the rolling terrain. Flannigan knew from experience with many young officers that their land navigation skills varied greatly, and Danton's ability to read a map diminished with distance from a known point. The terrain was undulating, lacking prominent features, which made positioning difficult. There were no obvious landmarks. Nevertheless, Danton dictated map coordinates to his RTO, to be encrypted and relayed back to the battalion along with the message, "Full House," code for having located the NVA.

Something had been bothering Flannigan about this mission. If detected, a platoon of eighteen men would have a hard time moving rapidly through this terrain. Reinforcements were at least an hour away, and clearings large enough to land helicopters were hard to find. If detected by the enemy, Recon would have to run, but where? Of course, Recon was expected to avoid detection, but he felt as if the platoon had been thrown into a shark tank to spy on the sharks.

Danton, however, seemed unconcerned. He put a fresh plug of Copenhagen under his lip and tucked his map back into his thigh pocket. "There's something you don't know, Flannigan," he said. "The highers believe an enemy sapper battalion has headquarters somewhere in this area. That's the only reason we were left here, to find it. The NVA chose not to take us on when we arrived and just pulled back, deeper into Cambodia. Now they've apparently resumed operations, and we need to know what's up on that hill. I'll be damned if I'm going to leave until I can bring back a full report on what we found."

What did a "full report" mean? And how pull it off without getting caught? "Okay, I'll take one man and a radio and see how close I can get," the sergeant said, hoping he could satisfy the lieutenant's curiosity and get the platoon extracted back to the base camp.

"No, I'll go. You stay put. I have to see for myself," Danton said.

Officers didn't normally separate themselves from their platoons, at least not intentionally. Danton never missed an opportunity to impress his superiors. Did he see this as another opportunity. Or did he have a death wish?

"I want to take the best man in the platoon with me," Danton said, "and that would be Jackson. He moves like a cat."

The two of them alone on a scouting mission? Flannigan didn't think so. "Why not take a couple of others, anyone but Jackson."

"We're quicker and quieter with two. Besides, if we get caught, it won't matter how many of us there are. And I want Jackson."

Jackson was on guard with two others at the edge of the crater when Flannigan stood over him. “Well, Top,” Jackson said, “we found ’em, so when do we get out of here?”

“The lieutenant wants to talk to you.”

“What does he want now?”

“He wants to take look-see up that hill.”

“What do that mean to me?”

“You are going up there with him to scout it out.”

“Alone?”

“The two of you.”

“That mutherfucker crazy, man. Why? Call in the air attack and let’s head for Camp Farrell.”

“Not your decision to make, Jackson. Now get ready. No ruck, just bandoliers and as many frags as you can carry. You’ll need your pack frame ’cause you’ll be humping a radio.”

“Ain’t happenin’, Top. If he wants to get greased, he can do it alone. I’m not goin’.”

The other two grunts nodded in agreement, and Flannigan himself thought it was a big mistake. Whatever was transpiring on that hill, why take unnecessary risks? Tell the generals what we have found and let them draw their own conclusions. But Danton was never satisfied, and once he’d made up his mind, you couldn’t change it.

Flannigan said, “Okay, soldier, I’m issuing you a direct order. Besides, if you don’t go, someone else will have to go in your place. That what you want?”

Jackson pondered it for a moment, ripped off his helmet, and threw it on the ground. “Damn it, Top, that ain’t fair.”

“Nothin’ fair in this man’s army, Jackson.”

Glowering, Jackson pulled two frags from his ruck, dropping them in his thigh pockets. Two more went into an ammo pouch on his pistol belt. He hung two bandoliers of M-16 ammo across his chest and, mumbling epithets, accompanied Flannigan to Danton’s position in the crater.

It was early afternoon when the officer and the grunt left the crater, Jackson carrying the “Prick 25” radio on a ruck frame. They had gone only a little over a hundred meters when they heard a truck approaching on the road and watched from hiding as it passed. A couple of dozen NVA troops sat in its bed, most of them slumped and dozing. How far had they traveled? The truck disappeared around a bend.

The two grunts continued the climb, concealed by thick undergrowth and guided by a growling engine and sounds of construction. As they drew near, voices became audible. To Danton, this was tantalizing; to Jackson, foreboding. They knew they were very near when they came upon a patch of freshly felled trees and tracks of a vehicle with large tractor-like tires. The timber had been harvested and dragged away, but for what purpose? Danton meant to find out.

He motioned Jackson to stop. “It’s got to be just ahead. Let’s get back to that road,” he whispered. Jackson followed him reluctantly as he angled to the right and regained sight of the road at a hairpin turn. Staying a safe distance away, they followed it around the curve and came upon a crew of NVA troops busily unloading the truck they had observed earlier.

"Back, back, back," Danton whispered and the two ducked back into a tangle of low palms on the shoulder of the road. "We're going to have to work our way around that truck to find out where all that ammo is going."

Jackson shook his head defiantly. "You go, you want to, dude. I've seen enough."

"What's the matter, Jackson, yellow?" Danton said.

"Ain't yellow, ain't crazy neither," Jackson replied.

"Look, I'm not putting up with any more of your bullshit, soldier," Danton snarled. "I need that radio, and you're stayin' right behind me. That's an order."

Jackson's blood was boiling. He was tempted to tell the lieutenant to go to hell and return to the platoon, but Danton would accuse him of cowardice and disobeying a direct order. No, he'd have to stay with the officer but only for now. The two circled through the jungle, giving the truck a wide berth. They reached a point where they could observe from hiding some kind of construction activity. The engine noise was coming from a backhoe, pushing soil into a pile. NVA troops and indigenous workers passed by carrying timbers on their shoulders. So that's it, Danton surmised, they're building bunkers. But he couldn't be sure.

"Okay, we've seen it; now let's get the hell outta here," Jackson whispered.

"Negative," Danton replied, transfixed. "If it's a bunker complex, it's a damn big one. If not, what is it? I've got to know."

"What difference do it make? Call in the air strikes."

Danton dismissed him as if he was an obstinate child. Watching at a distance through the trees was like peering through knotholes at a baseball game. They had windows to parts of the playing field but couldn't see the diamond. "We got to get closer. We can cross this open area and drop behind that bamboo thicket up there without being seen," Danton said coolly. "We'll make it easy. They won't be looking."

Jackson surveyed the fifty meters between them and the bamboo. The larger trees were sparse, the undergrowth low. They would have to sprint from tree to tree, then crawl. If someone in the NVA camp happened to be looking or out taking a leak or whatever, they might be seen. He didn't like the odds. "I ain't goin'," he declared.

Danton had had enough. He said angrily, "What d'you mean you ain't goin'?"

"What I said."

Danton was furious. "I'm ordering you, goddamn it."

Jackson just stared at Danton with burning eyes. "You've already done that. I ain't goin' any closer."

This was no place for an argument, and Jackson held the upper hand, at least for now. Danton had to think this through. He figured that, if he went alone, being spotted would be less likely. If the two of them were caught, the enemy would have both them and the radio, and they needed the radio in case they ran into trouble. "We're wasting time. I'll deal with you later. Report our situation to Top and wait for me here with the radio. And don't move. You got that?"

"Umm hmm."

Danton shed his two bandoliers and slid a single magazine into his left thigh pocket. Two frags went in the right one. M-16 in hand, he took off, sprinting from tree to tree, watching the NVA for the next opportunity to make a move. Jackson lost sight of him in waist-high palm and scrub. He must be crawling now, Jackson figured; that one crazy muthafucker.

Danton's head popped up like a prairie dog's until he neared his objective, then he bolted ten steps into a clump of bamboo. Well, Jackson concluded, he made it. Now let's see if he can get his sorry ass back. He unhooked the radio handset from his ruck strap, intending to raise Sergeant Flannigan. As he put it to his ear, the sergeant's voice broke through the static: "Big Eyes Six, this is Big Eyes Five. Need a sitrep. Over."

Jackson said, "We found 'em. Over."

"How many? Over."

"Too many. They buildin' somethin' near the top of this ridge. Over."

"Tell me exactly what you see. Over."

"Lots a' NVA carryin' logs, a little tractor pushin' dirt around. 'Bout it. Over."

"Okay, put Six on. Over."

"He ain't here. Over."

"Say again?"

"He headed off by himself."

"Where the hell did he go? Over."

"To get a closer look. Over."

"Without you and the radio? Over."

"Affirmative. Over."

"I don't know what's going on up there, but you get your butt and that radio to him on the double. Do you read me? Over."

"He told me to stay put. Half the gook army up there. They see us. We all fucked."

Flannigan was as angry with Danton as he was with Jackson. It was just like the lieutenant to take chances like this. There wasn't a damn thing he could do about it now. Moving the platoon forward would accomplish nothing. After years of combat experience, he knew that it was best to know what peril he faced and not go charging off half-cocked. He could only hope the lieutenant would return without alerting the enemy, and if he didn't, Jackson was right: they were all in big trouble.

"Okay, let me know the second he gets back," Flannigan said.

Two more trucks arrived with troops and ammunition in the ensuing hour and a half. Jackson was getting nervous. "What's he doin' up there? By now, we could have called in air strikes and split this AO," he mumbled under his breath. "But no. Oh, hell no. Not the LT. Fucking lifers always want more. More bodies. Count their bodies. Take 'em to the bank and cash 'em for another medal. I didn't sign up to get wasted on account of no honkey fool. Coulda stayed home and got that."

He heaped contempt on others too, everyone responsible for his miserable fate: the idiot general who had decided to leave Recon behind, the assholes in the rear who slept on clean sheets while they sent men out to bleed and die in the mud, those redneck politicians back in the States who wanted this damn war until they didn't. And here he was, fighting for people who had no use for his black ass.

He stood up to urinate but cut it short and dropped to the ground. At first, he wasn't sure, but yes, someone was definitely coming, closing on him fast, three Montagnards and a single soldier with an AK-47. On their current course, they would pass within a few meters of his position, and he worried a change in direction could bring them even closer to the shrubby palm understory that hid him. He held the grip of his M-16, ready to fire, and watched them approach.

One of the tribesmen carried a chainsaw, another an axe, and the third a machete. The soldier appeared to be very young, short, small boned, and very similar in appearance to other troops from the north Recon had killed in ambushes. A red star on his pith helmet and a red bandana around his neck said he was NVA. He casually carried his rifle by the barrel over his shoulder. The tribesmen were short, muscular, and round faced, their hair thick and black. They wore loincloths and filthy T-shirts, one of them decorated with the Adidas logo.

Jackson's mind raced through options, which were few. Using his rifle would only make things worse. He could spring on them with his Bowie knife, figuring he could easily take out the NVA, a much smaller man. But he couldn't predict what the tribesmen would do, whether they would bolt or use their tools to fight him.

He lay prone and held his breath, not daring to blink. The little procession passed within steps of where he lay in the undergrowth. One of the tribesmen looked in Jackson's direction and the grunt readied himself to leap, but the Montagnard turned his head without breaking stride. The others looked straight ahead, like preoccupied commuters on their way to work. He held his breath. They passed by him, and he exhaled.

Another hour passed with no sign of Danton. Back in the crater, Flannigan was feeling helpless, and very angry. The platoon could do nothing to help Danton if the lieutenant fell into enemy hands. He could only wait and hope for the best.

Gradually activity on the hill diminished until the entire operation seemed to go dormant, no voices, no sounds of machinery, no construction noise at all. The heat of the day had arrived, and perhaps they were taking a siesta, Jackson speculated. Then the reason became clear: a loud whump made the earth wince, and the blast wave from an explosion passed over him.

Meanwhile, Lieutenant Danton, hiding in a grove of bamboo, had been watching tribesmen and their NVA controllers digging a tunnel into the slope of the hill. Having no effective air force and spotty anti-aircraft defenses, the Northern army and the VC relied on a sophisticated system of tunnels for defense and concealment. What he was watching here made sense, considering the recent heavy US carpet-bombing of the Ho Chi Minh Trail in border areas.

He watched, mesmerized. NVA troops passed back and forth through his field of vision. He tried to count them but gave up, unable to determine whether he was double-counting. More arrived on foot and in two trucks. They had to be garrisoned somewhere up the road. Troop quarters, an ammunition depot, a hospital, a command center? All of these were plausible uses of the tunnel. Was this the sapper battalion detected in the area? Maybe the geniuses in intel at Long Binh could sort it out.

While he watched, tribesmen carried baskets of soil and rocks from the tunnel and emptied them for the backhoe loader to plow into a ravine. Several indigenous women were carrying infants on their backs in slings, indicating there were villages in the area, perhaps the very ones that had been precipitously abandoned before the invaders arrived. Were they Degar or Jarai of Vietnam or Khmer Loeu of Cambodia? The distinctions were lost on him. A more important question was, were they collaborators or forced laborers? The presence of civilians would complicate an air strike, with growing concern about "collateral damage." He was glad he had pressed on and now had visual confirmation of a specific target for an air strike.

He looked at his watch. He had been here over two hours. He rolled to his side and took the measure of the terrain he had to cover to reach Jackson and the radio. It looked at least one football field in length, his visual yardstick, and much farther than it had seemed earlier. He would have to run with his back to the enemy. At that moment, he saw construction activity at the tunnel stop and workers clearing the area, the same pause Jackson was observing. It's now or never, Danton decided, and he took off on a dead run just as an explosion shook the ground and the tunnel coughed dirt and debris from its mouth.

22
STIRRINGS OF MUTINY

Colonel Standley's Jeep jounced along an oiled dirt road past squat clapboard buildings immured with sandbags. He was on his way to the division headquarters, and he was ebullient. He was bringing General Taggart the first good news the battalion had in months. That fox Danton has found the enemy, and this time the element of surprise is ours, Standley was convinced.

Finishing the job seemed simple enough: Danton would safely retreat to an LZ for extraction under cover of air strikes. The plan seemed sound, but he wanted to be prepared for any eventuality. He went over the details in his mind: aircraft would have to be standing by to conduct the air strikes; helicopters would have to be at the airstrip on the border, ready to insert Delta Company if anything went wrong; and more troops standing down at the base camp would have to be ready to go back into Cambodia in the worst case.

At the division headquarters, General Taggart and his staff listened intently as Colonel Standley summarized Lieutenant Danton's report: a large tunneling project, a possible ammo and ordnance cache, a heavy concentration of troops in a staging area, possibly the headquarters of the sapper battalion mounting periodic attacks in the Central Highlands and along the coast.

Taggart studied a large topographical map of the area. "Interesting. Can we get more granularity? I mean, what do we actually have here? How many troops? Command indications? And what else is in the area? Civilians?"

"Lieutenant Danton thinks the enemy operation is spread out over the area. Hard to know, but this may be the heart of it. The abandoned villages we found earlier belonged to indigenous locals. Are they Khmer Rouge or just locals put to work by the NVA? Again, it's hard to say."

"That tunnel fascinates me," Taggart said, ruminating. "I'd sure like to know more about it before we hit it."

"What about those locals?" Standley cautioned.

"We need good targeting. Can your Recon boys get a fuller picture? Obviously, we have to be careful."

Standley stared at the map, but he wasn't seeing it; he was thinking. He said, "That won't be easy. The longer we leave the platoon in there, the more risk we lose them. I'd like to run it by Danton first."

General Taggart looked at his watch. It was nearly 1800 hours, not enough daylight left to pull Recon out anyway. "Okay, talk it over with him and get back to me."

Standley fretted on his way back to the battalion area. Recon's shit was hanging out a mile. He didn't want to lose a platoon. And putting civilians at risk raised concerns he didn't even want to contemplate. There was only one person who could give him cover on this: Danton.

As darkness set in, Recon's grunts lay like the spokes of a wheel on the rim of the bomb crater. The sounds of the NVA hung in the still night air: shouts, laughing, metallic banging, a truck that wouldn't start. Occasionally they observed points of light bobbing along the road—flashlights. There was movement, lots of it. The work on the tunnel was obviously continuing through the night.

Danton and Flannigan huddled under a poncho in the bottom of the crater where they could study a map with a flashlight. The red luminescence of its filter bathed their faces. Standley had gotten the response he might have expected from Danton: if the general wanted more intelligence, Recon would provide it if possible. Now Danton had to tell Flannigan, who expected the platoon would be calling in air strikes and heading for an LZ and extraction in the morning.

"There was a cassava plot here," Flannigan whispered, pointing at a spot near one of the abandoned villages. "Plenty of room for an LZ. I think we can be back there in less than an hour."

"Good. Let's get the coordinates back to the battalion," Danton said.

"I'll have everyone ready to move out at first light."

"Not so fast. I just got off the radio with Colonel Standley."

"Now what?"

"The highers have more for us to do before we leave."

"You can't be serious. What now?"

"Take it easy. They need better targeting for air strikes. All these villages have, you know, women and children. There's that civilian casualty thing."

"When has that bothered them? Hell, they've been carpet-bombing this area for months. We're sitting in a hole big enough to flatten a whole village."

"I don't ask questions; I just follow orders."

"I hope you told Standley we are sitting in the middle of an enemy stronghold. If we get caught, God help us."

"We're not going to get caught," Danton whispered assertively. "So listen up."

Danton's plan was to move east toward the nearby Tonle Son River, a major blue line, and do it under the cover of darkness. It had to be the main source of water for the local tribes and the NVA. There would probably be more villages, and what else? There was only one way to find out.

Flannigan listened skeptically. The platoon was already out of the range of the artillery stationed on the border. Moving a kilometer to the west would take them beyond the specified limit of the incursion. And just as concerning to the sergeant—extending the operation would not go down well with the grunts who had anticipated they would be withdrawing to an LZ for extraction in the morning to Camp Farrell and then stand down.

Flannigan attempted one more time to change Danton's mind. "I don't like this, LT. This mission's got way too much hair on it. Why not direct air strikes on that tunnel?"

"Jesus, Flannigan, you sound like an old woman."

"Yeah, and I'd like to get a little older."

Danton killed the flashlight. "This discussion is over. Get the squad leaders down here. I want Jackson's squad in the lead and him on point."

"After today?"

"Because of today. That man is going to follow orders or else."

In the pale light of a new moon, Flannigan picked his way along the crater's rim, rounding up the four squad leaders. They found Danton eating from a C-ration can. "Ham and motherfuckers," he grunted. "The low bidder who sold this slop to the Army should face a firing squad. Okay, gather 'round. I've got something to tell you."

The grunts greeted the news of their extended mission in Cambodia with disbelief. The platoon had accomplished what it was left in Cambodia to do. Staying any longer was insane. They were vastly outnumbered, and if discovered, they would be running for their lives with no route of escape. They would likely be run to ground and wiped out long before reinforcements could reach them.

"The gooks don't know we're here, and we're going to keep it that way," Danton said, reading their minds. "And here's how. We're going to move tonight, under cover of darkness."

The squad leaders moaned. Jackson mumbled, "You gotta' be shittin' me."

"What did you say, Jackson?" Danton demanded.

"I saw what's up on that hill, hundreds of 'em; eighteen of us. And we gonna stumble around in the dark up there? That is suicide. Tell them highers we ain't—"

"That's enough, Jackson. I'm still leading this platoon, and if I want your opinion, I'll ask for it."

"Well, you got it anyway, and count me out. I ain't goin'."

Danton grabbed a fistful of Jackson's shirt, pulled him nose to nose, and seethed, "You let me down once today already. You'll follow orders. Is that clear?"

"Don't touch me, you asshole," Jackson shot back, slamming his big hand into Danton's chest. The officer staggered back on his heels. Two of the squad leaders grabbed Jackson, pinning his arms.

"Keep your voices down, for chrissake," Flannigan said, stepping between the two. "Jackson, you're way out of line."

Jackson said, "This man boocoo dinky dow, Top. He'll get us all wasted."

Danton said angrily, "Sergeant, when we get back to base camp, I want this man charged with striking an officer and disobeying a direct order. You men are witnesses."

"That's *if* we get back," Jackson sneered.

Flannigan said, "Jackson, you're no longer squad leader. Get your butt back up to your position and send Sal down here to take your place."

"Fine with me," Jackson said, cursing under his breath.

Recon's grunts waited nervously to move out. A man can stay in the bush with little or no food and under constant pressure for only so long, and they were near exhaustion, running on adrenalin. A breath of wind brought the smoky scent of cooking fires, nuc mum, and whatever the Vietnamese were cooking up. The drone of a generator and occasional shouts joined the discordant nocturnal chatter of the jungle. Flashlights flickered through the trees several hundred meters away.

It was midnight when a delegation of five grunts, Jackson among them, arrived at Flannigan's position on the rim of the crater. They huddled around him, and he knew whatever they had to say, it wouldn't be good.

Jackson spoke first. "Top, them flashlights been movin' all around us. We sittin' in the middle of the NVA's hood, and we screwed if we do what the lieutenant says. So here's what it is. We ain't goin' along with his plan. We took a vote and—"

Flannigan said, "Hold it right there before you say something that's going to get you all in some real trouble."

"Come on, Top. Ain't no trouble worse than this. I say we pull back now, call in the air strikes, and get the hell out while we still can."

"Jackson's right, Top," said Sal Romano, Jackson's replacement as the squad leader. "We took a vote, and everyone agreed. We found them Dinks; now it's time to leave. We stay longer, they'll be on us like flies on shit."

Jackson said, "So we headin' for an LZ at first light, no matter what the LT says. He wants to stay here by himself, fine. But we need you to call the choppers to come and get us."

Flannigan said, "You're talking mutiny. You know that."

Jackson said, "Call it what you want."

These men were dead serious. Flannigan was a professional soldier. He would rather chew off his right arm than be involved in a mutiny. Granted, the odds were stacked against them, but when you're under orders in battle, you comply, no matter what.

"You men return to your positions. I'll talk to Danton," Flannigan said.

"Talk good, 'cause we di-di outa here in the morning, with or without him," Jackson said.

Flannigan headed down to Danton's command post with no idea what he was going to say. The lieutenant would issue a direct order, charge his men with cowardice, and promise court-martials, all too predictable. But here, deep in a Cambodian jungle, his threats were empty, his officer's commission as useful as a matchbook diploma; he needed the respect and confidence of his men, and he had neither.

Flannigan found Danton under his poncho with a flashlight, writing a letter. Was it to his wife, just in case? The lieutenant folded the letter and tucked it into his helmet liner. He said, "Everyone briefed, ready to go?"

"Not exactly," Flannigan said.

"Is there a problem?"

"I think it falls into that category."

"What's going on?"

Flannigan braced himself. "Seems that the men have taken a vote. They're heading for an LZ at first light."

For once, the eruption Flannigan expected didn't occur. It was too dark to see Danton's face clearly, but he knew the man was smoldering. Danton said, "Jackson's behind this, isn't he?"

"It's not just him."

"Of course, you informed them of the consequences and ordered them not to do it."

"Yes."

"I can have them locked in the slammer for twenty years."

"They know."

Danton got quiet again. Flannigan guessed the officer was weighing his options. Some or all of the platoon could defy a direct order, stripping him of any shred of authority he had left, and he couldn't really have them all charged with mutiny. The word itself implied a shameful lack of leadership, an embarrassment.

At length, he said, "And you, Sergeant Flannigan, what do you say?"

"I think they have a damn good reason to be worried."

"Worried? About what? Don't they get it? There was a reason the NVA didn't stand and fight when the battalion blew in and out of here a few weeks ago. They want us to think there's nothing here. They're protecting something big, something they don't want to lose."

"What more do we need to know? I mean why not pull back and call in air strikes?"

"Because I want to know what we've got here," Danton said. "Don't they get it? This could be the command center for that sapper battalion we've been chasing for months. We can hand it to the general on a silver platter. I need this, Flannigan."

He pulled a pouch of chew from his breast pocket and pushed a plug into his cheek. It galled him to negotiate with his men, but if they refused to follow orders here, there wasn't much he could do about it. All he needed was a little more time, one more sweep.

"Sergeant, I can't submit to this gross dereliction of duty, this, this . . . mutinous threat. However, I'm not an unreasonable man. I can make adjustments to my plan. We move toward the blue line tonight, arrive by early morning, and gather what intelligence we can. Then we pull back to an LZ for extraction before nightfall, say, 1800 hours. One more day—that's all I need."

"I don't think they're in a mood to dicker."

"Damn it, I'm not dickering. I'll inform the battalion and have air support standing by. We'll be back in Camp Farrell by tomorrow evening. And oh, throw this in. I'll see to it they get an in-country R&R, three days in Vung Tau. They can go fuck their brains out. Tell 'em. And oh, Flannigan, there is no taking sides here. You will support my command. Is that clear?"

"Yes, sir."

After a twenty-year career in the army, Flannigan never dreamed it would come to this. He despised this officer but owed him his obedience as long as what he wanted was lawful. "But there's one more thing," Flannigan said. "You need to drop this business of having Jackson sent to the stockade."

"The hell I will," Danton said. "I'm going to teach that kid a lesson."

"LT, listen to me. You want the men to this; you have to let it go."

Danton spat tobacco juice and slapped a mosquito on his neck. "Well, okay, but I want him transferred to a line company. He's more trouble than he's worth."

Flannigan was disgusted. When he had arrived in Vietnam on his first tour four years earlier, it was with men who had trained together in the States. There was unit cohesion, soldiers who would never think of defying their officers. Not that these late arrivals weren't good fighters or lacking in character. It was the war that was breaking the Army's back, destroying the Army as he knew it.

"Well?" Jackson said when Flannigan rejoined them on the lip of the crater.

"Well, he is willing to change his plan. Move to that blue line, see what we can see, then pull back and find an LZ for extraction. Air strikes for cover. So he wants one more day, and he's willing to throw in some in-country R&Rs when we get back to base camp."

"No deal," Jackson snapped.

Flannigan said, "Hold on. Let's think about this. He'll lay on the air strike and have the birds coming for us. He won't press charges against anyone."

Jackson said, "Give a shit. Tomorrow, next week, next year, all the same. I say we get out now, while we still can."

"What about the rest of you? He's trying to be reasonable."

"I think we need to take this back to the guys," one of the squad leaders said. "At least, I'm not willing to make the decision for my guys."

"Come on, bros, we ain't negotiatin' with that prick," Jackson said.

"We need to run it by the guys, man," one of the others agreed. "They need to have a say."

Flannigan sensed some of the men were vacillating. "Okay, you men talk it over, but make it fast. We haven't got much time."

The five split up and disappeared in the dark. When they were gone about an hour, Flannigan began to worry. The night was expiring and with it any hope of an agreement. Danton would be wondering. Since when did troops take a vote on following orders? This was unheard of, a gross dereliction of duty if not outright mutiny. He heard footsteps approaching. The squad leaders squatted around him.

Jackson's whisper was barely audible. "I think it's a big mistake, but okay, we do it on one condition. When we get back, Danton is gone from the platoon. He moves on. We all had 'nuff of that son of a bitch."

Flannigan was nonplussed. The deal was getting complicated. "Come on. Why would he agree to that?"

"'Cause he's got no choice."

"Let me understand this. You want him to request a reassignment."

"No request," Jackson said. "We refuse to hump out with him again."

"That's right," one of the others said. "And he has to make good on it. If he doesn't, we'll sit down on the next operation. And we need to know if you are with us or against us, Top."

This demand was too outrageous to succeed. If he took the men's side, he could face a court-martial himself. But if he took Danton's side, he'd lose the trust and respect of the men he cared about.

When Flannigan arrived at Danton's position, the lieutenant was again under his poncho, this time encrypting a report to the battalion headquarters. "Do we have an agreement?" Danton asked from beneath the poncho.

"They're okay with it, on one condition."

"No conditions. This little game is over."

"No, I think you should consider this. It might be best for everyone concerned."

"What is it?"

"They want you to put in for a transfer as soon as we get back."

There was a wheezing sound under the poncho. Flannigan took it for a laugh. He had rarely heard Danton laugh.

"Well, you just tell them I'm pleased to oblige. It just so happens that when I get back to base camp, I get my captain's bars and a company to command. Colonel Standley already approved it. In fact, he insisted on it. So you just tell them I agree, but that's all you tell them. No mention of my new assignment. You roger that?"

"Yes, sir."

The dead night air carried sounds from the NVA camp: a humming generator, a truck engine cranking, a rooster crowing, the lugubrious singsong of a Vietnamese soprano broadcast from Hanoi. The grunts silently checked their weapons and fell into a single file. They wouldn't need their rucks, which were left in the crater. It was too dark to see much more than two arms' length.

The enemy was now moving all around them on the road and on trails, streaming back toward positions it previously occupied closer to the border. On the previous day's hump, Flannigan had made mental notes of slash cuts and clearings spacious enough for helicopters to land and lift Recon out. If it could avoid detection behind a wall of air strikes, Recon might be able to reach an extraction point before the enemy knew what hit them.

The sergeant glanced at the thin crescent of a waning moon, believed to be a time to end a bad relationship. But for now,

Danton held on to his command, and his platoon followed him into the darkness. Holding an azimuth in the jungle at night was difficult at best, and where the platoon would find itself when the sun rose, no one could be sure—hopefully, not in enemy hands. Flannigan pulled his compass from his breast pocket and watched the heading. It was all he could do.

23
THE CALL COMES

To anyone who happened to be watching on the other side of the border, the grunts of Delta Company appeared to be engaged in routine patrols from an old special forces camp. Their actual mission was to be prepared to make an air assault back into Cambodia on minutes' notice. When Delta's Captain Gilman summoned his platoon leaders to report on the double, they feared the worst.

Gilman related the situation as he knew it: Recon had run into trouble. Heavily outnumbered, the platoon was engaged in an intense firefight. Fixed-wing aircraft and helicopter gunships were flying in support. Delta Company was to immediately air assault back into Cambodia, land in a cleared patch of the jungle about two kilometers from Recon, and link up in all haste.

Hoffman had put religion on hold years earlier when he had left home for college. Like the young Saint Augustine who prayed, "Lord, make me chaste, just not yet," he figured he would get straight with God later. Now, it seemed like a good time to pray.

Delta Company's men stood in formation on the dirt airstrip with a double issue of an infantryman's arsenal: belts of machine gun ammo wrapped around their bodies like Mexican bandits, extra M-16 bandoliers crossed on their chests, and rucks bulging with light anti-tank weapons, Claymore mines and fragmentation grenades, C-rations, and water. They'd been stalking the NVA for nearly a month, enduring hunger, thirst, filth, and sleeplessness, living like animals. Hoffman wondered, Are my eyes as hollow as theirs? He took a roll call:

"Dankovich."

"Here."

"Armijo."

"Yo."

"Schirado."

"Present."

"Sullivan . . . Sullivan." Hoffman looked up from his roster. "Where the hell is my RTO?"

"Jerking off," someone offered.

There were bursts of laughter in the ranks. "He's changing his battery, LT," someone in the rear blurted.

"I'm here, damn it," Sullivan shouted, shambling into the formation with his ruck in one hand and his radio and pack frame in the other.

"Glad you could make it," someone said.

"One of you assholes want to carry this fucking thing?" Sullivan fired back.

"Want to suck my dick?" another said.

"Okay, knock it off," Hoffman said. "I need you to be serious for a minute."

Humor was the infantrymen's antidote to dread. Cambodia was a netherworld of fleeting forms and incipient doom. They'd been there, and they did not want to go back. A dust devil worked its way across the runway's hardpan. Hueys idled at the end of the airstrip, and more circled above. The tropical rheostat was set to high, and the day's heat was building. At least air support would be unimpeded by the weather if they needed it. With all present and accounted for, Captain Gilman briefed his troops:

"Gentlemen, here are our marching orders. Recon is pinned down near an NVA tunnel complex. It's a klick or so west of the area we left two days ago. Our objective is to assault a nearby LZ, link up with Recon, and reinforce them until more troops can arrive. I won't minimize the difficulties involved. There could be a battalion of NVA in the area. We will establish and hold a defensive position until Bravo and Charlie companies can be lifted in from base camp."

A slick flew low over the formation, drowning out Gilman. He waited for it to pass and continued, "Forward air control has located a suitable LZ about one kilometer south of Recon's current position. Gunships are now prepping the area. We will move to link up with Recon as soon as we land. That's all I know at this time. Godspeed, and I'll see you on the LZ."

Three Hueys taxied down the strip and settled near the company formation. Hoffman's platoon ran to its birds and scrambled aboard. The grunts sat cross-legged, leaning back on their swollen rucks, cradling their weapons in their laps. The three slicks were quickly airborne and climbing over the trees, followed by another sortie. In minutes, the entire company was on its way.

Hoffman's bird bumped along on thermals high above the rolling heavily forested wilderness of Ratanakiri Province, Cambodia, one of the most remote and uninhabited areas of the country. A silver ribbon of river wound through the jungle, destined for its confluence with another stream and onto the Mekong. The air was refreshingly cool at several thousand feet, the rolling landscape post-card placid. The helicopters passed over a fire support base in the distance, and Hoffman could observe the artillery rounds leaving the canons and arcing toward their targets somewhere to the north.

The chopper was airborne no longer than ten minutes when it banked sharply and began a descent. The door gunner pulled the cocking lever of his M-60 and prepared to fire. Two F-4 Phantoms circled and dove in like crop dusters, leaving behind them geysers of black smoke. The grunts on board scooted their legs out the door and prepared to hit the ground running.

The slick skimmed the treetops, its blades slapping the air with the rhythm of jackhammers. Hoffman saw a large clearing in the jungle ahead, felt for the skid with his boots, and shifted his weight over his legs. He watched the ground come up and stepped off before it touched down, ran ten steps, and dropped into a recently cultivated plot. So there had to be a village nearby. As far as he could tell, the LZ was cold, a grunt's fervent prayer. The next three helicopters were already landing when he directed his men to take up positions in the tree line and set up security.

The entire company was inserted without incident. So far, so good. With the helicopters gone and quiet restored, explosions and small arms fire could be heard to the north. The rifle reports indicated disciplined shooting, no bursts of automatic fire, but there were explosions too. Well, Hoffman wondered, did Danton finally got the big battle he always wanted?

"I just raised Flannigan, Recon's platoon sergeant, on the horn," Gilman told his officers. "They're about eight hundred meters north of us, in this line of hills." He pointed to a coordinate on his topographical map. "Flannigan says they're pinned down in a bomb crater with KIAs and WIAs, nearly out of ammo. He estimates as many as several hundred NVA in the area, maybe a battalion."

"Jesus," Gildersleeve exclaimed.

"Yeah, it doesn't sound good. I've called for reserves from base camp as fast as they can get here, but Recon can't wait that long; we've got to move now."

Gilman assigned Gildersleeve's Third Platoon to take the lead. When the company reached Recon's position, it would secure a perimeter with the help of air support and hold off the enemy until relief from Camp Farrell arrived. Guided by the sound of battle, Delta Company moved in a column of twos. A patchwork of dense forest, tangled thickets, and dry streambeds stood between them and the embattled Recon. The troops moved as quickly as the terrain would allow, expecting the sickening sound of enemy fire directed at them at any moment.

Like the firing of a starter's pistol, the shots that rang out from the right of the column came as a relief of sorts. Several AK-47 rounds whizzed at Gildersleeve's point man, one of them striking him in the thigh and spinning him to the ground. The grunts behind him scrambled for cover, all but the medic. Reacting instantly, he shed his ruck and ran forward with his medical kit, ignoring shouts to stay down. The AK-47 cracked again, two rounds, both striking him in the chest.

It took a few agonizing moments to locate the source of the well-aimed shots, the doing of a sniper. The dense screen of foliage was like a window with one-way glass: the sniper could see them, but they couldn't see him. The grunts lay behind trees, heads down, firing blindly in the direction of the initial burst. Every attempt to peek from behind their cover drew fire from their tormentor who was so near they could hear a metallic click when he reloaded a magazine and changed his position.

Hoffman's platoon was in the rear of the column, not directly vulnerable. Gilman radioed instructions to maneuver to the right and attempt to flank the sniper. The rest of the company held fire while the Second Platoon crept forward, listening to the sniper's firing to get a fix on his location. This was a clever operator, not like a monkey in a tree, but on the ground, changing positions after every burst.

The platoon came to a small draw where the point man caught a fleeting glimpse of an individual disappearing into a stand of trees. He emptied a magazine at him, and the platoon gave chase but couldn't find him in the forest. Like a chameleon, a small man skilled in camouflage could hide in plain sight. He had done his damage and was finished for now.

The company moved forward again, now with Hoffman's platoon in the lead and Gildersleeve's platoon falling back with the dead and wounded. Led by the sound of gunfire and bombing runs of the F-4s, there was no need for a compass. The grunts neared the fighting. Smoke and the gassy odor of napalm hung in the air. Occasional shards of shrapnel zipped through the canopy. Now there was a risk from friendly fire, and Hoffman halted the column while he tried to raise Recon on the radio: “Tiger Five, this is Delta Two Six. Do you read me? Over.”

Flannigan’s voice shouted back, “This is Tiger Five. I read you, Lima Charlie. Where the hell are you?”

“Just to your east. Can you send up a flare? Over.”

“Affirmative. Here it comes.”

A parachute flare swished and popped above the canopy about sixty meters away. Hoffman pointed his compass at the sputtering flare before it disappeared into the trees.

“Tiger Five, Delta Two Six. We’re approaching from the southwest. We’re going to call off the fire support until we find you. Do you copy? Over.”

“Roger, but make it fast.”

“Okay, we’re coming in.”

24
A FATAL OBSESSION

Fishing boats bobbed at anchor just offshore. Medical personnel tossed frisbees or sunbathed on OD blankets beside pretty bikini-clad Vietnamese girls. The blades of helicopters coming and going scattered the shouts of men playing volleyball on the beach.

The war seemed very remote from the evacuation hospital at Qui Nohn where First Lieutenant John Hoffman and Master Sergeant Conner Flannigan had just finished a breakfast of bacon, eggs, and toast. They sat in wheelchairs at the hospital's entrance, across an airstrip paralleling the shore. The two had arrived by medevac two days earlier and were awaiting transport back to the States. It was the first chance they had to talk since the battle in Cambodia.

"At about 0300, we moved out of that bomb crater," Flannigan recounted. "We had maybe a few feet of visibility in the dark. We could hear the NVA jabbering like a troop of monkeys off to our right. I feared we would stumble right into them; I told him so, but he just kept pushing. Never listened, that man. Anyway, somehow, we reached the blue line before first light."

"Blue line?"

"Yeah, it was in the general direction he wanted to go, and when you can't see where the hell you are, it was a marker. We heard it before we reached it—well, what we actually heard was a pump pulling water from the stream. We had pretty good cover along its bank, so we hunkered down there and waited for daylight.

"It was still pretty gray when we made out two individuals approaching the stream. One of them squatted in the shallows and got busy with something. The other sat on a rock on the bank. With more light, we saw a Montagnard woman doing laundry. The other one was NVA, apparently watching her.

"Well, Danton, right away, he whispers to me, 'We're going to grab the woman.' I tell him, 'You gotta be kidding.' He doesn't even hear me. He figures we can jump the gook from behind, take him out, and snatch the woman. By the time anyone in the camp misses them, we're gone with her and everything she knows about the NVA operation.

"Well, under the circumstances, it was crazy, but there was one good thing about it. If we pulled it off, we got the hell out of there, and no more argument about that. So he picks three men, two to take out the NVA while he and another go after the woman. It was getting light, so they had to move fast."

Hoffman said, "So, was the NVA soldier armed?"

"Well, if he was, it wasn't in his hands or on his shoulder. He looked pretty laid-back, and why wouldn't he be? The two men assigned to take him out crept through the jungle to a point behind him, while Danton and his man waited where we were. That water pump made a lot of noise, and our boys had no trouble springing on the gook from behind. They cut his throat. The woman got up and tried to run, but Danton charged after her and tackled her in the stream. She screeched, and I knew this ain't good. She fought him hard and bit him when he tried to muzzle her with his hand.

"They dragged her up the bank to us. When I got a good look at her, I realized I'd seen her before, or else she's a dead ringer for the Montagnard gal we chased halfway across Vietnam . . . you know, the one led us right into Cambodia that last time. She's pregnant, too. Danton recognizes her and says she's coming back with us. You can imagine how happy the boys were about that. Our shit is hangin' out a mile.

"She is not going to come willingly, so we have her gagged and tied hand and foot. Then things really go to hell. Along comes another NVA trooper down the trail to the stream. He's armed, and he's in a hurry. Maybe he heard the screaming, maybe not, but he's looking for his buddy, and when he sees the body, he takes off back up the trail. No way we can stop him.

"We gotta get out of there, pronto. We untie the woman's ankles, but she sits on the ground and won't budge. I tell Danton she ain't worth it, but he has his trophy, and he isn't about to leave her behind. So he has a rope looped under her armpits and assigns two of our men to get her on her feet and drag her if necessary.

"I had a pretty good idea how to get back to the bomb craters where we could get extracted, so I took point; Danton and the prisoner fell to the rear. We hadn't gone far when word came up that the file had to stop. I go back and find Danton arguing with the men in the rear. The woman had been dragging her feet, doing whatever she could to slow us down. The guys had enough and wanted to tie her to a tree and leave her, but Danton wouldn't have it. He started throwing around his usual threats, but they meant nothing.

"So he ties the rope around her neck so he can yank her along like a dog on a choke chain. I told him she was with a child, and it wasn't right. He told me not to worry, he was just teaching her to cooperate and he wouldn't hurt her.

"Well, pretty quick, the Dinks are sprinting like deer through the trees, trying to cut us off. We are taking fire. No way were we going to outrun our chasers, so we had to get to a bomb crater and defend ourselves. We were running, trying to stay together, but it was a mad scramble. In some places, the jungle was so heavy I couldn't see more than three or four men behind me, and I was afraid we were splitting up."

"Awful," Hoffman muttered. It was easy for him to imagine.

"We came to an area we passed through earlier that'd been carpet-bombed. I headed for a large crater and jumped in. Eight or ten fell in after me, but the rest were strung out. Men straggled in, and I didn't know who was missing, too busy trying to organize a defense. Finally, Danton's RTO arrives without Danton. He tells me he looked back, and the lieutenant had fallen way behind with that woman. I chewed his ass for not going back to help them." Flannigan paused reflectively. "All the LT had to do was let go of the woman. He wouldn't do it."

"You tried," Hoffman said.

"Yeah, I tried. The next few hours in the crater we were hangin' on by our fingers. The gooks were lobbing grenades; we were wingin' 'em back. Four times they tried to overrun us. It was hand to hand when they reached the pit. If it weren't for the gunships, we wouldn't have made it. I directed fire as close as I dared, and I was prepared to call it in on top of us. The gunships were taking a lot of small arms, but they stayed with us. I saw one flame out, probably the one that crash-landed just across the border.

"When the birds left to refuel and reload, an F-4 showed up with napalm. Good thing. We were rationing our fire and didn't have many frags left. The two machine gunners were saving what they had left for another mass assault. That's when I heard from you on the radio. If you Delta guys hadn't reached us when you did, we'd have died in that hole, sure as hell."

Four soldiers in green T-shirts passed them carrying a basketball. Flannigan leaned forward in the chair, adjusting pillows behind him. He had a bullet wound in his shoulder and shrapnel in his back and buttocks. Hoffman was treated for shrapnel wounds in his neck and side. He suffered ear drum damage and had been rendered unconscious by a blast. For both men, the war was over. They'd be on their way back to the States in a few days.

"Danton—in a way I pitied him. I guess it had to end that way for him," Flannigan said.

"He knew what he was doing, and he did what was expected of him. More."

"I've seen a lot of medals given to fools, LT."

"Sometimes it takes a fool.'

"I won't argue that."

The two sat silently for a moment. A medevac chopper passed over them and landed on the hospital's pad. Orderlies rolled out a gurney and laid a man on it. They were in a hurry. Somewhere out there in the jungle, grunts were locked in battle.

"There's something I've been wondering about, LT," Flannigan said when the helicopter lifted away. "One of our guys said you volunteered to go look for Danton. Seemed suicidal, and hopeless in any case. We figured he had to be either dead or captured. What made you do it?"

"Not sure myself. My inclination was to think he finally got what he had coming, but it made me sick to feel that way. No one deserves to die like that. Somebody had to bring him back."

"And Jackson, of all people, goes with you. He hated Danton."

"Didn't hesitate. Just stepped up."

"Mystery to me, but you never know what's goin' on in these kids' heads. Where did you find Danton?"

"Very near where Jackson believed he might be, in a little depression where he'd taken cover. He looked to be wounded in the groin area and back and lost a lot of blood, but he was his usual congenial self. He says, 'Well, I'll be damned, Ivy League and Jackson, two of my favorite people.' He had a .45 in his hand, a rifle beside him, and empty M-16 magazines all over the place. There were NVA bodies scattered around. He must have held out until he had nothing left to fight with."

"And the woman, was she with him?"

"Right next to him, rope around her neck, as you said. Unconscious with a bad head wound. Still breathing but barely."

"Amazing they were alive. The friendly fire must have been coming in on top of them."

"Yeah, body parts hanging in the trees. It was grim. He said we had to bring her too. We told him no way; we had to get out of there fast."

"What was it about that woman?" Flannigan wondered.

"Beats me. He made a terrible fuss and said he wasn't leaving without her. He ordered us to bring her and resisted when we tried to lift him. Jackson had had enough. He pointed his weapon at the woman's head." Hoffman swallowed hard.

"He shot her?"

"Damn it, Top, I just couldn't let the kid live with that. I did it myself."

Flannigan said, "You did them all a favor."

Back at Camp Farrell, Captain Gilman sat behind a green metal desk in a small room in the double-wide trailer serving as the battalion headquarters. On the desk were a small tape recorder, a notepad, a pack of cigarettes, and an ashtray filled with butts. A single chair was positioned in front of the desk. There was a knock on the door, and a clerk peeked in: "Specialist 4 Jackson is here, sir."

"Send him in."

Jackson, his steel pot under his left arm, halted in front of the desk and waved a limp salute. "Specialist Jackson reporting as ordered, sir."

"At ease, Jackson," Gilman said unnecessarily, because Jackson already was. "Take a seat."

Jackson sat and dropped his steel pot on the floor with a clunk.

Gilman said, "You know why I wanted to see you?"

"Yes, sir. Cambodia."

"Specifically, events surrounding the death of Lieutenant Danton." He pushed a button on the recorder and checked to make sure the tape was turning. "Tell me how he got left behind."

"Didn't run fast enough."

"We can assume that, Jackson. Why wasn't he running fast enough?"

"You know already. Because of that Yard woman."

"And no one assisting him? Why?"

Jackson just shrugged.

Gilman insisted, "The Montagnard prisoner was found with Lieutenant Danton, just the two of them, alone. Why? Why were they alone?"

"She was slowing us down. We told him to cut her loose, but he wouldn't."

"So you and the others just left them behind?"

"No, sir. We didn't even know they were missin' 'til everyone got to the bomb crater."

"Everyone but Lieutenant Danton."

"Yes, sir."

From earlier interviews, Gilman knew about Danton's decision to extend the platoon's mission in Cambodia, to move at night nearer the NVA position, and to risk taking the woman prisoner. But Danton's tactical decisions, while questionable, were lawful and sound enough. That his men disagreed was immaterial. How Danton and the woman got separated from the others was harder to explain and difficult to work into the narrative Gilman was constructing.

"Okay, let's move forward to when you and Lieutenant Hoffman found him. Tell me what you saw, and don't leave anything out."

"Didn't you get that from Lieutenant Hoffman?"

"I'm asking the questions, specialist." Gilman tapped a cigarette from the pack of Camels and lit it with a short one smoldering in the ashtray. "Smoke?" he said, pushing the pack toward Jackson.

"No, thanks."

"I'll quit when I get home; at least that's what I tell myself," Gilman said, taking a drag and resting the cigarette on the edge of the desk because there was no room for it in the ashtray. He flipped back a couple of pages in his notepad, glanced at what he had written, and said, "I flew to Qui Nhon yesterday and spoke with Lieutenant Hoffman. Now I want to hear from you. So you and Hoffman backtracked and found Lieutenant Danton. Then what?"

"We found both of 'em about fifty meters away. Danton was messed up and bled a lot. Couldn't stand up. The girl was unconscious—a head wound."

"And you left her when you started back to the perimeter carrying Lieutenant Danton?"

"Yes."

"Why?"

"We couldn't carry 'em both."

"Tell me everything you observed in the area immediately around Lieutenant Danton, where he was, what he had done to defend himself. Give me the picture."

"He got himself some cover, not much, just a little low spot between some trees. The gooks must 'a rushed him several times 'cause there were dead ones around him, maybe ten; I didn't count. Looked to me like he used frags and used up all his magazines.

The air strikes were comin' in on top of him. The trees were pretty chewed up, and there were gook body parts. That's about all I can say about it."

Gilman prompted, "So he single-handedly held off the enemy long enough for Recon to reach the bomb crater. Right?"

"You say so," Jackson agreed indifferently.

"I'm asking what you say, Jackson."

"He killed a lot of NVA, him and the air support."

"So you immediately started back, you and Lieutenant Hoffman, carrying Lieutenant Danton. Is that correct?"

"Yes, sir."

"And at that point, the enemy had not broken contact," Gilman suggested.

"The Dinks were movin' through the jungle, all spread out, like they do when there are air strikes. We were tryin' to stay out of their way, takin' cover where we could. Every time we heard the Phantom, we'd hit the ground. I saw napalm on one run, and shrapnel was flyin' through the trees around us." Jackson folded his arms and looked at the floor, a thousand-yard stare.

"Take your time, Jackson," Gilman said.

"Somethin' big hit us. I don't know how long I was out, but when I opened my eyes, it was really quiet. My head hurt, and my ears were ringin'. I couldn't hear shit. I saw Hoffman and Danton layin' not far away, neither of 'em movin'. I crawled over to 'em. Hoffman was breathing but out cold. Danton—he was dead."

"You certain he was dead?"

"I know dead when I see it," Jackson shot back. "He had a hole the size of a fucking baseball in his back."

Gilman wrote on his pad. "Could it have been an enemy mortar?"

"The shit was flying everywhere. Could have been friendly fire from that F-4."

Gilman looked up from the pad. "Well, that's speculation. Must have been an enemy fire."

"Whatever," Jackson said, "don't mean nothin'."

Gilman said, "And after that?"

"After that, I carried the LT back to the defensive perimeter."

"That's quite a story, Jackson," Gilman said, dropping his pen and switching off the recorder. "Lieutenant Hoffman has put you in for a Distinguished Service Cross. You should get at least a Silver Star out of it. I'll see that it gets done."

"Don't bother."

"What?"

"All I want is out. I've had enough."

"Well, that's not mine to grant. You'll get the medal anyway. Someday you'll be proud you have it; show it to your kids."

Jackson picked up his steel pot. "Can I go now?"

"You're dismissed."

He saluted, did an awkward about-face, and walked to the door. As he left, Gilman said, "And Jackson, give yourself credit. That was a ballsy thing you did."

25
MILITARY JUSTICE

First Lieutenant Jack Hoffman got his requested stateside posting at Fort Lewis, Washington. There he would serve out the last four months of his active-duty obligation, close to home and only a few hours' drive to Vancouver, BC, where Susan had returned to help care for her ailing mother. He rented an apartment near the post, in a rabbit warren of buildings occupied almost entirely by military personnel and civilian employees. It would do for a few months.

Winter on the shores of Puget Sound was dreary enough, but an existential gloom hung over the fort. Though US involvement was winding down, there was little indication of it at Fort Lewis and nearby McChord Air Base, turnstiles for men going to and returning from Vietnam. The army continued to "process" draftees and recruits, pushing them through the meat grinder of boot camp and turning out green sausages. War protests outside the main gate had become almost routine. Jane Fonda was arrested in a sit-down the day Hoffman arrived.

At the personnel center, he found half a dozen junior officers, all back from Vietnam, waiting in the adjutant's office and discussing their new assignment preferences. "If you don't like what he's got for you, ask him what it would take for something better," one said.

"You're shitting me," another said.

"Shit, thee not. I've heard it works. What'r they gonna' do, send you back to Nam?"

It sounded apocryphal, but both men flashed a thumbs-up when they left the adjutant's office. Hoffman's turn came, and he reported to a captain sitting behind a desk, peering over piles of paper. "At ease, lieutenant," the captain said. "Hoffman, Hoffman," he mumbled as he thumbed through a stack of orders. "Why can't these clerks put things in alphabetical order? Ah here it is, the last assignment, Twenty-fourth Division. My division, too. It should have rotated home by now."

"We thought so, too," Hoffman said.

"No one knows what they're doing in this goddamn war," the captain said. He flopped open a binder. "Well, let's see what we have for you, lieutenant. There are several basic training positions open in North Fort: executive officer, Bravo Company. Report at 0730 tomorrow."

Putting recruits through their paces in the rain was the last thing Hoffman had in mind after a year humping in an Asian jungle. He considered what he had overheard in the waiting area about assignments. Should he try it? "Excuse me, sir, but have you got anything else? Something, well, indoors?"

"This isn't an employment agency, Hoffman," the captain said.

"I realize that, sir, but would you please take another look? Perhaps Johnnie Walker would help you find something."

"Are you trying to bribe me, lieutenant?"

"No, sir. Absolutely not. Just one member of the Twenty-fourth celebrating homecoming with another."

The captain checked his list again. "The judge advocate general's office—the JAG needs help with its caseload. Seems deserters are crawling out of the woodwork like mice in a burning house."

"I'm no attorney." A few hours' lecture on the Uniform Code of Military Justice in officer candidate school was the extent of his legal training.

"No sweat. You'll be a defense counsel, and they're all guilty anyway. The staff will walk you through what you need to do."

Well, it would be warm and dry and the hours regular. "Where do I report for duty?"

"Next door, the personnel center, 0800."

"Where would you like me to bring Johnnie Walker?"

"Lieutenant Hoffman, I don't know what you're talking about. But I'm in room 201 at the BOQ on the main post if you want to drop by for a drink."

The JAG occupied two floors of a World War II barracks crammed with metal desks. A dozen enlisted men pounded on typewriters. A specialist 5 near the door glanced up from his work. "Can I help you, sir? Oh, you're the new lieutenant," he said, seeing Hoffman's name tag. He identified himself as Paul Brisco and did not salute. He showed Hoffman to a desk. "You'll interview your clients here when the MPs bring them from the stockade. Do you have any legal background by chance?

"No."

"Then you're highly qualified. Winning these cases is not possible."

"How so?"

"Because they all plead guilty. The only evidence necessary for a guilty verdict is a morning report for the day the defendant was supposed to be on a plane to Vietnam."

"What if there was a good reason for a man's absence?"

"Oh, they all have a reason, but I advise against a not-guilty plea. You'll just piss off the judge for wasting his time. Besides, you'll get a chance to ask for leniency in extenuation and mitigation. These boys come up with stories their own mothers wouldn't believe."

"What about sentencing?"

"Dishonorable discharge and five years in the federal slammer. The judge sends them back to the stockade to stew on it overnight, then you go to the stockade with an offer: Leavenworth, or a seat on the next troop plane to Tan Son Nhut. Most take the airplane."

Brisco handed Hoffman a stack of manila folders. "Here are your clients. The clerks will arrange interviews. They'll also help you prepare for trial and answer any questions you have about courtroom procedures. And by the way, like me, every clerk here has a law degree. Two years and out, man. This ain't exactly a career opportunity."

"So I practice law while the lawyers do paperwork."

"Practice? Right."

The Army's upside-down way of doing things, but the job would keep him out of the weather. The trials went just as Brisco had said. His clients' stories were fanciful and often amusing, but the men had a right to say whatever they wanted in extenuation and mitigation. He found he enjoyed making them plausible, however outlandish they were.

The JAG office was closed on weekends, freeing him for the three-and-a-half-hour drive to Vancouver to visit Susan. He had been home only two weeks when he asked her to marry him. All the uncertainty that had darkened his world for the last three years was behind him. Perhaps it was the urgency of survival—no longer necessary—that drove him, but he was in a hurry, and he couldn't imagine living without Susan.

She, however, felt no such urgency. Not that she didn't love him, but he was just back from Vietnam, so why jump into marriage so soon? Why not have some fun, take some time to decompress and get to know one another? Not to mention the practical issues, like where they would live and what he would do for a living. What was the rush?

"Heck, we'll figure that stuff out together," he argued. "I'll move to Vancouver, find a job, maybe return to school. We can work out the practical details as we go along."

She smiled patiently. "What would you do in Vancouver? You really are a romantic."

"I'm serious."

"I believe you, but I need more time, and so do you, Jack, whether you know it or not."

Hoffman wondered if he was screwing this up, pushing her too hard. "Susan, you have been on my mind since the day we met. I don't think I would have survived if it wasn't for you. Please forgive me. I feel like a fool."

"Jack, in case you didn't hear me, I do love you. But please, we don't need any pressure now. Let's relax, let things settle, and get to know one another better."

That was November, and by January, Hoffman was glad they had waited. Life on the post was a grind, long hours of casework during the day and once-a-week assignments to post duty officer, a job that kept him driving around the fort checking buildings until he played the recording of reveille over loudspeakers at 0600.

Every day, poncho-draped young men stood in a seemingly endless line at the personnel center, waiting to be processed for transit to Vietnam. It was depressing, but in his final weeks of active duty, he felt a knot developing in the pit of his stomach. He would drive through the main gate a civilian soon, never to return, so why was he feeling so ambivalent? It was inexplicable. He was glad Susan wasn't there with him.

When his commanding officer summoned him, Hoffman had no idea why. The office was regulation Army, linoleum floors smelling of stale wax, bare walls, division, and American flags flanking a large desk, clear but for a neat stack of papers and two framed photos, which Hoffman assumed were of his wife and children. A sofa and coffee table looked as though they were left by accident by movers.

Hoffman came to attention three paces from his superior's desk and saluted. The colonel wore on his uniform the crossed rifles of the infantry, a Combat Infantry Badge, and rows of ribbons nearly to his shoulder.

"At ease, Hoffman. Let's sit on the sofa where we can chat," the colonel said amiably.

Now Hoffman was really curious. He noticed some documents and a small blue box on the spotless glass table top.

"Something to drink?" the colonel asked.

"No, thanks, sir." Hoffman hoped this would be short.

"I see you're about ready to leave us," the colonel said. He was a square-faced man with penetrating brown eyes and bushy eyebrows. He fixed Hoffman with that withering gaze mastered by senior officers.

"Yes, sir, in three weeks."

"You've made up your mind?"

"Yes, sir."

"Well, you're the sixth fine young officer I've lost this month. I'll be straight up with you. I've looked at your efficiency reports, your record in Nam, and your educational background, and I think you have a future in the Army. And although you are a reserve officer, I think you are regular army material. You fit the profile the army wants when this goddamn war is over."

Hoffman was caught flat-footed. "Thank you, sir; I appreciate the offer," he said, trying not to stammer, "but honestly, I hadn't planned on making the army a career."

"Hell, we're not asking you to make that decision now. Just one more year to think it over," he stressed. "This war has been hard on the Army, and we need good men. I've been in uniform now for more than twenty years and haven't regretted a moment of it. The Army has been good to my family and me. You married, Hoffman?"

"No, sir."

"Is there someone special?"

"Yes, sir, there is."

He pushed the papers and a pen to Hoffman and opened the blue box. Inside was a set of captain's bars. "Sign here, call her on the phone right now, and have her come and pin these on your shoulders."

Hoffman looked at the silver bars and tried to collect himself, choosing his words carefully. "Sir, thank you. I am grateful you think I'm deserving, but my lady and I are getting married. She would never go along with it, even for a year."

"You're sure?"

"Positive, sir."

He felt cowardly for using Susan as an excuse. He didn't know what he would do when he was a civilian again, but he had never given an Army career any consideration. The colonel leaned back, locked his hands behind his head, and gazed reflectively at the ceiling. "Well, lieutenant, I hate to lose you, but I wish you well."

As Hoffman left the room, he had a sinking feeling he was leaving something there, or rather someone, someone he had become. He headed for the JAG office where he had a few cases to wrap up. A squall blew in from Puget Sound, rain pelting the pavement. He pulled up the collar of his raincoat and splashed along in his patent black leather shoes, feeling water seep in along the seams. He had forgotten his galoshes, but he wouldn't need the shoes much longer anyway.

The day was as dark as his mood. When he reached the office, he rescheduled his appointments for the day and drove the Volkswagen he had just purchased over the Tacoma Narrows Bridge to the Kitsap Peninsula with no destination in mind. He just needed to get off the post, alone, soothed by the steady beat of the windshield wipers.

26
"THE WORLD"

By March, Susan's mother was back on her feet. Susan had a teaching position waiting for her in Sydney, but with Jack Hoffman now home in Seattle, the two had the decision to make. He maintained he was perfectly willing to move to Australia, but she balked at that.

"Honestly, Jack, that makes no sense. You wouldn't be happy there for long. What would you do? Besides, I never intended to stay more than a year or two in Sydney anyway. I can teach anywhere, and you have law school ahead of you. It would make more sense for me to move to Seattle."

"I'd be happy anywhere you are," he assured her, suspecting she wasn't entirely truthful about cutting short her sabbatical.

"Sweet of you, but let's be practical."

"You sure?"

"Perfectly."

Hoffman had $6,000 in his Soldiers' Savings Account, "blood money," he called it, held for him while he served his tour of duty in Vietnam. With $2,000, he had bought the Volkswagen Beetle, and with the remainder, he proposed to make a down payment on a house. They could live there together and share expenses. The two lovers spent weekends looking and found one they liked in

Ballard, a craftsman that needed a lot of work, but the price was right, and a VA loan made the payments affordable on a teacher's salary. His unemployment compensation, which military separation counselors had encouraged those returning to civilian life to take, would supplement her salary. He would return to school on the GI Bill.

It was April when Susan found a teaching position in an elementary school near the house, starting in September. Until then, she would waitress to help pay the bills, and Hoffman prepped for the law school admission test. The GI Bill allotment wasn't sufficient to cover the cost of his studies, let alone the cost of living, so he would have to work part-time to get through. He would take loans. It was going to be a heavy lift for both of them, but doable.

What he didn't tell Susan was he was souring on law school. The law to him was a default career, a respectable profession for lack of anything he'd rather do. And three years of legal studies after leading men in combat, never knowing whether a hail of bullets awaited him on the next LZ, in the next valley, around a bend in the trail, was like braking to a full stop from a hundred miles per hour.

Every morning he crammed for the test but couldn't concentrate. Frustrated and mentally blocked, he'd abandon the exercises and, instead, worked on the house or puttered on his sailboat, which he had taken out of storage and moored on Lake Union. He was in a foul mood, and Susan suspected something.

"Jack, are you going to be ready for the test? If you don't want to take it, then don't."

"Susan, I'm going to take that damn exam. Don't pester me about it, please."

He did take it, got a mediocre score, and applied to several local law schools. He wouldn't know for several months whether he was admitted. He searched the classifieds in the newspaper for jobs. An entry-level position in the sales department of a major pulp and paper company was open, so he visited the personnel department, filled out an application, and received a call to come in for an interview.

The only civilian suit he owned was six years old and felt like a straitjacket in the armholes and chest. The Army had given him a new body, and he needed a suit that fit. He purchased a dark-blue pinstriped suit, two ties, and three shirts, two white and one pink, a color the salesman assured him was in fashion. He couldn't see himself wearing it, but Susan liked it. On the day of his interview, he dressed and stood in front of the mirror. He felt like a clown. "Soldier, you are out of fucking uniform," he said to the image in the glass. He called for Susan. "Check me out. Am I appropriately corporate?"

"Very businesslike and very handsome." She brushed back his hair, which she had been trimming to save money. It nearly covered his ears. "Who's your barber, anyway?"

He pulled her close, and they kissed. "She's a lousy barber, but she's got great legs."

The company's headquarters were on the twentieth floor of a downtown office tower. He had the jitters, which annoyed him. This wasn't going to be a firefight. He made his way through the crowded lobby to a bank of elevators, trying to look inconspicuous. Doors opened. He stepped in with several other riders, not noticing until he reached for a button that this elevator was dead-ending on the tenth floor. He'd have to ride it down and take one going to the 20th. He looked at his watch. He had five minutes to spare, and the elevator seemed to be stopping on every floor.

When he finally arrived on the twentieth floor, the door opened to a carpeted lobby and a receptionist behind a high semicircular counter. A sandbagged bunker came to mind. The company's logo in polished brass was mounted on a mahogany-paneled wall behind her. The receptionist was answering calls with a headset. He waited and checked his watch again, trying not to appear as miserable as he felt. In two minutes, he would be late for his appointment. At that moment, an attractive young woman approached. "Can I help you?"

"I'm looking for the marketing department."

She had a nice smile. "I'm headed that way. Come with me." They threaded their way through an obstacle course of cubicles. Dozens of young men in white shirts, sleeves rolled up, ties loosened, sat at desks under fluorescent lighting, cradling phones to their ears. The floor appeared to be divided into sections; each one was served by a secretary equipped with an electric typewriter and a copy machine. For nearly three years, Hoffman had lived as an infantryman, outdoors, "in the field." Now he felt claustrophobic. White noise muted the sounds of voices and office equipment. Filtered air filled the space like a suffocating gas.

"Here we are," the young woman said, stopping outside a conference room. "Good luck with your interview." She disappeared into the maze of cubicles. How did she know I was here for an interview, he wondered. He felt like he had a sign on his back that said, "Kick me."

A secretary instructed him to have a seat on a couch outside the conference room. The door was open a few inches, and Hoffman glimpsed a slight pasty-faced fellow with a flattop haircut dressed in a white shirt and tie that seemed to be the regulation uniform. He looked like he hadn't left the office tower for fresh air in ten years, a corporate troglodyte.

Another man was already waiting on the couch, fidgeting with papers in a briefcase. A copy of *Gentlemen's Quarterly* lay on a coffee table. Hoffman thumbed through slick photos of male models posing in expensive clothes.

"They'll see you now, Mr. Coffin," the receptionist said, and Hoffman's sofa companion entered the conference room. The secretary closed the door behind him.

Fifteen minutes passed. Hoffman battled with himself: all these people, like rats in little cages . . . but we need the money . . . combat platoon leader sells toilet paper . . . well, you have to start someplace . . . working here would drive me dinky dow.

The door opened, and Coffin brushed by Hoffman without looking at him. The secretary went in and closed the door, emerging a minute later. "Mr. Hoffman, they will see you now."

"They?" Hoffman had seen only one.

The pasty-faced fellow about the same age as Hoffman introduced himself as Paul Rosen and offered a limp hand. He invited Hoffman to sit at the conference table and excused himself for a moment. Hoffman looked out the windows, the first he had seen since entering the building. The glassy façade of another office tower stared back blankly. Photos of paper mill stacks puffing smoke, maybe steam, and a few framed portraits of well-groomed, officious-looking men in their fifties and sixties hung on the walls.

Rosen returned with a colleague, also in his mid-twenties, who introduced himself as Jed Smith. His handshake was somewhat firmer than Rosen's, but he avoided eye contact. Hoffman couldn't imagine spending his life like these two in one of these buildings. The two sat opposite Hoffman, separated by six feet of polished wood. On the table in front of them were two documents, which from a distance, Hoffman recognized as his curriculum vitae. Rosen spoke first:

"I see you just completed your military service, but you have no prior civilian work experience. Is that correct?"

"Well, of course I've had temporary jobs, summers mostly, during school. As you can see, I entered the army fairly soon after graduation."

"Drafted?"

"No, volunteered for officer candidate school."

"Hmm. The position we're filling is in sales. I presume you looked at the qualifications we're looking for."

"I read the job description."

It was Smith's turn. "So, what assets do you bring to this job?" His tone was interrogatory.

"My understanding is, it's an entry-level position," Hoffman said. "I think my education and military experience reflect communication and decision-making skills. I'm confident I can handle the job."

Rosen said, "But do you think you have the aptitude for this kind of work? I mean, you personally."

"I'm not sure what you mean by aptitude. I held responsible positions in the Army. I led a platoon. I had to be adaptable to different situations. I'm a fast learner."

Rosen shrugged, picked up Hoffman's resume, and dropped it dismissively. "I'll be frank, Mr. Hoffman. Your military experience is just not relevant. You know, this Vietnam thing—we're curious. Why would anyone in their right mind volunteer for something like that?"

The question was so cold that it froze Hoffman's brain. His sphincter juddered, and his testicles felt like castanets, the familiar "pucker factor." He went into attack mode, visualizing a leap over the table, grabbing them by their necks, and taking them down. Don't do it, a voice inside him shouted. He had to get out of there, now.

"I don't like where this is going," he said, raging inside. "Thanks for your time."

He got up and left the room in a cold sweat, making his way blindly through the maze of cubicles. Now, where was that elevator? At one turn, he encountered the young woman who had shown him in.

"How'd it go?" she inquired cheerfully.

"Just great."

"Then maybe I'll see you here soon," she said.

"Somehow, I don't think so."

Seattle, his home, now seemed as foreign as the Asian jungle once did. A cold hand squeezed his heart as he joined the flow of pedestrians on his way to the parking structure. "Scumbags," he growled, still fuming over the interview. A couple walking in front of him looked back warily and sped up. Maybe he had made a big mistake leaving the Army where he had important duties, professional status, respect, and potentially a career.

When Susan asked about the interview, he demurred. "They were looking for someone with experience," he said dismissively. He gave up checking the job postings in the newspaper and took long brooding walks alone. And he drank. In the evenings, he would meet several other vets in a neighborhood bar. Susan was usually asleep by the time he came staggering home, reeking of liquor and cigarettes.

Susan began to wonder if she really knew this man. When she asked what was bothering him, he wouldn't talk about it. Once when she was doing the laundry, she found a bag of marijuana in the pocket of one of his shirts. That too? Okay, he was, after all, just back from the war. When he started school, the GI Bill would kick in, and he'd get his mind off of whatever was bothering him. He'd be challenged. They'd struggle through.

The first two notifications from prestigious law schools arrived in the mail, and neither surprised him: one rejection, one waiting list. The third came a few weeks later from a smaller less-esteemed school, accepting him. He showed the letter to Susan who was in the kitchen making coffee.

"Congratulations, darling," she said. "I knew you'd get in."

But he had been agonizing over it. He would be pushing thirty when he graduated in three or four years, which seemed an eternity. And Lord knew there were enough pettifoggers chasing ambulances in Seattle. The fact was, practicing law didn't interest him. Susan would just have to trust him to work something out. If necessary, he'd get a job in construction, something that paid well, until he decided what to do with his life.

"Susan, I've agonized over this, and I can't do it. My heart's just not in it."

She leaned against the kitchen counter, folded her arms, and closed her eyes. "Well, Jack, I can't say I'm surprised. What are you going to do?"

"I don't know, maybe back to school for an MA. Meantime, I'll find work. Just give me a little space to figure things out."

"Of course. Just talk to me. Don't do this alone."

They had occasionally been socializing with Paul and Jean Rankin. Paul, a university classmate of his who had obtained several deferments from the draft, had risen rapidly in the management of a chain of suburban newspapers. He noticed a change in his old pal and tennis partner: the Hoffman home from the war was not the easy-going, fun-loving, optimistic one he knew from college days. He was taciturn, listless, and moody when he should have been happy about resuming civilian life with a bright, delightful partner.

Rankin hadn't discussed his concerns with his friend, but when he heard Hoffman gave up on law school, he decided to suggest something—a long shot, but worth a try. When the couples were out for dinner one night, he baited the hook and made a cast. Maybe Jack was hungry enough to bite.

"So you gave up on the law, Jack. What now?"

"Maybe an astronaut."

"Seriously. What are you thinking?"

"Let's talk about something else," he said, annoyed.

"No, we're going to discuss this. Look, I have no idea what you've been through in that damn war, but it seems to me you have to put it behind you and move on."

Hoffman laughed. "Quite trite, Paul. Oh, did I say trite? I meant right. And yeah, you haven't a clue."

"Okay, so you had an awful experience, but you can't just sit and lick your wounds. I have a proposition. We have an opening in the newsroom in Bellevue. You used to write for the *Dartmouth*, good stuff too."

Rankin sold ads for the paper and recalled Hoffman wrote satirical columns for the campus newspaper. They were acerbic, witty, and popular.

"You gotta be kidding, Paul. Some self-absorbed gibberish for the college rag? That doesn't make me a journalist."

"Baloney. You could do this job in your sleep."

"With no degree in journalism and my only experience on a campus newspaper, I couldn't qualify for copyboy."

"Leave that to me."

"No, I don't think so."

Susan interjected, "Listen to him, Jack. Don't just dismiss it out of hand."

"What are we talking about here, a twenty-six-year-old cub reporter?" Hoffman asked disdainfully.

"Let's not be condescending, dude. Reporting local news is not like saving the world for democracy, but it has some socially redeeming value."

"You think that's why I went, to save the world? Where the hell were you, then?"

"Okay, well taken. That was a stupid comment. Why not give this a try?"

"So, what precisely would I be writing about?"

"City hall beat. You have a degree in political science, and you can write. The starting pay ain't great, but the job will keep you busy while you decide how you're going to make your first million."

Susan said, "Jack, please, take him up on it. What do you have to lose?"

Hoffman drew circles on the tablecloth with a spoon, an old habit. Though he liked to write, journalism wasn't something he had remotely considered, but he had to think about Susan and get off his butt. "Okay, I'll give it a try, but Clark Kent I'm not."

"Great," Rankin said. "I'll take care of the details and call you tomorrow."

A week later, Hoffman was pulling onto the freeway and heading to Bellevue every morning at 0645. The city council kept him churning out stories: homeless shelters, water projects, a new transit mall, and a bump in the city business tax. With the help of a friendly editor, he was quickly able to produce solid copy, an inverted pyramid. "Just pour the words into the mold," the editor said. The job was neither glamorous nor lucrative, but his coverage won him the respect of the people he dealt with at city hall, and writing op-eds gave him a feeling that he was making a difference in the community. Invariably, they spawned letters to the editor.

Meanwhile, the house needed attention. There was wallpaper to be stripped and floors to be sanded and refinished. Susan got a permanent teaching position in a Seattle middle school, and after a year on the newspaper's staff, he was considering a move to one of the larger dailies. To all appearances, he and Susan were a normal young couple launching a life together. Now, with some stability in their finances and house payments to make, the two married in a civil ceremony, witnessed by the Rankins.

But privately, she found some of his behavior odd. He didn't visit the bar as often as he once did, but he drank alone at home. He still had trouble sleeping at night and frequently woke with nightmares he wouldn't discuss with her. When the old house settled and snapped at night, he'd slip out of bed, remove a pistol from the nightstand, and search the dark house. He couldn't walk down the street without looking over his shoulder. And when reports from Paris or Saigon were in the news, he'd curse at the TV screen.

He refused to talk about what he had experienced in Vietnam. One day she found him in the basement going through the contents of his army footlocker.

"Jack, what are you doing?"

"Looking at all these uniforms. It must be a dozen sets of fatigues, caps, hats, belts, and four pairs of boots. How about this formal blue dress uniform? I never had occasion to wear it, not even once. Paid good money for it, custom tailored. They wanted us to look good, gentlemen by an act of Congress. I think I ought to get rid of this stuff."

"Really? Why?" She sensed he was conflicted.

"Just takes up space. Unlikely I'll ever get called back to active duty."

"I hope not. Is that even possible?"

"Remotely."

"You never mentioned that."

"Don't worry, babe. The only good that came out of that war was meeting you, and I'm keeping you. We'd move to Canada first."

Susan skeptically watched him place the starched, neatly folded fatigues back into the footlocker, along with a large envelope of snapshots, a box of his decorations, and his military records. He pushed the footlocker into a dark corner of the basement behind the furnace. There it lay like a coffin holding the embalmed remains of one First Lieutenant Jack Hoffman.

Memories weren't as easily laid to rest. Everyday occurrences brought images of Vietnam to mind: a drenching rain, the beating blades of a helicopter, a sudden loud noise, the boyish face of a soldier in the airport, and footsteps behind him on the street at night. Worst of all was that dream, the events surrounding the last minutes of Alan Danton's life.

"Bad dream?" Susan would mutter, awakened by his tossing.

"It's nothing; go back to sleep," he would respond.

Susan was patient, but he was hard on himself about one aspect of their relationship. How many long dark nights had he laid, rain soaked, beside a jungle trail, a Claymore mine detonator in his hand, staying awake thinking of her? He would try to visualize her smile, her eyes, her body, catch the scent of her hair, and recall the sweet sensation of holding her close. Their time in Sydney had been so short, and he had longed to be with her again.

Now that his longing was rewarded, he was failing her in bed. He was strung too tight and couldn't seem to relax and let it happen.

Vietnam flashbacks haunted him everywhere. The summer of his homecoming, the two hiked to Quartz Lake, one of his favorite camping spots in the Olympics. They made the seven-mile trek from the trailhead, mostly uphill, to a spot where he knew they would find solitude. A few days in the woods like in the years past. They would swim, fish, sleep under the stars, read, and relax.

As they started up the trail, he began to feel uneasy. They were doing something he had avoided in Nam: walking on a trail. He became hypervigilant again as if programmed to observe any sign of movement around him, any unnatural sound. Every turn in the trail suggested a potential ambush. It was completely paranoid to feel this way, he told himself, but he couldn't clear his mind.

Night brought no relief. A breeze licked the walls of the small tent. Was the sound he just heard windfall, or an animal, or someone approaching? He felt vulnerable with no view of what might be going on outside, and he regretted he had no weapon. Susan was sleeping soundly when he crawled from the tent and picked up a hatchet.

He stood barefoot on the forest floor, damp with dew, identifying likely avenues of approach to the camp. Stars blinked above the openings in a towering ceiling of Douglas fir. He sat with his back to the trunk of a large tree, far enough from the tent that it was unlikely he'd be spotted in the dark. Hatchet in hand, he assumed the role of a listening post, prepared to spring into action if need be.

At the break of dawn, he awoke to the sound of Susan's voice. "Jack, what on earth are you doing out here?"

He opened his eyes and looked at his wristwatch: 0630. He wondered how long he had slept. The air was crisp. A ribbon of fog stretched across the lake. "Couldn't sleep in the tent," he said awkwardly.

"So you sit out here all night? Really, Jack."

"I heard noises," he said, thinking truth was the best defense of his behavior.

"You can't do this, can you?" she said.

He stood up and stretched. "Look, Susan, I'll be fine. Just forget about it."

"No, let's leave. We can try this again some other time."

They packed up and left, and there never was another time.

The bombing of North Vietnam continued as North Vietnamese and US peace negotiators argued over the shape of the table. Meanwhile, the ground war began to evolve. The Desert Devils knew their grip on South Vietnam's central highlands was loosening. They had seen the NVA enclaves in Cambodia and struggled to intercept the constant flow of Communist troops on the labyrinthian footpaths through the mountains. Their perspective was quite different than that of the decision makers at home. The grunts knew that, when the last American soldier died in Vietnam, the mountains would belong to the little men from the north.

Meanwhile, Vietnam veterans were appearing on the streets of American cities. They were easily recognizable with their camouflage fatigues, jungle boots, shoulder-length hair, and angry eyes.

There were reports that the ranks of the infantry were filled with mental cases. It seemed that many in the public viewed them with the suspicion that they were the product of a failed war, that they had come home guilt-ridden, morally ambivalent, and potentially violent. Angered and feeling as if they bore the mark of Cain, many of them joined war protests, tossing their medals over the gate at the White House.

Hoffman was defensive about the character of the Vietnam vets. Sure, some guys were having reentry problems, but the vast majority of the vets came home to lead normal, productive lives. In an op-ed, he wrote that, of the nearly three million men and women having served in Vietnam, "Today, most started families and are holding down regular jobs. Many have returned to school, and more than likely, their coworkers and classmates aren't even aware they are Vietnam veterans."

He concluded the op-ed this way: "John F. Kennedy said after the Bay of Pigs, 'Victory has a thousand fathers, and defeat is an orphan.' The nation called its young men to take up arms in Vietnam. While many refused to answer the call, these chose to risk their lives in defense of their nation. If someone is to be blamed for this war, let it not be them. They accomplished all that was asked of them and more. This they know; this no one need tell them."

He wasn't surprised when the first letter that hit his desk was unsigned and had no return address. At the top of an otherwise blank page were two typewritten words: "Baby Killers."

The suburban newspaper had little career potential, but he found he enjoyed his work. The power of words appealed to him, and as he gained experience, he saw opportunities to move up in the profession to larger publications. Employed and comfortable in their new home, Jack Hoffman and Susan Lazard were settled into the routine of a married life eleven months after his return from Vietnam.

27
WALKING WOUNDED

The corrugated surface of Puget Sound glittered like foil in the morning sun. Commuter ferries plowed furrows across the bay. Tess was waiting in front of the hotel when he arrived. The doorman opened the car door for her, and she jumped in. "Whew, sprung from that windowless hotel on a day like this. Thank you."

"It's a good day to be on the water. Let's take the ferry to the Kitsap Peninsula."

"Whatever you say, tour guide." she said.

"I'll do my best to see your trust is rewarded," he said.

The line of cars at the ferry terminal was short, and they were soon on their way. As the boat left the landing, the two took the stairs from the vehicle deck to the stern platform and stood at the railing. The engine thrummed beneath their feet. A westerly wind raised whitecaps and blew a salty spray. Tess stood with Hoffman at the railing, taking in the receding skyline of Seattle.

"Do you dream?" she asked.

"Sometimes more than I'd like," he said

"I have one that keeps playing over and over. I'm on a ship, one of those huge tour boats, and I can't find my cabin," she said. "Subconsciously, I guess I feel trapped and can't figure out where I belong."

"Really? You sound pretty sure of yourself to me," he said. "You have a great career, successful; what do you want?"

"Good question. I don't know."

"Well, if you're unhappy, why continue?"

"I guess I believe in what I'm doing. One has to believe in something."

"I think you work too hard."

"You're right about that. I haven't taken a vacation in two years."

"So do it. I have a sailboat on Lake Union, and you can't get lost on it. Come back sometime, and we'll work on that dream."

"You're a kind man. Don't make any promises you don't intend to keep."

"Try me," Hoffman said, glancing at her. It was one of those moments when her resemblance to her father was unmistakable. He wasn't looking for it; it was just there. Though he was raised a Catholic and professed belief in life after death, he had long ago given up the notion that the spirits of the dead remain concerned about the lives of the living. And yet, the moment she walked into his newsroom and identified herself, he felt her father's presence.

As the boat neared the landing at Bremerton, Tess ran back out on the deck for a better view. "God, it's beautiful here," she said, breathing deeply. "The air is so fresh and clean. Do you sail much?"

"Used to, with Susan. Not so much lately."

"You say I work too much; what about you? How about taking some of your own advice and getting out on that boat?"

"Okay, you got me there. My daughter nags me about it."

"I work in the same dark world you do, and it can get depressing. That story you're covering is no fairy tale."

"Someone's got to tell the story. I have to wonder how these kids got so violent. Did we do it to them? I mean their parents have adjusted so well, with successful businesses, tight-knit communities, and stable families. Then there's this."

"I've lost count of the number of drug cases I've prosecuted, and with few exceptions, they follow the same pattern. If human beings feel they get shorted of the good things in life, they say to hell with everyone else and start doing what they think they have to do to get their share. They prey on one another mostly and end up in court where they meet people like me. I don't blame them for being angry. Would it surprise you if I carry sometimes?"

"You're full of surprises," Hoffman laughed. Beneath the hardcore prosecutor's persona was a fragile little girl. The war, three decades earlier, had killed her father and left her wounded, collateral damage. Hoffman suffered from the same wound. He knew the questions were coming, but he didn't know how he was going to answer them.

The ferry eased into the Bremerton landing. Hoffman drove off the ramp in a line of vehicles and pointed his car up the Kitsap Peninsula. "You're probably wondering where I'm taking you," he said.

"Not really. It's just good to get away, anyplace, even for a day. I'm so grateful to you."

"Happy to do it. When Susan and I were early married and strapped for cash, she would pack a picnic lunch, and we'd head up to a park where Admiralty Inlet joins Puget Sound. It's a pretty place. Hasn't changed much over the years."

"Back from the war, together again, in love. Sounds wonderful. What have I missed?"

"Not as idyllic as you imagine. We had a lot of adjusting to do. Now it's my turn to tell you it's not too late. You're young, free. There's really nothing stopping you from making some changes if that's what you want to do."

They passed the naval shipyard, heading north. "You must think I'm very unhappy, Jack, and maybe I am. But I'm taking steps. One of them is this mystery, my father I mean. It's something I have to get resolved. I didn't know what to expect when I walked into your little office a few days ago. Now I feel . . . I feel like I've known you for years. You've been so patient." Tess noticed a highway sign: Point No Point, 10 miles. "What a strange name," she said. "Is there a point or not?"

"Philosophically, that's the ultimate question," he said. "But geographically, yes. There's a lighthouse and a little park out at the tip."

"How did it get a name like that?" Tess wondered

"Most place names around here are either native American or given by some white guy with no imagination. An explorer was looking for an anchorage, but the water was too shallow, so there was no point in staying. Susan and I had a lot of fun with that name."

"It must be very hard for you, losing her I mean."

"Yeah."

"I'm so sorry."

"I'm grateful for every minute I had with her. That woman put up with a lot from me." He was saved from further discussion of that topic by the appearance of a grocery store. "Let's stop here and pick up a few things to eat at the park," he said.

Some brie, a baguette, and a bottle of cheap chardonnay would do for lunch. The clerk pulled the cork and provided paper cups. Thus provisioned, they proceeded to the lighthouse at the park. Visitors to the park were few in early spring. The two walked along the shore to a pile of driftwood and logs where they sat with Puget Sound licking the shore a few feet away. Hoffman sliced the cheese with his pocket knife and poured the wine.

They sat contemplatively under a bright spring sun, listening to the waves and the cries of gulls. Out on the inlet, trawlers pursued salmon while a few sailboats tacked lazily in the wind. Tess rolled her pant legs above her knees, took off her shoes, and buried her feet in the sand. "You're right, of course. I need to take better care of myself. If I hadn't been so compulsive, maybe I wouldn't have blown my marriage. I can't make that mistake again. I'm my own worst enemy."

"Tell me about your marriage," Hoffman said, poking the sand with a stick.

"We met in law school. When I passed the bar and landed a job with the DA, he wanted to start a family. I wanted to get my career established first. We were fine financially; he was making plenty at his firm, and I was the only female prosecutor in the office at the time. It was a plum job. If the men worked hard, I worked harder: twelve-hour days, weekends."

A sailboat tacked a few hundred yards offshore, canvass luffing. Farther out, a towboat crawled into the sound, pulling a barge with a load of sand.

"Every day, we passed one another in the house, like those boats, always in different directions. I'd come home dead tired and go straight to bed. We rarely spoke of anything but the checkbook. One day he confessed to having an affair for over a year and wanted out. I had no idea. Can't say I blame him."

"Now you're being hard on yourself."

"Maybe, but if I had given the relationship any effort at all, maybe I'd have a case to make for myself. You and Susan seem to have managed two careers, almost thirty years. That's impressive these days."

"Thanks to her. The early ones were the hardest on her. When I got home, I was . . . well, to put it in military terms, fucked up. It took years to admit how much that war messed me up."

"I find that hard to believe. You seem to have it together now."

"Ha, I've fooled you."

"Were you wounded?"

"My physical wounds weren't serious. That wasn't the problem."

"PTSD?"

Hoffman hesitated. "That's what they call it now, but all I knew was I couldn't get what happened over there out of my head. Just get over it. Besides, I was a commissioned officer. I had a college education. I wasn't some kid drafted from under the hood of a hot rod. More wine?"

"No, thanks."

Hoffman emptied the bottle into his cup. "More than you need to know. We came to talk about you and your dad. I'll shut up."

"No, please go on."

"The paper assigned me to do a series on returning vets. I visited storefront drop-in centers that were popping up, most of them run by vets. I sat through a few rap sessions and recognized my own behaviors in these guys. One fellow said that war took his innocence, and he was damn mad about it. I concluded no one who saw combat over there escaped some degree of trauma. You can't kill other people and watch your fellow soldiers die without asking why. When I was in training, it never occurred to me that I would hate it. Strange as it seems now, I never questioned what I would be asked to do."

"Well, at least my father was spared that. He apparently did a lot of killing."

"He did what he had to do."

"Oh, Jack, that's so facile. It would make me happy if I knew he hated it, too. Killing seems to be the thing you men do naturally. Loving, not so much. You obviously struggle with what you had to do. Did he?"

Hoffman looked at his watch. "It's going to get late, but if we leave now, we can stop for dinner and get back to Seattle by ten. Let's head back to the car." He took her hand and helped her to her feet.

"You haven't answered my question, sir," she said.

"Because I don't know the answer," he said. What was he supposed to tell her, that her father loved to kill, to rack up body count like scoring points in a war game, that he was careless with the lives of his men, and they hated him?

The restaurant Hoffman had in mind in Poulsbo sat above the bay. It had been one of Susan's favorites. He couldn't help glancing at their usual table when he walked in the door. He imagined her sitting there in the same chair.

The proprietor, Lawrence, rushed to greet him. "Mr. Hoffman, so very glad to see you again," he said enthusiastically. "We've missed you. How long has it been?" He looked quizzically at Tess.

"Lawrence, this Tess Danton, the daughter of an old colleague of mine," Hoffman said.

"Very pleased to meet you, Ms. Danton," Lawrence said. "How is Mrs. Hoffman?"

"Lawrence, Susan passed away two years ago."

"Oh, Mr. Hoffman, I'm so sorry."

"We had many memorable evenings here."

"We will miss her. I'll seat you at your table by the window if that's okay."

"Thank you, Lawrence."

The sky, the sound, the islands—the scene framed by the restaurant window was a palette of silver, green, and blue. Masts of sailboats bristled in the berths below. The conversation turned to her years in Columbus, living outside the gates of Fort Benning, the child of a dead hero. The constant unsolicited sympathy was overwhelming and unwanted. She attended the University of Texas on a track scholarship and was still running twenty miles a week. Hoffman said little, satisfied to let her talk about herself.

As evening approached, they set out for the ferry landing. On entering Bremerton, Tess cried out, "Jack, that sign we just passed—that's it."

"What?"

"The Turner Joy."

"Yes, it's mothballed here, a tourist attraction."

"Never mind that. When my father was in the Navy, he crewed on her. My mother hung an engraved plaque on the wall at home. I must have walked by that thing thousands of times. Do you mind if we take a look?"

"I think we have time before the next ferry if we don't stay long."

The ship's motto on a sign at the entrance of the museum read, "*Esse quam videri*," "To be rather than to seem." Appropriate, Hoffman thought. An attack on the Turner Joy by the North Vietnamese, subsequently determined never to have happened, was among grounds for the Gulf of Tonkin Resolution and America's intervention in Vietnam.

It was just before 5:00 p.m. when they arrived dockside. The destroyer, navy gray, sleek, and decks bristling with cannon barrels and electronic paraphernalia, stretched longer than a football field, the kind of power that was supposed to make victory inevitable. The visitors' gate was closing.

"I'm afraid it's too late to go aboard, Tess," Hoffman said.

"It's okay. I just want to get closer," she said. Grabbing her purse she leaped from the car and headed straight for the sea wall without him. She stood motionless at the railing, dwarfed by the massive ship. Minutes passed as Hoffman watched her.

He checked his watch again. If they were going to catch the next ferry, they would have to get going. He walked to her side, but she didn't acknowledge his presence. Finally, she turned to him and said, "I've carried a photo of him there, on the deck, for years."

She lifted from her purse a cigarette case and opened it. As far as he knew, she didn't smoke. She carefully removed a tattered black-and-white photo of a young sailor in a white uniform. Yes, no doubt about it; it was Alan Danton, smiling cheerfully, full of life, his face not yet wizened by war. It reminded Hoffman of a saint's patch of clothing or a sliver of bone preserved in a small reliquary. And why shouldn't she reverence him?

"He was a good-looking kid," Hoffman said.

"I have copies, but on this trip, I carried it for luck. He wrote on the back," she said, turning it over and reading, "'Missing you terribly. Tell our little angel Theresa Daddy will be home soon.'" She looked at it for a moment and returned it to the case. "It's all I have from him that mentions my name."

The sun was setting behind the Olympics. Couples strolled on a promenade in a waterfront park. The voices of children playing chimed the arrival of spring. A ferry left a trail of froth through the silky water as it churned away from Bremerton without Tess Danton and Jack Hoffman. They sat on a bench in the park, as far removed from the Cambodian jungle in 1970 as heaven from hell.

"I haven't pressed you all day about Dad," Tess said. "You've been so kind, and I wanted us to enjoy the day. But I'm running out of time here, and I have to know. Something about his death doesn't add up, something very strange that Captain Northrup told me. He said there may have been a woman with my father when he died."

Hoffman was taken aback. How much did Northrup tell her? "He wasn't there," Hoffman said.

"So, there was a woman," Tess declared. "Damn it, Jack, he wasn't but you were. You were with him when he died. I have a right to know everything."

Her father's decision to extend his platoon's mission in Cambodia, the near mutiny of his men, the taking of a captive, and his fatal obsession with the woman—these were matters unexplainable to the uninitiated. Soldiers just don't talk about them outside the brotherhood, even to family. Of one thing Hoffman was certain: Tess Danton should always believe her father was a hero, and Alan Danton should remain one. Hoffman should not deprive her of that.

"Yes, his platoon took her captive the NVA camp. He wanted to bring her back for questioning," Hoffman said, all true.

"That seems odd. The report implies he intentionally dropped back to fend off the NVA. What was she doing with him?"

The right questions. Hoffman felt as if he was being cross-examined. There had been enough lies about that war, but sometimes a lie is an act of mercy. "I can't tell you how the two of them ended up falling behind together. I only know what I saw with my own eyes when we got to him. Both of them were badly wounded. He had put up one hell of a fight."

For thirty years, Hoffman told no one what happened in the Cambodian jungle that day and his role in the woman's death. Sure, the Montagnard woman probably would have died anyway.

Arguably, ending her life was merciful. But technically, it was a homicide, a war crime. The nuns in school said murder was a mortal sin, a stain on the soul that required contrition. But he wasn't sorry. For him, there could be no absolution.

"The Army's report says you tried to bring him back to the defensive position. What about her?"

He said, "We were under fire. The enemy was moving all around us. We couldn't carry both of them, so we left her there."

The lie of omission is a commonly used tool when cleaning up accounts of combat. Tess pondered what Hoffman said. "I just don't understand it. Why would the others in the platoon leave the two of them behind, not attempt to help them?"

"The confusion that takes over is impossible to describe. They might not have realized he was gone. Under fire, you're just trying to protect yourself and the people around you," Hoffman said.

"Still, that doesn't explain how the woman ended up with him. Mr. Northrup told me my father liked the Montagnards. Perhaps he was trying to protect her."

"Certainly," Hoffman said, glad to have Tess think so. "When we found them, he wanted us to bring her back with us and made quite a fuss about it. But there was no way. We had to move fast, and we just couldn't carry them both. Besides, it was clear her head wound was fatal. It was, I guess, a kind of triage."

"Well, at least he cared," Tess said, fighting back the tears. "It's all so horrible. You risked your life for him . . . How can ever I thank you?"

"It's what we did for one another. I only wish we'd been able to bring him back alive."

She said, "This must be hard for you, I mean to have me question you this way. There are things I'm sure you'd rather forget. I won't bother you anymore."

"I'm afraid I haven't been much help," he said.

"More than you imagine," she said, wiping her eyes with a tissue she pulled from her purse. "I guess there are things I will never know about my father, but being with you makes me feel connected to him. You've been so patient with me. I hope he was as kind as you are."

"Alan Danton was a good man," Hoffman said. "He died trying to do the right thing as he saw it."

Tess said little on the return trip to Seattle. Would she ever find the peace she was looking for? Hoffman didn't know. Sometimes there are just no answers, and even if there are, what difference would they make? In war, acts of incredible nobility occur along with incidents of terrible depravity. God will have to sort it all out. Hoffman had done his best for his brother-in-arms and his daughter.

28
IT DOES MEAN SOMETHING

A phone message from the city desk awaited Hoffman when he arrived home. There had been developments in the shooting. He headed to Central Precinct where he found Sergeant Manny Fratanelli, head of the gang enforcement team, laying out a dozen eight-by-ten black-and-white photos on a table. The images, most of them headshots, were fresh from the dark room, still damp. Hoffman enjoyed an easygoing familiarity with the detectives who generally trusted him with the information they provided off the record and didn't expect to read in the newspaper.

"What's up, Manny? We heard you've made some arrests," Hoffman said.

Fratanelli kept arranging the photos fresh from the printer. "Appears Seattle wasn't big enough for two of these Asian gangs. Some hotshots from LA moved up I-5, invading our homeboys' turf. The usual, extortion, prostitution, drugs . . ."

Hoffman glanced at the photos. "Mind if I take a look?"

"Okay with me."

Hoffman glanced through the numbered images. Some were mug shots of expressionless young men, all Asians; others, images taken at different angles of the carnage at the bar. Some were shots taken at the port a week earlier of the pregnant young woman with the head wound. Next to it was a wide angle of the body of a male, sprawled under what appeared to be a bridge abutment.

Fratanelli noticed him lingering over the photo of the girl. "Yeah, that's the young lady we found down at the port. Pretty little thing. Kids don't have a clue what they're doing to themselves."

Hoffman's eyes moved to the next black-and-white, that of the male. He glanced questioningly at Fratanelli.

"Her boyfriend, a kid named Trinh. He was the top dog of a gang called the Green Vipers. His body turned up yesterday under the West Seattle Bridge. We think the girl accompanied him from LA. Her family filed a missing person's report at about that time. We're waiting for positive identification."

"Did they reside here?"

"Not sure. They're very mobile and move up and down I-5 like it's the Ho Chi Minh Trail. The local Bongs apparently decided to cut off the Vipers' head, and that's what started this. Witnesses saw four Bongs grab this Trinh and the girl as they were leaving the movie theater up on 132nd. The two were pushed into a car and driven off."

"Any suspects in custody?"

"Just for questioning. Claim they know nothing about it. The intruders from LA got more than even with the Bongs in that bar. AR-15s were the weapons used."

"It doesn't take long to empty a magazine, even on semi-automatic," Hoffman said.

"Speaking from experience?" Fratanelli gibed.

Hoffman ignored him. "What else can you tell me? On the record, I mean."

"Talk to the DA."

Hoffman returned to the newsroom, called the district attorney's office, and began to piece together elements of a story. Space was held on page one, above the fold, in the morning edition. Another reporter would help him run down as many details as possible. The city editor already had in mind for Hoffman an in-depth series on Asian youth. Hoffman figured it would require at least a month of research, interviews, and writing.

As he typed, he couldn't get the photo of the dead girl out of his mind. The city desk was waiting, and he was ready to hit the Send button when the phone rang. It was Tess Danton.

"Jack, it's Tess," she said unnecessarily.

It was good to hear her voice. The previous night, he had no idea what she was thinking, and he feared he had failed her.

She said, "I just wanted to thank you for yesterday. It was a beautiful day, and I apologize if I made you uncomfortable. I hope you understand."

"Don't worry about me," he said, somewhat relieved. How much had he told her? He couldn't remember exactly, but it wasn't much.

"I'd hoped to see you again before I left, but I just got a call from the office. A hearing was moved up, and I have to catch a red eye tonight. Today is out because I'm scheduled to give a presentation at a breakout session at the conference. Can't get out of it."

"I'll give you a lift to the airport," he said.

"You needn't bother."

"Tess, it's really no problem."

"Awfully nice of you, but I'll take a cab."

Her leaving gave him an empty feeling, like a parting from someone dear to him. “Okay, but call and let me know you arrived safely, okay?”

“You’re sweet. And Jack, I just want you to know you’ve been a great comfort to me. Like I said yesterday, somehow, I feel a kinship with you. I’m glad he had friends like you, that he wasn’t alone. It would be terrible to think he had died alone.”

“You can be proud of him, Tess,” he said.

“I am. If you’re ever in Austin, be sure to call.”

“Certainly,” he said, thinking the likelihood close to none. “And you know where to find me.”

“On your sailboat, I hope. You’re a great guy. If you don’t mind my saying so, I think Susan would like you to get on with your life and find someone to love.”

“You’re probably right.”

“Got to run. Love you, Jack.”

“Likewise, Tess. Have a safe trip.”

Then she was gone. He held the receiver to his ear for a moment and hung up.

That evening he stopped in at Central Precinct on the way home from an editorial meeting in the newsroom. The police were rounding up members of the Bongs for questioning. Any remaining Vipers were by then a thousand miles away on the I-5, a street without joy. Hoffman would work on his series on Asian youth, note their challenges and accomplishments, address common misconceptions, and stay out of the investigators’ way.

As he drove home, he was still perplexed. It was funny she came to him for help with the pain of her loss. He was a guy who was never able to help himself. He told her if she was unhappy, she should do something about it. Ha! Then she turned around and gave him the same advice.

The garage door closed behind his car. The cat watched him pass, disinterested. In the kitchen, he took a glass from the stack of dirty dishes on the counter, rinsed it, and dispensed ice from the refrigerator. He picked up a fifth of Bushmills at the liquor cabinet and proceeded to his study where he turned on a reading lamp, filled the glass, and settled into his recliner. He hadn't eaten, but he wasn't hungry.

He checked his watch: nine o'clock. She'd be landing any minute in Austin. "Well, Danton, congratulations," he said aloud. "You have a wonderful daughter there. I hope you're happy, 'cause this time, I really covered your ass." He drained the glass, refilled it, and turned off the light. "I'm getting hammered," he said to himself, and nodded off.

It was nearly midnight when he awoke with his heart pounding. The dream again: the woman lying in the fetal position with an open head wound; Alan Danton next to her, his face contorted in pain and anger; Jackson aiming his weapon at the woman. It always ended the same way, with the sound of a shot.